DARK LOVE

DARK LOVE

Edited by NANCY A. COLLINS,
EDWARD E. KRAMER and MARTIN H. GREENBERG

BCA
LONDON NEW YORK SYDNEY TORONTO

This edition published 1995
by BCA
by arrangement with Hodder and Stoughton

CN 4403

Typeset by Phoenix Typesetting, Ilkley, West Yorkshire.
Printed and bound in Great Britain by Mackays of Chatham PLC, Chatham, Kent.

This book is dedicated to the memories of
Jim Thompson (1906–1977)
&
Robert Bloch (1917–1994)
The Openers of the Way

–THE EDITORS

ACKNOWLEDGMENTS

I would like to thank Bill Malloy of Mysterious Press for his invaluable help, and Joe R. Lansdale, who volunteered Bill in the first place.

—NAC

CONTENTS

INTRODUCTION

There's a question – just one – that I'd like to ask the writers in this book:

Do you really let your parents read this stuff?

I ask because, while the writers themselves are nice enough – most of them, anyway, if you catch them on a good day – the stuff they've got in store for you is not. Some of it's bloody, some of it's sick, and none of it provides a shred of comfort.

In fact, the stories in this book plunge boldly into what another disturbing writer, back in the '20s, called 'some very strange psychological regions.' The writer was that old master, Arthur Machen, and he was talking about an early story of his own, 'The White People,' probably the most daring thing he'd ever written and still one of the best horror tales in the language. 'It contains,' he said, with wry understatement, 'some of the most curious work that I have ever done, or ever will do. It goes, if I may say so, into very strange psychological regions.' And he would speak of it no further, as if the tale unnerved even him.

These twenty-two chronicles of Dark Love venture into

similarly strange regions, only more explicitly and a great deal less politely; and though, to my knowledge, no one has ever handed out medals for Conspicuous Courage to mere writers, the twenty-two assembled here deserve some sort of credit for the sheer unflinching audacity with which they've followed their personal visions into manifestly dangerous territory. The tales in this volume respect neither taboos nor good taste; many of them set out to shock, and quite a few succeed. Whatever the world's reaction to them, one thing's for sure: they're not going to end up as episodes of *Tales from the Crypt* or some other TV show.

Yet love, good old human love, is undeniably their focus. They're even, in an odd way, romantic – assuming, of course, that there's something romantic about (to take just three examples) necrophilia, pyromania, and an unrequited passion for an eight-foot-long insect.

And why not? Even in real life, love can take some pretty odd forms.

Just a few minutes after I'd finished reading these stories, for example, a report came over the radio of an Ohio man who, back in 1964, was given a lift to Toledo by an eighteen-year-old girl. Apparently, over the course of the drive, he fell in love with her.

Romantic? You bet.

The man never saw the girl again – not for thirty-one years. But just last week, while reading the newspaper, he came across her name in an obituary of her mother, and managed to track her down. She's now, of course, a woman of forty-nine. According to the news report, he sent her four dozen roses and a stack of letters – thirty-one years' worth of letters, in fact. And when police searched his home, they found thirty-one years' worth of Christmas and birthday presents that, with admirable devotion, he'd been buying her year after year.

Yes, the police. It seems the woman has taken out an order of protection against this fellow, and he's currently under arrest for 'misdemeanor stalking.'

Still, as I said, it's a romantic story. Thoroughly human. We can all identify with it – some of us with the woman, some of us, admittedly, with the stalker.

Or take, if you prefer, a more sublime example: take the author of *The Divine Comedy.* Dante was barely nine years old when he first glimpsed Beatrice in the street – 'At that instant,' he wrote later, 'I may truly say that the spirit of life, which dwelleth in the most secret chamber of the heart, began to tremble with such violence that it appeared fearfully in the least pulses,' etc., etc. – and nine more years passed before he so much as exchanged a word with her. Yet these few chance encounters were all he needed; he spent the rest of his life celebrating his love for this 'most beautiful of the angels in heaven' whom he'd barely spoken to.

One more romantic, just to keep you in the mood: the artist Rockwell Kent. In 1929 he was strolling through a barren little fishing village in Newfoundland when, he says, 'I saw a girl's face at a window – just for a moment. I was ashamed to stare. And oh, I thought, how beautiful it would be to live here, and never go away – forever!' When, the next day, he set sail, 'I thought how never again I should see the girl in the square house at the turn of the path.'

And, by George, he never did. But years later, he was still dreaming about her.

Now, the only difference between those stories and the romantic little stories in this book is that, in the latter, the girl at the window would have a ravaged face and a knife clenched in her teeth, Dante would have orgasms over whipping Beatrice bloody, and the forty-nine-year-old focus of the Ohio man's affections would be dead by now. Dead? Her body parts would probably be scattered from Toledo to Tacoma.

Nothing the matter with that, of course. Each to his own, and all perfectly human. There's no love without obsession, this book seems to say, and obsession is the underlying theme of every story. If love is here, the stories ask, can lunacy be far behind? Make that *homicidal* lunacy; indeed, if there's one thing these stories make painfully clear, it's that down deep, down *real* deep, love and violence are as inextricably linked as Mom and apple pie. (And I speak as one whose mother has never made a decent apple pie in her life.)

The source of the fear in these stories is, in essence, the source of the fear in *all* horror stories: fear of the Other. Only in this case, in the twenty-two stories that follow, the Other looks remarkably like ourselves. He or she may be a hitchhiker, a pickup in a bar, or a bow-tied stranger in a crowded cafe; he or she may also be our co-worker, perhaps one we've secretly lusted after, or our neighbor, whether just across the alley or separated from us by the thinnest of walls. He or she may even be our lover or our spouse.

It's an unsettling thought, albeit on the printed page a pleasantly intriguing one. Once, around twenty years ago, while I was engaged in putting together a gothic romance magazine for women (it was called *Rosebud,* for the record, and died before its launch), I came across a scholarly article analyzing that particular genre's popularity. It had, I remember, a wonderful title, one that summed up the basic appeal not just of gothic romance but of a large segment of commercial suspense fiction: 'Somebody's Trying to Kill Me, and I Think It's My Husband.'

And who knows, maybe he is. Husbands murder wives (and ex-wives) all the time; wives return the favor. Even a handsome ex-football star turned actor – I'm speaking hypothetically, of course – may turn out to be a raving psychopath in the grip of a jealous obsession. The stories in this book remind us of a terrifying fundamental truth: that our understanding of our fellow beings is decidedly limited. We can never really know what's inside another person's skull; we can never know what demons are crouching just behind their eyes. Given the right pressures, the right family history, the right combination of heartbreak and hope – or given, perhaps, the right set of provocations supplied so abundantly by modern urban life – any one of us might be pushed beyond reason, over the edge, into the pit of psychosis.

I've been there myself. I remember walking the streets once, just after dawn, having lain awake all night in pain over a failing love affair, when I noticed that a woman I'd passed was eyeing me strangely. I realized, suddenly, that I'd been talking to myself – *but I didn't care.* I felt not a trace of embarrassment; the problems that preoccupied me seemed of far greater importance than what some stranger thought.

Looking back, it's clear to me that, at that moment, I was crazy. Nuts. Certifiable.

Could it happen again? Of course.

And it could happen – only with far more alarming consequences – to the harmless-looking fellow citizens we bump into every day on the street. They may well have a screw loose already; they may well be, as Machen once luridly suggested, 'lurking in our midst, rubbing shoulders with frock-coated and finely draped humanity, ravening like wolves at heart and boiling with the foul passions of the swamp and the black cave.'

More lethal still – potentially, at least – are those we believe we know most intimately; for intimacy makes us vulnerable. The therapists assure us that that's a blessing; a lot of us aren't so certain. Vulnerability is scary. Writing about the movie *Psycho,* a critic once noted that the reason the shower scene is so effective is that it exploits 'one of the archetypal moments of human vulnerability.' But surely there are many more such moments. Riding in an elevator with a stranger, for example. Using a public restroom. Picking up a hitchhiker. And most of all, climbing naked into bed with another human being, even one you think you know well.

It's this treacherous quality of sexual encounters – the supreme vulnerability they impose – that fuels the horror in this book. I was going to say, glibly, that horror makes strange bedfellows; but the lesson of these stories is that, ultimately, *all* bedfellows are strange bedfellows.

The bedroom, of course, holds other dangers as well. As visions of contemporary life, most of these stories allude in one way or another to the everpresent threat of AIDS. But viruses are really beside the point here. The stories demonstrate, among much else, that condoms or no condoms, sex isn't safe. And it never was.

It isn't pretty, either. I want to warn you right now that with very few exceptions, the descriptions of the sex act in the stories that follow, and of the people themselves – their fears and desires, their fantasies and needs, their all-too-mortal flesh and pitilessly observed reproductive organs – are so disquieting, so devastatingly unflattering, from writers male and female alike, that ugh to send anyone packing off to a monastery. No ltpeter or cold showers; the tales in this volume are a uasive argument for sexual abstinence than anything r hear from your doctor, your teacher, or your priest.

In ..., between the lethal danger and the sheer disgust, this book might actually have a salutary effect on the population problem. You'll find stories here calculated to raise eyebrows, goosebumps, and even a few laughs – but nary an erection. (Yes, there's humor here, all right, though it's of the blackest sort; and the main laughter one hears is the sinister cackling of the writers.) Just as second marriage has been called, waggishly, 'the triumph of hope over experience,' a similar challenge is presented here: if, immediately after finishing these tales, you still feel like getting down and dirty with another human being, it's clearly the triumph of biology over imagination.

However, if you're still determined to carry on the race (and I certainly hope you are), please heed one last warning, born of having immersed myself quite deeply in the contents of this book. Obey if you must those famous final words of *The Thing* – 'Keep watching the skies!' – and feel free each night, if you're so inclined, to look beneath the bed. Meanwhile, though, for safety's sake, keep an eye on something even closer, something midway between the heavens and the floor: that endlessly mysterious thing in bed beside you.

—T.E.D. KLEIN

Lunch at the Gotham Café

BY

STEPHEN KING

ONE day I came home from the brokerage house where I worked and found a letter – more of a note, actually – from my wife on the dining room table. It said she was leaving me, that she needed some time alone, and that I would hear from her therapist. I sat on the chair at the kitchen end of the table, reading this communication over and over again, not able to believe it. The only clear thought I remember having in the next half hour or so was *I didn't even know you* had *a therapist, Diane.*

After a while I got up, went into the bedroom, and looked around. All her clothes were gone (except for a joke sweatshirt someone had given her, with the words RICH BLONDE printed on the front in spangly stuff), and the room had a funny dislocated look, as if she had gone through it, looking for something. I checked my stuff to see if she'd taken anything. My hands felt cold and distant while I did this, as if they had been shot full of some numbing drug. As far as I could tell, everything that was supposed to be there was there. I hadn't expected anything different, and yet the room had that funny look, as if she had *pulled* at it, the way she sometimes pulled on the ends of her hair when she felt exasperated.

I went back to the dining room table (which was actually at one end of the living room; it was only a four-room apartment) and read the six sentences she'd left behind over again. It was the same, but looking into the strangely rumpled bedroom and the half-empty closet had started me on the way to believing what it said. It was a chilly piece of work, that note. There was no 'Love' or 'Good luck' or even 'Best' at the bottom of it. 'Take care of yourself' was as warm as it got. Just below that she had scratched her name.

Therapist. My eye kept going back to that word. *Therapist.* I supposed I should have been glad it wasn't *lawyer,* but I wasn't. *You will hear from William Humboldt, my therapist.*

'Hear from this, sweetiepie,' I told the empty room, and squeezed my crotch. It didn't sound tough and funny, as I'd hoped, and the face I saw in the mirror across the room was as pale as paper.

I walked into the kitchen, poured myself a glass of orange juice, then knocked it onto the floor when I tried to pick it up. The juice sprayed onto the lower cabinets and the glass broke. I knew I would cut myself if I tried to pick up the glass – my hands were shaking – but I picked it up anyway, and I cut myself. Two places, neither deep. I kept thinking that it was a joke, then realizing it wasn't. Diane wasn't much of a joker. But the thing was, I hadn't seen it coming. I didn't have a clue. What therapist? When did she see him? What did she talk about? Well, I supposed I knew what she talked about – me. Probably stuff about how I never remembered to put the ring down again after I finished taking a leak, how I wanted oral sex a tiresome amount of the time (how much was tiresome? I didn't know), how I didn't take enough interest in her job at the publishing company. Another question: how could she talk about the most intimate aspects of her marriage to a man named William Humboldt? He sounded like he should be a physicist at CalTech, or maybe a back-bencher in the House of Lords.

Then there was the Super Bonus Question: Why hadn't I

known *something* was up? How could I have walked into it like Sonny Liston into Cassius Clay's famous phantom uppercut? Was it stupidity? Insensitivity? As the days passed and I thought about the last six or eight months of our two-year marriage, I decided it had been both.

That night I called her folks in Pound Ridge and asked if Diane was there. 'She is, and she doesn't want to talk to you,' her mother said. 'Don't call back.' The phone went dead in my ear.

Two days later I got a call at work from the famous William Humboldt. After ascertaining that he was indeed speaking to Steven Davis, he promptly began calling me Steve. You may find that a trifle hard to believe, but it is nevertheless exactly what happened. Humboldt's voice was soft, small, and intimate. It made me think of a cat purring on a silk pillow.

When I asked after Diane, Humboldt told me that she was 'doing as well as expected,' and when I asked if I could talk to her, he said he believed that would be 'counterproductive to her case at this time.' Then, even more unbelievably (to my mind, at least) he asked in a grotesquely solicitous voice how I was doing.

'I'm in the pink,' I said. I was sitting at my desk with my head down and my left hand curled around my forehead. My eyes were shut so I wouldn't have to look into the bright gray socket of my computer screen. I'd been crying a lot, and my eyes felt like they were full of sand. 'Mr Humboldt . . . it *is* mister, I take it, and not doctor?'

'I use mister, although I have degrees—'

'Mr Humboldt, if Diane doesn't want to come home and doesn't want to talk to me, what *does* she want? Why did you call me?'

'Diane would like access to the safe deposit box,' he said in his smooth, purry little voice. 'Your *joint* safe deposit box.'

I suddenly understood the punched, rumpled look of the bedroom and felt the first bright stirrings of anger. She had been looking for the key to the box, of course. She hadn't been interested in my little collection of pre-World War II silver dollars or the onyx pinkie ring she'd bought me for our first anniversary (we'd only had two in all) . . . but in the safe deposit box was the diamond necklace I'd given her, and about thirty thousand dollars' worth of negotiable securities. The key was at our little summer cabin in the Adirondacks, I realized. Not on purpose, but out of simple forgetfulness. I'd left it on top of the bureau, pushed way back amid the dust and the mouse turds.

Pain in my left hand. I looked down, saw my hand rolled into a tight fist, and rolled it open. The nails had cut crescents in the pad of the palm.

'Steve?' Humboldt was purring. 'Steve, are you there?'

'Yes,' I said. 'I've got two things for you. Are you ready?'

'Of course,' he said in that purry little voice, and for a moment I had a bizarre vision: William Humboldt blasting through the desert on a Harley-Davidson, surrounded by a pack of Hell's Angels. On the back of his leather jacket: BORN TO COMFORT.

Pain in my left hand again. It had closed up again on its own, just like a clam. This time when I unrolled it, two of the four little crescents were oozing blood.

'First,' I said, 'that box is going to stay closed unless some divorce court judge orders it opened in the presence of Diane's attorney and mine. In the meantime, no one is going to loot it, and that's a promise. Not me, not her.' I paused. 'Not you, either.'

'I think that your hostile attitude is counterproductive,' he said. 'And if you examine your last few statements, Steve, you may begin to understand why your wife is so emotionally shattered, so—'

'Second,' I overrode him (it's something we hostile people are good at), 'I find you calling me by my first name patronizing and insensitive. Do it again on the phone and I'll hang up on you. Do it to my face and you'll find out just how hostile my attitude can be.'

'Steve . . . Mr Davis . . . I hardly think—'

I hung up on him. It was the first thing I'd done that gave me any pleasure since finding that note on the dining room table, with her three apartment keys on top of it to hold it down.

That afternoon I talked to a friend in the legal department, and he recommended a friend of his who did divorce work. I didn't want a divorce – I was furious at her, but had not the slightest question that I still loved her and wanted her back – but I didn't like Humboldt. I didn't like the *idea* of Humboldt. He made me nervous, him and his purry little voice. I think I would have preferred some hardball shyster who would have called up and said, *You give us a copy of that lockbox key before the close of business today, Davis, and maybe my client will relent and decide to leave you with something besides two pairs of underwear and your blood donor's card – got it?*

That I could have understood. Humboldt, on the other hand, felt sneaky.

The divorce lawyer was John Ring, and he listened patiently to my tale of woe. I suspect he'd heard most of it before.

'If I was entirely sure she wanted a divorce, I think I'd be easier in my mind,' I finished.

'Be entirely sure,' Ring said at once. 'Humboldt's a stalking horse, Mr Davis . . . and a potentially damaging witness if this drifts into court. I have no doubt that your wife went to a lawyer first, and when the lawyer found out about the missing lockbox key, he suggested Humboldt. A lawyer couldn't go right to you; that would be unethical. Come across with that key, my friend, and Humboldt will disappear from the picture. Count on it.'

Most of this went right past me. I was concentrating on what he'd said first.

'You think she wants a divorce,' I said.

'Oh, yes,' he replied. 'She wants a divorce. Indeed she does. And she doesn't intend to walk away from the marriage empty-handed.'

I made an appointment with Ring to sit down and discuss things further the following day. I went home from the office as late as I could, walked back and forth through the apartment for a while, decided to go out to a movie, couldn't find anything I wanted to see, tried the television, couldn't find anything there to look at, either, and did some more walking. And at some point I found myself in the bedroom, standing in front of an open window fourteen floors above the street and chucking out all my cigarettes, even the stale old pack of Viceroys from the very back of my top desk drawer, a pack that had probably been there for ten years or more – since before I had any idea there was such a creature as Diane Coslaw in the world, in other words.

Although I'd been smoking between twenty and forty cigarettes a day for twenty years, I don't remember any sudden decision to quit, or any dissenting interior opinions – not even a mental suggestion that maybe two days after your wife walks out is not the optimum time to quit smoking. I just stuffed the full carton, the half carton, and the two or three half-used packs I found lying around out the window and into the dark. Then I shut the window (it never once crossed my mind that it might have been more efficient to throw the user out instead of the product; it was never *that* kind of situation), lay down on my bed, and closed my eyes.

The next ten days – the time during which I was going through the worst of the physical withdrawal from nicotine – were difficult and often unpleasant, but perhaps not as bad as I had thought they would be. And although I was on the verge of smoking dozens – no, hundreds – of times, I never did. There were moments when I thought I would go insane if I didn't have a cigarette, and when I passed people on the street who were smoking I felt like screaming *Give that to me, motherfucker, that's mine!*, but I didn't.

For me the worst times were late at night. I think (but I'm not sure; all my thought processes from around the time Diane left are very blurry in my mind) I had an idea that I would sleep better if I quit, but I didn't. I lay awake some mornings until three, hands laced together under my pillow, looking up at the ceiling, listening to sirens and to the rumble of trucks headed downtown.

At those times I would think about the twenty-four-hour Korean market almost directly across the street from my building. I would think about the white fluorescent light inside, so bright it was almost like a Kubler-Ross near-death experience, and how it spilled out onto the sidewalk between the displays which, in another hour, two young Korean men in white paper hats would begin to fill with fruit. I would think about the older man behind the counter, also Korean, also in a paper hat, and the formidable racks of cigarettes behind him, as big as the stone tablets Charlton Heston had brought down from Mount Sinai in *The Ten Commandments.* I would think about getting up, dressing, going over there, getting a pack of cigarettes (or maybe nine or ten of them), and sitting by the window, smoking one Marlboro after another as the sky lightened to the east and the sun came up. I never did, but on many early mornings I went to sleep counting cigarette brands instead of sheep: Winston . . . Winston 100s . . . Virginia Slims . . . Doral . . . Merit . . . Merit 100s . . . Camels . . . Camel Filters . . . Camel Lights.

Later – around the time I was starting to see the last three or four months of our marriage in a clearer light, as a matter of fact – I began to understand that my decision to quit smoking when I had was perhaps not so unconsidered as it at first seemed, and a very long way from ill-considered. I'm not a brilliant man, not a brave one, either, but that decision might have been both. It's certainly possible; sometimes we rise above ourselves. In any case, it gave my mind something concrete to pitch upon in the days after Diane left; it gave my misery a vocabulary it would not otherwise have had, if you see what I mean. Very likely you don't, but I can't think of any other way to put it.

Have I speculated that quitting when I did may have played a part in what happened at the Gotham Café that day? Of course I have . . . but I haven't lost any sleep over it. None of us can predict the final outcomes of our actions, after all, and few even try; most of us just do what we do to prolong a moment's pleasure or to stop the pain for a while. And even when we act for the noblest reasons, the last link of the chain all too often drips with someone's blood.

Humboldt called me again two weeks after the evening when I'd bombed West 83rd Street with my cigarettes, and this time he stuck with Mr Davis as a form of address. He asked me how I was doing, and I told him I was doing fine. With that amenity out of the way, he told me that he had called on Diane's behalf. Diane, he said, wanted to sit down with me and discuss 'certain aspects' of the marriage. I suspected that 'certain aspects' meant the key to the safe deposit box – not to mention various other financial issues Diane might want to investigate before hauling her lawyer onstage – but what my head knew and what my body was doing were completely different things. I could feel my skin flush and my heart speed up; I could feel a pulse tapping away in the wrist of the hand holding the phone. You have to remember that I hadn't seen her since the morning of the day she'd left, and even then I hadn't really seen her; she'd been sleeping with her face buried in her pillow.

Still I retained enough sense to ask him just what aspects we were talking about here.

Humboldt chuckled fatly in my ear and said he would rather save that for our actual meeting.

'Are you sure this is a good idea?' I asked. As a question, it was nothing but a time-buyer. I *knew* it wasn't a good idea. I also knew I was going to do it. I wanted to see her again. Felt I had to see her again.

'Oh, yes, I think so.' At once, no hesitation. Any question that Humboldt and Diane had worked this out very carefully between them (and yes, very likely with a lawyer's advice) evaporated. 'It's always best to let some time pass before bringing the principals together, a little cooling-off period, but in my judgment a face-to-face meeting at this time would facilitate—'

'Let me get this straight,' I said. 'You're talking about—'

'Lunch,' he said. 'The day after tomorrow? Can you clear that on your schedule?' *Of course you can*, his voice said. *Just to see her again . . . to experience the slightest touch of her hand. Eh, Steve?*

'I don't have anything on for lunch Thursday anyhow, so that's not a problem. And I should bring my . . . my own therapist?'

The fat chuckle came again, shivering in my ear like something just turned out of a Jell-O mold. 'Do you have one, Mr Davis?'

'No, actually, I don't. Did you have a place in mind?' I wondered for a moment who would be paying for this lunch, and then had to smile at my own naivete. I reached into my pocket for a cigarette and poked the tip of a toothpick under my thumbnail instead. I winced, brought the pick out, checked the tip for blood, saw none, and stuck it in my mouth.

Humboldt had said something, but I had missed it. The sight of the toothpick had reminded me all over again that I was floating cigaretteless on the waves of the world.

'Pardon me?'

'I asked if you know the Gotham Café on 53rd Street,' he said, sounding a touch impatient now. 'Between Madison and Park.'

'No, but I'm sure I can find it.'

'Noon?'

I thought of telling him to tell Diane to wear the green dress with the little black speckles and the deep slit up the side, then decided that would probably be counterproductive. 'Noon will be fine,' I said.

We said the things that you say when you're ending a conversation with someone you already don't like but have to deal with. When it was over, I settled back in front of my computer terminal and wondered how I was possibly going to be able to meet Diane again without at least one cigarette beforehand.

It wasn't fine with John Ring, none of it.

'He's setting you up,' he said. 'They both are. Under this arrangement, Diane's lawyer is there by remote control and I'm not in the picture at all. It stinks.'

Maybe, but you never had her stick her tongue in your mouth when she feels you start to come, I thought. But since that wasn't the sort of thing you could say to a lawyer you'd just hired, I only told him

I wanted to see her again, see if there was a chance to salvage things.

He sighed.

'Don't be a *putz.* You see him at this restaurant, you see *her,* you break bread, you drink a little wine, she crosses her legs, you look, you talk nice, she crosses her legs again, you look some more, maybe they talk you into a duplicate of the safe deposit key—'

'They won't.'

'—and the next time you see them, you'll see them in court, and everything damaging you said while you were looking at her legs and thinking about how it was to have them wrapped around you will turn up on the record. And you're apt to say a lot of damaging stuff, because they'll come primed with all the right questions. I understand that you want to see her, I'm not insensitive to these things, *but this is not the way.* You're not Donald Trump and she's not Ivana, but this isn't a no-faulter we got here, either, buddy, and Humboldt knows it. Diane does, too.'

'Nobody's been served with papers, and if she just wants to talk—'

'Don't be dense,' he said. 'Once you get to this stage of the party, no one wants to just talk. They either want to fuck or go home. *The divorce has already happened, Steven.* This meeting is a fishing expedition, pure and simple. You have nothing to gain and everything to lose. It's stupid.'

'Just the same—'

'You've done very well for yourself, especially in the last five years—'

'I know, but—'

'—and, for thuh-*ree* of those years,' Ring overrode me, now putting on his courtroom voice like an overcoat, 'Diane Davis was not your wife, not your live-in companion, and not by any stretch of the imagination your helpmate. She was just Diane Coslaw from Pound Ridge, and she did not go before you tossing flower petals or blowing a cornet.'

'No, but I want to see her.' And what I was thinking would have driven him mad: I wanted to see if she was wearing the green dress with the black speckles, because she knew damned well it was my favorite.

He sighed again. 'I can't have this discussion, or I'm going to end up drinking my lunch instead of eating it.'

'Go and eat your lunch. Diet plate. Cottage cheese.'

'Okay, but first I'm going to make one more effort to get through to you. A meeting like this is like a joust. They'll show up in full armor. You're going to be there dressed in nothing but a smile, without even a jock to hold up your balls. And that's exactly the region of your anatomy they're apt to go for first.'

'I want to see her,' I said. 'I want to see how she is. I'm sorry.'

He uttered a small, cynical laugh. 'I'm not going to talk you out of it, am I?'

'No.'

'All right, then I want you to follow certain instructions. If I find out you haven't, and that you've gummed up the works, I may decide it would be simpler to just resign the case. Are you hearing me?'

'I am.'

'Good. Don't yell at her, Steven. They may set it up so you really feel like doing that, but *don't.* Okay?'

'Okay.' I wasn't going to yell at her. If I could quit smoking two days after she had walked out – and stick to it – I thought I could get through a hundred minutes and three courses without calling her a bitch.

'Don't yell at *him*, that's number two.'

'Okay.'

'Don't just say okay. I know you don't like him, and he doesn't like you much, either.'

'He's never even met me. He's a . . . a therapist. How can he have an opinion about me one way or another?'

'Don't be dense,' he said. 'He's being *paid* to have an opinion, that's how. If she tells him you flipped her over and raped her with a corncob, he doesn't say prove it, he says oh you poor thing and how many times. So say okay like you mean it.'

'Okay like I mean it.'

'Better.' But *he* didn't say it like he really meant it; he said it like a man who wants to eat his lunch and forget the whole thing.

'Don't get into substantive matters,' he said. 'Don't discuss financial-settlement issues, not even on a "What would you think if I suggested this" basis. Stick with all the touchy-feely stuff. If they get pissed off and ask why you kept the lunch date if you weren't going to discuss nuts and bolts, tell them just what you told me, that you wanted to see your wife again.'

'Okay.'

'And if they leave at that point, can you live with it?'

'Yes.' I didn't know if I could or not, but I thought I could, and I strongly sensed that Ring wanted to be done with this conversation.

'As a lawyer – your lawyer – I'm telling you that this is a bullshit move, and that if it backfires in court, I'll call a recess just so I can pull you out into the hall and say I told you so. Now, have you got that?'

'Yes. Say hello to that diet plate for me.'

'Fuck the diet plate,' Ring said morosely. 'If I can't have a double bourbon on the rocks at lunch anymore, I can at least have a double cheeseburger at Brew 'n Burger.'

'Rare,' I said.

'That's right, rare.'

'Spoken like a true American.'

'I hope she stands you up, Steven.'

'I know you do.'

He hung up and went out to get his alcohol substitute. When I saw him next, a few days later, there was something between us that didn't quite bear discussion, although I think we would have talked about it if we had known each other even a little bit better. I saw it in his eyes and I suppose he saw it in mine as well – the knowledge that if Humboldt had been a lawyer instead of a therapist, he, John Ring, would have been in on our luncheon meeting. And in that case he might have wound up as dead as William Humboldt.

I walked from my office to the Gotham Café, leaving at 11:15 and arriving across from the restaurant at 11:45. I got there early for my own peace of mind – to make sure the place was where Humboldt had said it was, in other words. That's the way I am, and pretty much the way I've always been. Diane used to call it 'my obsessive streak' when we were first married, but I think that by the end she knew better. I don't trust the competence of others very easily, that's all. I realize it's a pain-in-the-ass characteristic, and I know it drove her crazy, but what she never seemed to realize was that I didn't exactly love it in myself, either. Some things take longer to change than others, though. And some things you can never change, no matter how hard you try.

The restaurant was right where Humboldt had said it would be, the location marked by a green awning with the words GOTHAM CAFÉ on it. A white city skyline was traced across the plate glass windows. It looked New York trendy. It also looked pretty ordinary, just one of the eight hundred or so pricey restaurants crammed together in Midtown.

With the meeting place located and my mind temporarily set at rest (about that, anyway; I was tense as hell about seeing Diane again and craving a cigarette like mad), I walked up to Madison and browsed in a luggage store for fifteen minutes. Mere window shopping was no good; if Diane and Humboldt came from uptown, they might see me. Diane was liable to recognize me by the set of my shoulders and the hang of my topcoat even from behind, and I didn't want that. I didn't want them to know I'd arrived early. I thought it might look needy, even pitiable. So I went inside.

I bought an umbrella I didn't need and left the shop at straight up noon by my watch, knowing I could step through the door of the Gotham Café at 12:05. My father's dictum: if you need to be there, show up five minutes early. If they need *you* to be there, show up five minutes late. I had reached a point where I didn't know who needed what or why or for how long, but my father's dictum seemed like the safest course. If it had been just Diane alone, I think I would have arrived dead on time.

No, that's probably a lie. I suppose if it had been just Diane, I e gone in at 11:45, when I first arrived, and waited for

ood under the awning for a moment, looking in. The place bright, and I marked that down in its favor. I have an intense dislike for dark restaurants, where you can't see what you're eating or drinking. The walls were white and hung with vibrant impressionist drawings. You couldn't tell what they were, but that didn't matter; with their primary colors and broad, exuberant strokes, they hit your eyes like visual caffeine. I looked for Diane and saw a woman that might have been her, seated about halfway down the long room and by the wall. It was hard to say, because her back was turned and I don't have her knack of recognition under difficult circumstances. But the heavyset, balding man she was sitting with certainly looked like a Humboldt. I took a deep breath, opened the restaurant door, and went in.

There are two phases of withdrawal from tobacco, and I'm convinced that it's the second that causes most cases of recidivism. The physical withdrawal lasts ten days to two weeks, and then most of the symptoms – sweats, headaches, muscle twitches, pounding eyes, insomnia, irritability – disappear. What follows is a much longer period of mental withdrawal. These symptoms may include mild to moderate depression, mourning, some degree of anhedonia (emotional flatness, in other words), forgetfulness, even a species of transient dyslexia. I know all this stuff because I read up on it. Following what happened at the Gotham Café, it seemed very important that I do that. I suppose you'd have to say that my interest in the subject fell somewhere between the Land of Hobbies and the Kingdom of Obsession.

The most common symptom of phase two withdrawal is a feeling of mild unreality. Nicotine improves synaptic transferral and improves concentration – widens the brain's information highway, in other words. It's not a big boost, and not really necessary to successful thinking (although most confirmed cigarette junkies believe differently), but when you take it away, you're left you with a feeling – a pervasive feeling, in my case – that the world has taken on a decidedly dreamy cast. There were many times when it seemed to me that people and cars and the little sidewalk vignettes I observed were actually passing by me on a moving screen, a thing controlled by hidden stagehands turning enormous cranks and revolving enormous drums. It was also a little like being mildly stoned all the time, because the feeling was accompanied by a sense of helplessness and moral exhaustion, a feeling that things had simply to go on the way they were going, for good or for ill, because you (except of course it's me I'm talking about) were just too damned busy *not-smoking* to do much of anything else.

I'm not sure how much all this bears on what happened, but I know it has some bearing, because I was pretty sure something was wrong with the maître d' almost as soon as I saw him, and as soon as he spoke to me, I knew.

He was tall, maybe forty-five, slim (in his tux, at least; in ordinary clothes he would have been skinny), mustached. He had a leather-bound menu in one hand. He looked like battalions of maître d's in battalions of fancy New York restaurants, in other words. Except for his bow tie, which was askew, and something on his shirt, that was. A splotch just above the place where his jacket buttoned. It looked like either gravy or a glob of some dark jelly. Also, several strands of his hair stuck up defiantly in back, making me think of Alfalfa in the old *Little Rascals* one-reelers. That almost made me burst out laughing – I was very nervous, remember – and I had to bite my lips to keep it in.

'Yes, sir?' he asked as I approached the desk. It came out sounding like *Yais, sair?* All maître d's in New York City have accents, but it is never one you can positively identify. A girl I dated in the mid-eighties, one who did have a sense of humor (along with a fairly large drug habit, unfortunately), told me once that they all grew up on the same little island and hence all spoke the same language.

'What language is it?' I asked her.

'Snooti,' she said, and I cracked up.

This thought came back to me as I looked past the desk to the woman I'd seen while outside – I was now almost positive it was

Diane – and I had to bite the insides of my lips again. As a result, Humboldt's name came out of me sounding like a half-smothered sneeze.

The maître d's high, pale brow contracted in a frown. His eyes bored into mine. I had taken them for brown as I approached the desk, but now they looked black.

'Pardon, sir?' he asked. It came out sounding like *Pahdun, sair* and looking like *Fuck you, Jack.* His long fingers, as pale as his brow – concert pianist's fingers, they looked like – tapped nervously on the cover of the menu. The tassel sticking out of it like some sort of half-assed bookmark swung back and forth.

'Humboldt,' I said. 'Party of three.' I found I couldn't take my eyes off his bow tie, so crooked that the left side of it was almost brushing the shelf under his chin, and that blob on his snowy white dress shirt. Now that I was closer, it didn't look like either gravy or jelly; it looked like partially dried blood.

He was looking down at his reservations book, the rogue tuft at the back of his head waving back and forth over the rest of his slicked-down hair. I could see his scalp through the grooves his comb had laid down, and a speckle of dandruff on the shoulders of his tux. It occurred to me that a good headwaiter might have fired an underling put together in such sloppy fashion.

'Ah, yes, *monsieur.*' *(Ah yais, messoo.)* He had found the name. 'Your party is—' He was starting to look up. He stopped abruptly, and his eyes sharpened even more, if that was possible, as he looked past me and down. 'You cannot bring that dog in here,' he said sharply. 'How many times have I told you you can't bring that *dog* in here!'

He didn't quite shout, but spoke so loudly that several of the diners closest to his pulpit-like desk stopped eating and looked around curiously.

I looked around myself. He had been so emphatic I expected to see *somebody's* dog, but there was no one behind me and most certainly no dog. It occurred to me then, I don't know why, that he was talking about my umbrella, which I had forgotten to check. Perhaps on the Island of the Maître D's, *dog* was a slang term for umbrella, especially when carried by a patron on a day when rain did not look likely.

I looked back at the maître d' and saw that he had already started away from his desk, holding my menu in his hands. He must have sensed that I wasn't following, because he looked back over his shoulder, eyebrows slightly raised. There was nothing on his face now but polite inquiry – *Are you coming, messoo?* – and I came. I knew something was wrong with him, but I came. I could not take the time or effort to try to decide what might be wrong with the maître d' of a restaurant where I had never been before today and where I would probably never be again; I had Humboldt and Diane to deal with, I had to do it without smoking, and the maître d' of the Gotham Café would have to take care of his own problems, dog included.

Diane turned around and at first I saw nothing in her face and in her eyes but a kind of frozen politeness. Then, just below it, I saw anger . . . or thought I did. We'd done a lot of arguing during our last three or four months together, but I couldn't recall ever seeing the sort of concealed anger I sensed in her now, anger that was meant to be hidden by the makeup and the new dress (blue, no speckles, no slit up the side, deep or otherwise) and the new hairdo. The heavyset man she was with was saying something, and she reached out and touched his arm. As he turned toward me, beginning to get to his feet, I saw something else in her face. She was afraid of me as well as angry at me. And although she hadn't said a single word, I was already furious at her. The expression in her eyes was a dead negative; she might as well have been wearing a CLOSED UNTIL FURTHER NOTICE sign on her forehead between them. I thought I deserved better. Of course, that may just be a way of saying I'm human.

'Monsieur,' the maître d' said, pulling out the chair to Diane's left. I barely heard him, and certainly any thought of his eccentric behavior and crooked bow tie had left my head. I think that even the subject of tobacco had briefly vacated my head for the first time since I'd quit smoking. I could only consider the careful composure of her face and marvel at how I could be angry at her and still want her so much it made me ache to look at her. Absence may or may not make the heart grow fonder, but it certainly freshens the eye.

I also found time to wonder if I had really seen all I'd surmised. Anger? Yes, that was possible, even likely. If she hadn't been angry with me to at least some degree, she never would have left in the first place, I supposed. But afraid? Why in God's name would Diane be afraid of me? I'd never laid a single finger on her. Yes, I suppose I had raised my voice during some of our arguments, but so had she.

'Enjoy your lunch, monsieur,' the maître d' said from some other universe – the one where service people usually stay, only poking their heads into ours when we call them, either because we need something or to complain.

'Mr Davis, I'm Bill Humboldt,' Diane's companion said. He held out a large hand that looked reddish and chapped. I shook it briefly. The rest of him was as big as his hand, and his broad face wore the sort of flush habitual drinkers often get after the first one of the day. I put him in his mid-forties, about ten years away from the time when his sagging cheeks would turn into jowls.

'Pleasure,' I said, not thinking about what I was saying any more than I was thinking about the maître d' with the blob on his shirt, only wanting to get the hand-shaking part over so I could turn back to the pretty blonde with the rose and cream complexion, the pale pink lips, and the trim, slim figure. The woman who had, not so long ago, liked to whisper 'Do me do me do me' in my ear while she held onto my ass like a saddle with two pommels.

'We'll get you a drink,' Humboldt said, looking around for a waiter like a man who did it a lot. Her therapist had all the bells and whistles of the incipient alcoholic. Wonderful.

'Perrier and lime is good.'

'For what?' Humboldt inquired with a big smile. He picked up the half-finished martini in front of him on the table and drained it until the olive with the toothpick in it rested against his lips. He spat it back, then set the glass down and looked at me. 'Well, perhaps we'd better get started.'

I paid no attention. I already *had* gotten started; I'd done it the instant Diane looked up at me. 'Hi, Diane,' I said. It was marvelous, really, how she looked smarter and prettier than previous. More desirable than previous, too. As if she had learned things – yes, even after only two weeks of separation, and while living with Ernie and Dee Dee Coslaw in Pound Ridge – that I could never know.

'How are you, Steve?' she asked.

'Fine,' I said. Then, 'Not so fine, actually. I've missed you.'

Only watchful silence from the lady greeted this. Those big blue-green eyes looking at me, no more. Certainly no return serve, no *I've missed you, too.*

'And I quit smoking. That's also played hell with my peace of mind.'

'Did you, finally? Good for you.'

I felt another flash of anger, this time a really ugly one, at her politely dismissive tone. As if I might not be telling the truth, but it didn't really matter if I was. She'd carped at me about the cigarettes every day for two years, it seemed – how they were going to give me cancer, how they were going to give *her* cancer, how she wouldn't even consider getting pregnant until I stopped, so I could just save any breath I might have been planning to waste on *that* subject – and now all at once it didn't matter anymore, because I didn't matter anymore.

'Steve – Mr Davis,' Humboldt said, 'I thought we might begin by getting you to look at a list of grievances which Diane has worked out during our sessions – our exhaustive sessions, I might say – over the last couple of weeks. Certainly it can serve as a springboard to our main purpose for being here, which is how to order a period of separation that will allow growth on both of your parts.'

There was a briefcase on the floor beside him. He picked it up with a grunt and set it on the table's one empty chair. Humboldt began unsnapping the clasps, but I quit paying attention at that point. I wasn't interested in springboards to separation, whatever that meant. I felt a combination of panic and anger that was, in some ways, the most peculiar emotion I have ever experienced.

I looked at Diane and said, 'I want to try again. Can we reconcile? Is there any chance of that?'

The look of absolute horror on her face crashed hopes I hadn't even known I'd been holding onto. Horror was followed by anger. 'Isn't that just like you!' she exclaimed.

'Diane—'

'Where's the safe deposit box key, Steven? Where did you hide it?'

Humboldt looked alarmed. He reached out and touched her arm. 'Diane . . . I thought we agreed—'

'What we agreed is that this son of a bitch will hide everything under the nearest rock and then plead poverty if we let him!'

'You searched the bedroom for it before you left, didn't you?' I asked quietly. 'Tossed it like a burglar.'

She flushed at that. I don't know if it was shame, anger, or both. 'It's my box as well as yours! My *things* as well as yours!'

Humboldt was looking more alarmed than ever. Several diners had glanced around at us. Most of them looked amused, actually. People are surely God's most bizarre creatures. 'Please . . . please, let's not—'

'Where did you hide it, Steven?'

'I didn't hide it. I never hid it. I left it up at the cabin by accident, that's all.'

She smiled knowingly. 'Oh, yes. By accident. Uh-huh.' I said nothing, and the knowing smile slipped away. 'I want it,' she said, then amended hastily: 'I want a *copy*.'

People in hell want icewater, I thought. Out loud I said, 'There's nothing to be done about it, is there?'

She hesitated, maybe hearing something in my voice she didn't actually want to hear, or to acknowledge. 'No,' she said. 'The next time you see me, it will be with my lawyer. I'm divorcing you.'

'Why?' What I heard in my voice now was a plaintive note like a sheep's bleat. I didn't like it, but there wasn't a goddamned thing I could do about it. *'Why?'*

'Oh, Jesus. Do you expect me to believe you're really that dense?'

'I just can't—'

Her cheeks were brighter than ever, the flush now rising almost to her temples. 'Yes, probably you expect me to believe just that very thing. Isn't that *typical.*' She picked up her water and spilled the top two inches on the tablecloth because her hand was trembling. I flashed back at once – I mean *kapow* – to the day she'd left, remembering how I'd knocked the glass of orange juice onto the floor and how I'd cautioned myself not to try picking up the broken pieces of glass until my hands had settled down, and how I'd gone ahead anyway and cut myself for my pains.

'Stop it, this is counterproductive,' Humboldt said. He sounded like a playground monitor trying to stop a scuffle before it gets started, but he seemed to have forgotten all about Diane's shit-list; his eyes were sweeping the rear part of the room, looking for our waiter, or any waiter whose eye he could catch. He was a lot less interested in therapy, at that particular moment, than he was in obtaining what the British like to call the other half.

'I only want to know—' I began.

'What you want to *know* doesn't have anything to do with why we're *here*,' Humboldt said, and for a moment he actually sounded alert.

'Yes, right, *finally*,' Diane said. She spoke in a brittle, urgent voice. 'Finally it's not about what you *want*, what you *need*.'

'I don't know what that means, but I'm willing to listen,' I said. 'If you wanted to try joint counseling instead of . . . uh . . . therapy . . . whatever it is Humboldt does . . . I'm not against it if—'

She raised her hands to shoulder level, palms out. 'Oh, God, Joe Camel goes New Age,' she said, then dropped her hands back into her lap. 'After all the days you rode off into the sunset, tall in the saddle. Say it ain't so, Joe.'

'Stop it,' Humboldt told her. He looked from his client to his client's soon-to-be ex-husband (it was going to happen, all right; even the slight unreality that comes with *not-smoking* couldn't conceal that self-evident truth from me by that point). 'One more word from either of you and I'm going to declare this luncheon [illegible] gave us a small smile, one so obviously manufac- [illegible] und it perversely endearing. 'And we haven't even [illegible] ials yet.'

[illegible] first mention of food since I'd joined them – was just [illegible] he bad things started to happen, and I remember smelling salmon from one of the nearby tables. In the two weeks since I'd quit smoking, my sense of smell had become incredibly sharp, but I do not count that as much of a blessing, especially when it comes to salmon. I used to like it, but now I can't abide the smell of it, let alone the taste. To me it smells of pain and fear and blood and death.

'He started it,' Diane said sulkily.

You *started it,* you *were the one who tossed the joint and then walked out when you couldn't find what you wanted,* I thought, but I kept it to myself. Humboldt clearly meant what he said; he would take Diane by the hand and walk her out of the restaurant if we started that schoolyard *no-I-didn't, yes-you-did* shit. Not even the prospect of another drink would hold him here.

'Okay,' I said mildly . . . and I had to work hard to achieve that mild tone, believe me. 'I started it. What's next?' I knew, of course: the grievances. Diane's shit-list, in other words. And a lot more about the key to the lockbox. Probably the only satisfaction I was going to get out of this sorry situation was telling them that neither of them was going to see a copy of that key until an officer of the court presented me with a paper ordering me to turn one over. I hadn't touched the stuff in the box since Diane booked on out of my life, and I didn't intend to touch any of it in the immediate future . . . but she wasn't going to touch it, either. Let her chew crackers and try to whistle, as my grandmother used to say.

Humboldt took out a sheaf of papers. They were held together by one of those designer paper clips – the ones that come in different colors. It occurred to me that I had arrived abysmally unprepared for this meeting, and not just because my lawyer was jaw-deep in a cheeseburger somewhere, either. Diane had her new dress; Humboldt had his designer briefcase, plus Diane's shit-list held together by a color-coded designer paper clip; all I had was a new umbrella on a sunny day. I looked down at where it lay beside my chair and saw there was still a price tag dangling from the handle. All at once I felt like Minnie Pearl.

The room smelled wonderful, as most restaurants do since they banned smoking in them – of flowers and wine and fresh coffee and chocolate and pastry – but what I smelled most clearly was salmon. I remember thinking that it smelled very good, and that I would probably order some. I also remember thinking that if I could eat at a meeting like this, I could probably eat anywhere.

'The major problems your wife has articulated – so far, at least – are insensitivity on your part regarding her job, and an inability to trust in personal affairs,' Humboldt said. 'In regard to the second, I'd say your unwillingness to give Diane fair access to the safe deposit box you maintain in common pretty well sums up the trust issue.'

I opened my mouth to tell him I had a trust issue, too, that I didn't trust Diane not to take the whole works and then sit on it. Before I could say anything, however, I was interrupted by the maître d'. He was screaming as well as talking, and I've tried to indicate that, but a bunch of e's strung together can't really convey the quality of that sound. It was as if he had a bellyful of steam and a teakettle whistle caught in his throat.

'That dog . . . Eeeeeeee! . . . I told you time and again about that dog . . . Eeeeeee! . . . All that time I can't sleep . . . Eeeeeee! . . . She says cut your face, that cunt . . . Eeeeeee! . . . How you tease me! . . . Eeeeeee! . . . And now you bring that dog in here . . . Eeeeeee!'

The room fell silent at once, of course, diners looking up from their meals or their conversations as the thin, pale, black-clad figure came stalking across the room with its face outthrust and its long, storklike legs scissoring. No amusement on the surrounding faces now; only astonishment. The maître d's bow tie had turned a full ninety degrees from its normal position, so it now looked like the hands of a clock indicating the hour of six. His hands were clasped behind his back as he walked, and bent forward slightly from the waist as he was, he made me think of a drawing in my sixth-grade literature book, an illustration of Washington Irving's unfortunate schoolteacher, Ichabod Crane.

It was me he was looking at, me he was approaching. I stared at him, feeling almost hypnotized – it was like one of those dreams where you discover that you haven't studied for the bar exam you're supposed to take or that you're attending a White House dinner in your honor with no clothes on – and I might have stayed that way if Humboldt hadn't moved.

I heard his chair scrape back and glanced at him. He was standing up, his napkin held loosely in one hand. He looked surprised, but he also looked furious. I suddenly realized two things: that he was drunk, quite drunk, in fact, and that he saw this as a smirch on both his hospitality and his competence. He had chosen the restaurant, after all, and now look – the master of ceremonies had gone bonkers.

'Eeeeee! . . . I teach you! For the last time I teach you . . .'

'Oh, my God, he's wet his pants,' a woman at a nearby table murmured. Her voice was low but perfectly audible in the silence as the maître d' drew in a fresh breath with which to scream, and I saw she was right. The crotch of the skinny man's dress pants was soaked.

'See here, you idiot,' Humboldt said, turning to face him, and the maître d' brought his left hand out from behind his back. In it was the largest butcher knife I have ever seen. It had to have been two feet long, with the top part of its cutting edge slightly belled, like a cutlass in an old pirate movie.

'Look out!' I yelled at Humboldt, and at one of the tables against the wall, a skinny man in rimless spectacles screamed, ejecting a mouthful of chewed brown fragments of food onto the tablecloth in front of him.

Humboldt seemed to hear neither my yell nor the other man's scream. He was frowning thunderously at the maître d'. 'You don't need to expect to see me in here again if this is the way—' Humboldt began.

'Eeeeee! EEEEEEEEE!' the maître d' screamed, and swung the butcher knife flat through the air. It made a kind of whickering sound, like a whispered sentence. The period was the sound of the blade burying itself in William Humboldt's right cheek. Blood exploded out of the wound in a furious spray of tiny droplets.

They decorated the tablecloth in a fan-shaped stipplework, and I clearly saw (I will never forget it) one bright red drop fall into my water glass and then dive for the bottom with a pinkish filament like a tail stretching out behind it. It looked like a bloody tadpole.

Humboldt's cheek snapped open, revealing his teeth, and as he clapped his hand to the gouting wound, I saw something pinkish-white lying on the shoulder of his charcoal gray suitcoat. It wasn't until the whole thing was over that I realized it must have been his earlobe.

'Tell this in your ears!' the maître d' screamed furiously at Diane's bleeding therapist, who stood there with one hand clapped to his cheek. Except for the blood pouring over and between his fingers, Humboldt looked weirdly like Jack Benny doing one of his famous double-takes. *'Call this to your hateful tattle-tale friends of the street . . . you misery . . . Eeeeee! . . . DOG LOVER!'*

Now other people were screaming, mostly at the sight of the blood, I think. Humboldt was a big man, and he was bleeding like a stuck pig. I could hear it pattering on the floor like water from a broken pipe, and the front of his white shirt was now red. His tie, which had been red to start with, was now black.

'Steve?' Diane said. *'Steven?'*

A man and a woman had been having lunch at the table behind her and slightly to her left. Now the man – about thirty and handsome in the way George Hamilton used to be – bolted to his feet and ran toward the front of the restaurant. *'Troy, don't go without me!'* his date screamed, but Troy never looked back. He'd forgotten all about a library book he was supposed to return, it seemed, or maybe about how he'd promised to wax the car.

If there had been a paralysis in the room – I can't actually say if there was or not, although I seem to have seen a great deal, and to remember it all – that broke it. There were more screams and other people got up. Several tables were overturned. Glasses and china shattered on the floor. I saw a man with his arm around the waist of his female companion hurry past behind the maître d'; her hand was clamped into his shoulder like a claw. For a moment her eyes met mine, and they were as empty as the eyes of a Greek bust. Her face was dead pale, haglike with horror.

All of this might have happened in ten seconds, or maybe twenty. I remember it like a series of photographs or filmstrips, but it has no timeline. Time ceased to exist for me at the moment Alfalfa the maître d' brought his left hand out from behind his back and I saw the butcher knife. During that time the man in the tuxedo continued to spew out a confusion of words in his special maître d's language, the one that old girlfriend of mine had called Snooti. Some of it really *was* in a foreign language, some of it was English but completely without sense, and some of it was striking . . . almost haunting. Have you ever read any of Dutch Schultz's long, confused deathbed statement? It was like that. Much of it I can't remember. What I can remember I suppose I'll never forget.

Humboldt staggered backward, still holding his lacerated cheek. The backs of his knees struck the seat of his chair, and he sat down heavily on it. *He looks like someone who's just been told he's got cancer*, I thought. He started to turn toward Diane and me, his eyes wide and shocked. I had time to see there were tears spilling out of them, and then the maître d' wrapped both hands around the handle of the butcher knife and buried it in the center of Humboldt's head. It made a sound like someone whacking a pile of towels with a cane.

'Boot!' Humboldt cried. I'm quite sure that's what his last word on planet Earth was – 'boot.' Then his weeping eyes rolled up to whites and he slumped forward onto his plate, sweeping his own glassware off the table and onto the floor with one outflung hand. As this happened, the maître d' – all his hair was sticking up in back now, not just some of it – pried the long knife out of his head. Blood sprayed out of the head wound in a kind of vertical curtain, and splashed the front of Diane's dress. She raised her hands to her shoulders with the palms turned out once again, but this time it was in horror rather than exasperation. She shrieked, and then clapped her blood-spattered hands to her face, over her eyes. The maître d' paid no attention to her. Instead, he turned to me.

'That dog of yours,' he said, speaking in an almost conversational tone. He registered absolutely no interest in or even knowledge of the screaming, terrified people stampeding behind him toward the doors. His eyes were very large, very dark. They looked brown to me again, but there seemed to be black circles around the irises. 'That dog of yours is so much rage. All the radios of Coney Island don't make up to that dog, you motherfucker.'

I had the umbrella in my hand, and the one thing I can't remember, no matter how hard I try, is when I grabbed it. I think it must have been while Humboldt was standing transfixed by the realization that his mouth had been expanded by eight inches or so, but I simply can't remember. I remember the man who looked like George Hamilton bolting for the door, and I know his name was Troy because that's what his companion called after him, but I can't remember picking up the umbrella I'd bought in the luggage store. It *was* in my hand, though, the price tag sticking out of the bottom of my fist, and when the maître d' bent forward as if bowing and ran the knife through the air at me – meaning, I think, to bury it in my throat – I raised it and brought it down on his wrist, like an old-time teacher whacking an unruly pupil with his hickory stick.

'Ud!' the maître d' grunted as his hand was driven sharply down, and the blade meant for my throat plowed through the soggy pinkish tablecloth instead. He held on, though, and pulled it back. If I'd tried to hit his knife hand again I'm sure I would have missed, but I didn't. I swung at his face, and fetched him an excellent lick – as excellent a lick as one can administer with an umbrella, anyway – up the side of his head. And as I did, the umbrella popped open like the visual punchline of a slapstick act.

I didn't think it was funny, though. The bloom of the umbrella hid him from me completely as he staggered backward with his free hand flying up to the place where I'd hit him, and I didn't like not being able to see him. Didn't like it? It terrified me. Not that I wasn't terrified already.

I grabbed Diane's wrist and yanked her to her feet. She came without a word, took a step toward me, then stumbled on her high heels and fell clumsily into my arms. I was aware of her breasts pushing against me, and the wet, warm clamminess over them.

'Eeeee! You boinker!' the maître d' screamed, or perhaps it was a 'boinger' he called me. It probably doesn't matter, I know that, and yet it quite often seems to me that it does. Late at night, the little questions haunt me as much as the big ones. *'You boinking bastard! All these radios! Hush-do-baba! Fuck Cousin Brucie! Fuck YOU!'*

He started around the table toward us (the area behind him was completely empty now, and looked like the aftermath of a brawl in a western movie saloon). My umbrella was still lying on the table with the opened top jutting off the far side, and the maître d' bumped it with his hip. It fell off in front of him, and while he kicked it aside, I set Diane back on her feet and pulled her toward the far side of the room. The front door was no good; it was probably too far away in any case, but even if we could get there, it was still jammed tight with frightened, screaming people. If he wanted me – or both of us – he would have no trouble catching us and carving us like a couple of turkeys.

'Bugs! You bugs! . . . Eeeeee! . . . So much for your dog, eh? So much for your barking dog!'

'Make him stop!' Diane screamed. *'Oh, Jesus, he's going to kill us both, make him stop!'*

'I rot you, you abominations!' Closer now. The umbrella hadn't held him up for long, that was for sure. *'I rot you all!'*

I saw three doors, two facing each other in a small alcove where there was also a pay telephone. Men's and women's rooms. No good. Even if they were single toilets with locks on the doors, they were no good. A nut like this would have no trouble bashing a bathroom lock off its screws, and we would have nowhere to run.

I dragged her toward the third door and shoved through it into a world of clean green tiles, strong fluorescent light, gleaming chrome, and steamy odors of food. The smell of salmon dominated. Humboldt had never gotten a chance to ask about the specials, but I thought I knew what at least one of them had been.

A waiter was standing there with a loaded tray balanced on the flat of one hand, his mouth agape and his eyes wide. He looked like Gimpel the Fool in that Isaac Singer story. 'What—' he said, and then I shoved him aside. The tray went flying, with plates and glassware shattering against the wall.

'Ay!' A man yelled. He was huge, wearing a white smock and a white chef's hat like a cloud. There was a red bandanna around his neck, and in one hand he held a ladle that was dripping some sort of brown sauce. 'Ay, you can't come in here likea dat!'

'We have to get out,' I said. 'He's crazy. He's—'

An idea struck me then, a way of explaining without explaining, and I put my hand over Diane's left breast for a moment, on the soaked cloth of her dress. It was the last time I ever touched her intimately, and I don't know if it felt good or not. I held my hand out to the chef, showing him a palm streaked with Humboldt's blood.

'Good Christ,' he said. 'Here. Inna da back.'

At that instant the door we'd come through burst open again, and the maître d' rolled in, eyes wild, hair sticking out everywhere like fur on a hedgehog that's tucked itself into a ball. He looked around, saw the waiter, dismissed him, saw me, and rushed at me.

I bolted again, dragging Diane with me, shoving blindly at the soft-bellied bulk of the chef. We went past him, the front of Diane's dress leaving a smear of blood on the front of his tunic. I saw he wasn't coming with us, that he was turning toward the maître d' instead, and wanted to warn him, wanted to tell him that wouldn't work, that it was the worst idea in the world and likely to be the last idea he ever had, but there was no time.

'Ay!' the chef cried. 'Ay, Guy, what's dis?' He said the maître d's name as the French do, so it rhymes with *free,* and then he didn't say anything at all. There was a heavy thud that made me think of the sound of the knife burying itself in Humboldt's skull, and then the cook screamed. It had a watery sound. It was followed by a thick, wet splat that haunts my dreams. I don't know what it was, and I don't want to know.

I yanked Diane down a narrow aisle between two stoves that baked a furious dull heat out at us. There was a door at the end, locked shut by two heavy steel bolts. I reached for the top one and then heard Guy, The Maître D' from Hell, coming after us, babbling.

I wanted to keep at the bolt, wanted to believe I could open the door and get us out before he could get within sticking distance, but part of me – the part that was determined to live – knew better. I pushed Diane against the door, stepped in front of her in a protective maneuver that must go all the way back to the Ice Age, and faced him.

He came running up the narrow aisle between the stoves with the knife gripped in his left hand and raised above his head. His mouth was open and pulled back from a set of dingy, eroded teeth. Any hope of help I might have had from Gimpel the Fool disappeared. He was cowering against the wall beside the door to the restaurant. His fingers were buried deep inside his mouth, and he looked more like the village idiot than ever.

'Forgetful of me you shouldn't have been!' Guy screamed, sounding like Yoda in the *Star Wars* movies. *'Your hateful dog! . . . Your loud music, so disharmonious! . . . Eeeee! . . . How you ever—'*

There was a large pot on one of the front burners of the left-hand stove. I reached out for it and slapped it at him. It was over an hour before I realized how badly I'd burned my hand doing that; I had a palmful of blisters like little buns, and more blisters on my three middle fingers. The pot skidded off its burner and tipped over in midair, dousing Guy from the waist down with what looked like corn, rice, and maybe two gallons of boiling water.

He screamed, staggered backward, and put the hand that wasn't holding the knife down on the other stove, almost directly into the blue-yellow gas flame underneath a skillet where mushrooms which had been sauteeing were now turning to charcoal. He screamed again, this time in a register so high it hurt my ears, and held his hand up before his eyes, as if not able to believe it was connected to him.

I looked to my right and saw a little nestle of cleaning equipment beside the door – Glass-X and Clorox and Janitor In A Drum on a shelf, a broom with a dustpan stuck on top of the handle like a hat, and a mop in a steel bucket with a squeegee on the side.

As Guy came toward me again, holding the knife in the hand that wasn't red and swelling up like an inner tube, I grabbed the handle of the mop, used it to roll the bucket in front of me on its little casters, and then jabbed it out at him. Guy pulled back with his upper body but stood his ground. There was a peculiar, twitching little smile on his lips. He looked like a dog who has forgotten, temporarily, at least, how to snarl. He held the knife up in front of his face and made several mystic passes with it. The overhead fluorescents glimmered liquidly on the blade – where it wasn't caked with blood, that was. He didn't seem to feel any pain in his burned hand, or in his legs, although they had been doused with boiling water and his tuxedo pants were spackled with rice.

'Rotten bugger,' Guy said, making his mystic passes. He was like a Crusader preparing to go into battle. If, that was, you could imagine a Crusader in a rice-caked tux. 'Kill you like I did your nasty barking dog.'

'I don't have a dog,' I said. 'I *can't* have a dog. It's in the lease.'

I think it was the only thing I said to him during the whole nightmare, and I'm not entirely sure I *did* say it out loud. It might only have been a thought. Behind him, I could see the chef struggling to his feet. He had one hand wrapped around the handle of the kitchen's refrigerator and the other clapped to his blood-stained tunic, which was torn open across the swelling of his stomach in a big purple grin. He was doing his best to hold his plumbing in, but it was a battle he was losing. One loop of intestines, shiny and bruise-colored, already hung out, resting against his left side like some awful watch chain.

Guy feinted at me with his knife. I countered by shoving the mop bucket at him, and he drew back. I pulled it to me again and stood there with my hands wrapped around the wooden mop handle, ready to shove the bucket at him if he moved. My own hand was throbbing and I could feel sweat trickling down my cheeks like hot oil. Behind Guy, the cook had managed to get all the way up. Slowly, like an invalid in early recovery from a serious operation, he started working his way down the aisle toward Gimpel the Fool. I wished him well.

'Undo those bolts,' I said to Diane.

'What?'

'The bolts on the *door.* Undo them.'

'I can't move,' she said. She was crying so hard I could barely understand her. 'You're *crushing* me.'

I moved forward a little to give her room. Guy bared his teeth at me. Mock-jabbed with the knife, then pulled it back, grinning his nervous, snarly little grin as I rolled the bucket at him again, on its squeaky canisters.

'Bug-infested stinkpot,' he said. He sounded like a man discussing the Mets' chances in the forthcoming season. 'Let's see you play your radio this loud now, stinkpot. It gives you a change in your thinking, doesn't it? *Boink!*'

He jabbed. I rolled. But this time he didn't pull back as far, and I realized he was nerving himself up. He meant to go for it, and soon. I could feel Diane's breasts brush against my back as she gasped for breath. I'd given her room, but she hadn't turned around to work the bolts. She was just standing there.

'Open the door,' I told her, speaking out the side of my mouth like a prison con. 'Pull the goddamn bolts, Diane.'

'I can't,' she sobbed. 'I can't, I don't have any strength in my hands. Make him stop, Steven, don't stand there *talking* with him, make him *stop.*'

She was driving me insane. I really thought she was. 'You turn around and pull those bolts, Diane, or I'll just stand aside and let—'

'EEEEEEEEE!' he screamed, and charged, waving and stabbing with the knife.

I slammed the mop bucket forward with all the force I could muster, and swept his legs out from under him. He howled and brought the knife down in a long, desperate stroke. Any closer and it would have torn off the tip of my nose. Then he landed spraddled awkwardly on wide-spread knees, with his face just above the mop-squeezing gadget hung on the side of the bucket. Perfect! I drove the mop head into the nape of his neck. The strings draggled down over the shoulders of his black jacket like a witch wig. His face slammed into the squeegee. I bent, grabbed the handle with my free hand, and clamped it shut. Guy shrieked with pain, the sound muffled by the mop.

'PULL THOSE BOLTS!' I screamed at Diane. *'PULL THOSE BOLTS, YOU USELESS BITCH! PULL—'*

Thud! Something hard and pointed slammed into my left buttock. I staggered forward with a yell – more surprise than pain, I think, although it *did* hurt. I went to one knee and lost my hold on the squeegee handle. Guy pulled back, slipping out from under the stringy head of the mop at the same time, breathing so loudly he sounded almost as if he were barking. It hadn't slowed him down much, though; he lashed out at me with the knife as soon as he was clear of the bucket. I pulled back, feeling the breeze as the blade cut the air beside my cheek.

It was only as I scrambled up that I realized what had happened, what she had done. I snatched a quick glance over my shoulder at her. She stared back defiantly, her back pressed against the door. A crazy thought came to me: she *wanted* me to get killed. Had perhaps even planned it, the whole thing. Found herself a crazy maître d' and—

Her eyes widened. *'Look out!'*

I turned back just in time to see him lunging at me. The sides of his face were bright red, except for the big white spots made by the drain holes in the squeegee. I rammed the mop head at him, aiming for the throat and getting his chest instead. I stopped his charge and actually knocked him backward a step. What happened then was only luck. He slipped in water from the overturned bucket and went down hard, slamming his head on the tiles. Not thinking and just vaguely aware that I was screaming, I snatched up the skillet of mushrooms from the stove and brought it down on his upturned face as hard as I could. There was a muffled thump, followed by a horrible (but mercifully brief) hissing sound as the skin of his cheeks and forehead boiled.

I turned, shoved Diane aside, and drew the bolts holding the door shut. I opened the door and sunlight hit me like a hammer. And the smell of the air. I can't remember air ever smelling better, not even when I was a kid and it was the first day of summer vacation.

I grabbed Diane's arm and pulled her out into a narrow alley lined with padlocked trash bins. At the far end of this narrow stone slit, like a vision of heaven, was 53rd Street with traffic going heedlessly back and forth. I looked over my shoulder and through the open kitchen door. Guy lay on his back with carbonized mushrooms circling his head like an existential diadem. The skillet had slid off to one side, revealing a face that was red and swelling with blisters. One of his eyes was open, but it looked unseeingly up at the fluorescent lights. Behind him, the kitchen was empty. There was a pool of blood on the floor and bloody handprints on the white enamel front of the walk-in fridge, but both the chef and Gimpel the Fool were gone.

I slammed the door shut and pointed down the alley. 'Go on.'

She didn't move, only looked at me.

I shoved her lightly on her left shoulder. 'Go!'

She raised a hand like a traffic cop, shook her head, then pointed a finger at me. 'Don't you touch me.'

'What'll you do? Sic your therapist on me? I think he's dead, sweetheart.'

'Don't you patronize me like that. Don't you *dare.* And don't touch me, Steven, I'm warning you.'

The kitchen door burst open. Moving, not thinking but just moving, I slammed it shut again. I heard a muffled cry – whether anger or pain I didn't know and didn't care – just before it clicked shut. I leaned my back against it and braced my feet. 'Do you want to stand here and discuss it?' I asked her. 'He's still pretty lively, by the sound.' He hit the door again. I rocked with it, then slammed it shut. I waited for him to try again, but he didn't.

Diane gave me a long look, glarey and uncertain, and then started walking up the alleyway with her head down and her hair hanging at the sides of her neck. I stood with my back against the door until she got about three-quarters of the way to the street, then stood away from it, watching it warily. No one came out, but I decided that wasn't going to guarantee any peace of mind.

I dragged one of the trash bins in front of the door, then set off after Diane, jogging.

When I got to the mouth of the alley, she wasn't there anymore. I looked right, toward Madison, and didn't see her. I looked left and there she was, wandering slowly across 53rd on a diagonal, her head still down and her hair still hanging like curtains at the sides of her face. No one paid any attention to her; the people in front of the Gotham Café were gawking through the plate glass windows like people in front of the Boston Seaquarium shark tank at feeding time. Sirens were approaching, a lot of them.

I went across the street, reached for her shoulder, thought better of it. I settled for calling her name instead.

She turned around, her eyes dulled with horror and shock. The front of her dress had turned into a grisly purple bib. She stank of blood and spent adrenaline.

'Leave me alone,' she said. 'I never want to see you again.'

'You kicked my ass in there, you bitch,' I said. 'You kicked my ass and almost got me killed. Both of us. I can't believe you.'

'I've wanted to kick your ass for the last fourteen months,' she said. 'When it comes to fulfilling our dreams, we can't always pick our times, can w—'

I slapped her across the face. I didn't think about it, I just hauled off and did it, and few things in my adult life have given me so much pleasure. I'm ashamed of that, but I've come too far in this story to tell a lie, even one of omission.

Her head rocked back. Her eyes widened in shock and pain, losing that dull, traumatized look.

'You bastard!' she cried, her hand going to her cheek. Now tears were brimming in her eyes. 'Oh, you *bastard!*'

'I saved your life,' I said. 'Don't you realize that? Doesn't that get through? *I saved your fucking life.*'

'You son of a bitch,' she whispered. 'You controlling, judgmental, small-minded, conceited, complacent son of a bitch. I hate you.'

'Fuck that jerk-off crap. If it wasn't for the conceited, small-minded son of a bitch, you'd be dead now.'

'If it wasn't for you, I wouldn't have been there in the first place,' she said as the first three police cars came screaming down 53rd Street and pulled up in front of the Gotham Café. Cops poured out of them like clowns in a circus act. 'If you ever touch me again, I'll scratch your eyes out, Steve,' she said. 'Stay away from me.'

I had to put my hands in my armpits. They wanted to kill her, to reach out and wrap themselves around her neck and just kill her.

She walked seven or eight steps, then turned back to me. She was smiling. It was a terrible smile, more awful than any expression I had seen on the face of Guy the Demon Waiter. 'I had lovers,' she said, smiling her terrible smile. She was lying. The lie was all over her face, but that didn't make the lie hurt any less. She *wished* it was true; that was all over her face, too. 'Three of them over the last year or so. You weren't any good at it, so I found men who were.'

She turned and walked up the street, like a woman who was sixty-five instead of twenty-seven. I stood and watched her. Just before she reached the corner I shouted it again. It was the one thing I couldn't get past; it was stuck in my throat like a chicken bone. 'I saved your *life*! Your goddamn *life*!'

She paused at the corner and turned back to me. The terrible smile was still on her face. 'No,' she said. 'You didn't.'

Then she went on around the corner. I haven't seen her since, although I suppose I will. I'll see her in court, as the saying goes.

I found a market on the next block and bought a package of Marlboros. When I got back to the corner of Madison and 53rd, 53rd had been blocked off with those blue sawhorses the cops use to protect crime scenes and parade routes. I could see the restaurant, though. I could see it just fine. I sat down on the curb, lit a cigarette, and observed developments. Half a dozen rescue vehicles arrived – a scream of ambulances, I guess you could say.

The chef went into the first one, unconscious but apparently still alive. His brief appearance before his fans on 53rd Street was followed by a body bag on a stretcher – Humboldt. Next came Guy, strapped tightly to a stretcher and staring wildly around as he was loaded into the back of an ambulance. I thought that for just a moment his eyes met mine, but that was probably just my imagination.

As Guy's ambulance pulled away, rolling through a hole in the sawhorse barricade provided by two uniformed cops, I tossed the cigarette I'd been smoking in the gutter. I hadn't gone through this day just to start killing myself with tobacco again, I decided.

I looked after the departing ambulance and tried to imagine the man inside it living wherever maître d's live – Queens or Brooklyn or maybe even Rye or Mamaroneck. I tried to imagine what his dining room might look like, what pictures might be on the walls. I couldn't do that, but I found I could imagine his bedroom with relative ease, although not whether he shared it with a woman. I could see him lying awake but perfectly still, looking up at the ceiling in the small hours while the moon hung in the black firmament like the half-lidded eye of a corpse; I could imagine him lying there and listening to the neighbor's dog bark steadily and monotonously, going on and on until the sound was like a silver nail driving into his brain. I imagined him lying not far from a closet filled with tuxedos in plastic dry-cleaning bags. I could see them hanging there in the dark like executed felons. I wondered if he did have a wife. If so, had he killed her before coming to work? I thought of the blob on his shirt and decided it was a possibility. I also wondered about the neighbor's dog, the one that wouldn't shut up. And the neighbor's family.

But mostly it was Guy I thought about, lying sleepless through all the same nights I had lain sleepless, listening to the dog next door or down the street as I had listened to sirens and the rumble of trucks heading downtown. I thought of him lying there and looking up at the shadows the moon had tacked to the ceiling. Thought of that cry – *Eeeeee!* – building up in his head like gas in a closed room.

'Eeeee,' I said . . . just to see how it sounded. I dropped the package of Marlboros into the gutter and began stamping it methodically as I sat there on the curb. 'Eeeee. Eeeee. Eeeeee.'

One of the cops standing by the sawhorses looked over at me. 'Hey, buddy, want to stop being a pain in the butt?' he called over. 'We got us a situation here.'

Of course you do, I thought. Don't we all.

I didn't say anything, though. I stopped stamping – the cigarette pack was pretty well flattened by then, anyway – and stopped making the noise. I could still hear it in my head, though, and why not? It makes as much sense as anything else.

Eeeeeee.

Eeeeeee.

Eeeeeee.

Stephen King *is the author of thirty novels and many more short works of fiction. He lives in Maine with his wife, the novelist Tabitha King, but frequently visits New York City and lunches at the Gotham Café, where he pays special attention to the cutlery.*

The Psycho

BY

MICHAEL O'DONOGHUE

TITLES AND CREDITS
Crude white-on-black spray paint.

FADE UP ON:

INT: BEDROOM – MORNING

STRAIGHT-DOWN ANGLE ON THE PSYCHO lying in bed staring at the ceiling. He is blond, handsome, tall, and muscular. He wears black briefs and LOVE is tattooed on his arm. WE HEAR the soft ticking of an alarm clock on the bedside table.

The alarm goes off. As he sits up and shuts it off, WE SEE pills scattered on the table.

The room is shabby and disordered. There is a hot plate, a few pieces of Goodwill furniture, torn shades without curtains. The walls are scrawled with quotations about love – everything from the Beatles (ALL YOU NEED IS LOVE) TO Robert Browning (O LYRIC LOVE, HALF ANGEL AND HALF BIRD, AND ALL A WONDER AND A WILD DESIRE!) WE SEE some of these in TILTED, TIGHT SHOTS. On one wall is a giant handmade calendar with days Xed out. It's mid-February.

The Psycho gets dressed in makeshift combat gear including dog-tags and spit-polished army boots. Spotting an imperceptible fleck of dust on the gleaming toe of a boot, he carefully brushes it away.

He rips off a strip of bedsheet and ties it around his head.

He pulls an aluminum suitcase from under the bed. It is fitted with state-of-the-art guns. He tapes an automatic to his ankle, conceals a sawed-off twelve-gauge in his jacket, stuffs his pockets with ammo, and grabs an assault rifle.

The Psycho is ready to start his day.

INT: HALLWAY – MORNING

While locking the door, the Psycho sees the MILKMAN down the hall, a milk carton in each hand. He whips out the shotgun and cuts loose. The milk cartons explode as the man goes down.

The Psycho steps over the body and heads for the street.

EXT: STREET – MORNING

As he comes down his tenement steps, a pretty black HIGH SCHOOL STUDENT skates by, books slung over her shoulder. The Psycho squeezes off a burst that sends her crashing into the curb-side garbage cans, scattering her schoolbooks on the sidewalk. The skate wheels spin to a stop.

The Psycho strolls past her, eyeing a tall office building across the street. He walks toward the entrance.

INT: OFFICE BLDG. LOBBY – DAY

The Psycho crosses the lobby and steps into an empty elevator. A LITTLE BOY and GIRL get in after him. The Little Girl looks up at him and smiles. He smiles back. The doors close and WE SEE the floor indicator rise.

INT: TOP FLOOR – DAY

The bell dings as the doors open. The Psycho exits without a backward glance. The children lie sprawled on the floor.

The Psycho disappears into a stairwell door marked ROOF.

EXT: ROOF – DAY

The Psycho takes out a sniper scope and snaps it on the rifle. He braces against the building and sights on an elderly couple in the park.

Through the scope, WE SEE the OLD MAN in the crosshairs feeding PIGEONS. The rifle shot startles the pigeons, and the Old Man slumps on the bench.

The scope swings to sight on the OLD WOMAN.

EXT: STREET – DAY

TWO COPS are taking a coffee break in the patrol car as the second shot rings out.

MALE COP

Let's roll!

He peels out as his female Partner hits the siren.

EXT: OFFICE BUILDING – DAY

The cop car skids to a halt, and the Cops race into the building. WE HEAR sporadic rifle fire in the distance.

INT: LOBBY – DAY

The Cops rush into the lobby. A badly shaken SECURITY GUARD meets them.

GUARD
He's on the roof.
FEMALE COP
How do we get up there?
GUARD
(pointing the way)
Take the back stairs.

INT: STAIRS – DAY

The Cops run up the steps with drawn guns.

The sound of random gunfire gets louder. They reach the roof and, pressed against the wall, edge open the outside door.

EXT: ROOF – DAY

Encircled by spent cartridges, the Psycho unloads round after round on the unsuspecting city below. He doesn't hear the Cops sneak up behind him.

MALE COP
Freeze! Drop it!

The Psycho throws down the rifle.

As the Cop moves in to cuff him, the Psycho snakes out the ankle gun and blows him away. The other Cop fires but misses. The Psycho wings her. She tries to make it back to the stairs, but he nails her again and she tumbles down the steps.

INT: LOBBY – DAY

The Psycho leaves, ignoring the cringing Guard.

EXT: OFFICE BUILDING – DAY

He passes the abandoned cop car – doors flung open, cherry top whirling.

EXT: STREET – DAY

On his way home, he spies a pair of rabbits frolicking in a pet store window. He sprays the window with bullets, shattering the glass.

EXT: TENEMENT – DAY

He wearily mounts the front steps. It's been a long day.

INT: HALLWAY – DAY

He steps over the Milkman, careful to avoid the pools of milk splattered on the linoleum.

INT: BEDROOM– DAY

Unlocking the door, the Psycho enters his room, and tosses the guns aside. He picks up a can of spray paint and X's out the day on the calendar – February 14.

Sweaty, exhausted, he throws himself on the bed. In the STRAIGHT-DOWN ANGLE, WE SEE him staring at the ceiling.

WE SLOWLY PUSH IN on the Psycho.

He shuts his eyes. MUSIC begins – a scratchy old version of 'Funny Valentine.'

INT: HALLWAY – DAY

In a dreamy, drifting HAND-HELD ANGLE, WE SEE the Milkman twitch.

INT: OFFICE BLDG. STAIRS – DAY

WE FLOAT toward the Cop. She jerks alive and tries to stand.

EXT: PARK – DAY

The Elderly Couple start to move.

INT: BEDROOM – DAY

WE PUSH IN TIGHTER on the Psycho.

INT: HALLWAY – DAY

The Milkman gets to his feet. He presses the doorbell of the NEIGHBOR's apartment. She answers – a saucy woman in her forties – and gives him a big kiss.

EXT: STREET – DAY

A good-looking black HIGH SCHOOL STUDENT in a varsity jacket picks up the roller skater's books. A little chagrined, she sits on the curb adjusting a skate.

BOY STUDENT

Are you okay?

GIRL STUDENT

I'm fine.

He helps her to her feet, still holding the schoolbooks.

BOY STUDENT

I'll carry these.

INT: OFFICE BLDG. LOBBY – DAY

The elevator doors open, and the Little Boy and Girl exit holding hands.

EXT: PARK BENCH – DAY

The Old Man gives his companion a hug. She nestles her head on his shoulder.

EXT: OFFICE BLDG. – DAY

The Male Cop reaches under the car seat, pulls out a satin heart-shaped box of chocolates, and hands it to his Partner.

INT: BEDROOM – DAY

WE PUSH IN TO HEAD SHOT of Psycho. He grins.

EXT: PET STORE – DAY

Through the unbroken window, WE SEE, in addition to the pair of rabbits, dozens and dozens of baby bunnies.

INT: BEDROOM – DAY

WE PAN DOWN to the dogtags around Psycho's neck and MOVE IN FOR ECU. They read: CUPID.
MUSIC ends – 'Each day is Valentine's Day . . .'

FADE TO BLACK

Michael O'Donoghue *was born in 1940 and raised in upstate New York. After dropping out of college in the early sixties, he relocated to San Francisco, where he founded* Renaissance *magazine, funded by Bishop Pike, and published the likes of Charles Bukowski. After that, he relocated to New York City and began writing for the* Evergreen Review, *creating the legendary* Phoebe Zeitgeist *strip. Mike also served as the emcee at the Electric Circus, where he doled out hash brownies to the audience. His book* The Incredible Adventures of the Rock *kicked off the pet rock craze and attracted the attention of Christopher Cerf, who offered him a writing position at the infant* National Lampoon. *Michael went on to the National Lampoon Radio Hour, which led to his stint as head writer for* Saturday Night Live *during its early formative years, effectively reshaping late-night skit television as we know it. After leaving SNL, Michael spent his time writing various articles, collecting serial killer memorabilia, producing the cult film* Mr Mike's Mondo Video, *and scripting screenplays such as* Scrooged, *starring Bill Murray. His sudden, tragic death in 1994 from a cerebral hemorrhage silenced one of the most influential voices in post-modern American humor. His story, 'The Psycho,' is being made into a short film by black-comedy magicians Penn & Teller.*

Pas de Deux

BY

KATHE KOJA

SHE liked them young, young men; princes. She liked them young when she could like them at all because by now, by this particular minute in time she had had it with older men, clever men, men who always knew what to say, who smiled a certain kind of smile when she talked about passion, about the difference between hunger and love. The young ones didn't smile, or if they did it was with a touching puzzlement because they didn't quite see, weren't sure, didn't fully understand: knowing best what they did not know, that there was still so much to learn.

'Learn what?' Edward's voice from the cage of memory, deep voice, 'what's left to learn?' Reaching for the bottle and the glass, pouring for himself. 'And who'll do the teaching? You?' That smile like an insect's, like the blank button eyes of a doll made of metal, made from a weapon, born from a knife and see him there, pale sheets crushed careless at the foot of the bed, big canopied bed like a galleon inherited from his first wife – the sheets too, custom-made sheets – all of it given them as a wedding present by his first wife's mother: Adele, her name was and he liked to say it, liked to pretend – was it pretense? – that he had fucked her too, going from mother to daughter in a night, a suite of nights, spreading the seed past four spread legs and prim Alice could never compare, said Edward, with the grand Adele, Adele the former ballet dancer, Adele who had been everywhere, lived in Paris and Hong Kong, written a biography of Balanchine, Adele who wore nothing but black from the day she turned twenty-one and 'I don't understand,' he would say, head back, knee bent, his short, fat cock like some half-eaten sausage, 'what you think you can teach me, aren't you being just a little bit absurd?'

'We all have something to learn,' she said and he laughed, left the room to return with a book, *Balanchine & Me*: Balanchine in color on the cover, a wee black-and-white of Adele on the back. 'Read this,' putting the book into her hands. 'Find out how much you don't know.' Whiskey breath and settling back into bed, glass on his chest, big hairy chest like an animal's, he liked to lie naked with the windows open, lie there and look at her and 'Are you cold?' he would say, knowing she was freezing, that her muscles were cramping. 'Do you feel a draft?'

No, she could have said, or *yes* or *fuck you* or a million other responses but in the end she had made none of them, said nothing, got out. Left him there in his canopied bed and found her own place, her own space, living above her studio: dance studio, she had been away for a long time but now she was back and soon, another month or two she would have enough money maybe to keep the heat on all the time, keep the lights on, keep going. *Keep on going*: that was her word now, her world, motion at any cost. She was too old to be a dancer? had been away too long, forgotten too much, lost the fascistic grace of the body in torment, the body as tool of motion, of the will? *No.* As long as she had legs, arms, a back to bend or twist, as long as she could move she could dance.

Alone.

In the cold.

In the dark.

Sometimes when it got too dark even for her she would leave, head off to the clubs where for the price of a beer she could dance all night to thrash or steelcore, a dance different from the work she did at the barre: jerked and slammed past exhaustion, hair stuck slick to her face, shirt stuck to her body, slapping water on her neck in the lavatory through the smoke and stink and back out with her head down, eyes closed, body fierce and martyred by the motion; incredible to watch, she knew it, people told her; men told her, following her as she stalked off the floor, leaning close to her stool at the bar and they said she was terrific, a terrific dancer; and closer, closer still the question inevitable, itself a step in the dance: why was she dancing alone? 'You need a partner,' but of course that was not possible, not really because there was no one she wanted, no one who could do what she could do and so she would shrug, smile sometimes but mostly not, shrug and shake her head and 'No,' turning her face away. 'No thanks.'

Sometimes they bought her drinks, sometimes she drank them; sometimes, if they were young enough, kind enough, she would take them home, up past the studio to the flat with its half-strung blinds and rickety futon, unsquared piles of dance magazines, old toe shoes and bloody wraps and she would fuck them, slowly or quickly, in silence or with little panting yelps or cries like a dog's, head back in the darkness and the blurred sound of the space heater like an engine running, running itself breathless and empty and dry. Afterward she would lie beside them, up on one elbow and talk, tell them about dancing, about passion, about the difference between hunger and love and there in the dark, the rising and falling of her voice processional as water, as music, lying there in the moist warmth created by their bodies they were moved – by her words, by her body – to create it anew, make the bridge between love and hunger: they were young, they could go all night. And then they would look up at her and 'You're beautiful,' they said, they all said it. 'You're so beautiful; can I call you?'

'Sure,' she would say. 'Sure, you can call me,' leaning over them, breathing slowed, the sweat on her breasts drying to a thin prickle and see their faces, watch them smile, see them dress – jeans and T-shirts, ripped vests and camouflage coats, bandannas on their heads, tiny little earrings in silver and gold – and watch them go and before they go give them the number, press it into their hands; the number of the cleaner's where she used to take Edward's suits but how was it cruel, she asked herself, told herself, how was it wrong not to offer what she did not have? Far worse to pretend, string them along when she knew that she had already given all she had to give, one night, her discourse, she never took the same one twice and there were always so many, so many clubs, so many bars in this city of bars and clubs, lights in the darkness, the bottle as cold as knowledge in her warm and slippery grasp.

Sometimes she walked home, from the bars and the clubs; it was nothing for her to walk ten, thirty, fifty blocks, no one ever bothered her, she always walked alone. Head down, hands at her sides like a felon, a movie criminal, *just keep walking* through darkness, four a.m. rain or the last fine scornful drift of snow, ice like cosmetics to powder her face, chill to gel the sweat in her hair, short hair, Edward said she looked like a lifer: 'What were you in for?' as she stood ruffling her hair in the bathroom mirror, sifting out the loose snips, dead curls and his image sideways in the glass as if distorted, past focus, in flux. 'You don't have the facial structure for a cut like that,' one-hand reaching to turn her face, aim it toward the light like a gun above; that smile, like an abdicated king's. 'Once Alice cut her hair off, all her hair, to spite me; she denied it, said she only wanted a different look but I knew her, I knew that's what it was. Adele,' the name as always honey in his mouth, 'knew too, and she cut off *her* hair to spite Alice. Of course, *she* looked terrific, really sexy and butch, but she had the face for it. Bone structure,' almost kindly to her, patting her face with both hands, patty-cake, baby face, squeezing her cheeks in the mirror. 'That's what you don't have.'

And now this cold walk, each individual bone in her face aching, teeth aching, sound of the wind in her ears even when she was safe inside, door locked, space heater's orange drone and as late as it was, as cold as it was she stripped down to leggings, bare feet, bare breasts and danced in the dark, sweating, panting, the stitch cruel in her side, in her throat, in her heart, tripped by unseen obstacles, one hip slamming hard into the barre, metallic thud of metal to flesh, flesh to metal like mating, like fucking and she wished she had brought someone home with her, it would have been nice to fuck a warm boy in the dark but she was alone and so she danced instead, spun and stumbled and hit the barre, hit the barre, hit the barre until she literally could not move, stood knees-locked and panting, panting from fear of stasis as outside, past the yellowed shades, the sun at last began to rise.

Adele's book lay where she had tossed it, square and silent on the bathroom floor but one night, back from dancing and sick to her stomach – the beer, something had not agreed with her – from the toilet she picked it up, skimmed through the chapters, the inset pictures and although it was very poorly written – as a writer Adele had apparently been a fine dancer – still there was something, one phrase arresting like a blow, a slap in the face: *For me,* said Adele, *Balanchine was a prince. You must find your own prince, you must make him your own.*

Find your prince: Prince Edward! and she laughed, pants rucked down around her ankles, thin yellow diarrhea and she laughed and laughed but the phrase stayed with her, clung like the memory of motion to the bones and she began to look, here and there, at the young men at the clubs, look and gauge and wonder and sometimes at night, pinned and breathing beneath them, talking of hunger and love she would wonder what a prince was, how to see one: how one knew: was it something in the body, some burn, some vast unspeaking signal? The body does not lie: she knew this. And Adele – considering the small black-and-white picture, that arched avian nose, high bones to show like a taunt to life itself the skull inside the meat – had more than likely known it too.

The body does not lie.

Ten years old on the way to ballet class, forced by her mother's instigation: 'So you'll learn how to move, sweetie,' her mother so small and fat and anxious, patting her daughter's cheeks, round cheeks, small bony chin like a misplaced fist. 'So you'll be more comfortable with your body.'

'But I am comfortable,' sullen child's lie, head averted, temple pressed stubborn to the hot glass of the car window. 'Anyway I'd rather play soccer, why can't I sign up for soccer?'

'Dance is better,' the old car swung inexpertly into the strip mall parking lot, DANCE ACADEMY in stylized curlicue blue, cheap rice-paper blinds between MINDY'S DOG GROOMING and a discount hand-tool outlet. Smaller inside than it seemed from the street, ferocious dry air-conditioned cold and three girls listless at the barre, two older than she, one much younger, all in cotton-candy colors; from past the walls the sounds of barking dogs. The woman at the desk asking 'Will this be for the full semester?' and her mother's diffidence, well, we just wanted to try the introductory sessions, just let her try and see if she—

'I don't want to dance,' her own voice, not loud but the girls looked up, all of them, starlings on a branch, prisoners in a cell. 'I want to play soccer.'

The woman's gaze; she did not bother to smile. 'Oh, no,' she said. 'No sports for you, you've got a dancer's body.'

'Are you a dancer?' Shouted into her ear, that eager young voice. 'I mean like professionally?'

'Yes,' she said. 'No.'

'Can I buy you a drink? What're you drinking?' and it was one beer, then two, then six and they stopped on the way to her place, stopped and bought a bottle of V.O. – a princely gesture? – and sat in the dark doing shots as he undressed her, stripped like skin the moist drape of her T-shirt, her spartan white panties, her black cotton skirt till she sat naked and drunk and shivering, her nipples hard, all the light gone from the room and 'The way you move,' he said, kept saying, hushed voice of glimpsed marvels. 'Wow. The way you *move*, I knew right away you were some kind of dancer, right, I mean like for a living. Are you in the ballet? Are you—'

'Here,' she said, 'here, I'll show you,' and downstairs, hand in hand and naked in the dark, the lessening angle of his erection but he was young and it was easy, one or two or six little pulls and he was stiff as a board, as a barre, stiff and ready and she danced for him first, danced around him, Salome without the veils: rubbing her breasts against his back, trapping his thighs with her own and since he was drunk it took longer but not so very long, not much time after all before they were lying there, warmth's illusion and panting into one another's mouths and she told him the difference between love and hunger, between what is needed and what must be had and 'You're so beautiful,' he said, slurred words and a smile of great simplicity, a deep and tender smile; it was doubtful he had heard anything she had said. His penis against her like a finger, the touch confiding: 'So can I, can I call you?'

Dust, grains of dirt stuck to her skin, to the skin of her face against the floor. No prince: or not for her: her body said so. 'Sure,' she said. 'Sure, you can call me.'

When he had gone she went back upstairs, took up Adele's book, and began again to read it page by page.

No more ballet classes, dancer's body or no, she was out and now it was too late for tap or modern dance, too late for soccer and so she spent the summer with her father, dragging up and down the four flights of his walk-up, silent and staring at the TV: 'Why don't you go out?' Lighting up a menthol cigarette, he smoked three and a half packs a day; by the time she was eighteen he would be dead. 'Meet some kids or something.'

'There aren't any kids in this building,' she said. A musical on TV, the Arts in America channel; two women singing about travel and trains. 'And it's too hot to go out.' The air conditioner worked but not well; endless the scent of mildew and smoke, of her father's aftershave when he dressed to go out: 'Keep the door locked,' as he left, to whom would she open it anyway? Sitting up by the TV, chin in hand in the constant draft, the sound of traffic outside. In September he sent her back to her mother, back to school; she never went to a dance class again.

'It's a part-time position,' the woman said. She might have been twenty, very dark skin, very dark eyes; severe, like a young Martha Graham. 'The students – we have a full class load now—'

'How many?'

'Fifty.'

Fifty dancers, all much younger than she, all fierce, committed, ambitious. Toe shoes and a shower, the smell of hand cream, the smell of warm bodies: glossy floors and mirrors, mirrors everywhere, the harder gloss of the barre and *no*, a voice like Adele's in her head, *you cannot do this*: 'No,' she said, rising, pushing out of the chair so it almost tipped, so she almost fell. 'No, I can't, I can't teach a class right now.'

'It's not a teaching position,' sternly, 'it's an *assistant's*—'

Keep the shower room clean, keep the records, help them warm up, watch them dance, no, oh no. 'Oh no,' as she walked home, hands at her sides, *What were you in for?* Life: a lifer. Edward's number was still in her book, still written in black ink. She could not keep both the studio and the flat: the futon, the dance magazines, her unconnected telephone all moved downstairs, shoved in a corner, away from the barre. Sometimes the toilet didn't flush. The young men never seemed to mind.

Adele's book lay beneath her pillow, Balanchine's face turned down like an unwanted jack, prince of hearts, king of staves: and upturned black-and-white Adele, pinched nose and constant stare, our lady of perpetual motion.

'You look awful,' Edward said, stern as the young woman had been, there behind her desk: there in the restaurant, staring at her. 'Did you know that? Completely haggard.'

'Money,' she said. 'I need to borrow some money.'

'You're in no position to pay it back.'

'No,' she said. 'I'm not. Not now. But when I—'

'You must be crazy,' he said and ordered for them both, cream of leek and tarragon soup, some kind of fish. White wine. The server looked at her strangely; Adele could be heard to laugh, a little laugh inhuman, clockwork wound the wrong way. 'Where are you living now, in a dumpster?'

She would not say; she would not show him. He wanted to fuck, afterward, after dinner but she wouldn't do that either, arms crossed and mute and 'Where's all this from, anyway?' pushing back at the sheets, seemingly serene, not disappointed; his erection looked smaller somehow, fat but weak like a toothless snake, like a worm. The rooms were so warm, the bedroom as hot as a beating heart; the big bed still looked like a galleon, sheets and hangings cherry red and 'All this devotion,' he said. 'Suffering for your art. You never gave much of a shit about ballet, about dance when I knew you.'

That's not true but she didn't say it, how explain anything to him? and ballet of course brought up Adele: 'You've never even read her book on Balanchine,' scratching his testicles. 'If you cared about dance at all, you would.'

He was always a fool, advised Adele: *find your prince* and 'I need the money now,' she said. 'Tonight,' and to her surprise he gave it to her, right then, in cash; how rich he must be, to give so much so casually. Putting it into her hands, closing her fingers around it and 'Now suck me,' he said. Standing there naked, his cock begun at last to stir. 'That's right, be a good girl, suck me off.'

She said nothing.

'Or I'll take the money back.'

The bills were warm, warm as the room around her, warm as his hand around her own and in one motion she brought their linked hands, his own hand topmost to rise, fast and sharp to smash under his chin, hit so hard his hand jerked open, her hand free, the bills falling to the floor and gone then, shoving out the door with her fingers stinging and burning, burning in the cold outside.

Adele was silent.

'Do you—' One of the young ones, crouched between her legs, her canted knees on the futon with its one wrinkled sheet, its coverlet faded to the color of sand. 'Do you have condoms? Because I don't.'

'No,' she said. 'I don't either.'

His lower lip thrust out like a child defrauded, a pouting child. 'Well then, what're we going to do?'

'Dance,' she said. 'We can dance.'

She got a job at a used bookstore, erratic schedule, the hours nobody wanted and every hour, every minute a chafe, an itch unbearable to stand so still this way, medical textbooks and romance novels, celebrity bios and how-to books – once even *Balanchine & Me*, which she instantly stuffed into her backpack without thinking twice; why not? it was hers already and this a better copy, the photograph sharper, the pages not bent and soft and torn – taking money across the counter and she knew it was wrong, she knew it was not the right thing to do but sometimes she overcharged for the books, not much, a dollar here or there and pocketed the money, kept the change, what else could she do? The job paid nothing and took so much, stole time which she needed, had to have: no studio would hire her, no company until she was good enough, professional enough to teach and she had missed so much, lost so much time: she had to make up, catch up, keep working and there were only so many hours in the day, already she woke at six to dance before work, work all day and then out to the clubs at night for that other dancing that while exhausting somehow refreshed her, made her new again, ready to dance again so what else was there to do?

And sometimes – she did not like this either, but her world was full, now, of things she could not like – she let the young men buy things for her, breakfast, a bag of doughnuts, carry-out coffee which she drank later, cold coffee in the cold, walking to work at the bookstore and then somehow they found out about the stealing, she never knew how but they did and they fired her, kept her last week's wages to pay for what she had taken, and that night she danced as if she were dying, flailing arms and her head swinging in circles, she felt as if her neck would snap, wanted it to snap, break and let her head go flying to smash red and gray to silence against the wall: *no prince for you*, nothing, nothing from Adele even though she asked: *what would you do? tell me, I need to know, I have to know what to do* and afterward, alone and panting by the bar from which she could not afford to buy a drink, approached not by one of the young men, no prince but someone else, an older man in black jeans and a jacket who told her she was one terrific dancer, really sexy, and if she was interested he had a proposition to make.

'Naked?'

'Private parties,' he said. The smell of menthol cigarettes, a red leather couch above which hung a series of Nagle nudes and 'They never touch you, never. That's not in the contract, I'm not paying you for that. They're not paying *me* for that.' Gazing at her as if she were already naked. 'You ever wear make-up? You could stand a little lipstick. Do something with your hair too, maybe.'

'How much?' she asked, and he told her.

Silence.

'When?' she asked, and he told her that too.

Too-loud music, she brought her own tape player and a selection of tapes, twenty-two different choices from *The Stripper* to soft rock to thrash, she could dance to anything and it didn't matter as much as she had feared, being naked, not as bad as it might have been although at first it was terrible, the things they said, they were so different from the young men at the clubs, being naked must make the difference but after a while there was no difference after all or perhaps she had forgotten how to listen, forgotten everything but the feel of the music and that had not changed, the music and the sweat and the muscles in her body, dancer's muscles and she did four parties a night, six on a good night; one night she did ten but that was too much, she had almost fallen off the table, almost broken her arm on a chair's unpadded back and with that much work she had no time for herself, for the real dancing, alone at the barre, alone in the dark and the winter, it seemed, would last forever, her hands were always frozen, broken windows in her studio and she covered them over with cardboard and duct tape, covered them over with shaking hands and her hands, she thought, were growing thinner or perhaps her fingers were longer, it was hard to tell, always so dark in here, but she thought she might have lost some weight, a few pounds, five or ten and at the parties they called her skinny, or scrawny, *get your scrawny ass movin', babe* or *hey where's your tits?* but she had gone past the point of listening, of caring; had discovered that she would never discover her prince in places like this, her partner, the one she had to have: *find your prince* and although Adele made less sense these days, spoke less frequently still she was the only one who understood: the new copy gone to rags like the old one, reading between the lines and while she talked very little about her own life – it was a biography of Balanchine after all – still some of her insights, her guesses and pains emerged and in the reading emerged anew: she's like *me*, she thought, reading certain passages again and again, she knows what it's like to need to dance, to push the need away and away like an importunate lover, like a prince only to seek it again with broken hands and a broken body, seek it because it is the only thing you need: the difference between love and hunger: *find your prince* and find a partner, because no one can dance forever alone.

Different clubs now in this endless winter, places she had never been, streets she had avoided but she could not go back to some of the old places, too many young men there whose faces she knew, whose bodies she knew, who could never be her prince and something told her to hurry: time tumbling and burning, time seeping away and it was Adele's voice in her head, snatches of the book, passages mumbled by memory so often they took on the force of prayer, of chant, plainsong garbled by beating blood in the head as she danced, as she danced, as she danced: and the young men did not approach as often or with such enthusiasm although her dance was still superb, even better now than it had ever been; sometimes she caught them staring, walking off the floor and they would turn their heads, look away, did they think she had not seen? Eyes closed still she knew: *the body does not lie* but the ones who did speak, who did approach were different now, a fundamental change: 'Hey,' no smile, wary hand on the drink. 'You with anybody?'

I am looking for a prince. 'No,' she would say, surface calm and back at her place – it was the one rule on which she insisted, she would not go to them – the rigor of vision, letting the body decide—

'You got a rubber?'

'No.'

—and again and again the same report, no prince and no partner and indifferent she would slide away, sometimes they had not even finished, were still thrashing and gulping but these owned not even the promise of kindness and so were owed no kindness in return: indifferent she shoved them away, pushed them off and most grew angry, a few of them threatened to hit her, one or two of them did but in the end they cursed, they dressed, they left and she was left alone, pinprick lights through the cold cardboard, sweet uneasy smell from the space-heater coils: bending and flexing her feet and her fingers, all pared far past mere meat to show the stretch and grace of tendon, the uncompromising structure of the bone.

A weekend's worth of frat parties, at one place they threw beer on her, at another they jeered because she was so thin and would not let her dance, sent her away: it was happening more and more now, she might do two parties a night, one, sometimes there were no calls for her at all. In the office with the Nagle prints: 'What are you, anorexic or something? I don't deal, you know, in freaks, I don't want that trade. You want to keep dancing, you better start eating.'

What he did not understand, of course, what Adele understood superbly was that the meat was not necessary, in fact became a mere impediment to motion: see how much more easily she turned, how firmly in command of space, of vertical distance – *ballon*, dancers called it, that aerial quality also called elevation – how wedded she was to motion when there was less of the body to carry? Why sacrifice that for the desire of fools?

'You must weigh ninety pounds.'

She shrugged.

'Anyway you're lucky. There's a party next weekend, some kind of farewell party, the guy picked you out of the picture book. You especially he said he wants.'

She shrugged again.

'He wants you early, maybe a little extra-special dance – no touching, he knows that, but it's like a present for the guest of honor, right? So be there by eight,' handing her one of the go-to cards, three-by-five with an address and phone number.

Edward's address.

'Hey, I need a, I need a rubber or something. You got something?'

'No.'

'Hey, you're – you're, like, *bleeding* down there, are you on the rag or something?'

No answer.

'You should have taken the money,' Edward said, watching her walk in: the faux library, books unread, shelves full of silly crystal frogs, squat jade warriors, girls with ruby eyes. 'You look even worse than you did the last time I saw you, even worse than that ugly Polaroid in the book . . . I can't imagine you're getting much business; are you? Is this your idea of professional dance?'

She shrugged.

'Given up on the ballet?' and pouring wine, one glass; then shrugging and pouring another, go on, help yourself. The hired help. Like a maid, or a delivery boy; a prostitute. 'The man I spoke to said you don't have sex with your clients – is that true?'

'I dance,' she said. The room looked exactly the same, same quality of light, same smells; in the bedroom, on the bed the sheets would be red, and slick, and soft. 'I show up and I dance.'

'Naked.'

'In a g-string.'

'"Air on a G String",' sipping his wine. 'Can you dance to that? Does it have a good beat? *Christ*,' with real distaste as she removed her coat, 'look at you. You need a doctor, you're nothing but bones.'

'Is there a party?' she said. 'Or did you make that up?'

'No, there's a party but it's not here, not tonight. Tonight you can dance for me; if you're good I'll even tip you . . . is tipping permitted? or is it added on to the bill?'

She said nothing. She was thinking of Adele, Adele here in these rooms, choosing the bed linens, choosing the bed on which, Edward boasted, the two of them had made love before the wedding, before he and daughter Alice were even formally engaged: *the way her body moved*, he had said, *it was unbelievable* and 'Tell me about Adele,' she said, sting of wine on her lips, on the sores inside her mouth. Thread of blood in the pale wine. 'When was the last time you saw her?'

'What does that have to do with anything?'

'Just tell me,' she said.

It was here, he said, she was in town and we met for dinner, some Swedish restaurant, only four or five tables, best-kept secret in town but of course she knew, she always knew about everything. 'And after dinner we came back home,' he said. 'To our bed.'

'How old was she then?'

'What difference can that possibly make?'

'How old was she?'

'You know, looking at you now it's hard to believe I ever touched you. I certainly wouldn't want to touch you now.'

'How old was she?' and he told her, confirming what she had already known: like herself and the young men, the would-be princes, the parallel held true and there on one of the shelves – how had she missed it? a photograph of Adele, Adele at thirty maybe or maybe slightly older, that pinched stare relaxed now into the gaze of the true Medusa, queen of an older motion, sinuous and rapt and 'Finish your drink,' Edward said; his voice came to her as if from far away, the way Adele had used to sound. 'Finish your drink and you can go.'

Shall I go? to the picture of Adele who without perceptibly moving her lips said *no, no you must not go, that is the one thing you must not do* and bending, she took up the book, *Balanchine & Me* from the bag where the tapes were, the music, she had her own music tonight, Adele's humming voice in her head and 'Take a look,' she said to Edward, gaily, almost smiling, 'take a look,' and she began to strip, shoes and stockings, skirt and blouse, each piece shed deliberate as a blow and 'You're sick,' Edward said; he did not want to look at her. 'You're very sick, you ought to see a doctor.'

'I don't need a doctor.' Bra off, her flat breasts like airless pancakes, like starving people on TV and without music, without sound she began to dance: not the party dances, not even what she did alone with the barre but something different, more basic, closer to the heart of the bone and as she danced – panting, sweat down her sides and her face, sweat in her mouth and Edward standing glass in hand, staring and staring and she talked about the prince, the prince and the partner and all her seeking, all her lost and wandering ways: was she talking out loud? and then to the picture, the photograph of Adele: does he know? can he learn, will he ever understand?

The body does not lie, said Adele. *But he is trapped in his body. He was always there, for me, for you but he is trapped, he needs to get out. I could not help him get out so now you must. Get him out*

and 'Get out,' he said: her whirling body, one leg high, high, even with her shoulder, look at those tendons, that flex and stretch! The difference between lead and air, meat and feathers, hunger and love and 'Listen now,' she said: *listen now* and the little picture of Adele lit up, bloomed as if light rose from within, lit outward from the heart and with both hands she grabbed for the figurines, jade and crystal, frog and soldier and threw them to the floor, at the walls, up and down to smash and glitter, topple and fall and, shouting, he grabbed for her, tried to take her hands, tried to join the dance but *he is trapped* and 'I know,' she said to Adele, the glowing picture, 'oh I know,' and when he came for her again she hit him as hard as she could with the ball of her foot, karate kick, fierce and sure in the crotch to make him go down, fall, lie cramped and curled on the silence of the floor, curled about the red worm of his cock, the cradle of his balls: like a worm caught on the sidewalk, curling in panic in the absence of the earth.

The body does not lie, said Adele.

Edward gasping, a wet, weeping sound and she kicked him again, harder this time, a slow deliberate kick: *En pointe,* she said with a smile to the picture, and with one finger hooked the g-string from the cresting pelvic arch.

***Kathe Koja** is the author of* Cipher *(1991),* Bad Brains *(1992),* Skin *(1993), and* Strange Angels *(1994), and* Kink, *forthcoming from Henry Holt in 1996. Her short fiction appears in many anthologies as well. She lives in the Detroit area with her husband, artist Rick Lieder, and her son.*

Bright Blades Gleaming

BY

Basil Copper

I

Monday

I AM settling in. The room is not much. It is small and grubby, containing a bed with a very lumpy mattress. There are two dusty windows facing a narrow alley, and the gables of the opposite houses make the room seem even darker and smaller than it is. It would be airless in high summer and bitterly cold in winter. Fortunately, the season is in between, and I may have moved on long before winter. The landlady, Frau Mauger, is ill-favored and has the aspect of a grasping woman, but she seems to regard me without malice and has not charged me very much for the room. Perhaps something bad has happened here. We shall see. I must ask the other tenants.

So far I have seen only one: a tall, pale girl in a dark dress with her hair scraped back in a severe-looking bun, which only emphasizes the plainness of her features. She glides about between stairs like a wraith, pausing to look about her with large, affrighted eyes. She has nothing to fear from me; I am not at all attracted to that type. When I was negotiating terms with the landlady, Frau Mauger explained that the girl worked as a seamstress in the back rooms of one of the larger ladies' dress establishments in the city; but that she had been ill recently and had to stay in her room. She could not afford the doctor's bill and was worried that she might lose her situation.

Well, that is life nowadays. Things are bad everywhere. Berlin seems no different from any other place, except that it is larger and noisier. I spent some time this afternoon unpacking my things. I have only a brown leather suitcase and a large paper parcel. Though shabby, the former was originally of good quality, and Frau Mauger must have taken this into account because she cast suspicious eyes on me when I first arrived. It is true that I am unprepossessing and would not attract attention in a crowd, but perhaps that is an advantage in my position, for what I might have to do. My overcoat is shabby and my shoes down at heel, but I may be able to borrow some polish from a fellow lodger. I have little in the way of funds and must eke them out as best I may.

I am keeping these notes as a record of my thoughts and actions, for it may be important later on. I am hesitating whether or not to write to the newspapers. That did attract some attention in Cologne, where I stayed three months. Fortunately, an acquaintance warned me that the police were taking an interest in my inflammatory views and I moved on just in time. I must be more careful here and be sure not to attract too much attention. At first, at any rate. My father always said that I had a cunning that was almost supernatural; that I seemed able to foresee things before they happened. Poor man; it was tragic the way he died. And no one was ever able to work out how.

There is a very grubby calendar tacked to the plaster wall near my bed. For some reason the first months have not been torn off. I have removed these leaves and will use the reverse as writing paper and for my random jottings. I am feeling much better now and have opened one of the far windows in order to let a gentle breeze blow through this stuffy atmosphere. That is an improvement. By standing on one of the stuffed horsehair chairs, of which the room seems to have an abundance, I can just see the cobbled alley below and note a few pedestrians passing.

Now I am back at the bedside and annotating the calendar and bringing it up to date. I have crossed off the previous days and circled Monday so that I know where I am. I wonder why it is that one is never able to capture time and cause it to stop; or rerun events as one can in one's head? I should imagine the scientists and learned men of our society would have glib and facile explanations. It seems so simple to me and yet the process continually eludes them.

I stopped writing just now. It is late afternoon and the smell of cabbage soup is slowly permeating the atmosphere. It makes me realize that I am very hungry. I have had nothing since breakfast, which consisted of two small bread rolls and a cup of coarse black coffee. I have my wallet out and my imitation leather purse. I have locked the door from the inside and go over my monetary resources. Marks enough for the present, but what of the future? Should I stay in this evening and sample the cooking of the house? Probably not. The aroma wafting up the stairs is not such as to tempt a gourmet like me. But I will have to be careful. A small café in a discreet neighborhood and simple fare for the time being, I think.

Perhaps I could take breakfast here; have a very sparse lunch and reserve the evening for something more substantial. We shall see. But I need to keep up my health. Katrine said that I looked too thin and undernourished even for a medical student. I wonder where she is now. A nice girl, if a little on the thin side herself. But she helped me at a crucial time and made my stay in Cologne more pleasant than it would otherwise have been.

My head still hurts a little. It is probably the effect of that very bad wine I had at the *bahnhof* last night. It was the cheapest available, it is true, but it is always false economy to skimp on such things as wine. Food does not matter quite so much, as the digestive system is extremely resilient in a younger person, but bad wine leaves one with a headache and very much out of sorts. When I have tidied the room to my satisfaction, I light the lamp and look around with a little more satisfaction. It certainly makes it reasonably civilized now that most of my few possessions are in place.

I shake the lamp when the wick is burning evenly; the oil chamber is almost empty; although there is still light outside, it is very dark in here and I shall need the lamp for my note taking and reading in due course. I must ask Frau Mauger either to refill it or let me have a small supply of oil in one of those metal cans I saw stacked in her scullery; they were all marked with numbers in white paint, so they obviously referred to the rooms. There were twelve in all. So if every one was occupied there would be twelve lodgers in *toto.* That might be important to know.

I now place my case on the bed, open it, and inspect the contents most thoroughly. Fortunately, it has very strong locks of a non-standard pattern, so my possessions will be secure in case my room is entered in my absence. Frau Mauger has a passkey, of course, but naturally there will be a cleaning girl, so I must be very careful not to leave any of my writings about. Strong locks are the answer. They ensure privacy and hide things from prying eyes. Boarding houses and pensions are notorious for the latter. I had a friend once — but I digress. The story is too long and would take up too much time and paper if I wrote it all now. Perhaps one day when I am famous, I may even commit it to print. It is certainly worth the telling and might even be considered too bizarre for fiction.

I have noticed a small curtain in the corner of the room. I approach it and draw it back. Something I had not expected. There is an alcove with a fly-specked mirror on the rear wall. Beneath it a stone sink with a drain. And above it a large brass tap. I turn it and cold water gushes out. What a luxury for this place! I shall be able to perform my toilet in privacy. And when I need hot water for shaving, no doubt it can be procured from below. I must have hot water for that because my cutthroat has become blunted and I have not yet tried out one of the new types of safety razor. They say one's skin takes a while to get used to them.

I sit down on the bed again. So, my funds are sufficient for the next few weeks, if I go carefully. After that we shall see. I do know how to procure more but must be very circumspect this time. The affair in Cologne gave me a very bad scare, I can tell you. The memory of it makes me shiver yet. If it had not been for that old woman, no one would have known. Who would have thought that she would have such sharp eyes and hearing? But, as my father used to say, my 'native cunning' once again saw me through. Luck will not always last, I must remember. One has to temper necessity with extreme caution.

I get up once more and study myself in the mirror, bringing the lamp closer. No, the image presented is not too bad. I am not handsome, certainly. But I look passably respectable, and after a quick wash, using the sliver of soap in the metal bowl and the grubby towel, I should pass unnoticed in a crowd. And Berlin is full of crowds, thank God.

That makes me pause, though the phrase echoed only inside my head. Why invoke my Maker when I do not believe in Him? Curious, really. But perhaps only force of habit; things dinned into one by one's parents from an early age. How like an iron rack the world is! The more one stretches and tries to escape its grip, the more one is stretched in turn and the burning, tearing torture goes on.

But I must be calm. When I am carried away by such thoughts I sometimes am given to vocalizing them, and that is dangerous in such an establishment as this, with its loose-fitting floorboards and thin walls. I cross to the basin, run the water, and soak my fevered face in the blessed coolness. Ah, that is better! The headache and the aftertaste of the wine fumes have almost completely disappeared. I prepare to quit my lodging, but first make a final inspection to see that all is well. I must search out a small eating house in a secluded byway, where I shall not attract attention.

But not too secluded, because that will defeat the purpose. It is a fine point and must be met when I find the right place. But I shall know it. I always do. My unerring eye, as my mother used to say. I bend to polish my shoes with a fold of the tablecloth. One last look around, then I open the door to the mean landing with its frayed drugget and faded religious prints upon the walls. I step back inside, turn out the lamp, relishing the acrid smell of paraffin and hot metal and then carefully lock the door. I smile as I think of Frau Mauger. She has not asked me what I do for a living. That was a question that might have made me uneasy, as well as her.

I pocket the key and go down the creaky stairs. I see no one, though there is a faint murmur of voices from some of the ground-floor rooms. I let myself out through a side door, walk briskly along the alley and am swallowed up by the eddying crowds of suburban Berlin.

2

I have found the ideal place, a small café jammed in among narrow-chested buildings in an alley hidden away just off one of the main thoroughfares. It seems perfect for my purposes. Large enough for me to be fairly anonymous among the other clientele but small enough to allow me to see if there are any suspicious characters at adjoining tables. It appears to be frequented mostly by families containing a number of children, and commercial travelers of the unsuccessful sort. I can always tell the type, mainly by their air of abject hopelessness and their worn sample cases, which they deposit with such ridiculous care beneath their chairs. No unattended females.

The travelers, with their knowledge of defeat and their sunken eyes, make me realize how fortunate I am to be free from such absurd bondage. Free to practice my art, free to travel – when I am in funds, that is – free to select my friends, particularly women. I could expand on that subject but I have determined to keep this diary as coldly professional as I can make it. From my seat in the window of this small establishment I am well placed to watch the passing show. A constant stream of people of all types: young and old, men and women, children, girls, tramps and itinerants, all sway and undulate in a turgidly moving tide past the lace curtains of the window, where I can observe them closely without being noticed myself.

There is one particular girl who catches my eye; she is tall and well proportioned with a long dress which shows her bust to perfection. She has long auburn hair beneath her hat, which is worn well back from her broad, smooth brow. She could not be more than twenty or twenty-two, I should say. Several times she drifts up and down with the tide of humanity passing in front of my window, unaware of my intent gaze behind the concealing curtain. Is she merely perambulating like most of the passing throng? Or has she some other purpose? Perhaps a rendezvous with a friend or a person of the opposite sex? She is certainly not a prostitute. I know the type too well, and she bears all the hallmarks of the respectable working class.

I am becoming interested by this time, but my observations are interrupted by the waiter, a sallow-faced youth with prominent grease spots on his white shirtfront. My irritation is increased when the girl fails to reappear in front of my window. But I conceal my emotions, putting on my bland facade. I order my favorite sausage dish, which comes in a mound of creamed potatoes. Daringly, I order with it a glass of red wine, whose provenance is assured from past experience. I set to enthusiastically, and as the edge of my hunger is dulled and the warmth of the wine permeates my being, I am again able to take in the scene before me. But somehow it has lost its sparkle. The absence of the girl on whom my attention was focused makes a difference.

Instead, as the meal progresses and the patrons of the restaurant come and go, I begin to observe people at adjoining tables. There are three coarse-faced men near me, whose loud-checked clothing and fat, well-fed faces, together with their leather sample cases, proclaim themselves to my practised eye as commercial travelers of the more successful type. I watch them intently, noting the bulging notecase one produces. They are slightly tipsy and I note also that each has a carafe of red wine in front of him, the contents of which are replaced by the same sallow-faced waiter from time to time.

Their talk is of business mostly; I let the details pass but listen more intently when they lower their voices to whisper some coarse joke about this or that attractive woman who passes our window. I have them in their correct pigeon holes by now and arrange my own meal in order to be able to leave the café at the same time as this dubious trio. Their flushed faces and loud voices are drawing attention from the other customers by now. The *apfelstrudel* is quite delicious and in a moment of recklessness I order another portion with my second cup of the thick, sweet coffee in which this establishment specializes.

At last the meal is over and I spend some time scrutinizing the bill, while waiting for the party at the next table to leave. I count out the correct amount from my purse and leave a small tip on the table for the waiter, who, after all, has looked after me well. I will come here again tomorrow. The three men are on their feet now and walking somewhat unsteadily, weaving their way among the tables to the cash desk, where a frosty-faced matron with white hair, and wearing a severe black dress with a lace collar, presides over her ledger, with the paid bills crucified on a dangerous-looking metal spike at her elbow.

My friend has his thick wallet out now, laughing loudly at some joke uttered by his companions as he waits in the queue in front of me. As he makes an expansive gesture I bump into him as though by accident, catching his elbow. It is well done and I pride myself on my professionalism in such matters. He gives a muttered exclamation as his wallet hits the floor, spilling a sheaf of notes. I give him a mumbled apology as I grope downward, gathering up the notecase. I hand it back to him with further polite comments as he accepts my contrition good-naturedly. There is a moment of anxiety as he sifts the contents of the wallet, but he is looking only for the correct denomination with which to pay his bill.

I pay my own and hurry out, avoiding the small group on the pavement as they loudly discuss their plans for the evening. I too join the drifting crowds, though, unlike them, I do not pass and repass along the alley until I see that my companions have dispersed in the opposite direction. Then I go with the tide, enjoying the unaccustomed luxury of being quite at ease in my mind, noting the crowds, especially the women, trying to guess their professions or occupations. Here are wan shop girls, their pale faces alight with pleasure at being temporarily released from their bondage; mustachioed fathers of families with their buxom wives and slim daughters; young boys trundling iron hoops among the crowds, to the consternation of passers-by; and beggars, always beggars, of both sexes, lining blank walls where they intervene between the facades of shops; match sellers; wounded ex-soldiers, one with his mutilated stumps mercifully hidden by a blanket, resting on an improvised wooden cart pushed by an elderly woman, possibly his mother.

I drop a small coin into his cap and hurry on, avoiding his shamefaced thanks. I can afford to be a little more generous now. I finger the small bundle of crackling paper in my pocket, controlling my excitement until I return to my lodgings. Then I round a corner at the end of the alley. The girl is standing looking helplessly about her. I study her calmly, pretending to look in the window of a hardware shop. There is a mirror just behind a huge mound of zinc buckets, and I can see her clearly from where I am standing. She looks even more desirable than when I had first seen her through the café window.

She was standing uncertainly, clenching and unclenching her small fists in the white gloves all the while I observed her, which was for perhaps three to five minutes. Then she turned on her heel, as though she had made up her mind, and set off through the crowded street. I followed at a safe distance, keeping groups of people between us, stopping when she did and pretending to observe the contents of shop windows. But I do not really think my precautions were necessary. She was completely oblivious to my presence, as she was to all those about her.

We must have circled about for more than an hour, though time had ceased to have any existence. It was dusk and the lamplighters were lighting the street lamps when I realized we were once more back in the vicinity of the café where I had eaten. I was standing only a few yards from her, on the opposite side of the alley, but I might have been invisible for all the notice she took. Then there was a sudden scurrying of feet among the slowly thinning crowd which passed by at this dusky hour; a young man, hatless, his dark hair glistening beneath the lamps, rushed forward and swept the girl impetuously into his arms. People stared curiously as they passed, but the couple took no notice.

There were tears and broken sentences of apology; apparently the lover had been hours late for the assignation. Then they too passed away in the shuffling crowd, and I turned away with mingled feelings of rage and frustration in my heart. But I reined back my emotions and slowly came to myself again. A veil seemed to have come between me and the busy street. Later, I found myself on one of the main thoroughfares, and finally in the distance I could make out the great bulk of the Brandenburg Tor. I was then conscious that I had not eaten for some time, so I stopped at a cooked-meat shop and bought two large pork pies and two sweet buns for my supper.

These I carried back to Frau Mauger's. There was no one about as I let myself into the house by the side door; again, there was the murmur of voices from distant rooms and cracks of light showing beneath doors, but no one stirred. Gas jets burned palely in the scullery, and I took advantage of the moment to abstract one of the paraffin cans which bore the number of my room. Fortunately, it was half full and I carried it upstairs. Gaslight bleached the landing, so I had no difficulty in finding the small keyhole on my door. I left it ajar while I refilled and lit my lamp and then put the can away in a corner cupboard that smelt of damp and mold.

After I had relocked the door and drawn the curtains, I washed my hands at the basin in the alcove and sat down in one of the padded chairs to examine my haul. I caught sight of my excited face in the mirror as I counted out the notes. There were more than four thousand marks there! An incredible amount for perhaps five seconds' work. There would be enough there, together with what I already had, to keep me for weeks. I could concentrate on my great work with no need to worry about the cost of my accommodation or meals. There might even be time for some amatory adventures. I could not get the sweet face of the girl waiting in the alley out of my mind. I might see her again tomorrow or the day after.

I put the notes away in my leather body belt and sat down to my solitary supper, which I devoured with considerable satisfaction. When I had finished, I relaxed on the edge of my bed for a long time, preoccupied with my churning thoughts. I was aroused by a clock chiming midnight from a distant steeple. I undressed quickly, carried the lamp to the bedside table, extinguished it, and got beneath the coverlet. In three minutes I sank into a dreamless sleep.

3

Tuesday

This morning I sampled breakfast at Frau Mauger's for the first time. It is not something I should care to repeat in a hurry. I have seldom seen a more decrepit and quarrelsome crowd of boarders. There was watery soup served from a vast tureen in the middle of the table, which was covered with worn oilcloth, and the greasy aroma of stale leftovers was enough to put one off food for life. Hard rolls and some sort of sugary confection which passed for marmalade. While I digested this ill-favored start to the day, I studied my companions intently. To my disappointment, there was not a suitable girl among them. Or at least not one to set the heart racing.

Insipid coffee was being poured at this point, and I was momentarily distracted from the study of my companions in misfortune. An old man with a gray beard and a dark, clerical sort of garb, whom I understood to be a minor official at one of the great city museums; two rather elderly clerks in some ministry or other; an ancient with a ramrod-straight back, who wore the ribbon of some military decoration or other in his lapel, and whom a number of people at the table addressed deferentially as Herr Hauptmann. He is a typical, stupid, opinionated old man, pontificating to the table at large on long-ago battles in which he supposedly covered himself with glory. I very much doubt this. Such people should be wiped off the face of the earth. Even in wartime they are useless, merely squandering the lives of private soldiers. His narrow features and stupid white mustache fill me with disgust.

Apart from those mentioned there are several girls, none of whom is worth more than a passing glance. I am distracted from this sort of musing by the image of the girl I saw near the café yesterday. Perhaps I will see her again today. Who knows? Several times this military bore tried to catch my eye, but I was not to be drawn. As a newcomer I was obviously an object of greater interest than these familiar boarders, but I could sense the danger in this. I will not take part in any of these abominable so-called meals in future, but eat out. I can afford to do so. The increasing pressure of my body belt attests to this continually.

So I engaged instead in a somewhat muted conversation with a rather sullen middle-aged man on my right, without giving away anything about myself. He turned out to be some minor official at a local gas company office in the vicinity. He was lame also and unmarried, but I could feel no sympathy for him on those accounts. The old military gentleman continued with his fatuous monologue at the far end of the table, casting regretful glances at me from time to time, but I continued to avoid his unwanted attention and presently he desisted.

I excused myself from this dreadful meal as soon as I could and quitted the premises for the fresher air and the watery sunshine that gilded the rooftops, as though restored to life. A glass of bock in a crowded beer garden, as soon as I had reached a main hub of the city, fully restored my spirits and dissolved the aftereffects of the wretched meal from my taste buds. I lingered a while, watching the people about me as though with idle amusement, but in reality with a very definite purpose. I had not forgotten Angela, and I was looking for a definite type. But the hour I spent in this area of light-hearted amusement and idle chatter was absolutely wasted.

Either the woman of the type I wanted was in a party or perhaps with a young man, or was entirely unsuitable. It was almost as bad a situation as Frau Mauger's, and I sometimes despair of what appears to be the utter futility of my search. And to tell the truth, I am unprepared. I have no tools of my trade, having been forced to dispose of my last down a deserted well outside Cologne where they will never be found. Düsseldorf was even worse and I could find nothing there that satisfied me. Berlin is the only place. This is the city where I shall find everything I want: the woman or women, if I am lucky – and the necessary instruments for my purpose. Here I shall achieve my objective, surely, so that the whole world will ring with my name.

I then realize the waiter is hovering expectantly, and I order another bock. I make a few notes on a scrap of envelope while I await his return. As he places the glass upon the table I see, over his shoulder, the familiar figure of the girl passing the trellis work that frames the entrance to the garden. But as she turns in profile before me, I note that once again I have been mistaken. I rap the table angrily with my glass, causing an elderly lady nearby to glance in my direction. The girl I followed is becoming an obsession; I really must learn to curb my temper. I relax then and glance idly at the passing show.

Later. I have spent several hours at one of the great museums, where some distorted paintings by minor masters entrance me. How gorgeous it must have been to have lived in the Middle Ages, I feel. Then one could do as one liked, providing one was not a peasant! But to have the rights of the high, the middle, and the low . . . That must have been wonderful! Then I observe that one of the attendants is looking at me curiously and I hurry away. It would not do for anyone to become too interested in me. I am dressed quite respectably, of course, and am closely shaved with my hair brushed tidily. But I know from my own observations in the mirror in my room that my eyes glitter when I am roused. I must keep my lids half closed in order not to attract too much attention.

4

Wednesday

A great day! I have seen her again. Either she works at one of the premises in that narrow street where the café is situated, or perhaps lives or lodges there. And her name is Anna! A beautiful name, is it not? She was with a plain, dowdy sort of girl as I passed along the thoroughfare after lunch this afternoon, and I caught a fragment of their conversation as I followed close behind. But always keeping two or three people between myself and the two of them. That they are great friends goes without saying, because the girls have their arms entwined around each other's waists, as is often the way with bosom companions of the female sex.

Unfortunately, I lost sight of them in an open-air market and returned to the beer garden, where I consoled myself with wine on this occasion, and spent my time intensely scrutinizing all the people at the adjoining tables as well as the passersby. A fascinating occupation which never tires me. Unfortunately, the waiter has noticed my occasional habit of trimming my fingernails with my clasp knife. It is rather a large one and I keep it sharpened nicely, and he has an uneasy look in his eye that disquiets me in turn. I put it away casually, though my fingertips are trembling a little against the table surface.

He turns with some relief, and when he has gone into the restaurant on some errand or other, I drain the remaining inch of wine in my glass and move to a far corner of the vast forecourt, where there is an entirely new set of waiters, and I order another glass. I am concealed here by a potted palm and there is a low hedge in box trunking between me and the other section of the restaurant, and I see no sign of the waiter whose curiosity set my alarm bells ringing. But I must be more careful in future, though I am certain there is nothing in my dress or normal demeanor to single me out from the throng. I feel fine now and luxuriate in the warmth of the wine.

A military band is playing some old air in waltz time, and there is the scent of lime from the regularly spaced trees in the avenue.

Presently the sound of the band grows nearer, and I sense the quickening of interest in the crowd about me. Ah! There they are at last! The regimental band of the hussars, splendid in their tightly buttoned red and blue uniforms, their accoutrements glistening in the pale sunshine, while the plumes of the officers dance in the breeze. What a splendid sight! It sets the blood racing and I start to my feet, as do many others present. Girls are smiling and waving their handkerchiefs as the band passes, led by a solitary horseman on a white charger, and I see tears glisten on the cheeks of several old men standing stiffly to attention near me.

But the air of excitement dies within me. Their retreating backs and the supinely admiring attitude of the ancient military men remind me vividly of the odious old soldier back at my lodgings, and the afternoon seems to cloud over, even though the sun is shining as before. I sit myself down again as the music fades and am aware of several large beetles scuttling beneath my metal chair. They disgust me too, but I refrain from crushing them, as to me all life is sacred, save that of the detested human beings. I catch a young girl looking at me somewhat anxiously and hastily compose my features. The day seems grey and dusty as I presently quit the garden.

As I re-enter my lodgings this afternoon, as usual by the side door, and ascend the dimly lit staircase, I hear a board creak in the gloom. Then I see Frau Mauger standing near the door of my room. My suspicions about her are crystallizing. And they are reinforced when I see her hastily putting a large bunch of master keys behind her. I know what they are because I have already glimpsed them at her waist. She composes her features into what in a normal person would pass for a smile, when I come up.

'Ah, there you are,' she says with an air of embarrassment. 'I was hoping to find you. As you know, the rent is due by this evening.'

I have not yet been here a week, but I bite back the retort that all too readily springs to my lips. I merely nod and take my wallet up to the far end of the corridor, under the farthest gas jet. I keep a few notes in there for everyday needs. I extract the smallest note and take it back to her. I tell her that will cover the next fortnight. Greed struggles with pleasure in her face.

She will give me a receipt if I call in at her sitting room on my way out to dinner, she says. There is sarcasm in the latter part of the sentence, because she has guessed, quite correctly, that I have no wish to sample the so-called delights of her table. But I give her a thin smile and wait until she has descended the stairs, with a harsh rustling of skirts. Then I unlock my room, light the lamp, because little light penetrates into this place. I smile to myself in the semidarkness because the shade of the lamp is already warm. So she has been in the room.

I turn up the wick, relock the door, and examine my few possessions carefully. I see at once that my suitcase has been moved slightly from its original position. I examine the locks. All is well. I am convinced no one could open the case without either physically breaking the clasps or cutting out the leather. For the rest, there is nothing incriminating. I keep my written material, including my diary entries, with me at all times.

I wash and then relock my door carefully, leaving a stray hair from my collar across the crack of the jamb, after I have moistened each end with spittle. On my way out I pause at the door of Frau Mauger's sitting room. I can hear the faint clinking of coins. I enter at the same time as I rap on the panel. The woman almost leaps up from the table on which reposes a rusty tin box, a bundle of notes, and a heap of coins. There is fury in her eyes, but I explain in calm, clipped tones that I did knock before entering. She takes my lie with ill grace, knowing it for what it is. She mumbles something, pushes my change across the faded green baize cloth, together with a scribbled notation on a piece of grubby paper. I say nothing further as I leave the room without acknowledgment. The dusty air of the street tastes better than the stale odors of the lodging house.

I wander the streets idly, for an hour or two, enjoying the busy scene and the fresh breeze which ruffles my hair, while at the same time missing no attractive women who pass my field of vision. They are mostly drably dressed, being, I suppose, poor seamstresses or girls who work in offices or sweatshops, but now and again an attractive woman of the better class, elegantly dressed and with a sparkle to her eyes and a spring in her walk, attracts my rapt attention. But I conceal it well, glancing in shop windows while keeping an eye on the reflection of such a woman behind me. I am adept at this and have never yet been caught out, except on one occasion . . . But I decline to put this down on paper, as being of too intimate a nature.

I am looking for Anna, of course, but she does not seem to be abroad today. A pity, because I feel it is time I introduced myself. Under an assumed name, of course. It would never do to reveal my true identity. Far too — I was almost going to say incriminating, but that is the wrong word altogether. Revealing, perhaps? But that is not the right word either. I will leave a blank space here   There! If it comes to me, I can always insert it later. Ha! Ha! I am in an unusually merry mood today and on the lookout for adventure.

I am fortunate in that I am not short of money, thanks to that fool of a commercial traveler in the café. If I go on as I am going, I should have enough for another two months or so. If there is a God, I thank him for the constant supply of idiots of both sexes who always fortuitously seem to come my way.

I enter the old restaurant, perhaps with some idea of seeing Anna pass, and one of the waiters greets me as though I were an old friend. I order a bock to start with and under cover of one of the newspapers with which the proprietor kindly obliges the clientele, I study my companions. There are only a half dozen people in at this early hour of the evening, which is why I have chosen it, and as they are all sitting several tables away I am able to scrutinize them at leisure. An old bachelor, wearing some sort of velvet skullcap, is deeply engrossed in some political article while awaiting his order.

Why a bachelor? Or a widower, rather, which comes to the same thing. Because he wears a faded black armband on the left arm of his dark green velvet jacket. I turn my attention from him to two handsome women in the far corner, deeply engrossed in an animated conversation. Obvious lesbians because the younger, a fine-looking blonde girl, deeply feminine in her way, is wearing a low-cut gown and an imitation set of diamonds; I know they are paste, because I am experienced in these matters, but they are tasteful nevertheless and go well with her ensemble.

Her companion, certainly her 'husband,' is equally striking; in her late thirties, with masses of dark hair which has been cut in a mannish style, she wears a severe jacket of some dark material, also of a male cut, and with it a white silk shirt and a man's red tie. I notice also that both of them wear wedding rings and occasionally clasp hands across the table as they talk. I am fascinated with them and eye them for a long while until the waiter bringing their order distracts their attention and they observe my interest, whereupon I transfer my gaze to the other occupants of the large room.

These do not detain me long: two men of the working-class type with coarse clothing and loud laughs, and a sad-looking man in the corner with a professional air – he has silver hair and a long white beard and melancholy eyes. He has a book of poetry open in front of him and studies it with assumed interest while he furtively regards the lesbians over his soup from time to time. His dark hat and scarlet-lined cape hang from the mahogany stand behind his table, and his deep-socketed eyes seem to contain all the sorrows of the world.

Why do I know he is studying poetry? Because I have fantastic eyesight when I am absorbed in someone or something, and also, as he attempted to turn the page the book slipped and in retrieving it he revealed the flyleaf, which bore the tide in large black lettering. It was Baudelaire's *Les Fleurs du Mal*, one of my favorite works, which I have studied in translation many times in the silence of my solitary rooms. A divine work which should be in every man's – and woman's – possession.

But my order now arrives and I put aside my notes. A rare dish – not to say an esoteric one – featuring various varieties of sausage, cooked in unusual ways, together with fried onions and delicately grilled potatoes. How these Germans love their sausages! I have heard that they have no less than eight hundred different varieties in this country. That may be exaggeration, of course, but I have certainly seen a great many different types in shops and restaurants in the course of my wanderings. I was suddenly aware of the invasion of the pangs of hunger and set to without further delay.

It was during this stage of the meal that a minor tragedy occurred. I was engaged in taking a deep draught of bock when I caught sight of a familiar face passing the window. By the time I had realized it was Anna, the apparition had gone. I could not be certain it was she, and I caused a minor sensation by rushing to the restaurant door. But by the time I had pushed through a startled group of people who were just coming in, she had disappeared. I returned chastened to my seat and assured the agitated waiter that my sudden exit had nothing to do with the quality of the food or the service.

I was so upset by the incident that it took all the pleasure from the meal, and it was in a sullen and rather vindictive mood that I finished the repast. But by the time I had consumed a final cognac with my coffee, I had quite regained my good humor and eventually joined the groups of idlers on the pavement and, like a piece of driftwood on a tidal sea, allowed myself to be swirled this way and that until I finally ended up in an adjacent park where the band concert, held beneath strings of colored lamps, was really excellent and was still in full flood when I finally left them to it about eleven.

By contrast, my room at Frau Mauger's seemed more squalid than ever, and that night I sat long at my notes beneath the shaded lamp; I again checked my funds and found I still had plenty of cash in hand. In fact, enough for months more if I proceed frugally. I chuckled to myself at this; I had spent most of my life in extremely frugal circumstances, and certainly over the past dozen years had known real poverty until I learned to live by my wits and take my just dues from society.

But for the moment I am of two minds as to how to proceed; I had set my sights on Anna, but it now seems as though she will be more elusive than I had imagined. No one else interests me at the moment. At this point I break off these bleak thoughts and open up my suitcase. I forgot to mention earlier that I had carefully examined my door, and the hair I had placed across the jamb had been undisturbed. So I did not need to check my case. I sat examining its contents for quite a while. It does seem to me that I need some new instruments for the tasks I have set myself. But I have money enough and leisure enough to attend to this in due course. It is the problem of Anna that absorbs me. I am still thinking of her when I seek my bed.

Thursday

I had terrible dreams last night. They haunt me still. They may have been engendered by my interrupted meal. I occasionally suffer from indigestion, but nothing before had ever prepared me for the horrible parade of images that invaded my consciousness on this occasion. It began with something like a filmy gauze curtain waving in front of me. This gave way to Anna's face, which bore a sad, haunted look. Then I was back at Frau Mauger's, wandering the dusty, neglected corridors. I went to use the new toilet there. It is one of only two in the building, the other being Frau Mauger's.

I have that on the assurance of one of the residents; he is an old man, but how he came by this information I do not know. These places actually have porcelain sanitary ware. I was about to use the most intimate when, in a twinkling, what appeared to be thousands of bloated black spiders came swarming out of the water. I tried to scream, but my tongue seemed frozen to the roof of my mouth. Then the things were springing through the air; they were all over me, on my arms and shoulders, in my hair and then in my mouth.

I went mad then. I found something in my hands; perhaps it was a broom or a mop, seized in my frenzy from somewhere. I struck out blindly, crushing and smashing the things beneath my feet and with the weapon in my hands. They made a disgusting noise as I crushed them, and the air was full of the most nauseating odor. I, who love all animals and insects, was destroying the very things I had devoted my life to preserving! Thus shame was mingled with the horror. Blind rage had superseded my humanitarian instincts. Mercifully for my sanity, I woke in the calmness of my midnight room, my sheets soaked with perspiration.

I felt I had screamed aloud, but perhaps it had been only a half-strangled cry in my somnambulistic state, because there were no running footsteps in the corridor, no anxious voices or alarm being raised. But so vivid had been the anguish of my dream that I found the palms of my hands oozing with blood where my nails had cut into them. There were some traces on the sheets I found when I lit the lamp. I spent a half hour sponging them with a wet towel before I had erased the traces, and then I bound two handkerchiefs around my palms to stop any further emissions – with some difficulty, I might add.

When I was myself the following morning, I could not but come to the conclusion, somewhat wryly, that a convinced atheist like myself had now assumed the personification of a religious fanatic – that is, I bore all the signs of the stigmata! The irony would have been lost on someone without my sensibilities. But something happened today that went a long way toward restoring my spirits. This time I really saw Anna. She did not see me, as she was engaged in conversation when she passed the window of the café in which I was having a mid-morning coffee and a brioche, a habit to which I could soon become accustomed.

She was with the same girl I had seen her with before, and as I had paid my bill I drained my cup and followed them. They went in through the employees' entrance of a women's dress establishment, and I noted the time the business closed from a brass plaque screwed to the wall at the side of the front door. No doubt the girls had been delivering and collecting material, for they carried large cardboard boxes on which were engraved the name of the establishment. This was a great stroke of luck on my part, and I resolved to be nearby when the business closed for the day.

But that left me nearly seven hours to dispose of. I decided to have a late lunch; that way the day might not seem so long. That resolved, my footsteps took me on to one of the fashionable avenues of the city.

In one of the small side streets I made a remarkable find, in an extraordinary secondhand bookshop. There, in a remote corner of this vast establishment I discovered an old, musty volume called *The Pleasures of Pain*, privately printed by an obscure German academic. I was fascinated and determined to copy out some of the more striking passages. I borrowed the volume, as the proprietor was surrounded by potential customers, and carried the tome out under my jacket to read at my leisure. I intend to use it as a model textbook, and it has unlocked avenues in my mind of which I had never dreamed.

One of my fellow lodgers at Frau Mauger's is a minor clerical official at one of the city's largest slaughterhouses, and as I still had some six hours before I would see Anna, I caught a convenient public vehicle which passed only two streets away. My acquaintance was a little surprised to see me but at once fell in with my wishes. As I have previously remarked, I abhor all cruelty to animals and I had no wish to see actual slaughter taking place in this establishment, but I was curious as to the methods used in cutting up and preparing the meat. My fellow lodger took me to an iron gallery which overlooked one of the main abattoir areas, where the carcasses of dead animals came in on chains and were expertly dissected by giant fellows in bloodstained aprons, who wielded axes and razor-sharp knives with amazing dexterity.

I marveled at their expertise, and stayed a half hour, noting all their skilled movements with fascinated interest. I resolved to buy my acquaintance a glass or two of wine one evening soon and courteously saluted him on my way out. Back in the city center, I soon found a toy shop, where I purchased a number of female dolls of a certain type. On regaining the street I felt hunger pains and hurried to the nearest restaurant for a leisurely lunch. On emerging from the café, I turned aside and found a small court devoted to specialist shops.

I stopped halfway down, riveted to the pavement! Here was the establishment I had been vainly seeking. Bright blades gleaming in the dusty sunlight that struggled through the trees! Bright blades gleaming! Did not the poet somewhere write, 'How that glittering taketh me'? A medical establishment featuring surgical instruments and all doctors' medical supplies. The windows were full of them. Why did I not think of it before? Had I not been a medical student before the tragedy I have already mentioned brought my studies to an end? And I was positive that I could still carry off the role.

I glanced at my reflection in the window glass. I looked reasonably respectable, surely. And I could still remember most of the papers I had taken; I had specialized in surgery, though of course I would have had to have taken a medical degree before proceeding to that branch of the craft. It was with some diffidence that I entered the shop, the air of which was impregnated with that unmistakable odor of all the drugs and chemicals peculiar to hospitals. But I need not have worried. The dark-haired young man who advanced from the shadows at the far end of the counter looked just as diffident as I felt, and this bolstered my courage.

I made my needs known and was directed to a sort of corridor to one side where velvet-lined drawers opened to reveal gleaming surgical instruments. Curetting knives, slender scalpels, and some larger instruments for more serious work. I made my selection of five swiftly and confidently, and smiled at the shop man's professional chatter as he skillfully packed them for me. When I had paid and received my receipt, I stepped back onto the pavement full of confidence and good humor. My way stood clear before me now. I had given a false name and address, of course, and the assistant had not asked me for any identification. So I was convinced that I could not be traced.

Back in my room, I first secure the door, then unlock my case and remove some of the contents. These I display on the table with my new acquisitions; they make a splendid sight, lying gleaming in stray beams of pale sunlight that straggle in through the tops of the windows. When I have finished admiring them, I carefully rinse my new instruments in water and dry them with equal care. I have found that even the finest pieces of surgical equipment cannot give of their best if foreign bodies such as dust, grit, or lint are left clinging to the teeth or blades. And sure enough, I find particles of some substance like sawdust or paper packing adhering to these beauties during my ministrations.

When I have things to my satisfaction I lay out the dolls on the table, first removing their flimsy clothing. Of course, they bear no relation to the carcasses in the slaughterhouse, or to human beings, for that matter, but they are an approximation, which is better than nothing. I dissect them in an absorbed silence; I have lost none of my old dexterity, and soon the table is covered with sawdust, glass eyes, and arms severed at the joints.

Naturally, a great deal of these maquettes is made of porcelain and I cannot risk the cutting edges of the instruments on them, so it is not a true simulation. But it will do. When I have cleared up and replaced all the loose material in the cardboard and paper packing the shop assistant had provided, I was more or less ready.

Then I select those items necessary for my current tasks and lock the rest safely away. I have the chosen instruments in a sort of leather apron fastened to my belt, beneath my coat and outer garment as I leave my lodging. The last hours have passed in a dreamlike state, and I am hardly conscious of where my steps are leading me. I still have some half an hour before my rendezvous with Anna, and I take up my station in an empty doorway halfway down the street, in the direction in which I know she must come. At least that is the way she and her friend took whenever I glimpsed them from the café window. The only hindrance to my plan would be if her friend were with her. I must wait and see.

I meet Anna. That she is surprised to see me, there is no doubt. But I introduce myself and remind her of where we met before. We talk for a while. Then I leave her in a narrow alley and make my way back to my lodgings in a euphoric mood. But I have a terrible nightmare; I am in my room and it is raining blood. I am naked and drops are falling from the ceiling. I look in the mirror and see them streaming down my back. I scream then and find I am awake. But I am wet and sticky. The horror intensifies. Somehow, I struggle out of bed and light the lamp.

I am so appalled that at first I cannot open my eyes. I expect to see myself drenched in blood. But there is nothing! It is merely perspiration which streams down my face and body, drenching my night attire. The relief is so great that I sink to the floor. After a while I stagger to my feet. I am cold and my teeth are beginning to chatter, as much from emotion as from the chill of the night. I then creep to the door and listen. But there obtains a profound silence. So no one has heard the terrible noise I made and which must have woken me. Unless it was a silent scream such as must have occurred on the previous occasion I had a nightmare. A scream within a dream, as it were; a scream audible only to myself and not to the rest of the world. For that I must be thankful. I drag myself to bed and sleep fitfully until daylight.

Friday

Something is afoot this morning. There is crying in the street and some sort of commotion. I open my window and by standing on a chair am able to look down, which brings most of the alley below into view. There are crowds of people standing about as though something terrible has happened. Then a horse-drawn ambulance passes, going at a furious rate. The people in the street scatter to let it through. I leave the window open as I complete my toilet. When I again look, the people have dispersed and the thoroughfare has assumed its normal aspect.

About to leave for the day, I prepare to shut the door from the outside when I feel something sticky on the doorknob. My hand comes away scarlet. This gives me a great shock. Fortunately, there is no one in the corridor and it is not yet time for breakfast, so I rush back inside, wet my handkerchief at the tap, and wipe the handle clean. I find I am trembling as though with the ague. I go carefully along the passage but can see nothing further. I reenter my room and wash my handkerchief in cold water until it is clear of blood.

Then I drain the sink, wring out the handkerchief, and, wrapping it in a spare I take from my case, place the two in my trousers pocket, where the damp one will soon dry out. I keep a sharp lookout as I descend the stairs and out into the street but can find nothing incriminating. I make for the beer garden I have recently frequented and order coffee and rolls. It is far too early for wine, and I must keep a clear head.

The waiter who serves me is garrulous and obviously anxious to impart some news to me, but my attitude puts him off. Later he comes to serve a couple at a table nearby, and I hear the gist of their conversation. A girl has been found dead in a nearby street. Apparently she has been murdered. For some reason I become agitated. So much so, in fact, that I am about to depart without paying my bill. But the waiter catches my eye and comes over with the reckoning. I sink back into my chair, inexpressibly nervous and somewhat incoherent in my speech. The waiter looks at me curiously. He asks if I am unwell. I know the fellow is only being kind, and I go against my nature by thanking him and assuring him that it is merely a temporary upset.

Mollified, he moves off with the note I have given him, and when he returns with my change, I find I am so much out of character that I give him the sort of tip I would never normally give. He stammers his thanks, and when he has gone to serve some other customer I rise to leave the garden. But my upset is more serious than I thought because my legs give way beneath me. But if I move to another seat, a second waiter would only arrive to take my fresh order, so I remain where I am while I gather my strength and my wits about me.

I almost stagger out of the garden, but fortunately there is a public park almost opposite. Somehow I find the strength to cross the *strasse* and find an unoccupied bench in the pale sunshine. I sit there for a long time, a cool breeze ruffling my hair, until I am somewhat more restored to myself. When I eventually consult my watch, it is almost lunchtime, and I am shocked to discover how many hours have passed. I feel better then and, straightening my tie and tidying my clothing, I make my way to a rather smart restaurant on one of the main thoroughfares and enjoy a long and leisurely meal.

By this time it is early afternoon, but I now find a great reluctance to return to Frau Mauger's. Instead, I spend a couple of hours in the Zoological Gardens, where the feeding of the great carnivores with huge gobbets of meat fascinates me and I quite forget my earlier agitation. Their roaring notes of contentment are still sounding basso and cutting through the shrill cries of tropical birds as I step into the whirling chaos of carriages and iron-shod wheels. It is a great relief to reach the relatively quiet enclave where my lodging is situated.

The shadows are long on the ground as I let myself in the side door. I am proceeding quietly toward the staircase when I notice that the door of Frau Mauger's tiny office is open and a thin bar of lamplight is shining through. She comes to the door at the sound of my step, a worried look on her face. A man has been around questioning all her tenants, she says. She hopes there is nothing wrong. He has interviewed everyone except myself and a young clerk. Concealing my alarm, I ask what the man wanted. Frau Mauger shrugs. He said it was just routine, she replies. I ask her to describe the man. She again shrugs. An ordinary-looking person: middle-aged, wearing a black leather coat and a green homburg hat. He said he would call back tomorrow to finish his inquiries, she adds.

My heart thumps. A police agent! I know the breed only too well. I hope my inner turmoil is not showing on my face. But Frau Mauger's own features are impassive in the lamplight from the door. I tell her that I will be available in my room tomorrow afternoon, and that seems to satisfy her. She gives a third shrug, goes in, and closes the door. I mount the stairs with something approaching panic in my heart. I had forgotten to ask my amiable landlady whether the man had searched any of the rooms. Too late now. To return with that question would only arouse suspicion. Fortunately, my chamber seems undisturbed. I know now what I must do. I check my wallet again and make my preparations.

My case comes out from beneath the bed. I add to its contents and complete the packing by clearing my few possessions scattered about the room. When I have finished my arrangements, I put out the lamp and sit with thudding heart in the semi-darkness, like a hunted beast, until I hear the gong for supper and the slow, dragging footsteps of the hopeless inmates of this dismal lower-class prison as they make their way to the dingy dining room. Then I rise to my feet, give a last glance around, make sure I have everything, including my all-important diary notes.

I put on my coat, leave the key on the table, and go out, slowly and carefully closing the door behind me. I negotiate the stairs without attracting any attention and gain the side door. It is almost dark now and no one even glances at me as I join the thin stream of people passing. As soon as I have left the neighborhood, I quicken my pace. It would be fatal to delay. I will sleep in the *bahnhof* tonight. I know what I must do tomorrow. The way is now clear before me.

Later

I am in London. It seems a dirty and wretched place. Furthermore, despite the time of year it is damp and foggy, a condition which is exacerbated by the smoke from factory chimneys and from the wretched dwellings when the wind is in a certain direction. I am in a cheap lodging house in one of the small alleys off the street called the Strand. It is an almost exact replica of Frau Mauger's establishment, except that the food, if anything, is worse. I have scrutinized the Continental newspapers on sale at one of the great railway stations, but there has been nothing. That, at least, is a relief.

I have also changed my marks into English currency and was indignant at the exorbitant exchange rate. But I did not dare draw attention to myself and let the matter pass. I had a good crossing, fortunately. I saw nothing or no one suspicious in Calais or on the steamer. I was particularly careful when I arrived in Dover and took extraordinary precautions to avoid scrutiny, but neither then nor on the train to London did I see any sign that I was under observation. But it was with some relief that I found my present haven. And unlike Continental hotels and lodging houses, their English counterparts do not go in for the dangerous practice of police registration for their guests. That is something in which the British exhibit superiority at any rate.

My room here is very secure, with a strong lock and no less than two bolts on the door. Admirable for my purposes. The first night of my arrival I laid out my instruments and washed and polished them for my first major exploit. One that will elevate me to the front rank of famous men. Such bright blades gleaming! This room is sunny, or would be if the weather were clear, facing as it does the brown, muddy waters of the Thames, and the clatter of the busy traffic along the Embankment makes a soothing background to my thoughts.

I feel as though I am walking with destiny. Tonight I pack those instruments fitted for my purpose and lock the others away. I have taken every precaution. Rubber gloves from an ironmonger's shop, anonymous clothing. Though I do not think I shall be noticed, so abominable is the weather. For summer at least.

But this is England, a factor I keep forgetting. And it will be admirable for my purposes. I sit out the twilight at my window, waiting for dusk. It is very late coming in these latitudes. It is almost ten in the evening before I feel free to quit my lodgings, and gas lamps are glowing along the Embankment, insubstantial and ghostlike through the mist.

I purchased a smaller bag yesterday, which looks very much like one of those cases office clerks of the more impecunious sort favor. I am certain no one will notice me, particularly in this weather. I have spoken to one or two people at the lodging house and at the nearby railway station and gained certain important information. I take a last look around my room and prepare to set forth on my great adventure. I put a small tick against the soiled calendar that hangs on the wall above my table. It is August 6, 1888.

No one remarks me as I open the front door, which is left unlocked all night. I mingle with the passing crowds in the darkling street. The instruments make a faint clattering noise inside the case. Bright blades gleaming! Even in the darkness. But I must make sure in future that I muffle the sound by wrapping them firmly in cloth. I turn my steps eastward in the rapidly encroaching darkness. My acquaintances assure me that there is an abundance of whores where I am going. My informant has told me the exact spot where I can find a cab to take me to Whitechapel . . .

***Basil Copper** was born in 1924. His long and distinguished writing career spans many genres and more than eighty books. He is perhaps best known for his Mike Faraday mystery novels, and his continuing exploits of detective Solar Pons (originated by the late August Derleth). His short stories have been gathered in such collections as* From Evil's Pillow, Voices of Doom, *and* Here Be Daemons. *The Mark Twain Society of America has appointed him a Knight of Mark Twain for his 'contributions to modern fiction.'*

Hanson's Radio

BY

JOHN LUTZ

'I CAN prove that no man has ever set foot on the moon,' the voice from across the alley said. 'I have photographs of an area near Fort Colt, Arizona, that match in every respect the so-called official government photographs of the astronauts on the surface of the so-called moon.'

'Sam?' said Ina's voice from the bed. 'Sam? Why aren't you asleep? Does your leg hurt?'

'It doesn't hurt, it itches under this damned cast,' Sam Melish told his wife.

'Just suppose,' the Midnight Rider said, 'that someone moved some rocks around in the desert and arranged an area in Arizona to look exactly like the moon landing site. In other words, how do I know *your* photographs and not the government's aren't devious duplications?'

'Come back to bed, Sam,' Ina pleaded.

But Sam Melish tuned her out and continued listening to the radio blaring from the apartment across the alley. The man who lived there, Hanson, apparently slept with a dim nightlight on.

Sam could make out the massive shape of the hated gigantic portable stereo – the kind with good reason called boom boxes – where it was set on a table. It was long and dark, somewhat humped in the center, where its glowing dials seemed to glare at Melish like malevolent eyes.

'Sam?'

'Quiet, Ina. Please! I have no choice other than to listen to that noise monster across the alley, but you can give me some peace.'

But she couldn't, he knew. Ever since his leg had been broken when one of the aluminum-crushing machines fell on it where he worked as a bookkeeper at the City Waste Disposal Center, Melish had been confined to their tiny efficiency apartment, his right leg immobilized by a bulky cast. It wasn't the old-fashioned plaster kind; it was made of some sort of plastic. But it was permanent. That is, it would remain on his leg every uncomfortable second until the bone had mended and the doctor removed the cast. Right now his leg itched and he couldn't scratch it.

Yet that agonizing itch was no worse than the irritation in his mind, the outrage that crawled beneath his flesh and that he was equally helpless to scratch. The inconsiderate Hanson, in the fifth-floor apartment directly across the alley from Melish's, played his boom box at top volume constantly. Literally constantly! Around the clock!

During the day it was usually music, all types, but mostly rock or rap. At night it was sometimes music, sometimes inane twenty-four-hour talk stations. Melish could not escape the din. He'd tried wearing earplugs, but they barely reduced the decibel level and they gave him terrible headaches. Meditative concentration did nothing for him. During the past dreadful week Melish had come to hate the music as well as the disturbed and suspicious people who phoned in to such shows as the Midnight Rider's.

'Are you saying,' the caller asked incredulously, 'that you trust the government more than you trust me?'

But the Midnight Rider was too sly to fall into that trap. 'What I'm saying, Bill – it is Bill, right?'

'Right.'

'I'm saying that in this instance the evidence of a genuine moon landing outweighs your evidence, Bill. It's as simple as that.'

Bill would not be dissuaded. 'Anyone who'd trust the government more than a private citizen should leave this country and live in—'

'Turn it off!' Melish screamed. *'Turn it off!'* He stood teetering at the window on his crutches, glaring across the dark void above the alley.

After a few seconds, Hanson, a tall young man with bushy blond hair and hulking shoulders, came to the window and stood silently looking back at him. Melish could see him only in dim silhouette, a figure as unmoving and uncompromising as a statue.

'Off!' Melish shouted. *'Now!'* He staggered closer to the window on his crutches as if he might fly the width of the alley and smite Hanson like an avenging angel of blessed silence.

'Sam, my God, what are you trying to do?' Ina was behind him, clutching his shoulders to restrain him.

Melish saw the dark figure across the alley slowly raise a hand, then draw down the shade.

'Next you're going to tell me,' the Midnight Rider said at top volume, 'that the moon is really made of—'

'Gonna tell the man, *gonna make my* stand, *gonna do it* grand, *gonna . . .'*

Hanson had switched to a station blasting rap music.

Defeated, Melish fell back on the bed. The window air conditioner wasn't working, and perspiration soaked the sheets, glued his pajamas to him and stung the corners of his eyes.

'Want me to call the police, Sam?' Ina asked with compassion, though they both knew how he would answer her question.

'Why?' Melish asked. 'So they won't come for an hour? So when they do come, Hanson will turn down his stereo, then turn it back up as soon as they leave?'

Ina switched on the bedside reading lamp and stared down at him. She'd just turned forty and was attractive in a way she hadn't been as a younger woman. Her gaunt features had of late taken on a softer look. Her large brown eyes, always gentle, were now wise. She seemed deeply contented in a way that Melish didn't quite understand and knew he could never attain.

'Just look at you, Sam,' she said while he gazed up at her, 'look how you've let that noise wear you down.'

'It is wearing me down,' he admitted.

'Gonna do it right, *gonna make my* fight, *gonna see some* fright, *gonna . . .'*

'It's violent, that music,' Ina said. 'Why does he listen to it?' She seemed genuinely curious.

'Why does he listen to anything?' Melish said. 'Or everything? He tunes in to country-western, classical, talk shows, rock and roll, rap music, anything that's on the air. I think he's doing it to aggravate me. He knows about my broken leg; I've seen him staring over here through our window. Just standing and staring. This is a fifth-floor, walk-up apartment, so he knows I'm trapped here with this shattered bone. I'm not going to struggle down all those stairs, then back up them. I have no alternative! I have to listen!'

She didn't answer. Instead she switched off the lamp, and he heard and saw her shadowy figure walk around to her side of the bed. The springs whined and the mattress shifted as she lay down beside him.

'Try to get some sleep, Sam.'

'You can say that. You could always sleep through anything. A fire, a war . . . For you sleep is an escape mechanism.'

She touched his shoulder gently, and he knew she was smiling sadly at the truth of his words. And falling asleep.

'Gonna smoke some grass, *gonna kick some—'*

Melish wrapped the sweat-damp pillow around his head, then twined his arms around the pillow and squeezed, pressing its soft bulk as firmly as possible against his ears.

Hours later, he fell asleep to Handel's *Messiah.*

A warm breeze pushed in through the window the next morning while Melish and Ina were seated at their small wooden table eating a breakfast of low-fat cereal, toast, and coffee. Ina had spread strawberry preserves on her toast. Melish's toast was dry. Dr Stein had warned Melish sternly to watch his weight, his blood pressure, his cholesterol. That had been the day before Melish broke his leg.

Hanson's radio was blasting out a report from a traffic helicopter. 'Traffic approaching the bridges is backed up for miles,' said a woman over the background noise of the craft's rotors thrashing the air around her. 'Directly below us a truck and a car have had an accident and are blocking the west-bound lane. The drivers are outside their vehicles and they appear to be fighting.'

'This city,' Melish said around a mouthful of dry toast, 'has become hell.' He washed down the toast with scalding coffee that scorched his tongue.

'You used to love the city, Sam,' Ina said.

'I still do, but it has become hell.'

'It only seems that way to you because of your leg.'

Maybe she was right, Hanson thought. His leg did itch like crazy beneath the cast, as if a centipede were in its death throes down where he couldn't possibly reach it. He hadn't been thinking about the leg before she'd drawn it to his attention, but now it itched.

He shifted his weight over one of his crutches, levered himself up to a standing position, then slipped the other crutch beneath his arm. Across the alley he saw Hanson standing at his window, staring. When Hanson realized he'd been seen, he slowly backed away out of sight in the dimness of his apartment, like an apparition fading into another dimension.

'Hanson was watching us again,' Melish said. 'I think he's spying on us.'

'That's silly, Sam. Every time you've seen *him* looking over here, *you've* been looking over there. These apartments only have one window that looks out over the alley, and his and ours are directly across from each other.'

'Are you saying I'm getting paranoid?'

'No,' Ina said, 'what you are is edgy.'

Edgy, Melish thought. In his position, who wouldn't be edgy?

Hanson switched from local news, weather, and traffic to a station that played frenetic Latin music.

'You think he's not doing that to aggravate me?' Melish asked.

Ina smiled. 'Yes, he knows you can't mambo, Sam, and it's killing you.'

Melish saw that he was getting nowhere. He picked up the morning *Times* that Ina had brought in from downstairs and tried to read it. It was full of news about Latin America, so he set it aside.

It wasn't long before Hanson tired of the Latin music and switched to a talk show featuring a man who claimed that the president had once had sex with an extraterrestrial, noting that the president had not specifically denied the allegation.

Fifteen minutes later, Hanson tuned in to rap music. Melish recognized the recording artist, a young man known as Mr Cool Rule.

'*She be a police* snitch, *gotta off that* bitch . . .'

Melish tried not to listen. He watched as Ina finished with the dishes and left them propped in the yellow plastic drainer to dry. 'Why would a person have sex with an alien?' he asked.

'I don't know, Sam.'

'There would be the possibility of a rare socially transmitted disease.'

Ina wiped her hands on a dish towel, draped the towel over the oven handle, then said, 'I'm going out.'

'I'm going mad,' Melish said.

'We need food for lunch. Do you want anything in particular?'

'Anything,' Melish said. 'I can enjoy nothing, so I'll eat anything.'

Ina stared at him, shook her head, then left.

Melish heard the key and latch rattle behind her as she locked him in for security's sake. He worked his way to a standing position, then limped on his crutches over to the window that looked out on the street. After a few minutes, far below, he saw her foreshortened figure emerge from the building and walk toward Second Avenue and Fleigle's Market.

He was about to return to his chair when he noticed a figure on the other side of the street. Hanson. The man's stereo was blaring, and he wasn't even in his apartment! As Melish watched, Hanson began walking along the opposite side of the street, in the same direction as Ina.

Turning away from the window, Melish felt his fury grow. Here he was trapped and crippled and assaulted by sound, while Hanson blithely roamed the streets.

He picked up the *Times* again, thinking he might be able to read about Latin America now, but bile rose bitter in his throat and he hurled the paper back down. He limped to the refrigerator, got out the orange juice, and gulped some directly from its glass pitcher. The cool liquid felt good going down, and it soothed his burned tongue.

'*She the* mother *that cook my* brother.'

The pitcher slipped from Melish's hand and shattered on the tile floor. Glass fragments flew and orange juice flowed beneath the sink in a tidal wave.

Melish automatically started to stoop so he could right what was left of the pitcher and stop the flood of orange juice. The abrupt motion made him lose his balance. He caught himself on the sink, bumping his elbow painfully, and one foot slid in the juice and his pajama leg got soaked up to the knee of his uninjured leg.

There was only his fury now, his anger at himself for being so clumsy, his rage at the relentless barrage of sound that flew like sharp spears across the alley and assailed him in his home.

When Melish's father had died three years before, among the worthless junk and keepsakes Melish's siblings had foisted off on him was an old .22 hunting rifle. Melish had never known his father to hunt and had never seen him use the rifle, which had always been kept locked in the basement of the family home. The gun had been a gift to his father, and now Melish had it because he was the only brother or sister without children who might be endangered by its presence. Melish had years ago laid the rifle on the back of a closet shelf, tight against the wall, and forgotten about it.

Now he remembered it.

And he remembered placing the small box of ammunition in the drawer where he kept old sweaters he couldn't bear to discard.

Amazingly, he was almost nimble on his crutches as he got down the rifle and located the bullets. His hands, his fingers, were swift and purposeful as he loaded the magazine. Hanson was gone from his apartment, so there was no danger of doing harm to a fellow human. It was Melish versus the radio. No, it was civility versus chaos. Consideration versus callousness. Civilization versus anarchy.

Surely Melish was right to do this.

He worked the rifle's bolt action and jacked a round into the chamber.

Now that his mind was made up, he moved almost like an automaton, limping to the window, his right thumb hooked over the cross brace of his crutch, his fingers clutching the barrel as the rifle's wooden stock dragged across the floor. It was a small-caliber rifle that would make a sound not much louder than a sharp hammer blow. Hardly noticeable in this city that had become so raucous and rude, so ripe with sudden, unexpected danger. No one would, in fact, be able to hear the shot over the racket of Hanson's stereo.

His heart pounding against his ribs, Melish leaned the rifle against the wall. Then he dragged over a kitchen chair and arranged it in front of the window. He sat down, picked up the rifle, and rested its barrel on the sill.

Took careful aim.

'*She the one that* tell, *so she goin' to* hell.'

Melish squeezed the trigger.

The shot sounded like a palm slapping a flat surface. The hump-backed stereo seemed to move slightly on the table.

'*Throw the* switch *on the* bitch—'

Melish fired another round.

Silence.

Precious silence.

Peace.

Even before he opened the door to his apartment, Hanson knew something was very wrong.

The stereo was no longer playing, which meant the demons held at bay by its sound had somehow silenced it. No longer repulsed by the waves of life-saving noise, they had entered the apartment, the very place where Hanson lived. Now there was no sound protecting him. No sanctuary.

No peace.

God had forsaken him and sided with the administration.

Hanson slumped on the edge of the bed and began tearing at the flesh of his left hand with the nails of his right. Rage, sorrow, hopelessness swept over him.

He wept.

'It was an act of madness,' Ina said after Melish had told her what he'd done.

'It was an act of necessity,' Melish said.

But now that he'd calmed down, now that he could think in the silence, he was beginning to feel regret. He'd lost his composure. Acted like a wild animal protecting itself against attackers. This was a civilized society with rules, with laws, so that reasonable people could live alongside each other. He knew he should not have used the rifle.

'You might have killed the poor man,' Ina said, cleaning up the mess Melish had made when he dropped the pitcher of juice.

'He was out, or I would never have shot over there,' Melish said. 'I looked out the window and saw him down in the street, following you.'

'Following me?'

'Walking in the same direction, anyway.'

Fear crossed her dark eyes like a shadow. 'Why on earth would he follow me?'

'I don't know. I don't think he was actually following you. I said he was going in the same direction.'

'Well, you'd better apologize to him for what you did.'

'Are you kidding? What I'm going to do is stay quiet and hope he does the same.'

'He'll know what happened,' Ina said.

Melish knew she was probably right. It wouldn't take a ballistics expert to figure out who'd shot Mr Cool Rule and the Midnight Rider.

He lay in bed beside Ina that night in silence, but he didn't sleep.

In the morning, without the usual clamor of the news and traffic reports, he gazed across the alley and saw Hanson standing at his window staring at him.

Melish stared back, then shrugged apologetically and silently mouthed the words 'I'm sorry.'

Hanson gazed glumly at him for another few seconds, then lowered his shade.

Why had the man Melish shot the stereo? Hanson could think of only one reason. Melish had been possessed by the demons and become their agent.

And Ina, the woman who'd lain down with Hanson, was she also one of the possessed?

Their affair had begun months ago when they'd stared at each other from their windows, then met down in the street by accident. The attraction that had arced across the space between their windows was even stronger when they were close to each other, and neither of them had resisted it, though Hanson knew she was Melish's wife. A passion like an edict from God had gripped their souls and bodies, making Ina's professions of guilt and conscience seem absurd to Hanson.

He knew she thought he was strange. And dangerous. She was secretly afraid of him, but she liked that. He was so unlike Melish, who was so like every man. She had told Hanson once, whispered it hoarsely in his ear, that he was exotic. That was something Melish was not. Hanson hadn't told her about the building commissioner and the commissioner of public works and about the demons. He knew she would think they were something other than exotic and would be even more afraid of him, and she would refuse to see him again. That was a thought he couldn't bear.

When Melish was away at work they would use her apartment, sweating and grappling in the bed and sometimes on the floor. She would smell like wildness and make throaty sounds like an animal, and he could hear her even over the noise of his stereo roaring through the open window.

Then Melish had broken his leg and he was home all day, trapped in the apartment.

But Ina could leave. Hanson had followed her this morning, as she knew he would, and they'd been together in the park. Melish had no idea what his wife was.

But now Hanson understood what had happened, how the demons, once frustrated, were laughing at him. They had used Ina to seduce him and lure him away from his apartment. It had been part of the demons' plan that Hanson couldn't help staring at the woman's smooth flesh, her warm brown eyes, the gentle roll of her hips. How deceptive. How clever of the demons to compel him to watch her through her window and to want her until he ached in the core of him. They had been in her and they had used her to trick him. And they had possessed Melish and used him to destroy the noise that had been Hanson's salvation.

He thought about buying or stealing a new stereo, but he knew that wouldn't save him. The demons were in now, and they wouldn't leave. They'd been sent by the administration and they would accomplish their deadly task. It was all political, but it was lethal and on some level intensely personal. And if he moved to another apartment, they'd follow. They were in his clothes, and beneath his skin and inside his brain now like malignant tumors, and they were waiting and scheming and it was too late. He was doomed.

But it wasn't too late for Ina and Melish, also victims of the demons.

They could be set free.

It would be an act of kindness.

Hanson walked into the kitchen and removed from a drawer beneath the sink a wood-handled meat cleaver and a long boning knife. He was perspiring heavily in the heat, his T-shirt plastered to his flesh, but he shrugged into the green sports jacket he'd gotten from the Salvation Army and slid the cleaver up his right sleeve, the knife up his left. With his arms at his sides, he could curl the middle finger of each hand and keep both cleaver and knife out of sight, though the point of the knife hurt his finger and was probably causing it to bleed. That hardly mattered now. Destiny was walking in Hanson's clothes. He would deal the release of death to the man and woman as a kindness and a vengeance and a gift and then carve and eat their flesh corrupted by the demons and give himself screaming to the eternal fire.

Stooping slightly and holding his right forearm horizontal so the cleaver wouldn't drop from his sleeve, he opened the door and stepped out into the hall.

Both arms at his sides again, his weapons of fear and freedom concealed beneath his jacket sleeves, he trudged downstairs to the street.

The voices were between his brain and the inside of his skull now and were screaming at him all at the same time so it was as the Tower of Babel but the judgment and lightning of God would not be denied and Hanson would wield the steel and then embrace and breathe in the fire, the fire, the fire the fire the fire . . .

Ina happened to glance out the window and see him coming.

'It's Hanson,' she said. 'He's crossing the street, Sam. I think he's on his way here.' She slumped into the chair she'd just gotten up from and clasped her hands in her lap.

Melish heard the fear in her voice and was again ashamed of what he'd done. But maybe it was good that Hanson was coming. They would talk. Melish would apologize, explaining that in the heat and the noise and with his broken leg that never stopped itching beneath the cast, he had lost his head and acted rashly and wrongly. He would offer to buy Hanson a new stereo if he would promise not to play it too loud. Reasonable people could and would learn. These things could be resolved.

Melish and Ina stared at each other as they heard the sound of footsteps out on the stairs, then in the hall outside their door.

The knock was gentle and didn't seem angry.

Ina started to rise from her chair, but Melish motioned for her to sit back down.

He worked his way to his feet, leaning on his crutches, and hobbled to the door. He unfastened the chain lock, then turned the knob on the dead bolt, thinking that in the silence, in the peace, he and Hanson could talk and come to an understanding, two reasonable men. Neighbors should talk and get to know one another. Everyone had to live in this city together, had to learn to treat each other with consideration and perhaps, eventually, even with kindness. It was possible.

We should all hope.

When he opened the door, he was relieved to see that Hanson was smiling.

'Mr. Hanson,' he said, 'I'm glad you dropped by. I think we should talk.'

'I understand you're with the administration,' Hanson said.

***John Lutz** published his first short story in 1966 and has yet to look back. The author of over twenty-five novels and 300 short stories and articles, he is a former president of both the Mystery Writers of America and the Private Eye Writers of America. The creator of the Carver and Nudger series, his suspense novel* SWF Seeks Same *was the basis for the hit movie* Single White Female. *The winner of multiple Edgar, Shamus, and Trophee 18 awards, his most recent books are the new Nudger novel* Thicker Than Blood *(St Martins) and* Burn *(Henry Holt) featuring the Florida-dwelling Carver. His screenplay* The Ex, *adapted from his forthcoming novel, is scheduled to go into production in 1995.*

Refrigerator Heaven

BY

DAVID J. SCHOW

THE light is beatific. More than beautiful. Garrett sees the light and allows the awe to flow from him.

Garrett can't *not* see the light. His eyelids are slammed tightly shut; tears trickle from aching slits at both corners. The light seeks out the corners and penetrates them. It is so hotly white it obliterates Garrett's view of the thin veinwork on the obverse of his own inadequate eyelids.

He tries to measure time by the beat of his own heart; no good.

The light has always been with him, it seems. It is eternal, omnipotent. Garrett gasps, but not in pain, not *true* pain – no, for the light is a superior force, and he owes it his wonder. It is so much *more* than he is, so intense that he can *hear* it caress his flesh, seeking out his secret places, his organs, his thoughts, illuminating each fissure and furrow in his very brain.

Garrett slams his palms over closed eyes and marvels that the light does not care and offers no quarter. Garrett feels pathetic; the light, he feels, is unequivocal and pure.

Garrett has looked into the light and formulated a new

definition of what God must be like. He feels honored that he, among mortals, has been permitted this glimpse of the divine. His mind interprets the light as hot, though he does not feel the anticipated baking of his flesh. So pure, so total . . .

He has never in his pathetic, mortal life borne witness to a spectacle like it.

Finally, the light is too much. Garrett must avert his gaze, but he cannot. No matter which way he turns his head, the light is there, cleansing away agendas and guilt and human foibles and the mistakes of the past, as well as mistaken notions of the future. The light, forever, there in Garrett's head.

He reaches to find words to offer up to the light, and he can only find limited human conceits, like love.

A woman is in bed with her husband. They are between bouts of lovemaking, and the woman's eyes are hooded and blue in the semidarkness, with that unique glow – a radiance that tells the man he is all she sees, or cares to see right now.

She tells him she loves him. Unnecessarily. The words in the dark do him spiritual good anyway.

She touches his nose with her fingertip and draws it slowly down. You. I love.

He knows.

He is about to say something in response, if for no other reason than not to maroon her in their warm, post-coital quiet, stranding her alone with her words of love. He is trying to think of something sexy and witty and genuinely loving, to prove he cares.

He is on his back, and one of her legs, warm and moist on the softest part of the inner thigh, is draped over his. You are mine, the embrace says. You are what I want.

The man is still struggling with words that won't come. He misses his chance. If you miss the moment, other forces rush in to fill the dead air for you, and rarely does one have control or choice.

Later, the man thinks, if only he had spoken, none of the bad things would have happened.

There are some loud noises. The next thing the man knows, his wife is screaming and he is face-down, cheek bulled roughly against the carpet. His wife is screaming questions that will not be answered in this lifetime.

The man's hands are cuffed behind his back. He is lifted by the cuffs, naked, as lights click on in the bedroom.

He twists his head, tries to see. He is backhanded, very hard, by one of his captors. The image he snatches is of his wife, also naked, held by her throat against the bedroom wall, by a man in a tight business suit. With his free hand the suit is holding an automatic an inch from her nose and telling her in no uncertain verbiage to shut up if she knows what is good for her.

Like a bad gangster movie, thinks the man.

He sees all this in an eighth of a second. Then, *bang.* He hits the floor again, feeling the wetness of fresh blood oozing from a split eyebrow.

His ankles are ziplocked together – one of those vinyl slipknot cuffs used by police. Then he is hoisted bodily, penis dangling, and carried out of his own bedroom like a roast on a spit.

He fights to see his wife before his captors have him out the door. In this moment, seeing her one last time becomes the most important imperative ever to burn in his mind.

As he is hauled away, he says he loves her. He has no way of knowing whether she hears. He cannot see her as he speaks the words. In the end, the words come easily.

He never sees his wife again.

Donnelly regarded the box with a funny expression tilting his face to starboard. He took a long draw on his smoke, which made a quarter-inch of ash, then shrugged the way a comedian does when he *knows* he's just delivered a knee-slapper . . . and the audience is too stupid to appreciate it.

'So what did this guy *do*?' he said with artificial levity.

'That's classified,' said Cambreaux. 'That's none of your

beeswax. That, Chester, is a dumb question, and you oughta know better.'

'Just testing,' said Donnelly. 'I'm supposed to jump-quiz smart-asses like you to make sure there are no security leaks. So what did he do?'

'He's a reporter, from what I gather. He was in the wrong place at the right time with a camera and a tape recorder, neither of which we can find. They sent down orders to scoop him.'

'Very funny.'

'Scoop him up, I mean.' Cambreaux popped four codeine-coated aspirin like M&Ms. 'Do you have any more questions?'

'What did he see? What did he hear?'

'Let me ask *you* a question: Do you want to keep your job? Do you want me to lose *my* job?'

'That's two questions.' Donnelly was having fun.

'You asked two questions first.'

'Yeah, but your answers are cooler. You want a cigarette?'

'No.' Cambreaux really wanted the smoke, but thought this was a habit over which he should exert more control. There was a definite lack of things to do with one's hands down in this little, secure room, and he was grateful for Donnelly's company, this shift. 'They locked this guy in a cell for four days, your basic sweat-out. No phone calls. No go. So then Human Factors beats the crap out of him; still nothing. They used one of those canvas tubes filled with iron filings.'

'Mm.' Donnelly finished his cigarette and looked around for an ashtray. Finally he ground out the butt on the sole of his shoe. 'No exterior marks, except for a bruise or two, and your organs get pureed.'

'Yeah. They used a phone book, too.'

'And he read the phone book and said, "This has got a lot of great characters, but the plot sucks." '

'Boy, you got a million of 'em. And they all stink.'

'Thanks.' Donnelly patted himself down for a fresh smoke. It was a habit he swore he needed to quit. The pat-down, not the smoking. 'Then what?'

'Then what. They brought in Medical Assist. They tried

sodium pentothal; no dice. Then psychedelics, then electroshock. Still zero. So here we be.'

Donnelly looked twice. Yes, that *was* a kitchen timer on top of Cambreaux's console. Donnelly's wife had one just like it – round clock face, adjustable for sixty minutes. She used it to brew coffee precisely; she was fastidious about things like perfect coffee. Donnelly indicated the timer, then the big box. 'You baking him in there?'

'Yeah. He's not done yet.'

The box was about five feet square and resembled an industrial refrigerator. It was enameled white, steel-reinforced, and featureless except for a big screw-down hatch lock like the ones Donnelly had seen while touring an aircraft carrier. Thick 220-volt cables snaked from the box to Cambreaux's console.

'You got gypped,' said Donnelly. 'No ice maker.'

Cambreaux made the face he always made at Donnelly's jokes. Donnelly noticed – not for the first time – that Cambreaux's head seemed perfectly round, a moon head distinguished by a perfect crescent of hair at eyebrow level, punctuated by round mad-scientist specs with flecks of blue and gold in the rims.

'New glasses?'

'Yeah, the old ones were too tight on my head. Torture. Gave me the strokes, right here.' Cambreaux indicated his temples. 'Pure fucking torture. Man, you ever need any info out of me, just make me wear my old glasses and I'll kill my children for you.'

Donnelly strolled around the box, one full circuit. 'What do we call this?'

'The refrigerator. What else?'

'A *reporter*? Funny. Most journalists don't have the spine or the sperm for this sort of marathon.'

'If he'd talked, he wouldn't be here.'

'Point. Agreed.'

'What are you *staring* at, Chester?'

'I love to watch a man who enjoys his work.'

Cambreaux gave him the finger. 'You going to stand around admiring me all afternoon, or can I talk you into setting up a fresh pot on the machine?'

Cambreaux's timer went *ding.*

'I was waiting to see what happens when our reporter is done basting,' said Donnelly.

'What happens is this.' Cambreaux lifted the timer and cranked it back to sixty minutes.

Donnelly squinted at him. 'Jesus. How long have you been here today?'

'Six hours. New regs call for eight hours up.'

'Oh. Cream and sugar?'

'Just a spot of each. Just enough cream to discolor the coffee.'

'You're starting to sound like my wife.'

'Grope me and I'll shoot you in the balls.'

'This is probably a stupid question—'

'Guaranteed, from you,' Cambreaux overrode.

'—but can I get anything for our pal the reporter?'

Cambreaux pushed back from the console, the racketing of his chair casters loud and hollow in the room, like the too harsh ticking of the appliance timer. He winnowed his fingers beneath his glasses and rubbed his eyes until they were pink.

'Did I say this guy is a reporter? Scratch that. He *was* a reporter. When he comes out of the fridge, he won't need anything except maybe a padded cell. Or a casket.'

Donnelly kept staring at the box. It was just weird enough, the sort of anomaly you can't take your eye from.

'How about I just bring him a shot of good ole government-issue cyanide?'

'Not just yet,' said Cambreaux, touching his timer as if for inspiration, then jotting a note on a gray legal pad. 'Not just yet, my friend.'

Elapsed time has ceased to have meaning, and this is good for Garrett.

A relief. He has been released from what were once boundaries, and the mundane of the day-to-day. There is no day here, no night, no time. He has been liberated. Elemental input, and the limitations of his physical form, have become his sole realities.

He had once read that the next step in human evolution might be to a formless intellect, eternal, almost cosmic, undying, immortal, transcendent.

If the light had been God, then the cold is Sleep. New rules, new deities.

He is curled into a fetal ball like a beaten animal, shuddering uncontrollably while his lit-up mind wrestles with the problems of how to properly pay obeisance to this latest god.

His *bones* feel cold; his hands and feet, distant and insensate. Respiration is a knife of ice, boring in to pierce his lungs in tandem. He shallows his breath and prays that his rawed esophagus might lend the air a mote of metabolic heat before it plunges mercilessly into his lung tissue.

He is still merely mortal.

He knows the cold will not steal more than a few critical degrees of his core heat. The cold will not murder him; it is testing him, inviting him to discover his own extremes. To kill Garrett would be too easy, and pointless. He would not have survived the light only to perish by the cold. The cold cares about him, as the light had, as an uncaring god is said to care for the flock that is crippled, tormented, and killed . . . only to profess renewed faith.

The cold is intimate in a way that surpasses his mere flesh.

His fingers and toes are now remote tributaries of forgotten feeling. Garrett curls on his right side, then his left, to spell each of his lungs in turn, to stave off the workload of chilly pain by reducing it to processable fragments.

He allows the sub-zero ambience to flow *through,* not batter against, the inadequate walls of his skin. He thinks of the felled tree in the forest. He is here so the cold will have a purpose. He is the proof of sound in the silent, snowbound woodland; the freezing air needed him as much as he needed it to verify his own existence.

Huddled, then, and shivering, still naked, his blood retarded to a thick crawl in unthawed veins, Garrett permits the cold to have him. He welcomes its forward nature, its brashness.

Garrett closes his eyes. Feels bliss. Smiling, with clenched teeth, he sleeps.

On the dirty coffee table in front of Alvarado there were several items of interest: A bottle of Laphroaig scotch, a big camera, a snubnosed gun, and an unopened letter.

The camera was an autofocusing rig with flashless 1600 ASA color film and a blimped speedwinder, for silent work. Twenty-one exposures had been recorded in scant seconds. The Laphroaig was very mellow and half gone. The gun was a Charter Arms .44 Bulldog, no shots used yet.

Whenever the building made a slight nighttime noise around him, Alvarado tensed, his heart thudding briskly with anticipation. Moment to moment, he was safe . . . though the next moment might bring last call.

He had driven all the way into the San Fernando Valley to mail his preaddressed packets, copies of his precious tapes and photos. Now his backstop was secure, his evidence was damning, and the only reason he could think of for still hanging around his apartment was because he, too, felt damned. Soiled somehow.

New evidence waited inside his camera. Rawer, more toxic, dangerously good stuff to reinforce his already strong case.

Alvarado lifted the envelope and read the address for the thousandth time. It was a cable TV bill for Garrett, his next door neighbor. Once upon a time, the gods running computerized mailing lists had hiccuped, fouled their numbers. Rather than rectify the irritant with fruitless phone calls, Alvarado and Garrett had been trading mail for nearly a year now, sliding it beneath each other's respective doors when they were out. They both traveled a lot. The mail thing had become an after-hours joke between them.

Garrett was an ad agent for a publishing company. He toured his turf with a folio of new releases and pitched store to store. Alvarado had been staff at the *Los Angeles Times* until he was let go in a seasonal pruning, followed by a hiring freeze blamed on the latest recession. He made do as a freelancer until his time rolled 'round again; he had made his living professionally long enough to believe in karmic work rhythms. Freelancing had propelled him into some very odd new places. Alternative papers. Tabloids. Pop magazines.

Investigative journalism, self-motivated.

Now, if his backstop allies made proper use of the duplicate tapes and photos now safely in postal transit, Alvarado would be back on the map, big time. The waiting was not the worst part, though it *had* made his life pretty suspenseful during the past few hellish days.

Sometimes reporters got assassinated for their reportage. It happened, though the public rarely heard about it. Thus, Alvarado had emplaced his elaborate backstop network.

Sometimes reporters got *worse* than killed. Thus the gun, yes, loaded, and this quiet vigil in a dark room.

It had happened four or five days ago. Say a week. Alvarado's schedule and sleeptime had become totally bollixed, of combat necessity.

A week ago, he had heard a noisy commotion in the night. His damning photos and tapes had not yet been copied or mailed. He was awake from his snooze on the sofa in a silent instant, fully alert. At first he thought the disturbance was a simple domestic – Garrett and his wife or girlfriend having some temporary and loud disagreement in the middle of the night, as lovers sometimes do.

Alvarado's mind decoded the noises he heard. This was no argument.

He remembered grabbing his camera and moving to the balcony. After a second of hesitation he had stepped around to Garrett's adjoining balcony, and recognized immediately that very bad shit was going on inside.

He witnessed most of it through his viewfinder, focusing on the slit of light permitted by the curtains on Garrett's sliding door. He saw Garrett naked, trussed and manhandled by an efficiently fast goon squad in the very best J.C. Penney's Secret Service wash-and-wear. Garrett's wife or girlfriend, also naked, was being abused and threatened on the far side of the bedroom. The men moved like they had a purpose.

Twenty-one rapid-fire exposures later, Garrett was out, abducted, gone . . . and Alvarado was off to the mailbox with older, no less scary business. He had his own future to protect.

Now, tonight, Alvarado sat staring at the cable bill addressed to Garrett. He had received it. And Garrett had received a late-night visit intended for his neighbor.

Intended for *me*, Alvarado knew.

It was a coincidence almost divine, winning Alvarado the time to get his material to safety. Garrett had picked up the check, and perhaps that was why Alvarado was still hanging around.

Just like that, his life had become bad film noir. Here he was, drinking, fondling his gun, and fantasizing about the inevitable confrontation. Blam, blam, and in a blaze of glory *everybody* gets to be in the papers.

Post-mortem.

Provided the bad guys got the address right this time.

If the light was God, and the cold Sleep, then the sound was Love.

Garrett decides he is being tempered and refined for some very special purpose, duty, or chosen destiny. He feels proud and fulfilled. He cannot be the recipient of so many revelations for some nothing purpose . . . and so he pays very close attention to the lessons the sound brings him.

He is quite the attentive little godling in training.

The extremes he withstands are the signposts of his own evolution. He began as a normal man. He is becoming more.

It is exhilarating.

He eagerly awaits Heat, and Silence, and Darkness, and whatever he needed beyond them.

'You want to hear a funny?' said Cambreaux.

Donnelly felt he was not going to walk away amused. 'I do the jokes in this toilet.'

'Not as boffo as this: Our reporter? Janitorial collected him at three o'clock this morning. We've had the wrong guy in the refrigerator for a week.'

Donnelly did not laugh. He never laughed when he could feel his stomach dropping away like a clipped elevator, skimming his balls enroute to Hell. 'You mean this guy is *innocent*?'

Cambreaux's style did not admit of sheepishness, or comeback. 'I wouldn't say that.'

'Everybody's guilty of something, is that it?'

'No. I wouldn't say that our friend in the box is innocent. Not anymore.'

They both stared at the refrigerator. Locked inside was a man who had been subjected to stresses and extremes known to fracture the toughest operatives going. His brain had to be string cheese by now. And he hadn't *done* anything . . . except be innocent.

'Fucking Janitorial,' Donnelly snorted. 'They're always screwing up the work orders.'

'Bunch of gung-ho bullet boys,' Cambreaux agreed. Better to fault another department, always.

'So . . . you going to let him out?'

'Not my call.' Both he and Donnelly knew that the man in the box had to be released, but neither of them would budge until the right documents dropped down the correct chute.

'What's he on now?'

'High-frequency sound. Metered for – oh, *shit*!'

Donnelly saw Cambreaux rocket from his chair to grab the kitchen timer and hurl it across the chamber. It disintegrated into frags. Then Cambreaux was frantically snapping off switches, cranking dials down.

'Goddamn timer froze! It stopped!'

Donnelly immediately looked at the fridge.

'It was on too high for too long, Chet! Goddamn timer!'

Both of them wondered what they would see when the lid was finally opened.

Garrett feels at last that he is being pushed too far, that he must extract too high a price from himself.

He endures, because he must. He hovers on the brink of a human millennium. He is the first. He must experience the change with his eyes open.

The sound removed everything from Garrett's world.

Not too late at last, Garrett says *I love you.*

He has to scream it. Not too late.

Then his eardrums burst.

Cambreaux was drinking coffee in the lounge, shoulders sagging, elbows planted on knees, penitent.

'Ever hear the one about the self-protecting fuse?' said Donnelly. 'The one that protects itself by blowing up your whole stereo?' No reaction. 'I saw the fridge open. When did they take our boy?'

'This morning. I was on the console when the orders finally came down.'

'Hey – your hands are shaking.'

'Chet, I feel like I have to cry, almost. I saw that guy come out of the fridge. I've never seen anything like it.'

Donnelly sat down beside Cambreaux. 'Bad?'

'Bad.' A poisonous laugh escaped him. It was more like a cough, or a bark. 'We opened the box. And that guy looked at us like we'd just stolen his soul. He had blood all over him, mostly from his ears. He started hollering. Chet, he didn't want us to take him out.'

This didn't sound good, spilling from a professional like Cambreaux. Donnelly let out a measured breath, leavening his own racing metabolism.

'But you took him out.'

'Yes sir, we did. Orders. And when we got him out, he broke, and clawed his own eyes out, and choked to death on his tongue.'

'Jesus Christ . . .'

'Janitorial took him.'

'Disposal's the one thing those bozos are good at.'

'You got a cigarette?'

Donnelly handed it over and lit it for him. He lit himself one. 'Chet, did you ever read "The Pit and the Pendulum"?'

'I saw the movie.'

'The story is basically about a guy who gets tortured for days by the Inquisition. Right before he makes his final fall into the pit, he gets rescued by the French army.'

'Fiction.'

'Yeah, happy endings and all. We did the same thing. Except the guy didn't want to leave. He found something in there, Chet. Something you or I don't ever have a chance at. And we took him out, away from the thing he discovered . . .'

'And he died.'

'Yeah.'

They were silent together for a few minutes. Neither of them was very spiritual; they were men who were paid for their ability to do their jobs. Yet neither could resist the idea of what Garrett might have seen in the box.

Neither of them would ever climb into the box to find out. Too many reasons not to. Thousands.

'I got you a present,' Donnelly said.

He handed over a factory-fresh appliance timer. This one came with a warranty and guarantee. That made Cambreaux smile. A bit.

'Take it slow, old buddy. Duty calls. We'll have a drink later.'

Cambreaux nodded and accepted Donnelly's fraternal pat on the shoulder. He had just done his job. No sin in that.

Donnelly walked along the fluorescent-lit corridor, very consciously avoiding the route that would take him past the room where the refrigerator was. He did not want to see it hanging open just now.

He made a mental note to look up the Poe story. He loved a good read.

***David J. Schow** is a World Fantasy Award-winner and author of the novels* The Kill Riff *and* The Shaft, *and numerous short stories that have appeared in* Twilight Zone Magazine,

Night Cry, *and* Weird Tales *among many others. His non-fiction includes* The Outer Limits Companion *(recently revised) and on a monthly basis,* Raving & Drooling, *his opinion column for* Fangoria. *As a screenwriter he's penned the features* Leatherface: Texas Chainsaw Massacre III *and* The Crow. *His latest collection is* Black Leather Required.

Ro Erg

BY

ROBERT WEINBERG

THE clock in the hallway was striking eight o'clock as Ronald Rosenberg opened the door to his house. With a wan smile he nodded to himself. *On time as usual.* Slowly, he removed his coat and hat, unwound the wool scarf from his neck, and hung them up neatly in the nearby closet. By then his wife Marge's voice was drifting out of the kitchen.

'Is that you, honey?' she asked. Always the same question, night after night, month after month, year after year. Asked without thinking, without considering the foolishness of the remark. As if a burglar might answer otherwise. It was part of their daily routine. Their unchanging, uninspiring, dull, and predictable life together.

'Yes, dear,' he said, mentally sighing, 'it's me.'

Once, just once, he wanted to say, 'No, it's a fuckin' crook, come to steal your money and smash your skull, you dumb bitch.' But he knew better. The harsh words would upset Marge, and then he'd be forced to spend the entire evening apologizing, repeating over and over again how he shouldn't make such cruel remarks. Listening to her tell him how hard she slaved keeping his life running smoothly and how he didn't appreciate her efforts. Experience had taught him to keep such errant thoughts to himself.

'Dinner will be ready in five minutes,' Marge called. 'It's one of your favorites, beef stew and potatoes.'

Ron nodded, a resigned expression on his face. Thursday was always beef stew night. Just like Tuesday was always spaghetti and Friday was always chicken. Marge did everything strictly by routine. Organization was her life. Once she settled on a menu, she stuck to it for months at a time. The only variety in their meals was Sunday, when they went out for dinner. And even then, no matter what restaurant they visited, Marge consistently ordered the roast turkey dinner. With dressing, sweet potatoes, and salad. One glass of white wine. And apple pie for dessert.

Everything in Marge's life was planned, programmed, and perfect. She knew what she liked and how she liked it. Deviation from the norm was wrong, observing a schedule was right. Even their sex life was governed by a complicated series of rules and regulations, designed, Ron was secretly convinced, to make sure he did not receive more than a moment's worth of satisfaction from the act. More than once he had asked himself if he had married a woman or a robot.

With a shrug of his shoulders, he picked up the mail Marge had left on the lamp table in the hall. As per usual, she had sliced open all the letters but then placed them there for him to sort through. The mail was his job. Business for men, household duties for women. Marge was definitely not a feminist.

Most of the letters – advertisements, junk mail, and sincerely worded pleas asking for donations to one charity or another – went into the nearby garbage can. A short note from his brother complaining about his latest money problems Ron read twice, frowning as he did so. Chris was an inept businessman and a spendthrift. That he was in a deep financial hole was no surprise. That he also expected Ron to help him out of the jam was equally no surprise. Ron tucked the letter in his shirt pocket, vowing to call his brother after dinner.

The gas bill and electric bill followed into the same pocket. They would go on his dresser, to be paid tomorrow morning. Though Ron hated to admit it, in many ways he was just as much a creature of habit and routine as his wife.

One letter remained. He looked at it curiously. It was from a credit card company. Something about receiving a new charge card without having to do anything more than sign the enclosed application. Ron already had Visa and MasterCard and American Express. He saw no reason for another piece of plastic. Why would they even bother to ask?

Searching the front of the envelope for an explanation, he noted in annoyance that the application wasn't even addressed to him. It was for a Mr RO ERG. His eyes narrowed as he stared at the letter. The address was right. It was his. But the name was definitely wrong. No one named RO ERG lived in this house. Then, in a sudden flash of insight, he understood.

He was RO ERG. The computer at the credit card company offices had somehow taken the front two letters of his first name and final three letters of his last name to form this new person. Quite out of character, he grinned. The name RO ERG had a certain wild, untamed ring to it. He liked it. He liked it a lot. Uncertain of exactly why, Ron Rosenberg slipped the application to Ro Erg into his pocket behind the bills.

'Dinner's ready,' declared his wife, interrupting his wandering thoughts. 'Come and get it while it's hot.'

The form remained untouched the rest of the evening. Until, late at night, when Marge's steady, deep breathing indicated she was fast asleep. Quietly, Ron slipped out of their bed. Not that it mattered. He was the one who was a light sleeper. A million minor annoyances and worries kept him awake for hours. Marge dismissed as unimportant anything that wasn't an immediate threat. An earthquake wouldn't disturb her slumber.

Sitting in the bathroom, Ron carefully opened the envelope and studied the application within. It was exactly as he had suspected. The request was a mail-merge letter, generated by an unthinking computer program. In three different places he was referred to as 'Mr Erg.' Ron found the missive unintentionally hilarious when they commended Ro Erg on his outstanding credit record. Though he prided himself on never retaining a balance on any of his charge cards, Ron had never expected his frugality would entitle an imaginary entity to a $10,000 line of credit.

'Ten thousand bucks,' he whispered aloud, the numbers suddenly dancing through his head. That was a lot of money, a real lot of money. He closed his eyes, feeling strange. Feeling . . . excited. 'Ten thousand bucks.'

Ron was extremely cautious with his finances. After all, he had to support his wife, pay the mortgage on their house, and make the payments on their two cars. As well as save for the future. There usually wasn't much money left from his paycheck at the end of the month. Not that Marge believed in going out on the town anyway. Renting a movie on videotape was her notion of an exciting evening.

His face burning with suppressed excitement, Ron headed for the kitchen. All his life he had done what was right, what was proper. Now, for a change, he could do something crazy and no one else would know. The plastic card meant nothing. He would never use it. But just sending away for it was a small but still important act of rebellion. That was what mattered.

Grabbing a magnetic pen off the refrigerator, Ron scribbled 'Ro Erg' on the signature line of the document. Quickly, before he could change his mind, he placed the acceptance card into the postage-paid envelope and put it with the rest of the mail.

'Can't do any harm,' he murmured to himself as he settled back into bed. 'I'm just sending it in to see if they're stupid enough to follow through with the offer. That's the reason. The only reason.'

And though he continued to whisper that line until he finally drifted off into slumber, deep inside he knew all the while he was lying.

The card arrived two weeks later. It came complete with a ten thousand dollar credit limit and a promise of a PIN number to follow within a few days so that he could draw cash advances from ATM's. Casually, Ron tucked the charge card in his wallet and hid the page of terms beneath a stack of old bills in his files. He had never considered the possibility of a PIN number. And cash advances. Suddenly, his minor act of rebellion took on a whole new life of its own.

The identification number came three days later. Three long days, one of which was made infinitely longer by his brother's monthly visit. Tall and handsome, with broad shoulders and a winning smile, Chris always made Ron extremely uncomfortable when he was around. His sibling was everything that Ron was not. Chris was wild and carefree and extremely charming. He was also as dumb as a rock and proud of it.

Chris treated money as something to be spent as quickly as possible. It was an attitude that drove Ron crazy. Though they were brothers, Ron found his brother insufferable.

Annoyingly enough, Marge thought Chris was cute and only needed some time to 'mature.' It was Marge who continually insisted that Ron lend Chris money – money that disappeared without a trace and never a word about repayment. His wife, Ron had concluded long ago, was an easy mark.

Fortunately, Chris always arrived in the afternoon when Ron was still at work and departed right after dinner. Taking along with him another $100 of his brother's hard-earned cash.

'Damned bloodsucker,' said Ron as his brother drove off in a much nicer car than the one Ron owned.

'Ronald,' said Marge, her voice sharp. 'He's your brother. Give Chris a chance. Be patient. I'm sure he'll pay you back someday.'

Sure. When hell freezes over, thought Ron. But he knew better than to say the words aloud. That would only start them arguing. Ron hated fights. They gave Marge headaches and then they didn't have sex that night. And to Ron sex was one of the few things that made life bearable.

All was quickly forgotten the next night when Ron found the latest letter addressed to RO ERG waiting for him in the evening mail. Ripping open the envelope, he quickly scanned the enclosed letter and accompanying card. It was his Personal Identification Number and instructions for its use.

He chuckled with a combination of joy and relief. His brother's visit had been the final straw. There was a limit to how much badgering he could take. Before, RO ERG had been nothing more than a test of the credit card company's intelligence. The PIN card put a whole new spin on the game. For once Ron could outdo Chris at his own game. And he intended to do exactly that.

'Good news, honey?' asked Marge from the kitchen.

'Yes, dear,' answered Ron, 'very good news.'

The next afternoon, he called Marge and sadly informed her that he would be late for dinner. Extra work at the office, he explained, that had to be cleared up before he could leave for home. Ron was confident his wife wouldn't suspect a thing. In the past he often had stayed late at work. There was no reason she would suspect today it wasn't the truth. She didn't.

Informing his supervisor he needed the afternoon off to visit a friend in the hospital, Ron headed straight for the nearest cash station. Nervously, he inserted the RO ERG card and punched in the correct numbers for a thousand dollar cash advance. The entire transaction took less than a minute. Feeling slightly dazed, Ron stumbled away from the ATM with ten hundred dollar bills crammed into his pockets.

'A thousand smackers,' he muttered to himself, walking down the street. 'All mine, just by pushing some buttons!'

It was then that he had his first revelation about modern life. Society no longer cared about your background. People moved from one location to another so often that no one had real roots in their community. Relatives, schools, old friends, meant nothing. You were no longer defined by your past. Instead, the only thing that really mattered was the name of your credit cards. Those little pieces of plastic provided you with all the history you needed.

Dozens of people at work and in his neighborhood knew him as Ron Rosenberg. But the bank teller processing his charge receipt, the credit card employee handling his account, the postal worker sorting the mail, they knew him as Ro Erg. He was no longer merely one person. He was two separate entities sharing the same body – Ron Rosenberg and Ro Erg.

Shaken by his new grasp of reality, Ron tried to focus his thoughts on more immediate concerns. He had to consider what to do with the cash. If he brought the money home, Marge was sure to discover it. And thus learn about Ro Erg.

Ron couldn't let that happen. Ro Erg was his secret. And he meant to keep it that way. Anxiously, he hailed a cab. He needed a drink. But not in this neighborhood, close to his office where someone he knew might spot him.

'Take me to the airport,' he commanded the cabdriver, his voice shaking slightly. 'There's a bar up there. I forget the name. You know the one I mean. It's a quiet place. Where a guy can get a drink and be alone with his thoughts.'

'Sure, buddy,' said the cabbie with a laugh. 'I know the place. Max's joint. Right?'

'Right,' said Ron, settling back in the seat. 'That's the one.'

Max's place was The Red Garter and it was a dump. Dimly lit, with a dozen wooden booths hugging the far wall, its only saving grace was that it lacked a jukebox. Except for an old man whispering to a much younger woman at the end of the bar, there were no other customers. It was exactly the type of place Ron wanted.

'Scotch, on the rocks,' he told the lone bartender. 'Make it a double.'

Without thinking, Ron paid for the drink with a crumpled hundred pulled out of his pocket. The bartender stared at the bill for a moment, then with a loud cough and a shrug of his shoulders made change. It was as if he was trying to attract someone's attention to the money.

Lost in his thoughts about the meaning of identity, Ron hardly noticed when, a few minutes later, the old man at the end of the bar half fell off his chair and staggered out of the tavern, muttering obscenities the whole time under his breath. Nor did he give much thought to the man's female companion. Until she sat down in the chair next to him.

'Buy a girl a drink?' she asked in a soft voice.

'Sure,' he said with a shrug. The scotch had made him somewhat dizzy and a little light-headed. 'Whatever you want.'

'Gin,' said the woman to the bartender. 'Straight up.'

'Another scotch for me,' said Ron, gesturing to the cash still on the bar. 'Take it out of there.'

'My name's Ginger,' said the woman, sipping her drink. 'What's yours?'

Suspiciously, Ron turned and stared at the woman. There was little question to her profession. Ginger was dressed in a tight red dress that left nothing to the imagination. She wore black fishnet stockings and a pair of high-heeled black boots. The edge of her dress had ridden up to nearly the top of her thighs, but she made no effort to pull it down.

Her face was fairly attractive, though too much lipstick, blush, and eyeliner made her look cheap. And nothing could hide the hardness in her eyes.

Ron Rosenberg would have told her to stop bothering him. He was a married man and had no time for hookers. Ron never took chances, especially with women like Ginger. But it wasn't Ron who answered.

'I'm Ro,' he said hesitantly. 'Ro Erg.'

'Glad to meet you, Ro,' Ginger giggled, trying to sound seductive but not succeeding. She accepted his name without question. 'You look lonely. Need somebody to talk to?'

'I'm trying to . . .' began Ron, then paused, his words catching in his throat. Holding her drink in her right hand, Ginger had casually reached over with her left and placed it directly on his thigh. Smiling, she winked and gently squeezed her fingers.

Ron Rosenberg would have been panic-stricken. Aggressive women frightened him. But Ginger's hand wasn't resting on Ron's leg. Desperately, he clung to that thought. To the hooker he was Ro, not Ron. Ro Erg.

'My, my,' she murmured a few seconds later as her wandering fingers encountered his growing erection, 'you are a big one. How about if we retire to one of the booths in the back. We can *enjoy our conversation* without interruption back there.'

Licking his lips, Ro nodded. He knew he was acting crazy, but he didn't care. Besides, no one would ever know. This wasn't happening to Ron Rosenberg. He was Ro Erg.

Leaving a five for the bartender, Ro scooped up the rest of the money and followed Ginger to the farthest booth. She gestured him in, so their backs were to the bar. 'Nobody can see a thing from here,' she whispered, sliding in next to him. 'We're completely alone.

'But – but,' protested Ron, a measure of sanity emerging from his befuddled brain, 'the two of us are right out in the open. The bartender could come back here at any time.'

'Harry?' laughed Ginger. 'He knows what's going on. And he'll get his cut.'

Giving him no time to protest further, Ginger swiftly reached out with both hands for his clothing. In seconds, she unbuckled Ron's pants and zipped down his fly. He groaned in excitement as she reached into his trousers and pulled out his already erect cock.

'Nice,' she cooed, shifting slightly on the seat. The motion sent her dress riding up over her hips. Not surprisingly, she wasn't wearing anything underneath.

'Blow job costs fifty,' she said matter-of-factly, her fingers expertly massaging his rock-hard organ. 'If you want to fuck, it's a hundred. One twenty-five for both.'

'This can't be real,' said Ron, shaking his head in amazement. 'It can't be.'

'Wanna bet, sweetie?' said Ginger. Swiftly, she bent over and lightly placed her lips around the tip of his cock. Gently she sucked on the head. Once, twice, three times she flicked her tongue. She looked up at him and grinned. 'This is sex. This is real. How much are you gonna pay?'

It was then, bedazzled from the whiskey and sex, that Ron experienced his second revelation. Money was all that mattered. Ginger didn't care if his name was Ron or Ro or mud. She was a tramp, looking to make a quick buck satisfying a john's lust. His name, personality, history, meant nothing to her. Married or single, rich or poor, saint or sinner, Ginger didn't mind. All that mattered was money. A piece of plastic gave Ro Erg identity. Money gave him power. Those were the basic truths, the only truths that mattered, of modern life.

Ron Rosenberg would have been too consumed by guilt, worried that somehow, someway, Marge would discover this encounter, to continue. But it hadn't been Ron who withdrew the thousand in cash. The money wasn't his. It belonged to Ro Erg. Ginger hadn't been talking to Ron. She had asked Ro. And Ro answered.

'I'll take it all,' he declared, his voice thick with lust. He dug a wad of bills out of his pocket and handed Ginger a hundred and two twenties. 'Make it last a long time,' he said, 'and you can keep the change.'

Satisfied he had made the right choice, Ro Erg settled back on the bench and let Ginger take over.

Ron Rosenberg, the practical, cautious planner, secured a safety deposit box and mailing address at a nearby rental depot. A hundred dollar bill paid for the box and a place to receive mail. The cash remaining from Ro Erg's advance went into the box, along with a wallet containing the credit card. It was a lot safer here than at home, where it might be discovered by his wife.

After his encounter with Ginger, Ron knew there was no turning back. He was now a man with two identities – Ron Rosenberg and Ro Erg. Ron managed the important details while Ro enjoyed the results. It was a very satisfactory arrangement.

The new address for Ro proved important. Good news traveled fast in the credit card industry. A few months after activating his first charge card, Ro Erg received applications for two more. Again, each of them had ten thousand dollar limits, PIN numbers, and only required a signature for instant acceptance. He mailed in the documents for both.

Meanwhile, Ro learned the amazing truth about the power of plastic. Using the credit card as proof of his identity, he was able to obtain a charge card from a major department store. Using the two pieces of plastic, he was then able to get a new library card. With that and a mailing address, he was able to open a bank account. More chain store cards followed, as did further additions to his new identity. Day by day Ro Erg became more and more real. By year's end, Mr Erg had a dozen charge cards and nearly $50,000 in credit.

Always careful with money, Ron made sure that Ro never strayed too far into debt. He juggled money and cash advances from one account to another. He borrowed cash from one card to pay the minimum due on the second. Then used his line of credit from his third card to pay off the minimum debt on the second. He owed all of the companies something, but he made sure that he didn't owe any of them too much. Whenever there was a shortage of funds, he slipped some cash from Ron Rosenberg's paycheck into Ro's cash accounts to help balance the books. It was an elaborate pyramid scheme, but one that Ron knew he could operate for years as long as his alter ego didn't spend too lavishly or run up any major charges.

In the meantime, Ro Erg emerged more and more as a full-fledged personality. He was Ron's wild side, his suppressed side, the part of him that urgently desired to drink deeply of life's pleasures without regard to right or wrong. It was the segment of his character that had been repressed and contained by his overbearing wife. But Marge Rosenberg meant nothing to Ro Erg.

At night, lying in bed awake, the two halves of his personality, Ron and Ro, would engage in long, meaningful debates. Mostly, these arguments centered on what to do next. Ron, careful and cautious, wanted to maintain life the way it was. Ro, wild and headstrong, hated Marge and the stability she represented. He wanted to make a complete break with the past. But Ron wouldn't let him. And, though Ro presented powerful grounds for change, Ron refused to let his darker side take control.

As the weeks stretched into months, the conflict between the two conflicting sides of his personality grew more intense. Ro Erg no longer seemed satisfied with being merely the untamed element of Ron's personality. He wanted to be in charge. Day after day Ro struggled to take control of their shared body.

A cheap apartment paid in cash on a month-to-month basis served as their hideaway. It was here that Ro brought the hookers he picked up on the streets or in bars. Ginger was just the first of a long string of whores who provided him with sexual gratification. The one night a week that he had to work late stretched into two and sometimes even three. Marge never complained. If anything, she almost seemed pleased by his devotion to his work. Which should have made Ron suspicious. But it never did. He just could not imagine his plain, ordinary wife was any more than what he believed. It took a hooker to open his eyes.

'Wearing a wedding ring, I see,' remarked Candy, a bleached blonde with huge breasts and a talented tongue, late one night as she collected her hundred bucks from Ro. 'What's wrong, sweetie? Don't get enough from the wifey?'

'She's a cold, stupid bitch,' said Ro. 'Fucking for five minutes is a major effort for her.'

'Maybe,' said Candy with a nasty laugh. 'But you should keep an eye on her. Lots of times, things ain't what you think. You positive she don't got a stud of her own on the side? It ain't unusual for straying husbands to find out their wives been doing the same. Plenty of my johns' wives get their lovin' from the milkman.'

'We don't get our milk delivered,' replied Ron indignantly. Then his eyes narrowed as a sudden thought struck him and raced through his mind. Trembling with rage, his fingers clenched into fists. The truth hit him like a hammer between the eyes.

'But,' growled Ro Erg, 'there is my fuckin' brother.' Blood rushed to his face, turning his features bright crimson. Candy, licking her lips nervously, stepped back.

'Gotta leave, honey,' she gasped and, grabbing her purse, fled the room. Ro hardly noticed.

'My lazy son of a bitch brother,' snarled Ro. 'Not enough for him to rip off my hard-earned money. He has to fuck my wife on the side.'

Slowly, Ro shook his head from side to side in disbelief. Marge had ruined Ron's life for years with her control fetish. That she had been screwing his brother at the same time was beyond belief. But instinctively he knew the truth. The cold, unyielding truth. It was enough to drive a man insane.

'They'll learn,' he swore, his voice thick with anger. 'They'll find out soon enough you don't mess with Ro Erg.'

Two days later, as Ron ate breakfast, Marge informed him that Chris would be stopping by for dinner. He nodded, smiling gently as if recalling some secret joke.

'I'll be home around seven,' he promised as he dutifully kissed his wife on the cheek good-bye. 'Have a good day.'

'I'm sure I will,' she replied cheerfully, the tone of her voice confirming his most sickening suspicions.

Ron Rosenberg left his house, burning with repressed fury. However, it was Ro Erg – cold, calm, collected – who stopped at the bar on the north side of town to pick up the black market .45 automatic he had ordered the other night.

'Fully loaded and ready for use,' drawled the bartender, a big, bushy-bearded man named Jackson, as he handed over the weapon to Ro along with a box of shells. 'You know how to use it?'

'I was in the army for two years,' said Ro, checking the gun carefully. 'I know how to use it just fine.'

Then, as if seeking to deflect suspicion, he added, 'I work in a dangerous neighborhood. There's been a lot of muggings lately. I don't intend to be worked over by some crack head.'

'Sure,' said Jackson, the tone of his voice indicating he didn't care how Ro planned to use the automatic. 'Stay cool.'

'Thanks,' said Ro, 'I plan to.'

He spent the rest of the morning and the early part of the afternoon drifting from one bar to another. A drink here, a drink there, staying calm, letting the anger simmer deep in his belly. Only occasionally did a spark of Ron Rosenberg emerge into his consciousness, asking the inevitable question. 'Are you sure about this? Are you really convinced we're doing the right thing?'

'I'm positive,' said Ro.

At two, after finishing a roast beef sandwich and plate of french fries, he drove home. Not unexpectedly, he spotted his brother's car parked in the driveway. Drawing in a deep breath, he left his own auto a block away and walked back to the house.

The front door was locked. Carefully, Ro turned his key, trying to make as little sound as possible. He needn't have worried. The hallway and living room were deserted. But he had no trouble pinpointing his brother's location. Chris's cries of pleasure, emanating from the bedroom, rocked the whole house.

Coldly, Ro pulled out his gun and checked it over one last time. Deep in his mind, Ron sobbed uncontrollably. Ro ignored the voice. There was no pity in him. Ron had let Marge ruin his life. Ro was not going to let her do the same to him.

Satisfied the automatic was ready, he silently tiptoed down the hall to the bedroom. The door was half closed, giving Ro full view of the room without revealing him to the pair inside. Even expecting the worst, he felt sick with anger as he gazed on the scene within.

Chris was naked sitting on the edge of the bed. His face was raised to the ceiling, eyes clenched tightly together. 'Yes, yes, yes,' he was screaming passionately, his hands wrapped around Marge's head. His fingers were curled in her hair, urging her on. His legs were spread wide open.

Crouched on her hands and knees in front of Chris was Marge. Also nude, she was busily sucking on her brother-in-law's engorged cock. Her whole body shook with the bobbing movement of her head as she forced more and more of his swollen organ into her mouth. Her ass, facing Ro, swayed to and fro wildly with her every motion.

Ro's head throbbed with incredible pain. It felt as if his skull was about to explode. Throughout her marriage Marge had continually refused to perform oral sex on Ron. More than once she had expressed her absolute and total revulsion of the act. And here she was, sucking on Chris's cock with an all-consuming mania.

Furious, Ro's gaze fastened on the full-length mirror on the closet door directly across from Marge. Every few seconds she glanced at it, caught sight of her swiftly moving head, and then, as if excited by watching herself in action, redoubled her efforts. The dual image of Marge and her reflection both giving his brother a blow job wiped any possibility of mercy from Ro's thoughts.

'I'm close!' howled Chris, thrusting his groin forward so that the entire length of his organ disappeared into Marge's mouth. 'Now, now, *now!*'

Chris screamed in wordless ecstasy. His fingers clenched Marge's head in place, holding her immobile as his body shook with the force of his climax. 'I'm coming, I'm coming,' he shrieked as Marge's eyes widened in sudden shock as his cock exploded in her mouth. Half moaning, half gagging, she struggled to swallow his ejaculation.

Enveloped in lust, neither of them noticed Ro step quietly into the room. Chris, his eyes clenched shut, giggled in pleasure as Marge continued to suck passionately on his now spent cock. His first indication of trouble was when Ro pressed the cold steel of the gun barrel against his forehead. Chris's eyes widened in panic, but before he could open his mouth to beg forgiveness, Ro pulled the trigger.

The roar of the automatic filled the bedroom. Chris's head exploded like a ripe pumpkin hit with an ax. Fired from point-blank range, the powerful .45 removed most of his skull and forehead. Blood, brains, and gore erupted across his body and Marge's, soaking the bedsheets and the carpet like bright red paint.

Marge, her eyes still glazed and bewildered, looked up at Ro. Mouth still sticky with cum, she screamed. But there was no one there to help her.

'Please, Ron,' she cried. 'Forgive me! Please!'

'Sorry, Marge, but you got the wrong man,' declared Ro, pointing the automatic between her eyes and squeezing the trigger. He fired three times in succession, until there wasn't enough left of her face to be called a face.

Ro smiled. He felt good, real good. They deserved to die. Justice had been served. Now it was time for him to leave, before the police arrived.

He checked the room carefully. There was nothing here to connect him to the murders. Marge was Ron's wife, not his. Likewise, Chris was a total stranger. Ro Erg was in the clear. He had no motive for murder. No one had witnessed his crime.

It was then that he spotted Ron's face in the full-length mirror.

Stared deep into Ron's eyes and saw the fear lurking within. Watched as Ron glanced down at the two crumpled bodies on the floor and shuddered in revulsion. That's when Ro understood that he no longer could trust Ron. As long as he was around, Ro would never be safe. There was only one thing to do.

Slowly, methodically, Ro raised the gun he still clenched in his fist. Lifted it inch by inch, as Ron's face twisted in horror as he comprehended what Ro planned. But there was nothing Ron could do to stop him. With a nod of satisfaction Ro pressed the bloody nozzle of the gun to Ron's forehead. And pulled the trigger.

***Robert Weinberg** is the only two-time World Fantasy Award winner to be chosen as Grand Marshal of a Rodeo Parade. He is the author of six non-fiction books, nine novels, and numerous short stories. His* Louis L'amour Companion *was a bestseller in trade paperback and was recently reprinted in paperback. His latest fantasy novel,* A Logical Magician, *was published earlier this year. As an editor, Bob has put together nearly a hundred anthologies and collections.*

Going Under

BY

RAMSEY CAMPBELL

BLYTHE had shuffled almost to the ticket booth when he knew he should have sent the money. Beyond the line of booths another phalanx of walkers, some of them wearing slogans and some not a great deal else, advanced toward the tunnel under the river. While he'd failed to pocket the envelope, he never left his phone at home, and given the pace at which walkers were being admitted to the tunnel, which was closed to traffic for its anniversary, he should have plenty of time to complete a call before he reached the wide semicircular concrete mouth, rendered whiter by the July sun. As he unfolded the phone and tapped his home number on the keyboard, the men on either side of him began jogging on the spot, an action which the left-hand man accompanied with a series of low hollow panting hoots. The phone rang five times and addressed Blythe in his own voice.

'Valerie Mason and Steve Blythe. Whatever we're doing, it's keeping us away from the phone, so please leave your name and number and the date and time, and we'll tell you what we were up to when we call you back . . .' Though the message was less than six months old, it and Valerie's giggle at the end of it sounded worn by too much playback. Once the beep had stuttered four times on the way to uttering its longer tone, he spoke.

'Val? Valerie? It's me. I'm just about to start the tunnel walk. Sorry we had a bit of a tiff, but I'm glad you didn't come after all. You were right, I should send her the maintenance and then object. Let them have to explain to the court instead of me. Are you in the darkroom? Come and find out who this is, will you? Don't just listen if you're hearing me. Be fair.'

Quite a pack jogged between the booths at that moment, the man to his immediate left taking time to emit a triumphal hoot before announcing to the ticket seller 'Aids for AIDS.' Blythe turned his head and the phone to motion the woman behind him to pass, because if he stopped talking for more than a couple of seconds the machine would take him to have rung off, but the official in the booth ahead of him poked out his head, which looked squashed flat by his peaked cap. 'Quick as you can. Thousands more behind you.'

The woman began jogging to encourage Blythe, shaking both filled bags of her ample red singlet. 'Get a move on, lover. Give your stocks and shares a rest.'

Her companion, who seemed to have donned a dwarf's T-shirt by mistake, entered the jogging competition, her rampant stomach bobbing up and down more than the rest of her. 'Put that back in your trousers or you'll be having a heart attack.'

At least their voices were keeping the tape activated. 'Hold on if you're there, Val. I hope you'll say you are,' Blythe said, using two fingers to extract a fiver from the other pocket of his slacks. 'I'm just going through the booth.'

The official frowned in disagreement, and Blythe breathed hard into the phone while he selected a charity to favor with his entrance fee. 'Are you sure you're fit?' the official said.

Blythe imagined being banned on the grounds of ill health from the walk when it was by far his quickest route home. 'Fitter than you sitting in a booth all day,' he said, not as lightly as he'd meant to, and smoothed the fiver on the counter. 'Families in Need will do me.'

The official wrote the amount and the recipient on a clipboard with a slowness which suggested he was still considering whether to let Blythe pass, and Blythe breathed harder. When the official tore most of a ticket off a roll and slapped it on the counter, Blythe felt released, but the man stayed him with a parting shot. 'You won't get far with that, chum.'

The phone had worked wherever Blythe had taken it, just as the salesman had promised. In any case, he was still two hundred yards short of the tunnel entrance, into which officials with megaphones were directing the crowd. 'Just had to get my ticket, Val. Listen, you've plenty of time to post the check, you've almost an hour. Only call me back as soon as you hear this so I know you have, will you? Heard it, I mean. That's if you don't pick it up before I ring off, which I hope you will, answer, that's to say, that's why I'm droning on. I should tell you the envelope's inside my blue visiting suit, not the office suit, the one that says here's your accountant making a special effort so why haven't you got your accounts together. Can you really not hear it's me? You haven't gone out, have you?'

By now his awareness was concentrated in his head, so he didn't notice that his pace had been influenced by the urgency of his speech until the upper lip of the tunnel swayed to a halt above him. Hot bare arms brushed his in passing as the megaphones began to harangue him. 'Keep it moving, please,' one crackled, prompting its mate to declare 'No stopping now till the far side.' An elderly couple faltered and conferred before returning to the booths, but Blythe didn't have that option. 'That's you with the phone,' a third megaphone blared.

'I know it's me. I don't see anybody else with one.' This was meant to amuse Blythe's new neighbors, none of whom betrayed any such response. Not by any means for the first time, though less often since he'd met Valerie, he wished he'd kept some words to himself. 'I'm starting the walk now. Please, I'm serious, ring me back the moment you hear this, all right? I'm ringing off now. If I haven't heard from you in fifteen minutes I'll call back,' he said, and was in the tunnel.

Its shadow was a solid chill at which his body was uncertain whether to shiver, considering the heat which was building up in the tunnel. At least he felt cool enough to itemize his surroundings, something he liked to do whenever he was confronted by anywhere unfamiliar, though he'd driven through the tunnel several times a week for most of twenty years. Its two lanes accommodated five people abreast now, more or less comfortably if you discounted their body heat. Six feet above them on either side was a railed-off walkway for the use of workmen, with no steps up to either that Blythe had ever been able to locate. Twenty feet overhead was the peak of the arched roof, inset with yard-long slabs of light. No doubt he could count them if he wanted to calculate how far he'd gone or had still to go, but just now the sight of several hundred heads bobbing very slowly toward the first curve summed up the prospect vividly enough. Apart from the not quite synchronized drumming of a multitude of soles on concrete and their echoes, the tunnel was almost silent except for the squawks of the megaphones beyond the entrance and the occasional audible breath.

The two women who'd addressed Blythe at the booths were ahead of him, bouncing variously. Maybe they'd once been as slim as his wife Lydia used to be, he thought, not that there was much left of the man she'd married either, or if there was it was buried under all the layers of the person he'd become. The presence of the women, their abundant sunlamped flesh and determined perfume and their wagging buttocks wrapped in satin, reminded him of too much it would do him no good to remember, and he might have let more walkers overtake him if it hadn't been for the pressure looming at his back. That drove him to step up his pace, and he'd established a regular rhythm when his trousers began to chirp.

More people than he was prepared for stared at him, and he felt bound to say 'Just my phone' twice. So much for the ticket seller's notion that it wouldn't work in the tunnel. Blythe drew it from his pocket without breaking his stride and ducked one ear to it as he unfolded it. 'Hello, love. Thanks for saving my—'

'Less of the slop, Stephen. It's a long time since that worked.'

'Ah.' He faltered, and had to think which foot he was next putting forward. 'Lydia. Apologies. My mistake. I thought—'

'I had enough of your mistakes when we were together, and your apologies, and what you think.'

'That pretty well covers it, doesn't it? Were you calling to share anything else with me, or was that it?'

'I wouldn't take that tone with me, particularly now.'

'Don't, then,' Blythe said, a form of response he remembered as having once amused her. 'If you've something to say, spit it out. I'm waiting for a call.'

'Up to your old tricks, are you? Can't she stand you never going anywhere without that thing either? Where are you, in the pub as usual trying to calm yourself down?'

'I'm perfectly calm. I couldn't be calmer,' Blythe said as though that might counteract the effect she was having on him. 'And I may tell you I'm on the charity walk.'

Was that a chorus of ironic cheers behind him? Surely they weren't aimed at him, even if they sounded as unimpressed as Lydia, who said 'Never did begin at home for you, did it? Has your fancy woman found that out yet?'

He could have pounced on Lydia's syntax again, except that there were more important issues. 'I take it you've just spoken to her.'

'I haven't and I've no wish to. She's welcome to you and all the joy you bring, but she won't hear me sympathizing. I didn't need to speak to her to know where you'd be.'

'Then you were wrong, weren't you? And as long as we're discussing Valerie, maybe you and your solicitor friend ought to be aware she makes a lot less than he does now he's a partner in his firm.'

'Watch it, big boy.'

That was the broader-buttocked of the women. He'd almost trodden on her heels, his aggressiveness having communicated itself to his stride. 'Sorry,' he said, and without enough thought 'Not you, Lyd.'

'Don't you dare start calling me that again. Who've you been talking to about his firm? So that's why I haven't had my check this month, is it? Let me tell you this from him. Unless that check is postmarked today, you'll find yourself in prison for nonpayment, and that's a promise from both of us.'

'Well, that's the first—' Her rising fury had already borne her off, leaving him with a drone in his ear and hot plastic stuck to his cheek. He cleared the line as he tramped around more of the prolonged curve, which showed him thousands of heads and shoulders bobbing down a slope to the point almost a mile away from which, packed closer and closer together, they streamed sluggishly upward. On some days that midpoint was hazy with exhaust fumes, but the squashed crowd there looked distinct except for a slight wavering which must be an effect of the heat; he wasn't really smelling a faint trace of petrol through the wake of perfume. He bent a fingernail against the keys on the receiver, and backhanded his forehead as drops of sweat full of a fluorescent glare swelled the numbers on the keypad. His home phone had just rung when a man's voice said loudly 'They're all the same, these buggers with their gadgets. Can't be doing with them, me.'

There was surely no reason for Blythe to feel referred to. 'Pick it up, Val,' he muttered. 'I said I'd ring you back. It's been nearly fifteen minutes. You can't still be doing whatever you were doing. Come out, there's a love.' But his voice greeted him again and unspooled its message, followed by Valerie's giggle, which under the circumstances he couldn't help feeling he'd heard once too often. 'Are you really not there? I've just had Lydia on, ranting about her maintenance. Says if it isn't posted today her boyfriend the solicitor who gives new meaning to the word solicit, will have me locked up. I suppose technically he might be able to, so if you can make absolutely certain you, I know I should have, I know you said, but if you can do that for me, for both of us, nip round the corner and get that bloody envelope in the shit.'

The last word came out loudest, and three ranks in front of him glanced back. Of them, only the woman whose T-shirt ended halfway up her midriff retained any concern once she saw him. 'Are you all right, old feller?'

'Yes, I'm . . . No, I'm . . . Yes, yes.' He shook his free hand so extravagantly he saw sweat flying off it, his intention being to wave away his confusion more than her solicitude, but she advanced her lips in a fierce grimace before presenting her substantial rear view to him. He hadn't time to care if she was offended, though she was using the set of her buttocks to convey that she was, exactly as Lydia used to. The ticket seller had been right after all. The tunnel had cut Blythe off, emptying the receiver except for a faint distant moan.

It could be a temporary interruption. He pressed the recall button so hard it felt embedded in his thumb and was attempting to waft people past him when a not unfamiliar voice protested 'Don't go standing. There's folk back here who aren't as spry as some.'

'When you're my dad's age, maybe you won't be so fond of stopping and starting.'

Either might be the disliker of gadgets, though both appeared to have devoted a good deal of time and presumably machinery to the production of muscles, not only beneath shoulder level. Blythe tilted his head vigorously, almost losing the bell, which was repeating its enfeebled note at his ear. 'Don't mind me, just go round me. Just go, will you?'

'Put that bloody thing away and get on with what we're here for,' the senior bruiser advised him. 'We don't want to be having to carry you. We had his mother conk out on us once through not keeping the pace up.'

'Don't mind me. Don't bother about me.'

'We're bothered about all the folks you're holding up and putting the strain on.'

'We'll be your trainers till we all finish,' the expanded youth said.

'Then I ought to stick my feet in you,' Blythe mumbled as those very feet gave in to the compulsion to walk. The phone was still ringing, and now it produced his voice. 'Valerie Mason and Steve Blythe,' it said, and at once had had enough of him.

All the heat of the tunnel rushed into him. He felt his head waver before steadying in a dangerously fragile version of itself, raw with a smell which surely wasn't of exhaust fumes, despite the haze into which the distant walkers were descending. He had to go back beyond the point at which his previous call had lost its hold. He peeled the soggy receiver away from his face and swung around, to be confronted by a mass of flesh as wide and as long as the protracted curve of the tunnel. He could hear more of it being tamped into the unseen mouth by the jabbing of the megaphones. Of the countless heads it was wagging at him, every one that he managed to focus on looked prepared to see him trampled underfoot if he didn't keep moving. He could no more force his way back through it than through the concrete wall, but there was no need. He would use a walkway as soon as he found some steps up.

Another wave of heat, which felt like the threat of being overwhelmed by the tide of flesh, found him, sending him after the rhythmically quivering women. As far ahead as he could see there were no steps onto the walkways, but his never having noticed them while driving needn't mean steps didn't exist; surely a trick of perspective was hiding them from him. He narrowed his eyes until he felt the lids twitch against the eyeballs and his head ache more than his feet were aching. He poked the recall button and lifted the receiver above his head in case that might allow him to hook a call, but the phone at home hadn't even doubled its first ring when his handful of technology went dead as though suffocated by the heat or drowned in the sweat of his fist. As he let it sink past his face, a phone shrilled further down the tunnel.

'They're bloody breeding,' the old man growled behind him, but Blythe didn't care what he said. About three hundred yards ahead he saw an aerial extend itself above a woman's scalp as blonde as Lydia's. Whatever had been interfering with his calls, it apparently wasn't present in that stretch of the tunnel. He saw the aerial wag a little with her conversation as she walked at least a hundred yards. As he tramped toward the point where she'd started talking, he counted the slabs of light overhead, some of which appeared to be growing unstable with the heat. He had only half as far to go now, however much the saturated heat might weigh him down. It must be his eyes which were flickering: not as many of the lights as seemed to be. He needn't wait until he arrived at the exact point in the tunnel. He only wanted reassurance that Valerie had picked up his message. He thumbed the button and flattened his ear with the receiver. The tone had barely invited him to dial when it was cut off.

He mustn't panic. He hadn't reached where phones worked, that was all. On, trying to ignore the sluggishly retreating haze of body heat which smelled increasingly like exhaust fumes, reminding himself to match the pace of the crowd, though the pair of walkers on each side of him made him feel plagued by double vision. Now he was where the woman's phone had rung, beneath two dead fluorescents separated by one which looked as though it had stolen its glare from both. All three were bumped backward by their fellows as he jabbed the button, bruised his ear with the earpiece, snatched the receiver away and cleared it, supported it with his other hand before it could slide out of his sweaty grip, split a fingernail against the button, bruised his ear again . . . Nothing he did raised the dialling tone for longer than it took to mock him.

It couldn't be the phone itself. The woman's had worked, and his was the latest model. He could only think the obstruction was moving, which meant it had to be the crowd that was preventing him from acting. If Lydia's replacement for him took him to court, he would lose business because of it, probably the confidence of many of his clients too because they wouldn't understand he took more care with their affairs than he did with his own, and if he went to prison . . . He'd closed both fists around the phone, because the plastic and his hands were aggravating one another's slippiness, and tried not to imagine battering his way through the crowd. There were still the walkways, and by the time he found the entrance to one it might make sense to head for the far end of the tunnel. He was trudging forward, each step a dull ache which bypassed his hot swollen body wrapped in far too much sodden material and searched for a sympathetic ache in his hollowed-out head, when the phone rang.

It was so muffled by his grip that he thought for a moment it wasn't his. Ignoring the groans of the muscled duo, he nailed the button and jammed the wet plastic against his cheek. 'Steve

Blythe. Can you make it quick? I don't know how long this will work.'

'It's all right, Steve. I only called to see how you were surviving. Sounds as if you're deep in it. So long as you're giving your brain a few hours off for once. You can tell me all about it when you come home.'

'Val. Val, wait. Val, are you there?' Blythe felt a mass of heat which was nearly flesh lurch at him from behind as he missed a step. 'Speak to me, Val.'

'Calm down, Steve. I'll still be here when you get back. Save your energy. You sound as though you need it.'

'I'll be fine. Just tell me you got the message.'

'Which message?'

The heat came for him again – he couldn't tell from which direction, or how fast he was stumbling. 'Mine. The one I left while you were doing whatever you were doing.'

'I had to go out for some black and white. The machine can't be working properly. There weren't any messages on the tape when I came in just now.'

That halted Blythe as if the phone had reached the end of an invisible cord. The vista of walkers wavered into a single flat mass, then steadied and regained some of its perspective. 'Never mind. Plenty of time,' he said rapidly. 'All I wanted—'

A shoulder much more solid than a human body had any right to be rammed his protruding elbow. The impact jerked his arm up, and the shooting pain opened his fist. He saw the phone describe a graceful arc before it clanged against the railing of the right-hand walkway and flew into the crowd some thirty yards ahead. Arms flailed at it as though it was an insect, then it disappeared. 'What was that for?' he screamed into the old man's face as it bobbed alongside his. 'What are you trying to do to me?'

The son's face crowded Blythe's from the other side, so forcefully it sprayed Blythe's cheek with sweat. 'Don't you yell at him, he's got a bad ear. Lucky you weren't knocked down, stopping like that. Better believe you will be if you mix it with my dad.'

'Can someone pick up my phone, please?' Blythe called at the top of his voice.

The women directly in front of him added winces to their quivering and covered their ears, but nobody else acknowledged him. 'My phone,' he pleaded. 'Don't step on it. Who can see it? Look for it, can you all? Please pass it back.'

'I said about my dad's ear,' the man to his left rumbled, lifting a hammer of a fist which for the present he used only to mop his forehead. Blythe fell silent, having seen a hand raised some yards ahead of him to point a finger downward where the phone must be. At least it was in the middle of the road, in Blythe's immediate path. A few raw steps brought him a glimpse of the aerial, miraculously intact, between the thighs of the singleted woman. He stooped without breaking his stride, and his scalp brushed her left buttock. His finger and thumb closed on the aerial and drew it toward him – only the aerial. He was staggering forward in his crouch when he saw most of the keypad being kicked away to his left, and several other plastic fragments skittering ahead.

As he straightened up, a grasp as hot and soft as flesh yet rough as concrete seemed to close around his skull. The singleted woman had turned on him. 'Whose bum do you think you're biting?'

Any number of hysterical replies occurred to him, but he managed to restrain himself. 'I'm not after any of that, I'm after this.' The words sounded less than ideally chosen once they were out, especially since the aerial in his hand was rising between her legs as though magnetized by her crotch. He whipped it back, the grip on his skull threatening to blind him, and heard himself shouting. 'Look at it. Who did this? Who smashed my phone? Where are your brains?'

'Don't look at us,' said the woman with the increasingly bare and moist midriff, while the son leaned his dripping face into Blythe's. 'Keep the row up if you're after an ear like my dad's.' All at once they were irrelevant, and he let the aerial slip from his hand. There was at least one working phone in the tunnel.

As soon as he attempted to edge forward, the crowd swung its nearest heads toward him, its eyes blinking away sweat, its mouths panting hotly at him, and started to mutter and grumble. 'What's the panic? Wait your turn. We all want to get there. Keep your distance. There's people here, you know,' it warned him in several voices, and raised one behind him. 'Now where's he scuttling off to? Must be afraid I'll report him for going for my bum.'

The obstruction to his calls was about to turn physical if he couldn't find a way to fend it off. 'Emergency,' he murmured urgently in the nearest unmatched pair of ears, which after hesitating for a second parted their bodies to let him through. 'Excuse me. Emergency. Excuse,' he repeated, stepping up the intensity, and was able to overtake enough people that he must be close to the phone. Which of the clump of blond heads belonged to it? Only one looked real. 'Excuse me,' he said, and realizing that sounded as if he wanted to get by, took hold of its unexpectedly thin and angular shoulder. 'You had the phone just now, didn't you? I mean, you have—'

'Let go.'

'Yes. What I'm saying is, you've got—'

'Let go.'

'There. I have. Excuse me. My hand's in my pocket, look. What I'm trying to say—'

The woman turned away as much of her sharp face as she'd bothered to incline toward him. 'Not me.'

'I'm sure it was. Not my phone, not the one that was trodden on, but weren't you talking on the phone before? If it wasn't yours—'

She was surrounded by female heads, he saw, all of them preserving a defiant blankness. Without warning she snapped her head around, her hair lashing his right eye. 'Who let you out? Which madhouse have they closed down now?'

'Excuse me. I didn't mean to . . .' That covered more than he had time to put into words, not least the inadvertent winks which his right eye must appear to be sharing with her. 'It's an emergency, you see. If it wasn't you, you must have seen who it was with the phone. She was somewhere around here.'

All the heads in her clump jeered practically in unison, then used her head to speak. 'It's an emergency, all right, an emergency that you need locking up. Just you wait till we get out of here and talk to someone.'

That made Blythe peer at his watch. Sweat or a tear from his stinging eye bloated the digits, and he had to shake his wrist twice before he was able to distinguish that he would never reach the tunnel exit in time to find a phone outside. The crowd had beaten him – or perhaps not yet, unless he'd failed to notice it sending a message ahead that he was to be stopped. 'Emergency. Emergency,' he said in a voice whose edge the heat seemed determined to blunt, and when he thought he'd sidled far enough away from the woman who wanted to persuade him he was going mad, he let his desperation grow louder. 'Emergency. Need to phone. Has anyone a phone? Emergency.' A shake or a wave of the heat passed through bunch after bunch of heads, and each time it did so his right eye blinked and smarted. He was trying to sound more official and peremptory when his voice trailed off. At the limit of his vision the packed flesh beneath the unsteady lights had come to a complete stop.

He could only watch the stasis creeping toward him, wavering into place in layer after layer of flesh. It was his worse possible future racing to meet him, and the crowd had been on its side all along. As he heard a murmur advancing down the tunnel from the direction of the unseen exit, he strained his ears to hear what it was saying about him. He was feeling almost calm – for how long, he couldn't predict – when words in an assortment of voices grew distinct. The message was past him before he succeeded in piecing it together. 'Someone's collapsed in the middle of the tunnel. They're clearing the way for an ambulance.'

'Bastard,' Blythe snarled, not knowing if he meant the casualty or the crowd or the ambulance – and instantly knew he should mean none of them, because he was saved from the future he'd almost wished on himself. He began to shoulder his way forward. 'Emergency. Make way, please. Make way,' he was able to say more officiously, and when that failed to clear his route fast enough 'Let me through. I'm a doctor.'

He mustn't let himself feel guilty. The ambulance was coming – he could see the far end of the tunnel beginning to turn blue and shiver – and so he was hardly putting the patient at risk. The ambulance was his only hope. Once he was close enough he would be injured, he would be however disabled he needed to seem in order to persuade the crew to take him out of the crowd. 'I'm a doctor,' he said louder, wishing he was and unmarried too, except that his life was controllable again, everything was under control. 'I'm the doctor,' he said, better yet, strong enough to part the flesh before him and to blot out the voices that were discussing him. Were they trying to confuse him by dodging ahead of him? They had to be echoes, because he identified the voice of the woman who'd pretended she had no phone. 'What's he babbling about now?'

'He's telling everyone he's a doctor.'

'I knew it. That's what they do when they're mad.'

He needn't let her bother him; nobody around him seemed to hear her – maybe she was fishing for him with her voice. 'I'm the doctor,' he shouted, seeing the ambulance crawling toward him at the end of the visible stretch of tunnel. For a moment he thought it was crushing bruised people, exhaust fumes turning their pulse blue, against the walls, but of course they were edging out alongside it, making way. His shout had dislodged several voices from beneath the bleary sweat-stained lights. 'What did she say he's saying, he's a doctor?'

'Maybe he wanted to examine your bum.'

'I know the kind of consultation I'd like to have with him. It was a quack made my dad's ear worse.'

Could the crowd around Blythe really not hear them, or was it pretending ignorance until it had him where it wanted him? Wasn't it parting for him more slowly than it should, and weren't its heads only just concealing its contempt for his imposture? The mocking voices settled toward him, thickening the heat which was putting on flesh all around him. He had to use one of the walkways. Now that he had to reach the ambulance as speedily as possible, he was entitled to use them. 'I'm the doctor,' he repeated fiercely, daring anyone to challenge him, and felt his left shoulder cleaving the saturated air. He'd almost reached the left-hand walkway when a leotarded woman whose muscles struck him as no more likely than her deep voice moved into his path. 'Where are you trying to get to, dear?'

'Up behind you. Give me a hand, would you?' Even if she was a psychiatric nurse or warder, he had seniority. 'I'm needed. I'm the doctor.'

Only her mouth moved, and not much of that. 'Nobody's allowed up there unless they work for the tunnel.'

He had to climb up before the heat turned into sweaty voices again and trapped him. 'I do. I am. There's been a collapse, the tunnel's made them collapse, and they need me.'

He'd seen ventriloquists open their mouths wider. Her eyes weren't moving at all, though a drop of sweat was growing on her right eyelashes. 'I don't know what you're talking about.'

'That's all right, nurse. You aren't required to. Just give me a hand. Give me a leg up,' Blythe said, and saw the drop swelling on her untroubled eyelid, swelling until he could see nothing else. If she was real she would blink, she wouldn't stare at him like that. The mass of flesh had made her out of itself to block his plan, but it had miscalculated. He flung himself at her, dug his fingers into her bristly scalp, and heaved himself up with all the force his arms could muster.

His heels almost caught her shoulders. They scraped down to her breasts, which gave them enough leverage for him to vault over her. His hands grabbed at the railing, caught it, held on. His feet found the edge of the walkway, and he hauled one leg over the railing, then the other. Below him the nurse was clutching her breasts and emitting a sound which, if it was intended as a cry of pain, failed to impress him. Perhaps it was a signal, because he'd taken only a few steps along the way to freedom when hands commenced trying to seize him.

At first he thought they meant to injure him so that the ambulance would take him, and then he saw how wrong he was. He had an unobstructed view of the ambulance as it rammed its way through the crowd, its blue light pounding like his head, the white arch flaring blue above it as he felt the inside of his skull flaring. There was no sign of anyone collapsed ahead. The ambulance had been sent for Blythe, of course; the message had been passed along that they'd succeeded in driving him crazy. But they couldn't conceal their opinion of him, hot oppressive breathless waves of which rose toward him and would have felt like shame if he hadn't realized how they'd given themselves away: they couldn't hold him in such contempt unless they knew more about him than they feigned to know. He kicked at the grasping fingers and glared about in search of a last hope. It was behind him. The woman with Lydia's hair had abandoned her pretense of having no phone, and he had only to grab the aerial.

He dashed back along the walkway, hanging onto the rail and kicking out at anyone within reach, though his feet so seldom made contact that he couldn't tell how many of the hands and heads were real. The woman who was still trying to convince him he'd injured her breasts flinched, which gratified him. She and the rest of the mob could move when they wanted to, they just hadn't done so for him. The beckoning aerial led his gaze to the face dangling from it. She was staring at him and talking so hard her mouth shaped every syllable. 'Here he comes now,' she mouthed.

She must be talking to the ambulance. Of course, she'd used the phone before to summon it, because she was another of the nurses. She'd better hand over the phone if she didn't want worse than he was supposed to have done to her colleague. 'Here I come all right,' he yelled, and heard what sounded like the entire crowd, though perhaps only the tunnel that was his head, echoing him. As he ran the tunnel widened, carrying her farther from the walkway, too far for him to grab the aerial over the crowd. They thought they'd beaten him, but they were going to help him again. He vaulted the railing and ran across the mass of flesh.

It wasn't quite as solid as he had assumed, but it would do. The heat of its contempt streamed up at him, rebounding from the dank concrete of his skull. Was it contemptuous of what he was doing or of his failure to act when he could have? He had a sudden notion, so terrible it almost caused him to lose his footing, that when he raised the phone to his ear he would discover the woman had been talking to Valerie. It wasn't true, and only the heat was making him think it. Stepping-stones turned up to him and gave way underfoot – there went some teeth and there, to judge by its yielding, an eye – but he could still trample his way to the phone, however many hands snatched at him.

Then the aerial whipped out of his reach like a rod that had caught a fish. The hands were pulling him down into their contempt, but they weren't entitled to condemn him: he hadn't done anything they weren't about to do. 'I'm you,' he screamed, and felt the shoulders on which he'd perched move apart farther than his legs could stretch. He whirled his arms, but this wasn't a dream in which he could fly away from everything he was. Too late he saw why the woman had called the ambulance for him. He might have screamed his thanks to her, but he could make no words out of the sounds which countless hands were dragging from his mouth.

***Ramsey Campbell** is one of the premier dark fantasists currently working in the field. His first short story collection,* The Inhabitant of the Lake, *was published by Arkham House at the tender age of eighteen. He has since gone on to author such classics of modern horror as* The Doll Who Ate His Mother, The Face That Must Die, Midnight Sun, Obsession, Incarnate, The Nameless, *and* The Long Last. *A multiple World Fantasy, British Fantasy, and Dracula Society award-winner, he also reviews films for BBC Radio. Ramsey resides in Merseyside with his wife and two children.*

Hidden

BY

STUART KAMINSKY

CORRINE did not scream. It was more like a vibrating moan followed by a little wail as she ran down the stairs. She didn't let out a real scream till she was out the front door. She had saved her scream till she was sure someone would hear her.

I had pressed the record button of the tape recorder the second I heard her open the front door. It took her four minutes to change into her working clothes and use the downstairs bathroom.

Once she called, 'Mrs Wainwright?'

My parents' room was always the first one she cleaned. This Tuesday was no different, at least so far, than the four years of Tuesdays that had gone before it. It took her ten minutes to finish cleaning my parents' room. She would have taken half an hour if she thought my mother was home.

My room was second.

It was when she opened the door and stepped in that she made the wailing sound and ran.

As it was, the first real scream from the lawn was just a loud extension of the moan. It was the second one that must have howled down the street and through the open front door back up to me.

It was a little after nine. A little before four, I had driven my dad's car to Gorbell's Woods, walked north on Highland for another half mile or so, and dropped my father's favorite hat at the side of the street. Then I walked the two miles back, making sure no one would see me, not that anyone but a peeping insomniac would have in Paltztown.

Corrine was screaming almost steadily now, but her screams weren't as loud. She was probably running down the street now, neighbors cautiously looking through their windows, afraid the Wainwright maid had downed more than a few too many.

They didn't know Corrine. She was born again. A boor. I know she had at least one married daughter, Alice. Alice had come to help her mother once about two years ago, when I was twelve. Alice must have looked like her father. Corrine was a bloated wobbler. Alice was a skinny snorter. I could only imagine what kind of bird Corrine's husband, the part-time reverend, looked like.

The first neighbor to come, five minutes later, was Mr Jomberg, two doors down, retired, a heart condition. I didn't find out it was Mr Jomberg until later, but I'm surprised he didn't have a heart attack when he opened the door.

I recorded Mr Jomberg's 'Holy shit' and his footsteps hurrying unsteadily down the stairs.

Can shit be holy? Why not? Would God bother to exclude it? Would God be sure to include it? I've had the feeling since I was no more than ten that God, if there was one, worked to create the universe and people and when it came time for the little things, the details, God just said, 'The hell with it.' And God had a lot to do. New worlds out there every minute. New stars born. Old stars dying. Busy somewhere in the firmament. I was a forgotten detail, a the-hell-with-it. I figured that out too when I was ten and I almost drowned in the pool. I shouldn't have been left alone. I hadn't had a seizure for almost a year and I was in the shallow end, but I shouldn't have been left alone. I felt it coming, felt what Dr Ginsberg calls 'the aura.' I must have panicked, felt confused as my brain began to close down. Instead of heading for the side of the pool I took a step toward the deep end.

I woke up in the hospital. When I opened my eyes, my mother began 'Thank God'-ing though she never went to church and committed many a sin of omission. My father was there, sighing deeply. He touched my cheek. My sister, Lynn, a year older than me, had been pulled away from her friend's house.

'You okay?' she said, looking bored.

I nodded yes.

'No more swimming alone,' my father said.

My mother was supposed to have been watching me in the water. She had gone in the house to answer the phone. When she came out, I was almost dead.

That's when I decided I was a go-to-hell person.

You'd think that would depress a ten-year-old. If it did for a few seconds, I don't remember. I remember lying there and thinking, 'If there is no God, only people can punish me for what I do. If there is a God, he doesn't care what happens to me.'

That was my final seizure.

Before whoever listens to this says, 'That was the big day. Trauma time. The day we can trace it all back to. If only he had been given therapy. But now we understand. We can put it in a box with a label and forget Paul Wainwright. Even his name is easy to forget.'

The police came eight minutes and twenty seconds after Mr Jomberg went ballistic. I imagined him and Corrine on the front lawn, screaming, dancing in a crazy circle. If they make a movie, I strongly suggest they include the dancing scene, at least as a fantasy.

There were two policemen, one a man, one a woman. In case it's not clear on the tape, she said,

'Ahh, God.'

He said,

'Jesus. Call in.'

'God,' the woman repeated.

'Billie, call in,' the man said with a quaver in his voice. 'I'll . . . I'll check the house.'

They both left my room. I was hungry. I reached into the box next to me and took out two slices of bread. I put individual American cheese slices in the sandwich and placed the plastic that had covered them in the plastic container. I quietly snapped the container closed.

It's a little after one in the morning now. I can record all of this whispering into the microphone.

I had thought this out carefully. Lots and lots of premeditation.

In the ceiling inside my closet is a small trapdoor. It used to be the only way to get to the crawl space when my parents bought the house. They dormered the attic and made it a giant room for Lynn. I didn't mind. I like small spaces. Once I went with my mother and sister to Baltimore on the train. I think it was to console my Aunt Jean when her son died, but maybe it wasn't. I was just a kid, maybe three. My mother and sister complained about how small the sleeping space was in our little private room, especially when the two beds were open. I was in the upper. Even at three there was hardly enough room to turn over. I loved it. Wrapped in the dark.

The trapdoor in my closet. I hadn't forgotten. Walls were put up in the attic, on each side, to make it look and feel more like a room. The walls created unreachable spaces behind them. Narrow front-of-the-house to rear passageways. The trapdoor was forgotten by everyone but me. I locked my bedroom door and scrambled up, almost every night. I climbed quietly so Lynn wouldn't hear. I'd store things in the space and take naps in the darkness. One afternoon when I was home alone, I made a small hole in the wall, a very small hole so I could see most of the room. Then I went into Lynn's room and used the hand vac from the kitchen to pick up the few pieces of wood shavings I'd made making the hole.

I think of things. I plan ahead. I have a complete supply of nonperishable canned foods and drinks up here and a sealable plastic bucket where I can put my garbage. I chose foods that would have the least detectable smell. I have blankets, two pillows, and almost all my clothes piled neatly a few feet away. I have the small battery-powered television set that my parents kept in their room. And I have battery replacements. I checked with a flashlight for bugs for weeks before the morning I killed my parents and sister. The crawl space was clean.

The hardest part, the part I'm most proud of, is the fake ceiling, exactly the size of the closet ceiling. It fits perfectly. I made it in my room, tested it to see if it would work, how it would look. When I go through the trapdoor, I can reach the false ceiling where I prop it over my clothes rack. I reach down, pull the false ceiling up by the spring and handle I screwed into it and set the spring and bar in place in the trapdoor to hold the false ceiling in place. If someone looks in my closet, they'd see a ceiling. The only danger is if someone reaches up ten feet and pushes the ceiling. Not likely, but if they do climb up, the ceiling will wobble a little. They might think it's a little odd, but that's all.

There is plenty of air in my crawl space. Lynn's walls are wooden slats on plasterboard or something like that. There's a space between each of the slabs of plasterboard, a small space but enough.

But back to this morning.

Twenty more minutes and more police and a doctor.

'I've never seen it this bad.'

'Walters case, seven, eight years ago. Five in the family. Father did it. Ax, hammer, teeth. Bodies, parts all over the apartment.'

'Before my time, Barry.'

'Father's still in the funny farm, I think. God, will you look at this?'

'I'm lookin', Judd.'

I know what you're thinking. I'm not squeamish. I'll talk about it. You're wondering what I do for a toilet. Two things. I've got an emergency plastic bowl, a big one, with a pop-on top. If I can make it through the day, I'll go down at night, tonight, and use my own bathroom. I thought of everything. I made a checklist. I have a copy of it with me with a penlight and a supply of penlight batteries and even some replacement bulbs. I have books for during the day. All kinds of books, any kind of book, nothing that could form part of a puzzle to come up with a simple profile.

'He reads mysteries. That explains it.'

'He reads romances. That explains it.'

'He reads histories. That explains it.'

'He reads about knights with lances. That explains it.'

And then, from below, clear, the one with the rough voice, 'This is the son's room.'

'No sign of him unless some of these parts. No head, nothing that looks like a kid.'

'You got enough pictures there? I'd really like to get the hell out of here.'

'You wanna wait in the hall? Wait in the hall. I don't want some lawyer coming back at me a year from now. This is a big one.'

'We either find the kid's body in the next hour or he did it.'

'Prediction?'

'Experience. For Chri— Doc, what'd he do to that one?'

'Bad things, James. Let me work here. Go look for the boy, clues. Stop bothering me so I can get this done, these bodies out of here and back to the hospital.'

Two men left, out looking for signs of me. The doctor, left alone, talked to himself, probably into a tape recorder. I heard the click. It's on my tape. He said it was a pre-autopsy report, an 'on-site.' He talked slowly, forced himself to talk slowly or he had trouble breathing: 'All three victims are nude. Preliminary cause of death on female, age approximately 45, massive evisceration. All hair, from head and pubic area, shaved roughly, probably after death. Decapitated. Body on the floor. Head on the bed. Preliminary cause of death, male, same age, massive, repeated blows to the cranium, extensive brain damage. Multiple stab wounds. Preliminary cause of death on female, age fifteen to twenty, repeated, traumatic penetration of . . . No sign of bullet wounds on any of the victims, but the condition of the bodies is such that clinical examination will be necessary.'

He clicked off the machine and said,

'Animal. Animal.'

A few minutes later, the one with the rough voice and one or two others.

'Jesus,' said somebody.

'That's what they all say. Look around. Take it in. Do your job.

No blood in the hallway or anywhere else. They were killed in here. I'd say they were shot first.'

It was hard to hear the rest of the conversation. Someone was using a machine, sounded like a vacuum cleaner, in my room. I think they said,

'Neighbors don't report any noise, but . . .'

'You think after he killed the first one, the next one just came in here, saw the body and let herself—'

'Or himself . . .'

'Probably killed the man first. Easier to deal with the women.'

'What kind of kid lives in a room like this?'

'Shit, what kind of kid does something like this.'

'Place looks like a cell. No pictures, things on the table. Black blanket and pillows. I'll bet his clothes are neatly piled in the drawers and lined up perfectly in his closet.'

The sound of a drawer opening.

'What'd I tell you?'

The sound of someone opening the closet drawer right below me. I held my breath.

'I should have bet,' the rough-voiced man said right below me. 'It's the kid.'

New voice, shaky.

'Sergeant, wagon's on the way for the bodies. Can they bag 'em?'

'Ask the doc,' the rough-voiced one said, closing the closet door and making me strain now to hear what was going on in my room. The closed door had one advantage. It cut out most of the smell.

'Call in from Commer and Styles. They found one of the family cars. Identified by contents in glove compartment. Over in Gorbell's Woods, just off Highland. Driver side door open. Half a block farther, heading north, they found a hat on the side of the road. A kind of Greek fisherman's hat with the father's name on the sweatband.'

'He's heading out of town. On foot.'

'Why the hat? Why'd he take it? Why'd he toss it? Why'd he leave the car?' asked the sergeant with the rough voice.

They were all good questions.

'Can we go now, Sergeant? I mean downstairs.'

'Go. I'm stayin' a while.'

Footsteps leaving the room. A faraway sound of an ambulance siren. What was the point of the siren? What was the hurry?

The sergeant was breathing hard enough for me to hear him through the floor and door. He said something, too soft for me to hear, but it was angry. I'll listen to the tape later, maybe weeks from now when I can turn up the volume. I'm curious. Can you blame me?

Downstairs people were talking, arguing, using our phone. Beyond the wall two feet away from me, a pair of footsteps tracked around Lynn's room. I put my eye against the narrow slit between the plasterboard and planks. I caught a glimpse of blue uniform on a woman's body.

'Pretty kid,' said a young man's voice.

I was sure he was looking at Lynn's photographs of herself and her friends resting on her dressing table.

I couldn't see him or the policewoman who answered,

'Not anymore.'

They didn't stay in Lynn's room long. No more than a minute after they left I heard new voices below in my room.

'Oh, Lord . . .'

'They told you what it was like, Nate.'

'Yeah, but . . .'

Footsteps coming up the stairs.

'We set the bags. We set the gurneys. We—'

'Room's been printed and vacuumed,' the doctor said. 'That torso and the head go in one bag. Girl and the hand go in another bag. The woman in the corner . . . I'll help you.'

'Never done anything like this,' said the one called Nate. 'You know that, Russ? Old people who die in their sleep. Kid gets shot. Husband knifes . . . Nothing like this. Not in this town.'

'Give me a hand,' the doctor said.

The sound of a zipper. Good-bye, Dad?

I watched the eleven o'clock news, watched carefully. They won't really clean the room for a day or two. They'd close the door when the bodies were gone and seal off the room, probably sealed the whole house. Teams of police, possibly even South Carolina state troopers, possibly the FBI, would tear off tape, open doors, take more pictures, look at the blood, start looking for clues about where I might have gone.

They will find, in my second-from-the-top dresser drawer, under my sweaters, on the right, my notes and maps of New York City. I have circled neighborhoods with different color markers and made notes about them as places to visit or find an apartment. I have never been to New York City, never want to go. It's dangerous. It's dirty. It is where I want them to look for me.

Short-term plan: Be careful. Use the bathroom only late at night when I'm sure the house is empty.

Long-term plan: When I run out of food and clean clothes in about three weeks or a month, in the middle of the night, I climb down, use the large-container Krazy Glue to fix the false closet ceiling in place, and then get my bike and helmet wrapped in plastic and hidden five blocks away under the Klines' back porch. I wait till morning and, dressed like a morning biker complete with helmet, goggles, and armed with only a water bottle, I pedal out of Platztown, eating fast food on the way to Jacksonville, where I buy clothes, a shirt here, jeans there. I have $2,356 in my wallet. Most of it money I earned working in the Kash and Karry. Some of it from my mother's purse and father's wallet. I even know how to get a new identity, a Social Security card, a driver's license. I've seen it on television, read two books about it.

It has gone pretty much the way I planned. Busy with the police for about three days. A crew of women, Polish or Russian or something, came in to clean the room. After the clean-up, there were fewer and fewer until one day no one came. Days and nights reading, watching game shows, talk shows, movies and the news using my ear phones. The Channel Seven News, the team 'on your side' called what I had done 'gruesome' and 'beyond belief' after the national news anchor in Washington soberly reported on the horrid dread. People in Platztown are locking their doors and sleeping with their guns on the night table for fear I was still lurking in the night. There are photographs – of me looking like a grinning nerd, of my parents and Lynn looking like the next door neighbors of Rob and Laura Petrie.

The sergeant with the rough voice was part of a press conference on the second day. He looked fat and tired. His hair was curly and gray, and his sports jacket and unmatching trousers were badly in need of burning.

The mayor spoke at the conference, attended by reporters and television crews from as far away as Charleston and Raleigh. The mayor assured the world that the 'person or persons who committed this monstrous crime would soon be caught.' The chief of police was careful in answering a reporter's question. He said that I was certainly a prime suspect, but that I might also be the fourth victim, buried in the woods or, he hinted, kidnapped for the kidnappers' pleasure. A television reporter from Channel Seven asked, 'What if he had help?'

'No report of anyone in town missing,' said the chief with a knowing smile.

'Then whoever might have helped him might still be in town,' said the reporter. 'One of our own kids.'

'Not likely. We think Paul Wainwright is in Chicago or soon will be,' the chief said.

'How do you know?'

'Why Chicago?'

'Documents found in the suspect's room,' the rough-voiced sergeant, identified as James Roark, said.

'What documents?'

'Did he leave a diary?'

'He left his family dead, naked, and in little pieces,' Roark croaked.

At that point Channel Seven went back to Elizabeth Chanug in the studio. According to Elizabeth, there were 'apparently reliable' reports that the police knew with certainty that I was already in Chicago and they had narrowed the search down to certain specific areas in the city.

My favorite part, I almost missed it, was on Channel Ten. They interviewed people who knew me.

Mr Honeycutt, the school principal, to whom I have not

spoken more than twice in passing: 'A quiet boy. Outstanding student. Not a lot of friends.'

Miss Terrimore, the guidance counselor, a sagging lump of a creature trying to hold herself together with tailored suits: 'Without revealing confidences, about all I can say about him is that he was a bright, defensive, and clearly troubled boy.'

She had talked to me twice, and both times she popped menthol cough drops and barely looked up from the report she was filling out. It was in-her-office, how-you-doin'?, that's-fine, next. I could have waved an Uzi in front of her, and she would have wiped her nose and said, 'How you doin'?'

Jerry 'Turk' Walters, Turk the Jerk, dresses like a rapper, belongs in the crapper: 'Paul was in two of my classes this semester, three last. I sat near him 'cause everything is alphabetical, you know. And our names are close. Paul didn't talk much. Good student. A weird smile that gave me chills. No close friends. No real friends I knew about. But he helped me out a few times.'

Helped him out by letting him copy my homework regularly for two semesters.

Milly Rugello, pretty and mellow, dressed now in yellow, lips fine red and full for the camera, vacant eyes faking feminine concern: 'I wouldn't say we were friends. Actually, I didn't talk to Paul much. He was kind of creepy. But he never made any trouble.'

Creepy? Hindsight of the stupid. I was never, never creepy. I was clean-teethed and clean-clothed and normal, laughing when I should laugh, writing essays the teachers wanted, lamenting, although with regret and not anger, the plight of the hungry throughout the world, the spread of AIDS, the pervasiveness of bigotry. Man's inhumanity to Man.

I went to basketball games, football games, pep rallies, and even took my cousin Dorthea to the sophomore dance. Theme: A Touch of Springtime.

Milly Rugello
Lips like red jello,
Dressed all in yellow.
Hardly ever said hello.

Rugello, Milly
Skin like a lily,
Brainless and silly,
Oh, what I'd like to do to you.

Mr Jomberg, breathing heavy, trials of the heart and emphysema, dressed for the occasion in worn jeans and a flannel shirt with dominant reds and blacks, thumbs in his pocket, mountain man, folksy, neighborhood wise man: 'Wainwrights were decent people, always a good morning. The girl was bright, always friendly and polite, not like a lot these days. The boy?' Mr Jomberg shook his head sadly. 'An enigma. Always polite, showed a little interest in my garden, seemed to get on well with my dog. It's all a shock.'

Enigma? Had Mr Jomberg run to his thesaurus? Did he have an untapped vein of the mother lode of mindless clichés? Interest in his garden? Did Mr Jomberg live in Fantasyville? And the dog? I seriously considered eviscerating the snarling, foul, filthy-toothed rag.

Connie was kept from the cameras. A good thing too. She would have been useless, though she might have had a good word or two for me. I was always polite to Connie, I was always polite to everyone.

Day by day Channel Seven has even less and less about me and what I had done. The national news had abandoned me after three days. Channel Seven dropped the story today. There was no new news about me. There was nothing to report.

I've come down cautiously around two in the morning every other day, listened to be sure no one was in the house, used the toilet, washed myself, dried the bowl with toilet paper I had brought down with me, flushed whatever had to be flushed down, and went quickly back to the closet.

The first time down, on the third day, I had been, I admit it, just a little excited. Not frightened. Adventure. Challenge. Danger. I stopped in the middle of my room, the light of a three-quarter moon letting me know that the room had been cleaned, something I already knew from the sounds of the day. Bed against the wall, stripped to the springs. Dresser in the corner, everything cleared from the top. Desk empty now.

During the day, the policeman with the rough voice, James Roark, had brought my Aunt Katherine through the house. I heard the door to my room open.

'You gonna be all right, Mrs Taylor.'

She didn't answer. She must have shaken her head.

'I'll just stand here and give you a hand if you need it.'

Shuffling. A cardboard box opening? My imagination. Drawers opening. Things be swept into the box, clunking hurriedly off its sides. Aunt Katherine breathing hard. Her husband, my father's brother, had left her and Dorthea when I was a little kid. I wondered if he would read about this or see it on television or if he were dead. 'Were dead.' Got that? Subjunctive. Feed that to Mr Waldermere if you find it. You taught me well, Mr W. I listened. Promising future, huh, Mr W?'

My room looked like a tomb, drenched in gloom, waiting for the boom of doom, growing smaller, driving me into the corner where I could curl up like a pre-abortion in the womb.

I climbed back up and sealed myself in.

It is two weeks later on a Tuesday at two-twenty in the morning. I just dropped a green garbage bag of dirty clothes and another green garbage bag of food and garbage onto the floor of the closet. I propped the fake ceiling against the rods from which all my remaining clothing has long since been removed, and climbed down sneaker quiet. It took me fifteen minutes to seal the ceiling. I'm drenched in sweat. It's a hot night and the air conditioning isn't on. Why should it be? I left the television, radio, and all but one of the books sealed in the crawl space. I took a paperback copy of Lord Byron's poetry, which I've stuffed into my back pocket. I also took this tape recorder. I plan to chronicle my journey through life. Tape after tape after tape. Hundreds of tapes, maybe thousands. I'll leave them right out in the open, neatly catalogued, telling visitors that I plan to publish them someday.

Three years, five years, ten years, half a century from now when the house is remodeled or torn down – if it was not demolished in the next two months because no one wants to buy it – some unintentional archeologist would discover the traces of my deception in the crawl space.

Will they marvel at my cleverness or just call me mad? I have no illusions about people.

I am putting down the crinkling garbage bags to open the door. And then down the stairs, out the back door, through the alley, dropping the bags in the dumpster outside of Rangel and Page's Supermarket. Pickup on Wednesday morning. After that, with the coming of dawn, the morning biker, head down, tools down the highway and what I really am remains . . .

hidden.

Paul Wainwright walked gently down the stairs, feeling his way in the near total darkness, garbage bags tapping against his back, tape recorder clutched in his hand. In the living room, the nearby street lamp let a slash of filtered light through the downstairs curtained windows.

Paul had taken four steps toward the kitchen when he heard his father's voice say,

'Put them down gently, Paul.'

Paul dropped the bags and turned into the darkness of the living room.

'Go sit in the chair by the window,' his father said.

Paul's knees turned to pudding. For as long as a minute, he didn't move, and then the voice again from his father's favorite chair,

'Sit, Paul. Now.'

Paul made his way to the chair near the window and looked toward the voice of his father in the darkness.

'I've got to know why', his father said wearily.

'You're not my father,' Paul said.

'And for that I thank God,' the voice said.

'You're Roark, James Roark. Sergeant James Roark.'

Roark had almost dozed off when he heard the sound above him. A thud, followed by another thud. The thudding sounds were followed by shuffling and the slap of something – wood, plastic – against something hard. It could have been a burglar, but Roark didn't think so.

For the first week after the murders, he had slept two, three hours a night in patches. His wife had reminded him that they were going to visit their daughter at Mount Holyoke in two weeks and he had to apply for the vacation time. He had said yes and forgotten and then, when it came time to pack and leave, Roark had said no. He had to stay behind. He had to find Paul Wainwright.

His wife hadn't argued. She had seen Roark like this only once before, when they lost their first child before he reached his first birthday. Best to leave him alone. Best to let him heal. Best if it worked the way it had more than twenty-five years ago.

When his wife had left, Roark had taken his vacation and slept during the day with the sun coming into his room and the phone turned off. At night he had gone quietly to the Wainwright house, let himself in, and sat in the living room waiting, hoping for the boy to return, sure at times that he would, just as sure more often that he would not. He was certain that the boy had not gone to New York City. The hints were too obvious, the maps too hastily circled, the blood on the corner of one map that of the dead father, strongly suggesting that the maps had been put in the drawer after the father's murder. There had been no evidence of a young man of Paul's description going through any nearby town or getting on any bus, train, or plane. The family's second car was still in the garage. No, the chances were good that Paul Wainwright was still somewhere in or near Platztown. They had searched, asked and found nothing, and so Roark had clung to the hope that the boy would come back home when he thought it was safe, would come back home for clothes, hidden money, a last look. Nothing much, but Roark had a feeling. His feelings had been wrong in the past. Wrong more than they were right, but he had nothing to go on and a real need to justify the nights he was spending in the Wainwright living room. And now came the realization that Paul Wainwright had been hiding in the house, two floors above him for more than two weeks. In the slash of light from the window, the boy looked white and thin, his dark T-shirt pulsed with his beating heart.

'What's in your hand?' Roark said. 'Hold it up.'

The boy held up a small tape recorder.

'Put it next to you on the window ledge.' Roark went on rubbing his stubbled cheeks.

Paul put the tape recorder on the ledge.

'Now,' Roark said, 'play it.'

'I—' Paul began.

'Play it,' Roark insisted, and Paul pushed the rewind button. The two sat listening to the hum till the machine clicked and Paul hit the play button. Twenty minutes later, the machine clicked off.

'Doesn't explain much,' Roark said.

'That's all there is,' Paul said.

'There's no why to it,' said the policeman. 'I need a why.'

'When I was ten,' the boy said, 'I discovered that I had no feeling for anyone, none. My friends, family. They meant nothing to me. I didn't like them. I didn't hate them. I was just better than they were, smarter because I wasn't tied down by the confusion of—'

'Bullshit,' Roark interrupted.

'No. That's the truth.'

'Why did you, for chrissake, rape your own sister before you – before you—?'

'Because I could do it. I could do anything. I was excited by the power, the blood,' the boy said evenly.

'And your mother, Jesus, kid, what'd you tear out her heart with, your bare hands?'

'And a knife,' the boy said.

'Last question. Why did you have to stab your father not once but six times?'

'Fifteen,' the boy said. 'I stabbed him fifteen times.'

'The tape is bullshit, isn't it, son? You wanted to find a way to get caught and have someone listen to it. If I hadn't caught you tonight, you'd have found a way to get caught.'

Paul Wainwright tried to laugh, but it came out as a dry, choking sound.

'No one raped your sister, Paul, and no one tore your mother's heart out, but you're right. Your father was stabbed fifteen times.'

'I killed them,' Paul said, his voice breaking. 'And I almost got away with it.'

'Nope,' said Roark. 'Nothing about your life fits the kid on that tape or what happened in that bedroom. You want to know the way I figure it?'

'No,' said the boy.

'I'll tell you anyway. You came home a week ago Monday night from the Tolliver game. No one around but your father. He said something like, "Let's go up to your room. I've got something to tell you." You were feeling good, thought it was good news, bad news, who knows. You got up there and opened the door and saw what he had done to your mother and sister. You went wild with fear, anger. You hit him with the lamp, and when he went down you took the knife from his hand and you stabbed him, once for every year of your life.'

'The fake ceiling in the closet,' the boy tried. 'It took me—'

'Hell, you're a kid. My daughter had a hiding place in a cupboard. You've probably been climbing up there for years, hiding out, spying on your sister.'

Paul started to get up.

'Sit down, son,' Roark said. 'And don't get up till I get some more answers. I understand why you killed your father. He'd been seeing a shrink in Charlotte for a couple of years now. Plenty to show that he was a man in need of help. Between you and me and without the tape running, I'd say you could get yourself a good lawyer and sue the hell out of that shrink for not seeing where this was going.'

'I killed them,' the boy repeated.

'Why? I mean, why did you climb up there? Why did you make the tape? Why did you want us to think you'd killed them all?'

The boy was shaking now.

'I killed them,' he repeated.

'Take it easy. You cold?'

Paul shook his head no.

'Let me give it a try,' Roark said. 'My father's still alive and I've got kids. You wanted to protect your father's name.'

'I should have seen it coming,' Paul said softly. 'The little things he did, said. The anger, crying. I should have seen. My mother should have seen and my sister too, but they're not . . . they weren't . . .'

'As smart as you,' said Roark. 'It was your fault he killed them because you're smarter than they were and you should have stopped him?'

Paul said nothing. He hugged himself and began to rock in the filtered light from the street lamp.

'What about it being his fault, your father's?'

'He was sick. Someone should have helped him. He was a good husband, a good dad.'

'We're way out of my league here,' Roark said. 'I'll try once and leave it to the pros. You killed one person, your father, who murdered your mother and sister and was trying to murder you. You're not responsible for what he did. There's nothing you could have done to stop it 'cause there's no way you could have known he would lose it. Plenty of people see shrinks and behave wacky. I saw a shrink for years and I yelled at my family and behaved like an – you'll excuse my French – asshole.'

The boy kept rocking, tuning out. Roark had seen it before. He got up from his chair and moved to the boy's side, looking down at him. Roark took off his jacket and put it around the shivering boy's shoulders, though the room was warm and muggy.

'Let's go,' the policeman said, helping the boy up and pocketing the tape recorder.

Paul gave him no trouble. They stepped past the two green garbage bags.

'I just thought . . .' Paul started and looked around the room. 'I just thought . . .' he repeated, looking up at the thick Irish face of the policeman and trying to speak through his tears, 'that there are some things, some things that should stay . . .' And the policeman finished as he put his arms around the boy, ' . . . hidden.'

Stuart M. Kaminsky *is the author of thirty-three novels. His mystery series include those featuring Russian Inspector Porfiry Petrovich Rostnikov, Depression-era Hollywood private eye Toby Peters, and the acerbic Abraham Lieberman. He won the Mystery Writers of America's Edgar Award for his Rostnikov novel* A Cold Red Sunrise. *His book* Exercise in Terror *was made into* Hidden Fears, *starring Meg Foster, and* When The Dark Man Calls *was made into* Frequence Muerte, *starring Catherine Deneuve. A Professor of Motion Picture, Television & Recording Arts at Florida State University, Kaminsky also wrote the dialogue for Sergio Leone's epic gangster picture,* Once Upon A Time In America, *and scripted the screenplay for* A Woman in the Wind, *starring Colleen Dewhurst.*

Prism

BY

WENDY WEBB

SOME came forth and talked to her. The others stayed deep in her mind and hid. Like she was hiding. Janie would kill them if they came out, she might kill the ones who dared to speak now. Janie might even kill her, if they came too close and hurt with their words. She retreated further into a dark corner of her mind to wait. To watch.

'Bad girl, Janie. You were bad today. Very, very bad. Now you have to pay the price.' The serrated knife sawed back and forth across her wrist.

Janie felt no pain as she watched the tiny grooves of the knife shred skin and bring blood – pain was someone else's responsibility. She felt no remorse in her act today, just bitterness in it being discovered by the righteous Tatum.

Of course Tatum would know, she knew everything. They all did. Eventually.

The knife slipped to the floor. Tatum didn't move to pick it up. Good. Maybe the punishment was complete.

Janie tugged at her Sunday school dress, tight across her

developing chest, and smeared dark blood on soft green velveteen. Snow flurries, carried on a sudden gust of wind, floated through the broken kitchen window overlooking the cracked cement stoop and the dark woods of the backyard, then settled softly on her black patent leather shoes.

Tina came then, squatting like a frog balancing on a lilypad, and watched the little flakes melt to water. 'Look, Janie. See how pretty they are? Mommy would like it. Beau, too.' Her interest waned as quickly as it appeared. 'Let's color. I have a new box of crayons.' Then, grudgingly, as was her way, she added, 'We'll share.'

Janie dismissed the little girl as no more than a toddler unaware of little around her except her own immediate needs, and wrapped her arms around her chest. The kid was one of the new ones. And an annoying one at that. She shuddered with the drop in temperature the broken window had allowed and felt her anger grow again. There was enough to do without worrying about a whining child who wanted to color.

'Look at this mess, will ya? Just look at it. And Sunday company coming any minute.' Betty snorted in disgust, picked up glass fragments and flung them into the trash can under the sink. She pulled an uprooted violet out of a pile of house plant soil scattered in clumps across the floor and held it out accusingly. 'What is this? Some new approach to horticulture? Save it for that television broad Hazel. I got everything I can do to keep your room clean.' She snatched up a single navy blue pump, a torn jacket, and a severed paisley tie, and threw them into the coat closet. 'It's a good thing your mother and Beau can't see this mess.' She pulled her thumb across her neck and winked. 'They wouldn't like it a bit. Not one bit. So, let's just call it our little secret.'

She whisked a handful of ice cubes from an overturned tumbler into her open palm, tossed them carelessly over her shoulder toward the sink, then sniffed the air. 'Whiskey. And today being the Almighty's day.' The fallen high-back chair was righted and shoved under the table. It stopped short of flush with the table edge. ''Course, it doesn't matter to them one way or the other.

When it's time, it's time. And it's always time.' A blast of cold air pierced her green velveteen dress. 'Damn, it's cold.'

'Janie,' Tina whined, 'I'm cold. And I want to color. Can we color now?'

Tatum spoke knowingly. 'No coloring today, Tina. Janie was a bad girl. A bad girl who deserves what she gets. And more.'

Janie eyed the knife, now lying on the floor. Maybe she deserved to be punished and maybe she didn't. A faint smile touched her lips.

Cold wind ripped through the room, crashing countertop trinkets to the floor. Potting soil rolled across the cracked linoleum and soaked up blood at the knife's edge under the table.

Her smile turned to a scowl. If it hadn't been for her, levelheaded, take-command Janie, they'd still be in this mess. All of them. Someone had to take matters into her own hands. Certainly *she* wouldn't. Unless you called hiding like a coward doing something.

They called her cold, aloof, and had never been anything else to her. Because she deserved nothing more, Tatum had whispered to her in the dark of their room, because she had earned nothing less. Janie had rolled over on the hard floor and curled into a tight ball, anger seething, growing.

But on the hard floor, *she* shivered uncontrollably, knowing that the pain in her ankles, knees, and elbows would mean bruises tomorrow. A few more to add to the growing quilt-work. If only she had a blanket, just a small one, or a towel, to take the edge off. There were plenty around for Mother and her new lover, nothing for her. Even the midnight prowl for warmth, with a return to the linen closet before dawn, had been a mistake. Their eyes missed nothing – 'Discipline,' her mother had said, and Beau agreed – and their hands left nothing on her untouched for the crime. Only the X-rays would prove that now, and the insistent whispering of Tatum with her cold 'I told you so.'

It was a lesson repeated over and over again in both words and actions. From the adults, then finally from Tatum.

She would awake to frigid water from the well drawn for a bath, then be sent outside for hours in the snow-covered woods wearing last summer's clothes. Stiff from the cold, and numb with Tatum's constant taunting, she was called in for a supper of frozen food tossed at her in rapid succession. Whatever she could catch and hold was hers, until their adult patience ran thin and the thawing food was thrown away.

Tina had come then, for the first time. The little one cried and rubbed her empty stomach; then as her child's rage bubbled, she stamped her foot. Adult eyes saw the scene and their hands took action. She screamed with the realization as the closet door closed and locked, and heard their muffled laughter from the other side. Tatum had talked to her as a mother to a wanton child. 'I hope you've learned something from this. You're a bad girl, and bad girls are always punished. Always. Your mommy and Beau won't like you if you're bad.' She paused then, as if to let this sink in. Her eyes narrowed with new thought. 'Janie put you up to this, didn't she? I knew it. It's always her fault. She never learns, but she will now. Won't you, Janie?'

Janie shifted her eyes from the darkening, moist soil at her feet to the locked closet door, and remembered.

Tina cringed. 'Please. I'll be good. I promise. Don't let it happen again, Janie. Pulleeeze.' Her wail ended suddenly.

'Damn.' Betty hoisted her arms to her hips. 'The second my back is turned, it looks like a bomb went off in this place.' She released a long martyr sigh and reached in the closet for a broom. Its bristles worked savagely across the floor, *whisk-whisk-whisk,* in a contest with the wind. Marching to the broken window, Betty stared with contempt at the gray skies. 'I hate winter, ya know it? Muddy shoes, damp clothes, being stuck in the house with a bunch of tyrants. Never can make them happy. Their eyes see everything, things that aren't there most of the time, if you ask me. Still, I suppose it's a roof over my head.' Her voice dropped to a whisper. 'Got nowhere else to go.' Her broom came down under the table edge with a wet thud. 'I still hate it.' She took a tentative sweep across the floor with a last look out the window, then turned her full attention to the work. Her eyes widened. Blood smeared in an arc where the bristles met linoleum. Her lips peeled back in a sneer. 'Did I say I'd keep your secret? Well, forget it, honey. I may be the last to know, but I'll be the first to tell.' Her face softened suddenly, pleaded. 'I hafta. I got nowhere else to go.'

Tatum surfaced, smiled knowingly. 'You deserve what you get. Bad girls always do. Give me your wrist.' She dropped the broom and foraged under the table for the knife.

Janie stood and laid the knife carefully on the table. Clotted blood and soil stuck to it like icing on a chocolate cake. Anger filled her, traveled up her spine and exploded in her head. Who was Tatum to threaten her with punishment and then try to carry it out? It wasn't for her to decide. And it wasn't up to Betty to tell all either. In fact, it was none of their damn business what she did or didn't do. If they chose to interfere, meddle in what she knew was right, then it was up to her to stop it. Stop them.

Confusion crowded in. They knew her scheme and were planning to fight back by taking over. All of them. She blinked, tried to think straight. Fragmented thoughts surfaced and threatened to relieve her of control. She shook her head and tried to force the thoughts back to their dark, murky depths again.

You must be punished.

Aw, I'll clean it up. C'mon.

Bad girl, Janie. Very, very bad.

Who'll clean your room?

The knife, Janie. Give me the knife.

She reached for the filthy knife, ran it broadside against her green velveteen dress, and held it high to catch the sparkle of the kitchen light. She took a deep breath and let calm settle over her. She was in charge now, she was the one who made the rules. And although she hadn't created them, she could end their miserable existence. All of them.

Who could stop her? Certainly not the hiding one. *She* cringed in the dark corner of the mind and tried to make herself very small and insignificant. Almost invisible.

There was only one thing left to do.

She plunged the knife into her skinny belly.

It tickled. Almost.

A light smile fell across her lips before she blacked out.

Pounding. There. At the front door. Insistent pounding that brought her to weak consciousness.

They mumbled to themselves, banged on the front door until it cracked but held, and shouted out for someone to answer. Their footsteps left the front porch and quickly rounded the corner of the house to approach the back door.

Her belly hurt, a stinging, burning hurt. Tears ran down her face. She raised her head ever so slightly and saw the torn, bleeding bodies under the table. 'Mother? Beau?' She twisted away from them and stopped with the searing pain.

A face loomed in the broken window, then a second. The first turned away with a retching sound, the other screamed for help.

She whined. Nothing would help them now, it was too late. Too late. 'Momma?' The whine turned to a wail, a keening of horrible realization, then stopped, cut short.

The newest one, a baby, sat up in an awkward, swaying attempt at balance, then reached out to touch a still hand for a game of pat-a-cake. Her lips jutted out in a pout when they wouldn't play.

They were cold. Somebody had made them cold.

***Wendy Webb** is an Atlanta-based writer who has traveled the globe and, as a registered nurse and a professional educator, has worked in China and Hungary. An interest in acting landed her roles in movies such as S.P Somtow's* The Laughing Dead, *as well as work with the Atlanta Radio Theater. Her short stories have appeared in the* Shadows *series of anthologies,* Women of Darkness, Confederacy of the Dead, *and* Deathport. *She is the co-editor of the* Phobias *anthologies published by Pocket Books and the forthcoming* Gothic Ghosts *anthology from Tor Books.*

The Maiden

BY

RICHARD LAYMON

'I DON'T know about this,' I said.

'What's not to know?' Cody asked. He was driving. His car was a Jeep Cherokee, and he had it in four-wheel drive. We'd been bouncing along a dirt road through a forest for about half an hour, it was dark as hell out there except for the headlights, and I didn't know how much farther it might be to our destination, a place supposedly called Lost Lake.

'What if we break down?' I asked.

'We aren't gonna break down,' Cody said.

'It sounds like the car's shaking to pieces.'

'Don't be such a weenie,' said Rudy, who sat in the passenger seat.

Rudy was Cody's best pal. They were both a couple of pretty cool guys. In a way, I felt very honored that they'd invited me to come with them. But I felt nervous, too. Maybe they'd asked me to come along because I'm the new kid in school and they just wanted to be nice and get to know me better. On the other hand, maybe they planned to screw me.

I don't mean screw in the literal sense. There was nothing the least bit funny about Cody or Rudy, and they both had girlfriends.

Rudy's girl wasn't much. Her name was Alice. She looked like someone had taken hold of her by the head and feet, then stretched her out till she was way too long and skinny.

Cody's girl was Lois Garnett. Everything about Lois was perfect. Except for one thing: she *knew* that she was perfect. In other words, she was a snot.

I had a bad case of the hots for Lois, anyway. How could I not? All you've got to do is look at her, and she'll drive you crazy. But I made the mistake of getting caught, last week. She dropped her pencil on the floor in Chemistry. When she bent down to pick it up, I had a view straight down the front of her blouse. Even though she had a bra on, the view was pretty terrific. The problem is, she looked up and saw where my eyes were aimed. She muttered, 'What're you looking at, asshole?'

'Tit,' I answered. I can be a wiseguy sometimes.

It's a good thing looks can't kill.

Boyfriends can, though. Which was one reason I was a little bit worried about going off into the woods in the middle of the night with Cody and Rudy.

Nobody had mentioned the incident, though.

Not so far.

Maybe Lois hadn't told Cody about it and I had nothing to worry about.

On the other hand . . .

I figured it was worth the risk. I mean, what was the worst that could happen? It's not like they would actually try to kill me just for looking down Lois's blouse.

What they *said* they wanted to do was set me up with some gal.

I had been eating my lunch in the quad, just that afternoon, when Cody and Rudy came over and started talking to me.

'You doing anything tonight?' Cody asked.

'What do you mean?'

'He means,' Rudy said, 'we know this babe that thinks you're hot stuff. She wants to *see* you, know what I mean? Tonight.'

'Tonight? Me?'

'Midnight,' Cody said.

'You sure you've got the right guy?'

'We're sure.

'Elmo Baine?'

'You think we're morons?' Rudy asked, sounding steamed. 'We *know* your name. *Everybody* knows your name.'

'You're the one she wants,' Cody said. 'How about it?'

'Gosh, I don't know.'

'What's not to know?' Rudy asked.

'Well . . . Who is she?'

'What do you care?' Rudy asked. 'She wants you, man. How many babes want you?'

'Well . . . I'd sort of like to know who she is before I make up my mind.'

'She told us not to tell you,' Cody explained.

'Wants it to be a surprise,' Rudy added.

'Yeah, but I mean . . . How do I know she isn't some sort of a . . . you know . . .'

'A dog?' Rudy suggested.

'Well, yeah.'

Cody and Rudy looked at each other and shook their heads. Then Cody said, 'She's hot stuff, take my word on it. This might be the best offer you ever get, Elmo. You don't wanta blow it.'

'Well . . . Can't you tell me who she is?'

'Nope.'

'Is she someone I know?'

'She knows you,' Rudy pointed out. 'And she *wants* to know you a lot better.'

'Don't blow it,' Cody told me again.

'Well,' I said. 'I guess . . . okay.'

After that, we made plans about where and when I would meet their car.

I didn't ask if 'anyone else' would be going with us, but I figured there was a chance they might show up with Alice and

Lois. The possibility had me really excited. As the day went on, I got myself so sure Lois would come along that I pretty much forgot all about the mystery girl.

I fixed myself up and snuck out of the house in plenty of time to meet the car. When it showed up, though, it didn't have anyone in it except Cody and Rudy. I guess my disappointment must've showed.

'Something wrong?' Cody asked.

'No. Nothing. I'm just a little nervous.'

Rudy grinned at me over his shoulder. 'You sure smell good.'

'Just some Old Spice.'

'You'll have her licking you.'

'Cut it out,' Cody told him.

'So,' I said, 'where are we going? I mean, I know you're not supposed to tell me *who* she is, but I'm sort of curious about exactly *where* you're taking me.'

'Can we tell him?' Rudy asked.

'I guess so. Have you ever been out to Lost Lake, Elmo?'

'Lost Lake? Never heard of it.'

'You have now,' Rudy told me.

'Is that where she lives?' I asked.

'It's where she wants to meet you,' Cody said.

'She's sort of a nature girl,' Rudy explained.

'Besides,' Cody said, 'it's a great place for fooling around. Way out in the woods, a nice little lake, and you've got all the privacy in the world.'

That crummy dirt road seemed to go on forever. The Jeep shook and rattled. Branches or something squeaked against the sides. And talk about dark.

There's nothing like a forest when it comes to darkness. Maybe that's because the trees block out the moonlight. It was like driving through a tunnel. The headlights lit up the stuff just in front of us, and the taillights made a red glow out the back window. Everything else was black.

I was okay for a while, but I started to get more and more

nervous. The deeper into the forest we went, the worse I felt. They'd told me that the car wouldn't break down, and Rudy had called me a weenie for even asking. A while later, though, I went ahead and said, 'Are you sure we aren't lost?'

'I don't get lost,' Cody said.

'How are we doing on gas?'

'We're fine.'

'What a pussy,' Rudy said.

What a shithead, I thought. But I didn't say it. I didn't say anything. I mean, we were out in the boonies and nobody knew I was with these guys. If I made them mad, things might get pretty drastic.

Of course, I realized that things might take a turn for the ugly, anyway. This whole deal could be a setup. I hoped not, but you just never know.

The trouble is, you can't make any friends at all if you don't take a chance. Whether or not a friendship with Cody and Rudy was worth this much of a risk – and I was having some real doubts about that – an in with them would mean an in with Lois.

I could just see it. There might be triple dates: Cody and Lois, Rudy and Alice, Elmo and Mystery Girl. We would travel crowded in the Jeep. We'd sit together at the movies. We'd go on picnics, have swimming parties, maybe take camping trips – and fool around. My actual partner would be Mystery Girl, but Lois would be right there where I could watch her, listen to her, and maybe more. Maybe we would trade partners sometimes. Maybe we would even have orgies.

No telling what might happen if they accepted me.

I guess I would do just about anything to find out – even take a ride into the middle of nowhere with these guys, where they might be planning to leave me stranded, or beat me up, or worse.

I was pretty scared. The deeper we got into the woods, the more I suspected a bad time from these two. But I kept my mouth shut after Rudy called me a pussy. I just sat there in the backseat and worried and kept telling myself that they didn't have a good enough reason to really demolish me. All I'd done was take a look down Lois's front.

'Here we are,' Cody said.

We had come to the end of the road.

Ahead, lit by the white beams of the headlights, was a cleared place big enough for half a dozen cars to park. There were logs on the ground to show you where to stop. Off beyond the parking area, I saw a trash barrel, a couple of picnic tables, and a brick fireplace for barbecues.

Ours was the only car.

We were the only people.

'I guess she isn't here yet,' I said.

'You never know,' Cody told me.

'There aren't any other cars.'

'Who says she drove?' Rudy said.

Cody steered toward one of the logs, stopped, and shut off the engine.

I couldn't see any lake. I almost made a crack about it being lost, but didn't feel much like joking around at the moment.

Cody shut off the headlights. Blackness dropped on us, but only for a second. Then both the front doors swung open, making the overhead light come on.

'Let's go,' Cody said.

They both climbed out. I did, too.

When they shut their doors, the light inside the Jeep died. But we were standing in the open. The sky was spread above us. The moon was almost full and the stars were out.

Shadows were black, but everything else was lit up, almost like a dirty white powder had been sprinkled around.

That was one extremely bright moon.

'This way,' Cody said.

We walked through the picnic area. I've got to tell you, my legs were shaking.

Just past the tables the ground slanted down to a pale area that reminded me of how snow looks at night – only this seemed dimmer than snow. A sand beach? It had to be.

Beyond the curve of the beach, the lake was black. It looked beautiful, the way the moon made a silvery path on the water. The silver came straight at us from the far end of the lake. It stretched past the side of a small, wooded island and came all the way to the beach.

Cody had said that this place had 'all the privacy in the world,' and he was right. Except for the moon and stars, there were no lights in sight: none from boats on the water, or from docks along the shores, or from cabins in the dark woods around the lake. The way things looked, we might've been the only three people for miles around.

I wished I wasn't feeling so nervous. This could be a great place if you weren't here with a couple of guys possibly planning to mess you over. A great place to be alone with a really terrific babe, for instance.

'I don't think she's here,' I said.

'Don't be so sure,' Rudy told me.

'Maybe she changed her mind about coming. I mean, it's a school night, and everything.'

'It's gotta be a school night,' Cody explained. 'Too many people here, weekends. Look at this, we've got the whole place to ourselves.'

'But where's the girl?'

'Jeez,' Rudy said, 'will you knock off the whining?'

'Yeah,' Cody said. 'Relax and enjoy yourself.'

Just then we walked out on the sand. After a few steps both the guys stopped. They took off their shoes and socks. I took off mine, too. Even though it was a warm night, the sand felt cool with my feet bare.

Next, they took their shirts off. There was nothing wrong with doing that; they're guys and the night was warm and a soft breeze was blowing. But it made me so nervous, I got a cold wad in the pit of my stomach. Cody and Rudy had really fine physiques. And even in the moonlight you could see they had good tans.

I untucked my shirt and unfastened the buttons.

They left their shirts on the beach with the shoes and socks. I kept mine on. Nobody said anything about it. As we walked down the sand toward the water, I almost decided to go ahead and take my shirt off. I wanted to be like them. And I sure liked the way the breeze felt. I just couldn't do it, though.

We stopped at the water's edge.

'This is great,' Cody said. He raised his arms and stretched. 'Feel that breeze.'

Rudy stretched, flexed his muscles, and groaned. 'Man,' he said, 'I sure wish the babes were here.'

'Maybe we'll come back Friday, bring 'em. You can come, too, Elmo. Bring your new honey and we'll have ourselves a big ol' party.'

'Really?'

'Sure.'

'Wow! That'd be . . . really neat.'

It was exactly what I wanted to hear! My worries had been stupid. These two were the greatest pals a guy could have.

A few more nights, and I'd be right here at the beach with Lois.

I suddenly felt terrific!

'Maybe we oughta just, you know, put off everything till then,' I said. 'My, uh, date . . . she isn't here anyway. Maybe we should just leave, and we can *all* come Friday night. I wouldn't mind waiting till then to meet her.'

'That'd be okay with me,' Cody said.

'Same here,' said Rudy.

'Great!'

Smiling, Cody tilted his head sideways. 'Wouldn't be okay with *her,* though. She wants you tonight.'

'Lucky bastard,' Rudy said, and slugged my arm.

Rubbing my arm, I explained, 'But she isn't here.'

Cody nodded. 'You're right. She's not here. She's *there.*' He pointed at the lake.

'What?' I asked.

'On the island.'

'On the *island?*' I'm no expert on judging distances, but the island looked pretty far out. A couple of hundred yards, at least. 'What's she doing *there?*'

'Waiting for you, lover boy.' Rudy punched my arm again.

'Quit it.'

'Sorry.' He gave me another slug.

'Cut it out,' Cody told him. To me, he said, 'That's where she wants to meet you.'

'There?'

'It's perfect. You won't have to worry about anyone barging in on you.'

'She's on the *island*?' I was having a fairly difficult time believing it.

'That's right.'

'How'd she get there?'

'She swam.'

'She's sort of a nature girl,' Rudy said. He'd pointed that out once before.

'How am *I* supposed to get there?'

'Same way she did,' Cody said.

'Swim?'

'You know how to swim, don't you?'

'Yeah. Sort of.'

'Sort of?'

'I mean, I'm not exactly the world's greatest swimmer.'

'Can you make it that far?'

'I don't know.'

'Shit,' Rudy said. 'I knew he was a pussy.'

Screw you, I thought. I felt like slamming him in the face, but all I did was stand there.

'We don't want him drowning on us,' Cody said.

'He won't drown. Shit, his *fat*'ll keep him up.'

Part of me wanted to pound Rudy for saying that, and part of me wanted to cry.

'I can swim to that island if I want to,' I blurted out. 'Maybe I don't want to, that's all. I bet there isn't even any girl there.'

'What do you mean?' Cody asked.

'It's just a trick,' I said. 'There isn't any girl, and you know it. It's just a trick to make me try to swim to the island. Then you'll probably drive off and leave me, or something.'

Cody stared at me. 'It's no wonder you don't have any friends.'

Rudy nudged him with an elbow. 'Elmo here thinks we're a couple of *assholes.*'

'I didn't say that.'

'Yeah, right,' Cody said. 'We try to do you a favor, and you think we're out to screw you. Fuck it. Let's go.'

'What?' I asked.

'Let's go.'

They both turned their backs to the lake and started walking up the beach toward the place where they'd left their stuff.

'We're leaving?' I asked.

Cody glanced back at me. 'That's what you want, isn't it? Come on, we'll take you home.'

'To your mommy,' Rudy added.

I stood my ground. 'Wait!' I called. 'Hold on, okay? Just a second. Let's talk this over, okay?'

'Forget it,' Cody said. 'You're a loser.'

'I am not!'

They crouched and picked up their shirts.

'Hey, look, I'm sorry. I'll do it. Okay? I believe you. I'll swim to the island.'

Cody and Rudy looked at each other. Cody shook his head.

'Please!' I yelled. 'Give me another chance!'

'You think we're a couple of liars.'

'No, I don't. Honest. I was just confused, that's all. It's just strange. I've never had a girl . . . like, *send* for me. Okay? I'll go. I'll do it.'

'Yeah, all right,' Cody said. He sounded reluctant, though.

They tossed their shirts down. As they walked back to where I was standing, they kept shaking their heads and looking at each other.

'We don't wanta be here all night,' Cody said to me. He checked his wristwatch. 'What we'll do, we'll give you an hour.'

'And then leave without me?'

'Did I say that? We're not gonna leave without you.'

'He does think we're assholes,' Rudy said.

'I do not.'

'If you're not back,' Cody said, 'we'll yell or toot the horn or something. Just figure you'll have about an hour with her.'

'Don't keep us waiting,' Rudy warned. 'You wanta screw her till dawn, do it some time when we ain't your chauffeurs.'

Screw her till dawn?

'Okay,' I said. I faced the water and took a deep breath. 'Here goes. Anything else I need to know?'

'Are you planning to keep your jeans on?' Cody asked.

'Yeah!'

'I wouldn't.'

'They'll drag you down,' Rudy pointed out.

'You'd better leave them here.'

I didn't like the sound of that at all.

'I don't know,' I said.

Cody shook his head. 'We aren't gonna take them.'

'Who'd wanta *touch* 'em?'

'The thing is,' Cody went on, 'those jeans'll soak up a lot of water. They'll get damned heavy.'

'You'll never make it to the island in 'em,' Rudy said.

'They'll sink you.'

'Or *she* will.'

'What?'

'Don't listen to Rudy. He's full of crap.'

'The Maiden,' Rudy said. 'She'll get you if you don't swim fast enough. You gotta lose the jeans.'

'He's just trying to scare you.'

'The *Maiden*? There's a maiden who's gonna get me or drown me or something?'

'No no no,' Cody said. He scowled at Rudy. 'Did you have to go and mention her? You idiot!'

'Hey, man. He wants to keep his jeans on. He keeps 'em on, he'll never stand a chance of out-swimming her. She'll nail him, for sure.'

'There's no such thing as the Maiden.'

'Is, too.'

'What are you two talking about?' I blurted.

Cody faced me, shaking his head. 'The Maiden of Lost Lake. It's some bullshit legend.'

'She got Willy Glitten last summer,' Rudy said.

'Willy got a cramp, that's all.'

'That's what you think.'

'That's what I know. He ate that damn pepperoni pizza just before he went in. That's what killed him, not some stupid ghost.'

'The Maiden ain't a ghost. That shows how much you know. Ghosts can't grab you and . . .'

'Neither can gals who've been dead for forty years.'

'*She* can.'

'Bull.'

'*What are you two talking about?*' I snapped.

They both looked at me.

'You wanta tell him?' Cody asked Rudy.

'You go ahead.'

'You're the one that brought it up,' Cody said.

'And you're telling me I'm full of shit. So you tell it your way. I'm not saying another word about her.'

'Would *some*body please tell me?'

'All right, all right,' Cody said. 'Here's the deal. There's this story about the Maiden of the Lost Lake. Part of it's true, and part of it's bull.'

Rudy made a snorty noise.

'The true part is that a gal drowned out there one night about forty years ago.'

'The night of her senior prom,' Rudy added. He'd broken his word about keeping his mouth shut, but Cody didn't call him on it.

'Yeah,' Cody said. 'It was prom night, and after the dance was over her date drove her out here. The whole idea was to fool around, you know? So they park in the lot back there and start in. Things get going pretty good. Too good for the gal.'

'She was a virgin,' Rudy pointed out. 'That's how come they call her the Maiden.'

'Yeah. Anyway, it's all getting out of hand, as far as she's concerned. So to slow things down, she says they oughta go and take a swim in the lake. The guy figures she means a skinny dip, so he's all for it.'

'Nobody else was around,' Rudy said.

'That's what she thinks, anyway,' Cody said. 'So they climb out of the car and start stripping. The guy takes off everything. Not her, though. She insists on keeping her underwear on.'

'Her panties and bra,' Rudy explained.

'So they throw their clothes in the car and run down here to the beach and go in the lake. They swim around for a while. Play games. Splash each other. That sort of thing. Then they get hold of each other and, you know . . . things start getting hot again.'

'They were still in the water?' I asked.

'Yeah. Out where it isn't very deep.'

I wondered how he knew all this.

'Pretty soon she lets him unhook her bra. It was the first time he'd ever gotten that far.'

'Finally got to feel her titties,' Rudy said.

'He figures he's died and gone to heaven. And he figures he's finally gonna score. So then he tries to pull her panties down.'

'He was gonna put it to her, right there in the lake,' Rudy explained.

'Yeah. But then she tells him to stop. He doesn't listen, though. He just goes ahead and tries to pull her panties down. So she starts fighting him. I mean, this guy is bare-ass naked and probably has a boner to beat the band, so she *knows* what's gonna happen if he gets her panties down. And she isn't about to let it. She pounds on him and scratches him and kicks him until she finally manages to get loose and head for shore. Then, just when she's wading out of the lake, her boyfriend starts shouting. He yells, "Guys! Quick! She's getting away!" And all of a sudden these five other guys come running down the beach at her.'

'They're his buddies,' Rudy explained.

'A bunch of losers who hadn't even *gone* to the prom. The guy, the Maiden's date? He'd collected five bucks from each of them and set up the whole deal. They'd driven out earlier that night, hidden their car in the woods, then waited around, drinking beer. By the time the guy showed up with the Maiden, they were plastered out of their minds . . .'

'And horny enough,' Rudy added, 'to fuck the crack of dawn.'

'The Maiden never had a chance,' Cody said. 'They caught her while she was running up the beach, and they held her down while her prom date banged her. That was part of the deal, that he'd get to go first.'

'Didn't want no sloppy seconds,' Rudy explained.

'After him, all the rest of them took turns.'

'Two or *three* turns each,' Rudy said. 'Some of 'em nailed her in the butt, too.'

'That's . . . awful,' I muttered. It *was* cruel and terrible – which made me feel guilty about how the story made me sort of hard.

'She was messed up pretty good by the time they were finished with her,' Cody explained. 'They hadn't beaten on her, though. There were four or five of them holding her down the whole time, so they never had to punch her out or anything like that. They figured she'd look all right once she'd washed up and gotten dressed. The plan was for the boyfriend to drive her back home just as if nothing had happened. They figured she wouldn't dare tell on them. Back in those days, you looked like the town slut if you got yourself gang-raped. She'd be ruined if she tried to get them in trouble.

'So they tell her to go in the lake and clean herself up, and while they're thinking everything's gonna turn out great, she goes stumbling into the water and wades out farther and farther. Next thing they know, she's swimming hellbent for the island. They don't know if she's trying to escape or wants to drown herself. Either way, they can't let it happen. So they go and swim out after her.'

'All but one,' Rudy said.

'One of the guys didn't know how to swim,' Cody explained. 'So he stayed on shore and watched. What happened is, the Maiden never reached the island.'

'She almost made it,' Rudy said.

'Had about fifty yards to go, and then she went under.'

'God,' I muttered.

'Then the *guys* went under,' Cody said. 'Some were faster swimmers than others, and they were spread out pretty good. The guy on shore, he could see them in the moonlight. One by one they each sort of let out a quick little cry and splashed around for a few seconds, and vanished under the water. The gal's prom date was the last to go. When he saw his buddies were going down all around him, he turned tail and tried for shore. He made it about halfway. Then he yelled out, "No! No! Let *go* of me! Please! I'm sorry! Please!" Then, down he went.'

'Wow,' I muttered.

'The guy who'd seen it all, he jumped in one of the cars and went speeding for town. He was so drunk and shook up, he crashed after he got out to the main road. He thought he was dying, so he confessed while they were taking him to the hospital. Told everything.

'It was a couple of hours before a search party made it back here to the lake. And you know what they found?'

I shook my head.

'The guys. The boyfriend and his four buddies. They were stretched out side by side, right here on the beach. They were all naked. They were lying on their backs with their eyes wide open, gazing up at the sky.'

'Dead?' I asked.

'Dead as carp,' Rudy said.

'Drowned,' Cody said.

'Jeez,' I said. 'And it's supposed to be the Maiden who did it? She actually drowned *all* those guys?'

'You couldn't exactly call them guys anymore,' Cody said.

Rudy grinned, then chomped his teeth together a couple of times.

'She *bit* off their . . . ?' I couldn't bring myself to say it.

'Nobody knows for sure *who* did it,' Cody said. 'Someone or something did. I'd say she was the most likely candidate, wouldn't you?'

'I guess.'

'Anyway, they never found the Maiden.'

'Or the missing weenies,' Rudy added.

'People say she drowned out there on her way to the island, and it was her ghost that took vengeance on those guys.'

'It's not her *ghost*,' Rudy said. 'Ghosts can't do shit. It's *her*. She's, you know, like "the living dead." A zombie.'

'Bull,' Cody said.

'She just sort of hangs around out there under the water and waits till a guy tries to swim by. Then she goes for him. Like she did Willy Glitten and all those others. She gets 'em by the dingus with her teeth—'

Cody elbowed him. 'She does not.'

'Does, too! And pulls 'em down by it.'

I suddenly laughed. I couldn't help it. I'd been pretty wrapped up in the story, and actually believing most of it, up till Rudy said that about the Maiden turning into some sort of a dick-hungry zombie. Maybe I can be a little gullible sometimes, but I'm not a complete dope.

'You think it's funny?' Rudy asked.

I quit laughing.

'You wouldn't think it's so funny if you knew how many guys have drowned trying to swim out to the island.'

'If they drowned,' I said, 'I'll bet it wasn't because the Maiden got them.'

'That's what *I* say,' Cody said. 'Like I told you, only part of the story's true. I mean, I'm willing to believe the business about the girl getting raped and then drowning. But the rest of it, I think somebody made it up. I don't think it's true about the guys getting *picked off* when they went after her. Much less that she bit off their cocks. I mean, that's complete bull. It's just somebody's idea of poetic justice, you know?'

'You can believe whatever you want,' Rudy said. 'My gramps was there with the bunch that found the guys that night. And he told my dad about it, and my dad told me.'

'I know, I know,' Cody said.

'And he *didn't* just tell me it to scare me.'

'Sure, he did. 'Cause he knows you're just the kind of guy that might pull a stunt like those jerks.'

'I never raped nobody in my life.'

'That's 'cause you're scared you'll get your whang bit off.'

'I sure won't go swimming in *there*,' Rudy said. He stuck an arm out and pointed at the lake. 'No way. You believe what you want, the Maiden's in there and she's just waiting.'

Cody, looking at me, shook his head. 'She *is* out there, I guess. I mean, I think she did drown that night. But that was forty years ago. There's probably nothing much left of her by now. And she doesn't have anything to do with the drownings we've had. People just drown sometimes. It happens. They get muscle cramps . . .' He shrugged. 'But I sure won't hold it against you if you've changed your mind about swimming out to the island.'

'I don't know.' I stared out at it. There was a lot of black water between me and that patch of wooded land. 'If so many people have drowned . . .'

'It's not that many. Only one guy last year. And he'd just finished wolfing down a pepperoni pizza.'

'The Maiden got him,' Rudy muttered.

'Did they find his body?' I asked.

'No,' Cody said.

'So you don't know if he'd been . . . eaten.'

'I'd bet on it,' Rudy said.

I looked Cody in the eyes. They were in shadows, actually, so I couldn't see them. 'But *you* don't believe any of the stuff about the Maiden . . . you know, waiting around in the lake to, uh, do that to guys who swim by?'

'You've gotta be kidding me. Only dorks like Rudy believe in crap like that.'

'Thanks, pal,' Rudy said to him.

I took a deep breath, and sighed. I looked once more toward the island, and saw all that blackness along the way. 'I guess maybe I'd better skip it,' I said.

Cody gave Rudy an elbow in the side. 'See what you did? Why didn't you keep your big mouth shut?'

'*You* told him the story!'

'*You* brought it up in the first place!'

'He had a right to know! You can't just send a guy out like that without warning him! And he was gonna wear his *jeans*! Your only chance is if you can outswim her, and you can't do that with jeans on.'

'Okay, okay,' Cody said. 'Anyway, it doesn't matter. He's not going.'

'We shouldn't have tried to make him in the first place,' Rudy said. 'The whole idea was dumb. I mean, you-know-who's as hot as they come, but she ain't worth *dying* for.'

'Well,' Cody said, 'that's what she wanted to find out, isn't it?' He turned to me. 'That's the main reason she picked the island. It was supposed to be a test. What she told me, if you aren't man enough to make the swim, you aren't man enough to deserve her. The thing is, she didn't figure on Bozo here shooting off his mouth about the Maiden.'

'It's not that,' I said. 'You don't think I believe that stuff, do you? But, you know, I'm really not such a great swimmer.'

'It's all right,' Cody said. 'You don't have to explain.'

Rudy said, 'We just gonna leave now?'

'Guess so.' Cody turned toward the lake, cupped his hands to the sides of his mouth, and yelled, 'Ashley!'

'Shit!' Rudy blurted. 'You said her name!'

'Ooops.'

Ashley?

I knew of only one Ashley.

'Ashley Brooks?' I asked.

Cody nodded and shrugged. 'It was supposed to be a surprise. And you weren't supposed to find out at all if you didn't make the swim.'

My heart was slamming.

Not that I believed a word of it. Ashley Brooks could not possibly have the hots for me and be waiting for me on that island. She was probably the one girl in school who was just as stupendous as Lois. Beautiful golden hair, eyes like a summer morning sky, a face to dream about, and a body . . . a body that didn't quit. Talk about *built*!

But her personality wasn't at all like Lois. She had a kind of innocence and sweetness that made her seem like she was from another world – almost too good to be true.

I couldn't come close to believing that Ashley even knew I existed.

She was too much to hope for.

'It can't be Ashley Brooks,' I said.

'She knew you'd be shocked,' Cody told me. 'That's one reason she wanted us to keep it secret. She wanted to see the surprise on your face.'

'Oh, sure.'

Facing the island again, Cody called out, *'Ashley!* Might as well show yourself. Elmo's not interested!'

'I didn't say that!' I gasped.

'Ashley!' Cody called again.

We waited.

Maybe half a minute later, a white glow appeared through the trees and bushes near the tip of the island. The glow seemed to be moving. It was very bright. It probably came from one of those propane lanterns people use on camping trips.

'She's gonna be awfully disappointed,' Cody muttered.

A few more seconds passed. Then she stepped out onto the rocky shore, the lantern held off away from her side – probably to avoid burning herself.

'And you thought we was liars,' Rudy said.

'My God,' I muttered, staring at her. She was awfully far away. I could only make out vague things. Like the goldness of her hair. And her shape. Her shape *really* caught my eye. At first I thought she was wearing some sort of skin-tight garment – tights or leotards maybe. If that's what she had on, though, it must've been the same color as her face. And it must've had a couple of dark spots where her nipples belonged, and a golden arrowhead pointing down at . . .

'Holy shit,' Rudy said. 'She's butt naked.'

'Nah,' Cody said. 'I don't think . . .'

'Sure is!'

She raised the lantern high. Then her voice drifted over the lake. 'Elll-mo? Aren't you coming?'

'Yes!' I shouted.

'I'm waiting,' she called. Then she turned around and walked toward the woods.

'She *is* naked,' Cody said. 'Man, I don't believe it.'

'*I* do,' I said. She was out of sight by the time I got my jeans off. I kept my boxers on. They were a little limp in the elastic, so

I hitched them up as I headed for the water. I glanced back at the guys. 'See you later.'

'Yeah,' Cody muttered. He seemed distracted. Maybe *he* wanted to be the one going to the island.

'Swim fast,' Rudy said. 'Don't let the Maiden get you.'

'Sure,' I said.

As I waded into the lake, I could still see the pale light from Ashley's lantern and knew she was in the woods, just out of sight, naked and waiting for me.

The night was pale with moonlight and stars. A warm breeze drifted against my skin. The water around my ankles felt even warmer than the breeze. It made soft lapping sounds and climbed my legs. In my loose boxer shorts I felt almost naked.

I trembled as if I were freezing, but I wasn't cold at all.

It was just from too much excitement.

This can't be happening, I thought. This sort of thing just doesn't happen to guys like me. It's too fabulous.

But it is happening!

I'd seen her with my own eyes.

As the warm water wrapped my thighs and I imagined how she would look close up, I could feel myself rise hard and slide out through the fly of my boxers.

Nobody can see, I told myself. It's too dark, and my back's to the guys.

A couple more steps, and the lake water took me in. It was all soft, sliding warmth. I shivered with the pleasure of it.

'Better get *moving*!' Rudy yelled. 'The Maiden's homing in on you.'

I scowled over my shoulder at him, angry because he'd shouted and ruined the mood. He and Cody were still standing beside each other on the beach.

'You can quit trying to scare me,' I called. 'You just want to make me chicken out.'

'She's too good for you, barf bag.'

'Ha! Guess *she* doesn't think so.'

The water was up to my shoulders by then, so I shoved at the bottom and started to swim. Like I said before, I'm not the greatest swimmer in the world. My crawl pretty much stinks. I've got an okay breast stroke, though. It's not fast like the crawl, but it gets you where you're going. And it doesn't wear you out. Also, you can see where you're going if you keep your head up.

I like the name, breast stroke. But most of all I like how it feels to be gliding softly through the water that way. The warm fluid just slides and rubs against you, all over.

Or would, if you didn't have anything on.

Like boxer shorts. They were down low on my hips, clinging, trapping me. They wouldn't even let me spread my legs enough for good kicks.

I thought about taking them off, but didn't dare.

Anyway, they didn't have me *completely* trapped. I was still sticking out the fly, and I loved having it out and feeling the caress of the water.

This was all the more exciting because of the Maiden.

The risk.

Offering her bait.

Taunting her with it.

Not that I believed for one minute in all that garbage about the Maiden drowning guys and devouring their whangs. It was like Cody said: bull. But the idea of it turned me on.

You know?

I didn't believe in her, but I could picture her. In my mind, she was sort of suspended in the darkness maybe ten feet below me, her head about even with my waist. She was naked and beautiful. In fact, she looked sort of like Ashley or Lois. She was down there, drifting on her back, not swimming but keeping pace with me, anyhow.

The darkness didn't matter; we could see each other through it. Her skin was so pale that it seemed to glow. She was grinning up at me.

Slowly, she began to rise.

Rising to the bait.

I could see her gliding closer. And I knew she wasn't going to bite. The guys had it all wrong. She was going to suck.

I kept breast-stroking along, imagining the Maiden coming up and latching on. The guys had meant the story to scare me. It *had* scared me. But the mind is a great thing. You can turn things around. With a bit of mental legerdemain I'd changed their dong-chomping zombie into a seductive water nymph.

But I told myself to stop thinking about her. What with everything else – the sexy prom night story, seeing Ashley naked, the feel of the warm water – I was so excited that the last thing I needed was to imagine the Maiden underneath me, naked and ready to start sucking.

I had to think about something else.

What'll I say to Ashley?

That gave me a quick scare, until I realized there wouldn't be much need to say anything. Not at first, anyway. You swim to an island for a rendezvous with a naked girl, the last thing you do is chitchat.

I raised my head a little higher and saw the glow of the lantern. It was still among the trees, just in from shore.

I'd been making good progress. I was past the halfway mark.

Getting into Maiden territory.

Yeah, right.

Come and get it, honey.

'You better quit dawdling and get your ass in gear!' Rudy shouted.

Yeah, right.

'She's gonna get you! I'm not kidding!'

'You'd better swim faster!' Cody yelled.

Cody?

But he doesn't believe in the Maiden. Why's he *telling me to swim faster?*

'Move it!' Cody shouted. 'Go!'

They're just trying to scare me, I told myself.

It worked.

Suddenly, the water no longer felt like a warm caress; it gave me chills. I was all alone on the surface of a black lake where people had drowned, where rotting bodies lurked, where the

Maiden might not really be dead after forty years and where she might be a sharp-toothed, decayed huntress with nothing in her head except revenge and a taste for penis.

Mine shrank like it wanted to hide.

Even though I knew there was no Maiden coming after me.

I started swimming hard. No more breast stroke. I churned up a storm, kicking like a madman, windmilling my arms, slapping the water. There were shouts from behind me, but I couldn't make out the words through the noise of my wild splashing.

Head up, I blinked water out of my eyes.

Not much farther to go.

I'll make it! I'm gonna make it!

Then she touched me.

I think I screamed.

As I tried to twist away from her hands, they scurried down from my shoulders, fingernails scraping my chest and belly. They didn't hurt me. But they made me tingle and squirm. I quit swimming and reached down to get them away from me. But I wasn't fast enough. Gouging some skin, they clawed at the band of my shorts. I felt a rough tug. My head went under. Choking, I quit trying to grab the Maiden. I reached up as if trying to find the rungs of a ladder that would lead me to the surface, and air. My lungs burned.

The Maiden dragged me lower and lower.

Dragged me down by my boxer shorts.

They were around my knees, then around my ankles, then gone. For a moment I was free.

I kicked for the surface. And got there. Gasping, I sucked at the night air. It took both hands to tread water. I swiveled around. Spotted Cody and Rudy standing on the beach in the moonlight. 'Help!' I yelled. 'Help! It's the Maiden!'

'Told you so!' Rudy called.

'Tough luck,' called Cody.

'Please! *Do* something!'

What they did, it looked like they each raised a hand into the moonlight and flipped me off.

Then a pair of hands underneath the water grabbed my ankles. I wanted to scream. But I took a deep breath, instead. An instant later, they yanked me down.

This is it! She's got me! Oh, God.

I clutched my genitals.

Any second, her teeth . . .

Bubbles came up.

I heard the gurgling sound they made, and felt sort of a tickle as some of them brushed against my skin.

For a second I thought the bubbles might be gas escaping from the Maiden's rotting carcass. She'd been dead forty years, though. The rotting should've been over and done with, long ago.

My next thought was *air tanks.*

Scuba gear!

I stopped kicking. I squatted, reached down between my feet, made a sudden lunge with both hands, and caught hold of some equipment that I think turned out to be her mouthpiece. I gave it a tug for all I was worth.

She must've taken in a mouthful when I did that, because the rest was fairly easy. She hardly fought back at all.

From the feel of things, she was naked except for her face mask, scuba tank, and weight belt. And she wasn't any corpse, either. Her skin was slick and cool, and she had wonderful tits with big, rubbery nipples.

I hurt her pretty bad, right there in the lake.

Then I towed her ashore at the side of the island, so the guys wouldn't be able to see us. From there I dragged her a few yards to the clearing where she'd left her lantern.

In the lantern light I saw who she was.

Though, of course, I'd already guessed.

After doing her Ashley routine to lure me over, Lois must've gotten into her scuba gear real fast and snuck into the lake for her Maiden routine.

She looked great in the lantern light. All shiny and pale, her breasts sticking out between straps. She'd already lost the face mask. I took off her tank and belt so she was naked.

She was sprawled on her back, coughing and choking and having spasms, which made her body twitch and shake in ways that were very neat to watch.

I enjoyed the show for a while. Then I started in on her. This was *the best.*

For a while she was too out of breath to make much noise. Pretty soon, though, I had her screaming.

I knew her screaming would bring Cody and Rudy to the rescue, so I started swinging her weight belt. It caved her head in nicely, and finished her off.

Then I hurried to the tip of the island. Cody and Rudy were already in the lake and swimming fast.

I planned to take them by surprise and bash their heads in, but guess what? I was spared the trouble. They got about halfway to the island. Then, one at a time, they let out squeals and went down.

I couldn't believe it.

Still can't.

But they never showed up.

I guess the Maiden got them.

Why them but not me?

Maybe the Maiden felt sorry for me, the way I was being abused by my supposed 'friends.' After all, we'd both gotten betrayed by guys we'd trusted.

Who knows? Hell, maybe Cody and Rudy suddenly got cramps, and the Maiden had nothing to do with it.

Anyway, my little excursion to Lost Lake turned out way better than I ever would've dreamed.

Lois was stupendous.

It's no wonder people like sex so much.

Anyway, I eventually sank Lois and her gear in the lake. I found the canoe she must've come over in, so then I climbed aboard and paddled back to the beach. I took Cody's Cherokee most of the way home.

I wiped it to get rid of fingerprints. Then, for good measure, I set it on fire. I made it home just fine, with a while to spare before dawn.

***Richard Laymon** is the author of over twenty-five horror novels and sixty short stories. He has received Bram Stoker award nominations for three of his books:* Flesh, Funland, *and* A Good, Secret Place. *Recent novels include* The Stake, Savage, *and* Quake. *Dick is a native of Chicago, lives in Los Angeles, and makes his living as a writer thanks to the British.*

You've Got Your Troubles, I've Got Mine . . .

BY

BOB BURDEN

I AM not well. They should have never given me this job, but this is my mission. I must sell vacuum cleaners door to door.

Vacuum cleaners! It is ridiculous, there must be some mistake, I am still recuperating from my illness. I raised an objection to the manager, but he said I was a handsome, enterprising young man and I would do fine.

Then, on the way out, he pinched my ass.

I farted.

This particular jobs program was never meant for one like me, just out of the nuthouse and hardly cured! They said I am all right now, they said I wouldn't hurt anyone.

But surely I am a victim of some clerical error, some blockhead of a bureaucrat was blundering carelessly through his boring day. The fools have sent me to sell vacuum cleaners and I'm still beset by terrible dreams, having visions, hearing voices, and behaving oddly. I find myself shouting things for no reason. I find myself making faces when people aren't looking right at me. I find myself writing so small that I couldn't read the words myself.

I'm not fit for this job.

I see water and I worry about drowning in it. I see birds and I think they might just fly down and pluck out my eyeballs with their beaks and gobble them up. When people talk to me sometimes, I often cannot understand what they are saying, like they are talking in a foreign language or their words are blurred and, later, I can't remember what they have said.

Sometimes, I just stop and stare, transfixed, at a spot on the pavement, not knowing what it is or how it got there.

I fear my feet might fall off at any time.

As the members of our sales crew are dropped off at the various streets assigned them, I am pensive. And when they come to my street I have a loathsome, foreboding feeling. I get out of the car – I am alone now – I stand on the sidewalk, the car drives off, and I am alone with no one in sight for as far as the eye can see. I look around.

I hear noise from open windows, radios, and TVs playing; blocks away a car goes across the street. I want to throw the vacuum cleaner down, smashing it on the pavement, but somehow I go on.

My first building, an old and worn apartment, is nothing special. Maybe there are two or three people here who will buy vacuum cleaners. Yes, I would love to show up at the end of the day with more sales than everyone else. During the training session over the last week, I said little and kept to myself. I think they had no idea I was a madman, at least most of them, and I chose to keep it that way.

These apartments were built after World War II, filled with fresh young optimistic couples just starting out, who went to the movies three nights a week and ate lots of pot roast. After twenty years the apartments were slums. Now the building is renovated and full of fresh young optimistic couples again.

In the long hours of the afternoon every apartment building hallway is like a hallway of the dead. Inside these sepulchers there are ghosts, the echoes of the people who are at work.

I feel the wallpaper as I walk along. I will start on the top floor and work my way down.

But on the top floor no one seems to be home, until the last door. A bright and cheerful woman answers. She has a clean face and friendly eyes.

Before she can say no, I am talking . . .

'Hello, how are you – and how are you today – isn't it a beautiful wonderful day – my name is Ron, (not my real name of course) and I'm here to demonstrate our new Keeno-Kirby-Turbo Household Cleaner – perfectly free . . .'

'But, sir . . .'

'Excuse me, sir . . .'

Never minding her protests I drone on endlessly with my monotonous ramble that never stops, no pause, no periods, no commas.

She tries to say something: 'I'm sorry, sir . . .'

Her cheerfulness soon fades to a blank face – what is it? Melancholy? Fear? Regret? I talk faster and faster. She backs up now, with a look in her eyes; almost horrified. She puts her hand to her mouth. I have seen this look before. Something is not right. It makes me nervous when they do that; it means something, always bad, will happen . . .

I keep talking as I have been trained, flooding her with words. I have spent hours memorizing all this. My words are to answer her every objection before she asks it.

She backs up slowly as I move forward into the room. Around the room we go, she backing up, myself in close pursuit droning on.

Then she stumbles.

Her feet, tangled in the vacuum cord as we circled around the room . . .

Ah! *She is falling out the window!* Right in front of my eyes – my God – a big picture window – no screen – *we are four floors up*— Oh! She grabs a curtain – curtain ripping – her ass goes perfectly out the wide-open window – head bumps but clears window top – oh, no! It all happened so fast . . .

I feel panic! Fear! A bad, sick feeling. I put my hands up near my ears – yell, 'No!'

No! I look down out the window. She is lying on the pavement, obviously dead, legs and head twisted at odd angles like a broken doll. A small stream of blood is starting. Damn, I feel bad now . . .

Oh, oh, what have I done, what have I done?

I gather my vacuum and things and head out.

There's some money and a shopping list on a shelving unit by the door. 'I'm sure she won't be needing this now,' I think, and grab the money.

I close the door behind me. No one will know. Surely, if I just leave . . . But wait! What if she's still alive?

I rush down the stairs.

Below on the street, I am disoriented. Which side of the building am I on?

There she is. Oh, look at this. A stream of blood, her brains coming out. No . . . she's dead.

I notice now what a pretty woman she was, young and clean. Her golden locks are awry, her face is on its side, mouth open, eyes staring off.

At this moment I have a bad thought. It occurs to me to stick the vacuum cleaner nozzle up her cunt. Just out of the blue, strange ideas hit me at dramatic or horrible moments like this.

No! I push the horrible thought out of my mind! I shudder in disgust at it! What an awful thing to do.

But then it occurs to me that if I commit cunnilingus on her – some people still feel and hear for minutes, even hours, after their death – that it shall soothe her last moments of her life with pacific and benign bliss. Yes!

I hardly know her, yet I feel like I know her now. I set my vacuum down and go to it. It is a strange thing to do, but I feel so sorry for her. It never occurred to me that what I was doing was wrong. They say that's one my problems: differentiation. It is sometimes hard for me to tell right from wrong. And what of her . . . If she is dead, totally dead, then what I'm doing right now is useless, in fact, quite ridiculous perhaps, but what if she is still alive? Is she really enjoying this last moment? Or is she thinking about a blouse she wanted to buy, or her young husband, or some more cleaning she had to do, perhaps a soap opera she will now miss?

Suddenly! A voice from above!

'Hey, you! What the hell are you doing down there?' A man in a window above yells down at me.

Panic!

Startled!

Running!

I run away! I never looked up, more than out of the side of my eye. I run and I run and I . . .

For quite a while I run. Up and down streets, sidewalks, alleys all over town.

My fleet young body carries me!

My feet fly!

Brummmm! I'm a jet!

Brmm! I'm flying, soaring.

After running for a long time, I am far away across areas and neighborhoods. I stop at a fence out of breath . . . I put my hand to my chest, feel my heart beating . . . I am in a suburb. I am in the little road or alleyway that runs down between the back of the houses in rows. The houses are clean 1940s and '50s bungalow types, not super big but well kept and mostly painted white. In front of me, a man working in his garden . . .

'Hey, sonny – you all right there?'

He's talking to me! His kindness almost makes me sob.

'Come on, you better sit down . . . Are you okay?'

IF I TELL HIM, *'I-I just killed a woman' – he says 'What?' I say, 'It was horrible – an accident, of course – but her . . . brains – I saw her brains on the sidewalk . . .' He says 'I've never seen brains, what color were they?' No, I shall not tell him that* – instead I say, 'Please could I have a glass of water . . .'

I follow him into the house. I told him my name was Randall.

The glass he gives me seems very small – not a proper glass of water at all.

I eye him suspiciously.

I drink the tiny glass of water.

'Could I have some more?'

'Eh?'

'Oh, I'm sorry, *could I please have a glass of water.*' (Please and thank you are the magic words.)

He waits a minute, as if considering it. 'No. I'm afraid that's all I will give you.'

I get mad . . . This man looks like he was a woodpecker in another life. I feel persecuted and hurt at this dour turn of events. My head spins inside, not really thinking anything, just the feelings charging around, up and down, in and out.

Why does it always become this, this *bullshit*! Grrrr, I growl. Why can't anything ever be just nice and normal for me? I look at him, he looks back, cagey, sizing me up, rude man, shorter than me, that shrimp, his stupid face and this stupid kitchen!

We eye each other saying nothing. I hear the wall clock ticking . . .

So *stomp!* – I step on his foot. 'Ouch! Hey!' I run out of the house . . . slam the door.

Running . . .

Not far away, I remembered that I left my vacuum cleaner back there, there by the fence . . .

He is still in the garden. I creep on my belly like a commando . . . My new suit getting soiled . . .

Kids coming down the alley on bikes. One of them ran over my leg and laughed, but I keep on silently, crawling . . .

Yes, I want to leap up and chase that kid, push him over into some bushes – the fantasy shoots through my head, I wanted to kill him – I look back at him that way. But I keep on. I am dedicated to the mission now.

The vacuum cleaner. I have it. So easy. I am responsible for this equipment.

Now I have it and there's nothing the old man can do about it! He is working in his garden again. Now I stand up and yell over the fence, 'HEY!' right in that old man's face!

Startled, he does a double-take! Gloating, I brandish the

vacuum cleaner and all its rattling hoses! The old man brandishes his hoe. In a flash I am gone and don't look back.

A few blocks down, I stop and catch my breath, my feet slapping the pavement as I slow down. I set down the vacuum cleaner, breathing hard, bent over, hands on knees . . . whewww!

The exhilaration courses through me. I haven't had so much fun all day! What a weird old man he was! Wouldn't give me any more water, but I feel lucky to get away, wow . . .

I see a 7-Eleven down at the corner, on a main drag that cordons off this subdivision. Walking. The man at the counter eyes me as I come in. Buy some cookies and chocolate milk and, for no reason, some baseball cards. When I was young, I had a shoe box full of baseball cards, and I remember one time, I was in a corner newsstand and there was this kid who had a twenty dollar bill from his mother to buy baseball cards. It was his birthday, and he was buying pack after pack, twenty packs at a time for a dollar, opening them right there in the store, and he only had to get Ted Williams and Bob Friend and he had a complete set, and all the kids were gathering around at the spectacle and we all shared the excitement of the orgy of seeing him buying the cards and open them, and I looked at his clothes and he was a rich kid and I saw the car out there a big one, clean and sparkling, and I remember thinking that that's what rich kids do on their birthday . . .

Walking along with my vacuum cleaner, I stop and sit down on the curb. The cards I had just bought are in this heat-sealed, silvery plastic packaging, not anything like the old pressed wax paper I had as a kid. I opened the pack and – *hey!* – the ball players look different, they are rather normal-looking and like yuppies, kind of sterile. I remember how ugly and goofy they looked in 1963, and these new ones didn't look like them at all. I get this weird feeling come over me, like what was I doing here. I feel stupid and then real all alone. I look out at the traffic going by and tiny cars off in the distance, and some men were paving a pothole a few blocks that way and the sun was bright and . . .

And then I lifted the pack to my face and smelled the smell, that baseball card smell of pasteboard and printing and brittle bubble gum and . . . mmmmm. I came back down to the world again and everything was all right.

I lugged my vacuum cleaner across an empty lot to a big, shaded elm where I sat at the foot of the great trunk. I felt a breeze. I threw the chocolate milk carton away, then the baseball cards. I sailed them as far as I could, aiming at nothing in particular but just see how far I could go . . .

But then I do something on compulsion! I stand and go back into the neighborhood! First I hide the vacuum cleaner in some shrubbery. Soon I come upon the old man in his backyard. From a distance I watch him. Sneaking, I creep up on the fence. Without warning I pop out of the bushes and yell: 'Hey!' as loud as I can, and run away laughing. He was startled and threw his hoe up in the air. I hide.

Ten minutes pass. From farther down the alley I pop up and yell, 'Hey!' again. I feel an excitement, an exhilaration, and the poor man is confounded by this 'guerilla warfare.' After two more 'Heys!' he goes in the house.

With stealth and cunning I sneak up on the side of the house. He is on the phone. 'There's some son of a bitch guy in the neighborhood acting odd . . . I think he's mentally disturbed . . . Yes, please send someone . . .'

The police!

I'm gone.

But before I get out of the neighborhood, I am crossing a corner, and zap! – going the other way, on the next street over – a *police cruiser*! And they see me, I think. Evasive action!

A game of cat and mouse. Through backyards, bushes, car ports, laying flat in a ditch, I elude them.

A few times they catch a glimpse of me, but I am fleet. A few times the police drive by while I am hiding, and on slowly. They are looking for me.

After a while the police leave.

Back at the 7-Eleven, with my vacuum cleaner retrieved, I look up the old man's name in the phone book (got it off his mailbox) and drop a quarter. The phone rings.

'Hello?'

'Hey!'

That night I slept in the shrubbery in the industrial park where the vacuum cleaner offices were located . . .

As I walked there, I cross unfamiliar sectors of the city. I creep at night. The night is real. The night is the whir of bugs in the wood, the dew, the landscape – the whole landscape – the whole night – the whole civilization is covered with dew – and every leaf, every rock in the road, every roof and windowsill – and the cars – you can write on the cars, leave messages – strange cars going by – who's in them – what are they doing – where are they going – people wandering around in the middle of the night . . . It's all a mystery.

The next morning I feel renewed and chipper. Really ready to work. Sure I look a little bad after sleeping on cedar chips in the bushes and the damp from the dew, but that was no reason to fire me on the spot. My hair is mussed up, sticking up weird like anyone who's just woke up.

The crews were assigned, but I was left off. Mr Bellows, the boss, the man I farted at before, would not look me in the eye. I couldn't catch his glance, and so I raised my hand.

'Mr McFadden?'

'I don't have an assignment, Mr Bellows . . .'

'I'll discuss this with you in a little bit, Mr McFadden . . .'

'Am I fired? Are you—'

'I told you that we would discuss—'

'Shit! You can't fire me yet! I haven't had a chance!'

Maybe they know about the woman falling out of the window or the old man with the glass of water? No.

When I object further he accuses me of being drunk.

I told them I had buried the vacuum cleaner in a safe place and would tell them where it was all in good time. I am yelling and screaming and do not know what I say. It's coming out of my mouth before I even think about it. My vacuum cleaner sat over on the other side of the room bedecked with leaves and pine straw and cedar chips and fertilizer. Mr Bellows stared at it, then I did, then we looked each other in the eye.

I threw their stupid lamp on the ground as I stormed out.

Outside, I stand in the parking lot, calming down. I walk. I look back. Everyone is looking at me out of the window.

For a while I wander aimlessly.

Office parks have a certain artificial ambience, especially if you walk through them as a stranger, not knowing what is going on in any of these offices. It can give you the feeling of deadness, of nothing going anywhere, of nothing meaning anything and it can even be a little frightening.

I walk in to another office, across the office park. The receptionist greets me with a cheery voice, only glancing up from her typing at me. 'Can I help you sir . . .'

'Abbb . . .' The company's name on the wall is UTIMUM SYSTEMS, INC. in polished steel letters, and I have not the vaguest idea what they do here.

She looks up. I must look distressed. Her tone changes to one of concern. 'Is there anything wrong . . .'

'Yes. Ummm . . . there's something wrong with my brain!' I sound panicked, troubled . . .

She looks at me with more fear than concern. Perhaps she now noticed my disheveled appearance, messed-up hair, and overall dampness from sleeping in the bushes and dew.

I turn and leave.

Returning to my apartment, I am cautious. Walk by once to scope it. I find nothing suspicious: no one is waiting for me, there is no note on the door from the landlord telling me to come down to his office – the authorities haven't been here yet.

Usually I can get away with three 'acts or incidents' before they come looking for me. If I space the 'incidents' apart far enough, it will be six times or even nine, but always they come on an increment of three. In the world of the fates, three is a common denominator of some sort. I read that computer systems work on a binary system that is two digits, and the fates have a 'trinary' system as you look at it in perspective. Perhaps when our computers evolve to a three-digit system we will be on a better footing with fate and deal with it scientifically. We will someday master our fate.

I lay down on my bed.

The flimsy drapes blow in the wind.

Outside I hear the world going on: cars, brakes, buzz, horns . . . somewhere off in the distance a pile driver is pounding.

The world is going on without me, and I feel that now. The world is out there, going on without me. What a strange feeling.

If only I could master my fate! This 'furnished' apartment will soon be costing me $250 a month when the state's allocation runs out. Cheap, but it's in a bad area and the furnishings, heh . . . a chair, a table, a squeaky, sunken bed, a dresser that the drawers are hard to get out and people have scratched and scrawled words and initials on. The air-conditioning unit in the window makes a noise when it runs, like a helicopter engine about to throw a rod.

I think back on the mental hospital.

They did not cure me at that place. They sent me out too soon. Would they ever cure me? No. I've come to accept it.

This new State Medical System is for the birds. They just put me in there until I cooled down, until I fulfilled some sort of quota, and then they sent me out with this jobs-program thing.

Selling vacuum cleaners door to door, indeed! SMS is a disaster. They don't do anything for you, just pass you through the apparatus, stamp your form and pass you on to someone else.

How could they ever imagine that the government bureaucracies could run the health care industry? People are getting stupid in this country. Sure, they go to school and memorize facts and figures, learn to enter data in computers and produce splendid reports, but common sense and simple logic is lacking.

Where once the masses looked to religion to save them, now they look to government and doctors. It's like since the 'God is dead' thing in the sixties; medicine is a new religion and its magic wand will wave and everything will be all right. It will be years till they sort it all out. That Clinton guy got his. I read that he's out now and back in Arkansas. They have him driving a bookmobile for the community-service part of his sentence. Now, that would have been a perfect job for me, but I'm sure all the cushy bookmobile jobs have a waiting line a mile long after the last administration's debacle.

I think of what I've done today. Not proud of it. In my head I can see the woman with her brains, the old man with his glass of water, the look on Mr Bellows' face. Maybe, in another time, we all would have been friends.

Sometimes these thoughts come into my head out of nowhere. Things I have done haunt me, and sometimes things I haven't even done! Embarrassing moments, tragedies, social errors. You try to push them away – No!

I shouldn't have said that!

I shouldn't have said that!

No, I shouldn't have done that!

Why did I say that – why, why did I do those terrible things – everyone is looking at me – the feeling that I am no longer one of them – suddenly the jig's up!

I was never one of them. Maybe once I was . . . a long, long time ago . . . but I can't remember it well now . . . almost like I was someone else then. What happened to me.

The things you have done, bad things, they scream into your ear . . . the torment of those thoughts scream around in my head! I scream them out of me – I think of something, relive it in my mind, all the details come back to me like a TV show, and I scream *'Noooo!'* and I push it away!

Sometimes, especially in public, you have to say something to get the thoughts out, cover them up! When they're too much, I just have to sing!

In the line at the grocery store: 'Oh, what a beautiful morning! Oh, what a beautiful day!'

You are singing it altogether too loud, too weird . . .

People are staring at you, your mind is spinning . . .

Well, I'll just have to master my own fate! Cure myself. It's that simple! At least I'm not in that stupid mental hospital anymore. Just have to adapt now. Like I learned in the service, adapt to the environment around you, blend in . . .

YES!

Yes! That's it! I can cure myself! Fuck those incompetents and nabobs! I will do a better job of curing me than them, with all their degrees and reference books and technical words. I'll come back and show them someday. I'll have a big car, a restored late-sixties muscle car, yess! A convertible and nice clothes, stylish and casual and a gorgeous honey on my arm and . . . Fuck even going to see them, they can see me on TV, 'Hey! Wasn't that the guy who . . .'

I get a spoonful of peanut butter and eat it. When I'm hungry sometimes a spoonful or two can keep you going a few more hours without feeling hungry again.

I am happy for a moment! For a moment I feel good again. I will cure myself somehow, not to show them but for myself. I stand in front of the mirror. Look at myself. That is me. At least I am good-looking, dashing even.

Now I spring to life with new energy, jump up from the bed again. The room does not look so bleak; take a shower, wash the dishes in the sink, and clean the kitchenette, no time to clean the whole apartment . . .

I go to the closet and survey my clothes.

My shirts are nothing to write home about, but I have some wonderful pants. In my excitement I take out all my pants, take them off the hangers, and arrange them on the floor.

I stand back and enjoy the arrangement of my pants.

I glow with pride.

That night I had a special dinner party to go to. I do not remember exactly, but someone had invited me, or maybe somewhere I overheard someone talking and wrote it all down.

I did my best to improve my appearance, since the way I had slept the night before left something to be desired.

I do not want to miss the dinner. I am famished.

I have high hopes for this affair, hopes of meeting a better class of people, perhaps even a nice woman with good manners and a soft voice. I think of good things to converse about: weather, politics, polo . . . surely they play polo here. This is my chance. I want so much to better myself, and mix with the lofty and landed class of people.

At the party, the guests eyed me oddly and I kept to myself. Everyone was dressed better than I was. One whispered to another that the sleeves of my shirt had no cuff links and were kept together with Scotch tape – and the pants had no hem, as if they had been worn right out of the store they were bought in (which they were).

During dinner no one talked to me. At one point a piece of conversation reminded me of a joke I had heard.

As I told my joke, people listened to me at first, then gradually they started in their own conversations like they didn't care about my tale . . .

Soon everyone was back talking off in their own little worlds . . . I was mortified.

Before I even got to the punch line I fell silent!

No one cared.

I look at my soup.

I was depressed. This whole thing was not going well. I grew petulant, brooding, and began to feel myself under the table . . .

I'll show them. I spill my bowl of soup.

'Oooops!'

'Hey!'

Everyone stares. They're all looking at me. Now I feel how much I do not know these people. I do not like these people, the way they are looking at me, staring . . .

The hostess must have had an eye on me all along. The others look shocked, but she looks angry, eyeballing me like Ben Turpin. She evidently saw me spill the soup on purpose, and then it begins. She is screaming, yelling at me. She saw me do it and knew it wasn't a mistake. Then, like always, I couldn't understand what she was saying, my mind shut off in some way.

Now she's standing, face red, she is pointing at the door. She saw me spill the soup on purpose! She knows!

So there it is, now! I am to be humiliated. Kicked out in front of everyone. The sinking feeling. I look down at the lines of soup as it runs across the clean white tablecloth.

I throw my salad plate against the wall and leave.

As I pass through the other room on my way out, people who were not eating and had not seen what happened, but heard the commotion, stared at me like I was some wild animal in a cage – some kind of two-headed beast – I hated that.

Outside I stood and looked back out of the side of my eye. I could feel them talking inside – 'Who was that man?' 'Who invited him?' – I would show them a thing or two.

One hour later, I return with a special outfit. I have on my Indian outfit: loincloth, bandanna with two or three feathers in it, face paint, a bow and arrows, moccasins. First I peeked in the windows, spying on them. They are having fun, after-dinner banter – no one seems sad I left. They're all so happy!

A bedroom window upstairs is open. I shoot an arrow in. No one was in there, for I heard nothing but the clatter of the arrow as it falls to the floor. Will I sneak in through that window? I try to climb the brick walls, but it's no good.

Next, I write things on the house. Using my face paint tube, I write things like 'Down to the pedantic assholes who do not care.' 'Assholes live here.' 'The hypocrites are taking over everything.'

Being almost naked made me feel savage, crazy, and aroused. When I had an erection I strode in to the party, right in the front door, with a certain pompous, regal flair, like a noble chieftain of the ancient Indian Nations.

There I was, standing in the middle of the party for what seemed like the longest few seconds.

I wanted some punch.

There were gasps and some giggles when various women saw my huge boner lifting up the front flap of my loincloth. A gradual hush fell. With the stern face of a savage brute, in silent, solemn Indian stance I lift the cup of punch to my lips.

Then the hostess recognized me and began yelling and screaming again!

I whirled – drawing an arrow—
And shot wildly—
All mayhem ensued!

Rapidly, I began discharging my arrows!

A woman standing next to the hostess was hit in the eye and screamed like a chicken! Ahh, my friends, it was a wild, wilderness scene that broke loose in this great lodge of snobby coots, I say! The arrows flew and found their mark. There was screaming and disorder as the curs panicked and stumbled over each other to flee my wrath. When my arrows were spent, I had my knife.

Brandishing now! Indian yell! Out through the kitchen, where people stood moments before, chatting, I made my escape out the back door. With grace and agility I cleared hedges and a brick wall. I remember the flash of a neighbor's face in a window of a house I went past. My moccasins flew across the perfectly manicured lawns like the wind, for I was the last wild Indian in the world and this was the noble savage's last great victory, the massacre, at the Brentwood Estates, April 14, in the year of our lord, 1996 . . .

Members of the party give chase in their cars . . . I hear the telltale sound of a big luxury Detroit monster, bottoming out as it bounces at the end of a driveway and glides in pursuit. They're after me! By now I'm in the hedges and brush, running low at a squat. The cars are in the distance, across the lawns. They scour the area, meet at the crossroads and in far-off, serious-toned voices yell from car to car.

But I elude them easily.

Later . . .

My room! What a mess – what a terrible mess! I am depressed and the prospect of cleaning up the rest of the place leaves me cold. I see my pants on the floor, as I arranged them, and feel good.

I am reminded that this place is mine. It now has my own personal design despite its basic run-of-the-mill qualities. I survey the kitchen, sparkling clean. A messy house, but a dream kitchen, yes!

At first I am disturbed at the contrast – then a twinge of despair – a feeling of upset – embarrassed – then my eyes go bright – what a beautiful mess!

Everything is perfectly a mess, perfect random – strewn . . .

I couldn't stage it this good, the random way things have fallen: the jeans half inside-out on the floor – the sock coming out of one leg – the underwear still partially in the seat – the sneakers in different directions, one on its side – the pile of papers and magazines by the bed, totally disheveled, leaning over, precariously ready to fall.

I love this mess – I embrace it with all my soul – I plummet down on the bed, into the middle of it, the perfect picture of mess – and I am the centerpiece!

I muss up my hair – laugh – turn on a stupid TV station I never watch – I let drool run out of the side of my mouth – I'm enjoying my mess now . . .

Later, late that night, at the Waffle House I made a new friend. Donny was a person I had met or knew vaguely from somewhere, over the last two weeks since I'd been out and on the loose. I recognized him sitting there at the counter, recalled his name, and called him over. If I had not remembered his name, the whole course of the night would have been changed and thus my life and his too.

We sat and talked. He didn't like the job he had either, working in a graveyard, and when he heard that I quit my job that day, he agreed to quit his too. I think he may be retarded. At the very least, he is a slow learner, but he is honest and tells the truth to anyone who asks. He is that sort of quiet person, prone to keeping to himself, and I doubt anyone much ever even talks to him. He probably hasn't had a proper conversation in months.

Donny is a short fellow who wears overalls, a plaid shirt, and sneakers that don't match. His baseball cap is worn low over his eyes, giving Donny at first a sinister appearance, then the appearance of being just stupid. He talks slow and almost unsure of himself, like Michael J. Pollard, and if ever someone was to do the life of Donny on the silver screen, Michael J. Pollard would be perfect for the role.

I related to him, in confidence, the things that had happened to me that day. He loved the stories. He had never dreamed of dressing up in a wild Indian outfit but he thought it was probably a good idea, as long as you only did it now and then. He said he often became aroused whenever he saw a pizza or, to some extent, anything round – that he fought it all the time! He says there's a white spot on his heart, but the doctors don't know what it is. He thinks he won't live long, but then again he might.

It is very late in the night, everything's closed now, but we decide to go to a whorehouse. This one Donny knows of that's open all night. A whorehouse, what a wonderful idea. From the description it is in a real crummy area of town but, sure, I would go. I would even let him borrow my Indian outfit. I still have it with me in my coat pocket. It's a great disguise, as it takes up so little room and you can hide it anywhere.

On the way to the brothel, Donny stops at a dumpster behind a flower shop and gets some discarded flowers to give the girls . . . He pulls the dead petals off as we walk.

He says he can't fix his car because he goes to the whorehouse too much. Poor fellow. His need for the most basic form of love, a monetary love, has left him in hardship.

The brothel is in an old building on the side of a hill, with a couple of mobile home additions jammed onto it, a real architectural disaster. The old manager woman (the madame, I guess) eyed Donny suspiciously, and then me. They knew Donny from before. Donny chose a girl he had had before. She gave him a special rate because she was so ugly, and he would put a brown paper grocery bag over her head. She let him do that.

One woman eyed me, smiling. She had a tooth missing, and when she burped I smelled beer . . . No. Not her . . .

I chose a girl who is rather pretty, but who talked too much and proceeds to tell me everything she had done in her life. I had to tell her to stop talking for a while. We went to her private room, which had teddy bears, roaches from joints, empty pop cans, and posters of rock stars I'd never heard of. The whole room smelled like shampoo and glue. What we did then is a private matter, and I will not relate such details at this time.

When I was done, I waited for Donny in the sitting room.

After a while I thought about walking on home by myself but got reading the magazines.

Eventually, I must have dozed off.

I remember waking up to a commotion. It is many hours later, the wee hours of dawn, sunlight was coming in the windows and I had fallen asleep with a copy of *Gorgeous Gash* in my lap . . .

There was screaming and yelling down the hall, and I went to see. It was Donny. He had done something and the whore was angry and flailing! She was hitting Donny with his hat.

'Look at my tit! Look what you did to it. You rat bastard! Look at it! Look at it!' The woman shrieked up at the top of her lungs.

Her left breast was wizened, suckled, and hanging oddly. It was sucked out like a prune and flopped there as I stared in horror at it. Poor Donny was in a spot and looking quite ridiculous in the wild Indian outfit. The feathers were bent from her hitting him, and the paint was smeared on his face. He stood there dumbly, like Stan Laurel, getting hit. The paint from his face was also smeared on her tit and made it look even more gruesome and sucked out. A big, burly guy I took to be the bouncer came up fast. She yelled, pleading and outraged, at the bouncer: *'Look at my tit! Look at my tit! This bastard fell asleep with my tit in his mouth and sucked on it all night long! It's all sucked out!'*

Other people from the whorehouse came up in the hall. Donny just stood there, sheepish, groggy, and stumbling, hardly awake, but knowing that he had again done *something* wrong. He stood there dumbly, getting hit with his own hat!

'Perhaps it was an accident . . .' I ventured.

The bouncer looked at me like he would kill me! I stopped talking and looked away!

I slipped off. I must find something.

I went back down the hallway. Coming out of one room, a thin, dark little man with wavy, perfect black hair and a sheet wrapped around his waist stopped me in the hall and asked, 'What is it? Is it a raid? Is someone dead? Will the police come?' By his voice I could tell he was from India . . . and then our eyes met . . . I saw it in his eyes . . . he saw it in mine . . .

He was like *me* – quite out of his head . . .

There is a communion of the insane. This communion of insanity is sacred. We are friends and brothers instantly, like two masons or two undercover agents in a foreign land.

His eyes tell me this.

'Listen, I need to create a diversion or something . . .'

'You are in trouble, sir?'

'My friend, he . . .'

'Oh my, yes! I will help you now. Please wait, please!'

He disappeared back into the room, then came out hastily dressed and more prepared for an emergency.

And in his hand . . .

. . . a *hand grenade*!

He strode down the hall to the center of the commotion and faced the scene, holding the hand grenade up like an Olympic torch. I was stunned. No one else seemed to noticed him till he started talking, and I watched speechless.

'Please, everyone! It is my great misfortune to inform you that I have a *bomb* here! Please do not accost that little man any longer!' He holds the grenade aloft and has pulled the pin and it is sizzling.

Everyone runs. The bouncer, the whore with the floppy, wizened breast, a few more whores and customers who have joined in the scene, everyone, including Donny!

'Donny!' I shout angrily! He turns and sees my face. 'This *way*!' I yell at him.

Donny joins us, me and my new confederate, as we race down the hallway. The Indian man stops, goes back a few steps, and throws the fizzing grenade into a room piled high and full of laundry.

Outside, we duck as a window explodes above our heads, and

blasted feather pillows, burning sheets, towels and underwear fly across the parking lot. Quick, into the Indian guy's car.

'Gentlemen, let me introduce myself. I am Professor Agar Boshnaravata!'

'Pleased to meet you, Professor! I'm Carl and this is Donny!' I always use different names, my driver's license says Ulysses McFadden, but I am amongst friends now, and Carl is really my name.

Donny says 'Hi . . .'

'I see, Donny, that you are an Indian also!' says Agar.

'Huh?' replies Donny.

'It's a joke, Donny . . . er, it's a joke . . .' I say.

We drove off into the bright day on the road to new adventures. Suddenly, after weeks of having no friends, now I have two.

But are we really on the road to wild, high adventure or on the highway straight to hell . . . ? I neither know nor care now. I just roll my hand out the window and feel the air going by in the morning light, see the pavement blurring by, see a young child off in the distance by a swing set . . .

***Bob Burden** has been writing estranged literature for twenty years now and love-hating every minute of it. He is an award-winning writer, cartoonist, poet, performance artist, and master of the bizarre. Bob's whimsical, horrific tales will twist your mind, sell your dreams, and take a hard left turn when you're expecting a right. In the '70s he invented his own literary form, which he called 'Electra Fiction.' In the '80s he brought surrealism to the comics medium with his cult hero The Flaming Carrot, and in the '90s he designed the first three-piece suit made entirely from rubber bands. Watch for his upcoming works* Wipe Out, Dinner in the Rain, *and* Ninety Days Same as Cash.

Waco

BY

GEORGE C. CHESBRO

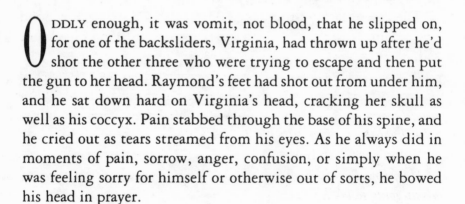

ODDLY enough, it was vomit, not blood, that he slipped on, for one of the backsliders, Virginia, had thrown up after he'd shot the other three who were trying to escape and then put the gun to her head. Raymond's feet had shot out from under him, and he sat down hard on Virginia's head, cracking her skull as well as his coccyx. Pain stabbed through the base of his spine, and he cried out as tears streamed from his eyes. As he always did in moments of pain, sorrow, anger, confusion, or simply when he was feeling sorry for himself or otherwise out of sorts, he bowed his head in prayer.

'Dear Heavenly Father—'

Yo.

Raymond's head snapped up. He looked around, saw no one. 'God . . . ?'

Over here.

Raymond looked to his left, toward the window, where a huge vulture sat perched on the sill, its black and crimson head cocked to one side, studying him with its yellow eyes.

Raymond slapped a hand over his own eyes, thrust out the other. 'Get thee from me, Satan!'

He waited a few seconds, and when he heard a rustling of feathers he opened his fingers a crack and looked toward the open window. The vulture flapped its wings in a kind of shrugging motion, then hopped around as if to fly off.

Have it your way, schmuck. It's your nickel. You called me.

'Wait!'

The bird twisted and curled its long, wattled neck, looked back at Raymond from beneath one outstretched wing.

What's the problem, Putz?

'You're not . . . Satan?'

You mean that hell guy some of you folks believe in?

'Uh . . . Yeah.'

Born only half cooked, never made it out of intensive care. You can't expect a poor devil like Satan to keep truckin' for very long when you keep upstaging him.

'What are you talking about?'

The great black vulture hopped back around to face Raymond once again. Now the creature's yellow eyes seemed soulful, almost sad.

It never ceases to amaze me how any human with even a smidgeon of awareness of what the people on this planet routinely do to each other would worry his pea brain for one little second about ending up in some other unpleasant place called hell. Sheesh.

'I don't want to burn!'

Hoo, boy. I could have a bit of bad news for you. But not to worry about going to Hell.

'You're saying hell doesn't exist.'

The enormous vulture slowly shook its head.

You're a real pisser, Raymond. I'm afraid you've missed my point.

'What are you?'

God's the name, comedy's my game.

'You can't be God. You're a vulture.'

Everybody's a critic. Somebody's got to clean up this mess you've made. I've designated the vulture as your planetary bird. What, you want I should have done my burning bush routine? Trust me on this: Before very long, you're going to have all the heat you can handle.

'What do you mean?'

In about five minutes those ATF and FBI boys outside are going to start to bulldoze this place, and then your nutso leader is going to torch the bunch of you.

'You're talking about David?'

The guy you let play hide the sausage with your wife and daughter.

'But David is your son!'

You have got to be kidding me.

'David . . . isn't your son?'

The Meshugah can't even play decent guitar. You think any kid of mine couldn't at least play as good as Hendrix?

'What about Jesus?'

The man had steel balls the size of watermelons. Him I liked. We used to talk a lot.

'But Jesus was your son, wasn't he? By the Virgin Mary?'

Look, schmuck, first of all, if I did decide to have a kid with one of you humans, the woman I chose as the mother certainly wouldn't be a virgin when I'd finished with her. Male gods like a little nooky as much as the next guy. But I never had any children. I've got some emotional problems, and I didn't want to risk passing them on. You people have enough problems. Some of the other gods used to have an occasional roll in the hay with humans, but their progeny were nothing to write home about. It didn't really work out. I mean, how many people can earn a living throwing the discus?

'What . . . other gods?'

There used to be a whole slew of us. We shared responsibilities. One handled crops, another storms, another the oceans. That kind of thing. There was even a kind of forest ranger. A cast of thousands. If you wanted something taken care of you prayed to the particular god in charge of that operation. Gods didn't answer prayers much more in those days than I do now, but at least you had a local representative.

'What did you do back then?'

Local maintenance. I was the superintendent of buildings and grounds. The bigwigs wouldn't give me any on-line earth responsibilities. Said I was too unstable. They were right, of course. You wouldn't want to be around me when I'm in a snit.

'What happened to the others?'

I killed them. I am a jealous God.

'How did you kill them?'

Cut them off from their supply of faith. It takes a lot of believers to keep a decent-sized god alive.

'You . . . cut off their supply of faith?'

Yeah. It took some doing, but a word here and a word there to the right people did wonders. While the others were busy doing their jobs, I'd come down here and talk to certain humans about there being only one God – me. My main man Moses was a joy to talk to. The man had a great ear for gossip, and an imagination like you wouldn't believe. He was truly an inspiration. The rest, as they say, is history.

'But there is a heaven?'

Home sweet home.

'And you'll take us there?'

Nooooo. I don't think so, Raymond. I don't have the power to do that: I never did have much of an aptitude for dealing with humans, which is why I was put in charge of buildings and grounds. But even if I did have the power to move you into my neighborhood, I'd be a fool to do it. Visiting with you from time to time is one thing, but I'd end up nuttier than I already am if I had to live with you. Sheesh.

'But you created us!'

Whoa, boss. You can't pin that one on me. You're not only a bloodthirsty, murderous crew of nest foulers, but your species has a serious design defect. The vast majority of you have a genetic predisposition to superstition, to believing some of the most breathtakingly preposterous things in order to justify your insane behavior. Insanity does beget insanity, you know, much like what you've got in your head ends up what you're sitting in.

'If you didn't create us, who did?'

Beats me. The fact of the matter is that you created me, and you keep me alive. I think you just kind of developed like all the other things on this planet.

'But where will I go when I die?'

You're not going anywhere, kiddo. It's lights out. End of the line. That's why they call it dead.

'You mean . . . this life is all I've got?'

Had. What did you want for your nickel?

'But David says the world is going to end now, and we're the only ones who will be saved!'

Sheesh. Your putz leader is just a meshugah like all the rest of you. I thought I explained that. The only difference is that he's an active loony, and the rest of you are passive loonies. The only thing in the world that's going to change after he torches you is that people are going to be telling jokes about the fried wackos in Waco. Did you hear the one about—?

'What do you mean by active and passive loonies?'

It's the difference between the foot and the grape. Taken as a whole, your species is psychotic. The fact that you're sitting there in a pool of blood on top of the skull of a woman whose brains you've just blown out while you carry on a conversation with a vulture is an excellent example of what I'm talking about.

'But you said you were God!'

I am. But most people talk to me when I'm not around to listen, not when I actually appear to them. I expected you'd have a heart attack. Talking to vultures who talk back is not usually considered a sign of mental health.

'I want to get out of here!'

That's the first reasonable thing I've heard you say. Maybe you should climb out this window like the four people you just killed were trying to do when you shot them.

'I can't move! I think I broke my tail bone.'

Pity. To finish answering your question, passive loonies like you don't really know what you want, except that you always want something different from what you've got. And you expect me to give it to you. It's the same all over the planet. On the other hand, active loonies like your leader know exactly what they want, and sooner or later they manage to round up enough passive loonies to give them a shot at it. Usually active loonies want power, or money, or to kill a lot of people they don't like, or control television programming. But all your resident active loony ever wanted was to be a rock star, and the only reason he wanted that was so he could schtup a lot of women. But that plan didn't work out, because the man's got no talent. So he did the next best thing, which was to gather up a bunch of passive loonies he could convince he was God so he could at least schtup all the women and children in that group. You're not going to be pleased with the outcome of this, but the fact of the matter is that, as active loonies go, your boy is really small potatoes. The damage he's done to other people is relatively limited. I'm here to tell you that there are some real doozies out there.

'I don't want to burn to death!'

Then you'd better shoot yourself.

'I don't have any bullets left!'

Suddenly there was a grinding sound from the floor below, and the building began to shake. The vulture turned its head, looked down.

Time's up. The boobs have come to do some serious boob hunting. Adios, schmuck.

'Help me! I don't want to die!'

'Raymond, who the hell are you talking to?'

Raymond turned his head toward the doorway, where his leader stood with a pistol in one hand and a can of gasoline in the other. The man's long, light hair hung about his face in greasy ringlets, and his eyes gleamed.

'David, they're here!'

'I know,' the man said, and grinned. 'But we won't be for long. It's time for the Rapture and the world to end, just like I prophesied. Boy, are they ever going to be sorry they messed with me. I asked you who you were talking to.'

Raymond pointed toward the giant bird still perched on the windowsill. 'That's God, David! I've been talking to God!'

'What, are you crazy? That's just a vulture.'

'Father, speak to him!' Raymond shouted at the vulture. 'Tell him what you told me!'

He can't hear me, Raymond. He believes his own publicity. He thinks he's God.

'David, I've had a vision! I'm having a vision! I think maybe you should reconsider your course of action. Can we talk about this?'

The bright-eyed man's response was to raise his revolver and fire off three shots. The vulture's head exploded in a fountain of blood and gore, and its great, feathered carcass fell off the sill and onto the floor with a loud thump. 'What the hell's the matter with you, Raymond? Here we are getting ready to go to heaven, and you're sitting on your ass talking to a vulture. Nice job saving these others, by the way. They're going to be thanking you in a few minutes.'

'David, I've been having some serious second thoughts about what we're doing here. God said the world isn't going to end at all, and that all that's going to happen is that people are going to be telling jokes about us.'

The man walked over to Raymond, stood over him. 'Get up off your ass, Raymond. I need your help.'

'I can't, David! I hurt my back!'

'Then you can go first,' the bright-eyed man said as he splashed gasoline over Raymond's head and body. *'We're outta here!'*

George C. Chesbro is the creator of the Mongo mystery series. His latest book is Bleeding in the Eye of a Brainstorm.

The Penitent

BY

John Peyton Cooke

'EVER since I was a young girl I've wanted to torture a beautiful young boy.' That was Marie's pickup line on me, whispered devilishly in my ear before I had even seen her face – and it worked. It meant she knew about Donald Fearn and Alice Porter. It also meant she had made a snap judgment about me based solely on my appearance. It didn't offend me; she happened to be correct, though I resembled half of the other people who regularly hung out at the Belfry and probably most of them weren't into half of what I was into.

She twisted my multipierced ear painfully as she took the bar stool next to mine. I winced and cried out, 'Ow!' and rubbed my ear to soothe it, counted to make sure none of the silver rings had fallen out.

'My name's Marie.' Her voice was high and feminine, honey smooth, sincere – not what one would expect from an out-of-nowhere ear-twister. 'What's yours?'

'Gary.' Looking at her, I had this sudden, intensely pleasure-ful sensation, as if someone were plunging a long hypo full of adrenaline straight into my aorta. It was not only her beauty that stroked me but her attitude.

Marie was smiling broadly, filterless Camel dangling, her eye-lined eyes boring into mine, irises glistening orange in the candle flame from the bar, eyebrows arched like an arch fiend, hair flat black and stringy but falling only as far as her shoulders, unlike mine, which came to the small of my back. She was all in black from her clinging sleeveless shirt to her narrow jeans to her boots. Her wide leather belt was shiny with sharp chromium studs that would be painful to anyone on the receiving end. She wore only three earrings but many bracelets and necklaces, black rosary beads, filigreed silver crucifixes inlaid with obsidian. The tattoo on her shoulder arrested my eyes: a Madonna and child, colorful and Raphaelesque, exquisitely inked.

While I was so distracted, Marie yanked me forward by my nose ring and planted one of her cigarettes in my mouth and lit it up for me, then shoved me back to an upright position, smiling playfully.

'Gary,' she said, and coyly blew smoke in my face. 'You know I'm not joking, what I said.'

'Wasn't that Donald Fearn's statement?' I said. 'After they caught him. Only you switched the genders around.'

'You know what happened to Alice Porter, then.'

'Of course,' I said. 'I know all about it.'

We found that we had a mutual interest in the case – not so surprising when you consider that it was not only sensational and semi-famous but local. We also shared the same taste in true-crime paperbacks and Anne Rice novels and bloody horror movies and punkish-metal, death-obsessed music. We both had come to the Belfry, which some wise saint had constructed in an old Gothic stone church in a depressed and dangerous part of the city. The club draws a batty crowd and has managed to remain minatory enough to scare away the army dudes, college frat rats, sorority mice, and other vermin.

I asked Marie why she had tried that line on me.

'Because you looked like a likely victim.'

I admitted that I was.

'And I wanted to get to you before someone else did.'

'Ever since I was a young boy I've wanted to torture a beautiful young girl.' That was what he said, Donald Fearn, back in 1942, before he was sent on to the gas chamber in the state penitentiary up at Canon City. What he had done to seventeen-year-old Alice Porter beggars description – but only a sadist would see fit to do so. All I'll say is that awls, nails, and wire whips were among the tools the deputies recovered from the bloody crime scene, along with the charred pile that was Alice's clothing, and when they hauled the girl's body out of the old dry well . . . well, as they say, that is a deep subject.

I grew up in Pueblo, about fifty miles from where Alice Porter's murder took place and about forty miles from where Donald Fearn was gassed by the people of Colorado more than fifty years ago. My grandpa worked in the steel mill here that covers our rooftops with soot and lends our air its ocher tint and rotten-egg smell – and happened to have produced the sturdy nails that were found among Donald Fearn's 'torture kit.'

Before his death Gramps would often indulge my pathological curiosity by saying, 'Gary, I ever tell you about that candy striper that was murdered up at that old Penitente church back in forty-two?' I would pull up a chair and tell him to go ahead, and we would do some rare transgenerational bonding. Gramps knew such stories would do little Gary no harm. Little Gary was always picked on by the other kids – a wimpy, scrawny, unhealthy-looking waif who never caused any trouble and would never so much as harm the hair on a poor little precious fly. Little Gary's interest in the gory monster movies that came on TV late Friday nights over KWGN out of Denver only showed that he had a healthy, active, normal imagination.

When I was a wee tot, the state DHS deemed my mother unfit to raise me for reasons no one has ever seen fit to tell me. I suspect she was hooked on smack, or else she smacked me around, or else she had a boyfriend who would smack me around on her behalf. The *Father* line on my birth certificate is typed in with a simple X, so either she didn't know who he was or I was an immaculate conception. I'm fairly certain he was not God but probably a Chicano, because I've got that mixed-up look to my complexion, dark coffee-bean eyes, glossy black hair, and I've always taken on a deep, reddish tan when I'm out in the sun for a couple of minutes. Anyway, my grandparents were given the right of ownership, and they were perhaps more tolerant with me than real parents would have been. As they got older, they even put up with my loud, evil music: their hearing was shot. At sixty-nine Gramps had a massive coronary that boosted him up to heaven with the power of a Saturn V rocket. Grandma keeps on ticking, all by herself over in that dirty little old tar-papered bungalow near the steel plant. I visit only when I want to borrow her car.

I can't say exactly how it is that I ended up who I am. Even if I suffered abuse at the hands of my mother or her boyfriend, that's no reason for me to be necessarily drawn to pain. In kindergarten the girls liked to knock me over on the playground, each grab a limb, and carry me around like a jungle captive, but I don't think that's why I enjoy submitting to the power of a woman. When I was a little older, the other boys used me as their victim when we played Star Trek, with me getting caught and tied up in all sorts of creative ways, but I doubt if that has anything to do with my interest in ropes and chains. As I grew old enough to enter the shady world of the adult bookstore without being carded, I would scan the varieties of girlie magazines and dildos on the walls, but my eyes were always drawn to the fetish mags, and only those in which the women had enslaved the men. No one ever taught me to find this appealing; it was the same natural instinct that draws the duck to water, the bat to the cave, the moth to the flame.

Most people's tastes are predispositions, things bred in the bone, biological hardwiring, genetic programming as inescapable as Fate. Certain things are scheduled to go off at certain times and you can't buck it, you have to give in. If you try to resist your genes, you're going to short out your circuit board and go careening over the edge, which I suppose is what must have happened to Donald Fearn.

'Ever since I was a young boy I've wanted to be tortured by a beautiful young girl.' There it was. It was out. I'd said it. Marie had asked me to do my own twist on Donald Fearn's confession, to modify it any way I chose, and to 'be honest about yourself.' But she had known all along who she was dealing with. She had smelled my quivering sweat from a mile away, across the crowded church floor, through the smoke and haze. She had found the hand that fit her black glove.

'Where else are you pierced, Gary?' she screamed over the music, which sounded like Grandma's washing machine amplified to the *n*th. The faces hovering around us were ghostly, cadaverous, pale makeup and bloodshot raccoon eyes.

'That's all.' What I had were the eight rings in the left ear, ten in the right, and the one in my nose – not one of those dainty things through the side of a nostril but a heavy silver door knocker hanging down in the middle like on the snout of a Spanish *el toro.*

Marie hooked her forefinger up through it again, and I found myself staring at her sharp, black-lacquered nail as it danced in the flickering light. 'I love this one,' she said, tugging not so gently. 'You mean to tell me you don't have one here?' Her other nails grasped my left nipple. 'Or here?' She pinched the right. 'Or here?' She tweaked my navel. 'Or here?' She grabbed the bulge in my jeans, found the head of my cock, squeezed it. 'Nothing?'

'No,' I said. Someone had returned with the hypo and stuck the needle straight into my heart muscle. I'd been considering getting other piercings, but I had no one to share those parts of my body with, so I hadn't seen the point in forking over the cash. Body piercing can be expensive, and I was living on my meager unemployment checks after having been laid off from my meat-butchering job at the King Soopers five months ago. My first ear piercing was done in high school, free, by a girl named Snookie with a needle and a cork. I had my later earholes done with a gun at Spencer Gifts down at the mall, which is fairly cheap, and I did my nose myself one night when I was dead drunk on pepper vodka. If left to my own devices, I might have done the rest of myself myself, but on the night Marie grabbed me, I had not.

'I don't feel any others,' Marie said. 'Show me.' She pulled my shirt up to just under my armpits and ran her nails up my chest. The posers around us stopped their conversation and turned to see. 'Little pink titties,' she said, grabbing and stretching them as if they were Silly Putty.

I winced. Marie smiled and began flicking my nipples with her sharp nails. My cock was trying to grow, but there was no room left in my jeans. She dragged her claws down my skin, leaving long red abrasions, her pearly teeth glowing wetly. There's no greater turn-on than the beatific grin that spreads across a sadist's face as she's hurting you.

'You mark easily,' she said. 'I love that.' She slapped me smartly across the face, knocking my jaw loose and making me bite my tongue. I tasted blood. My heart skipped a beat. My cock found the room it sought. 'A nice red glow,' she said. With her sharpest nail, she slashed four quick strokes on my chest as if it were the mark of Zorro:

Her finger was red with my blood. She stuck it in my mouth and had me lick it off. She wiped more drips off my chest and smeared them into my lips. She pulled my shirt back down; it soaked up my blood. She grabbed me by my nose ring and hopped off her bar stool, tugging me down off mine.

'Where are you taking me?' I asked, floating in a strange endorphin delirium. She had given me but a taste of what I most desperately craved, like a pusher offering a minuscule free sample of what he had loads of in his truck. She placed her hand in my crotch and felt my hardness: proof, if she needed it, that I was no pretender.

'I don't want to give these vultures a free show,' she whispered in my ear. Her teeth clamped down on my earlobe as if she were ready to bite it off. 'I'm taking you back to my place, Gary. You're going to like it there.'

I followed along eagerly as she pulled me through the crowd, down the cast-iron circular staircase, out the back door, down the dark-alley shooting gallery where people of indeterminate sex were huddled together in the shadows, passing a rubber hose around to see how snugly it could be tied off on each other's upper arms. She took me to her '74 Ford Maverick, held my wrists behind my back and locked them into a set of Spanish-style handcuffs, had me curl up in the trunk, slapped a strip of duct tape over my mouth, slammed the lid down, *chunk,* and shut me in the heavenly darkness.

The night of the murder, April 22, 1942, Donald Fearn's wife was at the hospital, in labor with their third child. Fearn himself was twenty-three, a railroad mechanic. The only reason we even know about him today is because his battered blue Ford sedan happened to get stuck in the mud on the morning of the twenty-third on his way back from killing Alice Porter. A farmer hauled him out with his tractor, and when the deputies later came around asking if he'd seen anything funny, the farmer was able to give them a precise description of car and driver. Otherwise, the murder would have remained a mystery, and Marie would never have had such a clever thing to say to make me come to attention.

Donald Fearn had never even spoken to Alice Porter until the night he picked her up off a Pueblo street on her way home from her nursing class, in the midst of a drenching thunderstorm. A witness heard her scream and vaguely saw her get into a car with someone, and that was the last anyone other than Fearn saw of her alive. Fearn took her out to an abandoned village and bound her to the altar inside the old *morada,* a church that had been built by a devout Catholic sect of Hispanos known as the Hermanos Penitentes. He spent the entire night torturing her while the storm raged and the lightning flashed outside. When he was done, Alice was not dead, but he could hardly allow her to identify him to police, so he struck her head with a hammer and dumped her body down the well. The rain that had provided him enough cover to snatch her had also created the mud that trapped him like a fly on tack paper and led to his ultimate confession, prosecution, and eventual and everlasting asphyxiation.

It was on Good Friday of this year that Marie and I paid our visit to the ghost village to investigate the scene of the crime, like a macabre Nancy Drew with one half of the Hardy Boys literally in tow (she had taken to dragging me around everywhere with my neck in a padlocked dog collar attached to a short leash). I'd read every one of the Hardy Boys books when I was still prepubescent, but even then I had got an almost sexual kick out of those scenes where the two teens were tied up back to back with handkerchiefs stuffed rudely in their mouths. I always imagined they were me, always envied them their predicament, always imagined much worse things waiting for them than what they ever got. Why had none of the villains ever stripped them, strung them up by their ankles, and taken a good cat-o'nine-tails to their virginal flesh?

We arrived as the sun still lingered over the Sangre de Cristos. The dry earth was sun-warmed even though the snow had only recently melted across the plateau. The wind racing down off the mountains was arctic cold, but we both wore our leather jackets, and the bite on my cheeks felt good. The village was a hodge-podge of leaning wooden shacks and old adobe huts skirted by drifts of cinnamon sand. Sagebrush grew everywhere. Tumble-weeds rolled down the barren streets. There were no old movie theaters or general stores or gas stations; the town had been dead for nearly a century.

'I expect to see Clint Eastwood riding in,' I said.

'It'll take more than Clint on a horse to save you,' Marie said, and gave a sharp tug. 'Come on, Gary.'

The *morada* stood on a hill a hundred yards to the east of the village, the old wooden cross askew atop the roof. It had not been built in the style of the old Spanish missions but was low and squat, narrow at front and back and long on the sides, with the exact shape and outsized proportions of a great stone sarcophagus. Only one slit for a window, like a gun port, graced the long side, the hand-textured adobe glowing like fire in the sun's last rays.

Marie led me up the cemetery path, past the many rows of weathered wooden crosses planted in the earth, to the *morada* entrance, a worm-eaten old door of solid, adzed timbers.

'This is it,' she said. 'Where it all happened.'

The sunlight fell away, and I glanced over my shoulder to see the village lost in shadow down below, the looming Sangre de Cristos now in silhouette. Donald Fearn had been here. He had known exactly where he was taking his victim. He had come prepared, had known precisely what he was going to do, had probably planned it and fantasized about it for days, weeks. Marie had been looking forward to this night for a long time as well, but she had wanted to wait until Good Friday to do me up right.

The date was significant – nothing to do with Donald Fearn but with the Penitentes, the sacred brotherhood whose secret, bloody rites had taken place within this most special house of worship every year for more than a century before the psycho from Pueblo ever grabbed poor Alice by the hand and pulled her screaming into his Ford and dragged her up to the *morada* and pushed her finally through his looking glass.

Before meeting Marie, I'd been staying in a cubbyhole at the Y, and when she told me to move in with her, I obeyed like an old family pet. I had a backpack and an old cardboard suitcase, mostly clothing and jewelry, and a few paperbacks and some cassette tapes and my Walkman and earphones. Marie had a studio apartment with bunk beds handcrafted out of two-by-fours and plywood, with sturdy hooks and eye screws at strategic locations. She'd had a male roommate who had 'vanished,' she said, a few months previously – she thought to Seattle but didn't know for sure. He hadn't called, she didn't care. He was a jerk, she said. He had raped her once. She told me to take the top bunk.

She brought me here for that first night of ecstasy, when I had been her captive, her plaything to be bound and unbound at her whim, to be pinched, pin-pricked, mummified, probed, whipped. After I moved in, we spent a great deal of time in the apartment stretching my limits. We seldom had regular sex; usually, when she had bound me or hurt me in a way that satisfied her, she would quietly masturbate.

Our relationship became centered on my transformation. She wanted me to enjoy more piercings and tattoos, and to that end we made periodic visits to the shop run by Federico, a paunchy, handlebar-mustached queer Hispanic leatherman who could do both cleanly and professionally, who had done Marie's masterful Madonna and Child. We could not afford to do everything at once, and we had to wait for me to heal before making each further major alteration. Federico made no effort to hide the fact that he enjoyed illustrating my hide and poking holes through my nether parts, and Marie got off on watching him work.

The process took months, but by the time we went to visit the *morada,* I had rings along my eyebrows, three studs through the tip of my tongue, two hefty rings in my nipples linked by a short chain, rings through my navel, and a whole series starting from my anus, across my tender frenum, along the ridge of my scrotum, up the shaft of my cock, and ending at the head with a massive, weighty Prince Albert of which I was proudest of all and which kept me in a permanent state of semi-erection. Though Marie let me keep the hair on my head, since she liked it for hair bondage, she routinely shaved my body baby smooth with a straight razor, which helped uncover my new tattoos: a green two-headed snake slithering out of my sphincter and onto my left glute, a dragon wrapping itself around one arm, an Egyptian scarab on my other bicep, eternal flames burning at my pubes.

My other tattoos were symbols Marie had appropriated from the Hermanos Penitentes. Crossing my left nipple:

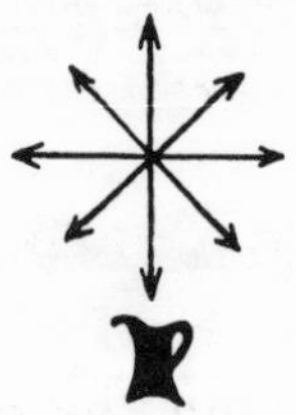

Double-headed arrows in a St Andrew's Cross superimposed over the cross of the crucifixion, the arrows symbolizing the authority of God, the cup to catch and preserve the blood of the Cristo. My right nipple was crossed similarly:

The cross and four nails of the crucifixion. In the center of my chest, where Marie had slashed her temporary M, she had Federico etch the most elaborate of Penitente marks:

The cross represents the brotherhood itself, with the mallet used on the Cristo, the spiked whip that scourged His back, the nails that skewered His limbs, and the cross of thorns with which He was crowned. On my back Marie had Federico tattoo the cross upon which St Andrew died a martyr:

Once worn by many of the Penitente men, it symbolized those brothers who were prepared to make no less of a sacrifice in the name of the Cristo.

On our last trip, when the last of the tattoos was finished, Marie thanked Federico for all his hard work. He said it had been his pleasure. As he was applying the gauze bandage to the fresh wounds he had carved into my skin, he turned and said to Marie, '*Ecce homo,* eh?'

Marie sized me up from head to toe and smiled at the sight of what she had wrought.

It took both of us to muscle the door open. It was twilight, and the light within the *morada* was blue and dim and fading fast. Marie turned on her flashlight and waved the narrow beam around the barren chapel. The interior was strewn with crushed beer cans, empty whiskey bottles, spent condoms – we were not the only people to have come here in the last fifty years. The low ceiling was hung with thick cobwebs, and I thought I caught a glimpse of a bat hanging in a corner. The altar at the head of the room was hewn out of the same sturdy timbers as the door. The chamber would have once been decorated with simple handcrafted icons – carved figures of the bleeding Cristo, images of the Virgin and the saints in frames of cheap tin. The Penitentes had been a poor people.

Marie led me up to the altar. 'Look at this.' With her bright beam she pointed out rust-colored stains that might once have been blood. She touched it, and some of the dusty flakes came off on the pads of her fingers. She wiped it on her jeans. 'So much for Alice Porter.'

My heart beat faster, strenuously. I could no longer find the tiny window, and realized the sky had gone black.

Marie yanked me forward and kissed me, thrusting her tongue inside to toy with my heavy studs. She reached up under my shirt and tugged on my nipple chain, slid my leather jacket over my shoulders and down onto the floor. She turned her flashlight off, plunging us into a void.

'Gary,' she said, 'are you ever going to get it.'

She pushed me back onto the altar and stretched me out spread-eagled. She roped my wrists and ankles with a strong, itchy hemp. The knots were expert, inescapable, tight enough to impede my circulation. When we'd first met, she had not made her knots so tight, but we had both discovered that I preferred them restrictive. I could feel my veins throbbing. She secured the ends down below so that I felt as if I were on a medieval rack. Then she took a pair of sharp Fiskars scissors to my jeans, underwear, and T-shirt, cutting them from my body, leaving me naked, cold, exposed.

Then she left. 'I've got to go get the rest of my kit out of the car,' she said, and took the flashlight with her.

For Marie, part of the thrill was playing mind-fuck, and I knew from experience that she was going to leave me like this for much longer than she would need to go down the hill. She would want me to think she was never coming back. But no matter how much I trusted her, how secure I was in the knowledge she would return, I couldn't help but panic.

I tried the ropes, but I had no room to move, no leverage, no strength that would amount to anything. The wind whistled through the *morada* and made the door creak. I heard a small animal scrabble in the corner. I could picture Marie sitting in the shelter of her car, thinking about me, thrusting fingers in her vagina, laughing maniacally.

Finally I heard her car door slam shut. But she was not coming back up the hill. She started up her engine, let it warm up for a few minutes, and then drove off. The sound of her car died out a few minutes later.

I was alone. No one but Marie knew where I was. I thought of the Spaniard in Poe's 'Pit and the Pendulum,' the prisoner of the Inquisition, bound on a cold slab in the darkness, awaiting the giant cutting blade as it swished through the air over his belly, gradually descending, driving him further into madness as the rats gathered below in the pit, waiting for the entrails to come.

The fantasy grew stronger, and I imagined Marie standing over me in a gray cowl, her hand on the lever controlling the giant apparatus, her eyes widening in ravenous blood lust.

I had a raging erection, but I could not touch it. It flopped on my belly like a beached whale, a drop of precum at the tip, the silver rings along the shaft clinking dully and echoing off the walls.

'Marie,' I whispered, and smiled. I knew she was not done with me. I closed my eyes and fell asleep.

'What I love about the Church is the pageantry and ritual,' Marie had told me once at the apartment. My grandparents had been Baptists, and they had stopped forcing me to go to church after my immersion, and I'd never given any religion much thought after that, until I met Marie, who had come to believe in her own personal brand of Christianity. I had come to believe in Marie.

'I'm sure it's not what it was in the days of the Latin mass,' she said. 'They're losing members, so they think they have to change, do everything in English, get involved in politics, become more "relevant" to the daily lives of their parishioners. That's why they're losing members! They've taken out the links to the past, removed themselves from the eternal mysteries that held it together. That's why I was drawn to the Penitentes.'

'You and Donald Fearn,' I said.

'But he got it all wrong,' she said. 'He may have heard vague stories about them or read the hysterical writings of Protestant missionaries who attacked the rites of the Penitentes only as an excuse to rail against popery. Donald Fearn thought they practiced ritual torture on each other and human sacrifice on the order of the Aztecs – unfortunately for Alice Porter. He was ignorant of their heritage.'

Marie told me their rituals had roots deep in the past, further than the medieval *flagellante,* further even than the early, primitive Christians, all the way back to the devotees of the goddess Diana in ancient Hellas, who scourged their own backs in her worship. The Archbishop John B. Lamy of Santa Fe, in the 1850s, tried to brand the Penitentes as heretics and have them excommunicated. But the Church gave in, recognizing them as devout believers, not devil worshipers, though explicit instructions were laid down that they were no longer to crucify any more of their brethren with spikes. By the time settlers came into the West and sneaked a forbidden peek at Penitente ceremonies, they were merely tying their chosen Christ up on the cross, but the blood still flowed down their backs from the sharp bite of their *picadors*.

The Penitentes were simple peasant farmers throughout the Rio Grande Valley and along the Sangre de Cristos, descendants of Spanish settlers in New Mexico dating back to 1598. Their sects had grown only in the rural areas away from the population centers of Santa Fe, Albuquerque, and El Paso – regions where there were too few Franciscan friars to go around. Many of the Franciscans spent more time trying to convert the Pueblo Indians than actually tending to their own flock, and some extorted huge fees for the performance of baptism, matrimony, and burial services. The rule of the Spanish territories became increasingly secular, and with the Mexican Revolution in 1820 all Spanish Franciscans were remanded to Spain – without being replaced. The rural settlements were set adrift with no spiritual guidance until the lands were annexed by the United States during the middle part of the century, by which time the Penitentes were firmly steeped in their own unique tradition.

'The Penitente women were not allowed into the circle,' Marie explained. 'But after the Last Supper on the morning of Holy Thursday, and all through Good Friday, they sang their *alabados* – rapturous, mournful chants of ecstasy and grief, the Virgin's wailing over the loss of Her Son. They sang outside the *morada* while the men were holed up inside, smoking and praying and selecting the one among them who would become the Cristo. They understood that without the darkness there could be no light, without suffering no rapture. Out of tragedy came not despair but salvation. Out of humility, dignity. Out of penance, redemption. Out of misery, ecstasy. Out of death, life. And glory.'

'Poor Donald Fearn,' Marie said, looming over me in the light from the Coleman lantern that stood between my legs. She thrust her awl deep into one of my ear holes, stretching it open with a wrench of pain and a trickle of blood. She removed the awl and inserted a thick Pueblo nail into my newly expanded hole. I clenched my teeth and drew in a sharp breath, but I could feel myself growing harder. The pain was everything I had been hoping for.

Marie had returned after perhaps an hour, waking me up with a stinging slap of her palm against my abdominals.

'If Donald Fearn were alive today,' she continued, 'he might have found some girl who would go along for the ride willingly, without his having to dump her down a well.'

This kind of talk was common for Marie when she had me at her mercy. She liked playing the part of the master criminal, telling the hero exactly what she was going to do to him rather than simply killing him in the first place and getting it over with. It upped the ante of the encounter, added a further element of danger and uncertainty.

'Look at Jeffrey Dahmer,' she said, working the blood-lubricated awl into my nose hole. 'He wanted sex slaves, but he went about it all wrong. He tried to do home lobotomies with a power drill, hoping his victims would become zombies who would answer his every beck and call. But they kept dying on him instead. He could never get it right.'

She had all my ear holes plugged with nails, and now she fit a thicker, longer one through my nose. She was turning me into a tribesman of the industrial jungle, plunging nails through every existing hole. The blood was dripping into my nasal cavity and down my throat, and I kept having to swallow it or I would choke. My breathing grew heavy; I tried to control it to keep from passing out. She would continue even if I were to fall into unconsciousness, and I didn't want to miss any of it.

'Dahmer could have gone to those same bars where he got his victims – or placed a personal ad in a magazine – and found any number of willing "slaves" who'd return week after week and do whatever he wanted as long as he didn't kill them. It just seems like such a waste.'

'But he also wanted to eat them,' I reminded her.

'Take this, my body,' she said. 'Drink this, my blood, the blood of a new covenant.'

The thick nails went in, replacing the rings at my eyebrows, nipples, navel, frenum, scrotum, and along the length of my penis and at last through the tip of my cock where my glorious Prince Albert had been. My shaft was warm and wet with blood, looking like an erotic pincushion. Every piercing throbbed, my ripped flesh screaming in pain. I made little cries as she worked, tried instinctively to squirm away from her fingers even though this was exactly what I wanted. My body was receiving pain, but my brain told me it was pleasure. Anyone who likes spicy-hot Mexican food has enjoyed a similar response. Bodybuilders grow addicted to their body's own painkilling chemicals after they've ripped their muscles to shreds from heavy lifting. Many people are masochists without even knowing or without admitting it to themselves. Others are sadists without recognizing the fact.

Marie and I were liberated. We knew ourselves. But neither of us knew how far the other was willing to go.

'I don't think I'll ever understand you,' she said as she grabbed the heavy, curved upholstery needle and threaded it with a thin strip of rawhide. 'You come to me for abuse. That's what this is, really. You want me to tie you up and beat you, knock you around, abuse you. It's what you live for. I'll never see what you get out of it. I cringe if I have a hangnail or a paper cut, but you look at it as if it's some precious gift from God.'

'It is,' I said.

'Any last requests?'

I looked up at her longingly but had no more to say.

She poked the needle through the corner of my mouth and began sewing my lips shut. When she was done, she tied off the rawhide firmly. She ran her hands along my chest, over my sensitive tattoos, and twisted the nails in my nipples as if she wanted to rip them free.

I tried to scream, but it was horribly muffled.

'See?' Marie said. 'Now no one can hear you. I guess we're ready.'

She untied my limbs, and I lay there immobile until the circulation returned. The preliminaries were finished. Now was time for the main event. She yanked me by the leash to a sitting position, then off the altar and onto my feet.

'Come, Gary,' she said. 'Now is your time. You must answer the call of your destiny.'

Marie led me outside by the light of her lantern. I was naked, tattooed, wounded with nails, the products of my dead grandfather, the tools of the carpenter, the Penitente symbol of the Cristo's suffering. The frenzied wind off the mountains chilled my flesh and made the sagebrush dance in Marie's light. The earth beneath my bare feet still retained the warmth of the sun. More stars were out than I had ever seen, staring down from the heavens, our only witnesses.

I breathed heavily through my nose, swallowing blood. My tongue toyed with the rawhide that sealed my lips. All my senses were heightened, but I was weary, dizzy, my knees weak. Blood trickled down the inside of my thighs, dripped onto the sand. I followed Marie over the hill, my eyes dreamily focused on the lantern as it swayed back and forth like a railman's signal.

We found the well hidden beneath a flimsy square of plywood. Marie knelt down and shoved it aside, shone her lantern down into its depths. 'This is where she died,' she said. 'Come take a look. Don't be afraid.'

I took tiny steps toward the brink, and Marie encouraged me a little farther. I tried to see the bottom, but the light illuminated only the earthen sides, leaving a gaping blackness. I teetered, felt as if I would fall in, but Marie caught me.

'I've got you, Gary,' she said. 'I've got you.'

Marie grabbed something from her bag and revealed it to me in the light. It was a *picador* – a many-stranded whip of braided cactus fibers, on the ends of which were attached sharp, jagged chunks of obsidian. She gave it to me, clasped my hands around it. I knew what to do with it.

She walked ahead of me but looked over her shoulder as we made our procession toward the Penitente *calvario,* which stood in the darkness a hundred yards from the *morada.*

I walked as I had seen in the photographs of Penitentes, hunched over with my back bared to the sky, my long hair dangling down in front, and brought the *picador* down heavily onto my back. Each obsidian rock was a small razor drawing blood. Marie grinned gleefully back at me. I did it again and again, over alternate shoulders. With each stroke Marie chanted an 'Our Father' or a 'Hail Mary.' I showed myself no mercy, one flagellation for each step I took, perhaps as many as a hundred until we reached the cross.

My back was a river of blood. The Penitentes had not gone completely naked but had worn white cotton breeches to catch the red flow. I had no such garments, so my buttocks and most of my legs were wet. The wind froze me as if I had just taken a shower and walked out into the cold night.

'You are Penitente,' Marie said, though a real Penitente would not have had my piercings – that was her own fetish, inspired by Donald Fearn and her own fertile imagination.

I collapsed at Marie's feet, but she hauled me back up to help her lift the cross out of its hole. It was nine or ten feet tall, built of the same sturdy timbers as the door and altar of the *morada,* weathered, silvered, cracked by storms. Someone had already done some digging around it, and I saw a shovel and another bag of equipment lying nearby. At first I feared Marie had asked some unknown other to join us, but then I realized this was where she must have come while I was asleep, when she wanted me to believe she had deserted me. She grabbed one side and I the other, and together we lifted the massive cross until it toppled over, kicking up a cloud of dust that was scattered by the wind. My limbs were shaking from the cold, pale from the loss of blood, sapped of strength, soon to fail me altogether.

'You are the Chosen One,' she told me, fixing me with her gaze. 'The Cristo reborn. It is your destiny to atone for the sins of men.'

A voice in the back of my mind noted that she had not said man or mankind but *men.* But that warning voice was lost in a cloudy haze, of no help to me now. I was so steeped in blood there was no turning back.

She laid me out to the cross. The cold, gritty wood was painful against my back. I stretched my limbs out along the crossbar, breathing through my nose, relaxing, drifting. The stars swirled above me as in a time-lapsed photograph.

'I made this out of roses,' she said, and placed the crown of thorns on my head. 'Look up at me.' In one hand she held a large wooden mallet; in the other, four iron railroad spikes. Despite the cold, despite my weak state, my cock was erect. I had no power and no desire to resist.

Marie knelt over me, her face glowing. She set the spikes down and grabbed a heavy leather blindfold from her bag. Her eyes were dark, impenetrable. I wanted to tell her how much I loved her. I wanted to thank her.

'Gary,' she said, stroking my cheek. 'You have made me so happy.' She pressed her lips against my mouth, painfully, and when she came away her chin was dripping with my blood. She gave me a warm good-bye look, put the cold blindfold over my eyes, and buckled it firmly in back of my head.

I felt the first spike rest in the palm of my hand for what seemed an eternity before she struck, driving through flesh, shattering bone, hammering deep into the wood. An otherworldly scream passed through me, unheard by her except as a whimper through my nose. Blood spilled out of the wound, and I blacked out.

I was jolted back to awareness as the cross fell into its hole, pulled into place by Marie and some rope. My hands and feet were bloated, throbbing masses skewered and held fast. My head lolled to one side, hair damp and billowing in the wind, cock erect and pointing up toward the heavens.

'Oh, yes,' Marie was saying, far down below, her voice rapturous, lost in herself. 'Gary, you are the One! You are a demigod! The Cristo lives in you, through your suffering and sacrifice!' She was breathing heavily, moaning. Though I could not see, I knew she had removed her clothes and was fingering herself.

My love for her was unbounded.

She screamed and said, 'I'm coming, Gary! Oh, this is for you, my love, I'm coming, coming . . .'

My mind dreamed up the scene, but instead of Marie, it was the Virgin Herself, Her hands gone up Her robes, Her eyes closed, mouth open, tongue stroking Her lips in sexual awakening. I was gone from the cradle, grown, the condemned man on the cross, looking down on My Mother as she came, staining the robes with Her juices. My cock exploded in a wrenching orgasm, shattering my fantasy, reacquainting me with the pain. The warm cum dribbled down my spasming shaft.

Below all was silence. I wondered if Marie was okay. I heard her gather her clothes from the dust, rise to her feet. Then up came a great wailing cry, mournful, grief-stricken, wrenched out of the depths of her throat. I imagined her tearing out her hair like a woman of Hellas.

I wanted to tell her to shed no tears. The cold wind had numbed me, freezing the blood on my back and along my legs. I wanted to tell her to be not afraid. I forgave her her trespasses. She knew not what she had done.

Sobbing, she gathered her tools from the base of the cross and tossed them into her bag. Her footsteps went running off down the hill, and her wailing turned to dark laughter that wafted up on the wind. In the distance I heard her engine sputter to life, and then she drove away. I waited, spent, contented, fulfilled, knowing Marie would return. I drifted off into glory.

'What in the name of—' said the sheriff's deputy who found me. They cut me down with a chainsaw. I had no power to move or to speak, but I was vaguely aware of my surroundings. He and the other deputies lowered the severed cross gently and unbuckled my blindfold. It was still dark, but the deputies had flashlights and lanterns. One of them used his pocketknife to cut the stitches on my lips. EMS workers jimmied loose the spikes, released me from the cross, put me on a gurney, and took me to the ambulance the deputies had called in from Canon City, where they took me to a hospital.

'Marie,' I mumbled. 'Marie, Marie . . .'

'Is that who did this to you?' asked the deputy, who was riding along with me, while the EMS guys worked on bandaging my wounds, removing my decorative nails.

I chose not to answer the deputy's question.

I was in and out of the hospital for months and had countless operations on my shattered hands and feet. Grandma took care of me at her home while I healed. I told the deputies and my grandma that I had been kidnapped by some crazy man in the back alley behind the Belfry. I gave them a description but said I had been blindfolded, it had been dark, and I had only a rough idea what he looked like. Outwardly, to them, I agreed whenever they said I had gone through a horrible ordeal. They said I was lucky, but they meant lucky they had stumbled across me, lucky I was alive.

'We always take a peek up at the old *morada* on the night of Good Friday,' one of them said. 'There's always someone up to no good. I never seen anything like this, myself. The old-timers talk about some strange sex murder happened years back, but I'd be surprised if it was any worse than this.'

I knew I was lucky, but I kept it to myself I'd had a strange, transcendental experience, thanks to Marie. I owed her. I would follow her anywhere, do anything for her – if only I knew where she was. She had disappeared that night at the ghost village, gone off in her Maverick and vanished. Perhaps she had gone to her ex-roommate in Seattle, the one she said had raped her. Maybe she forgave him now.

When I was eventually able to get around on my own, still with the assistance of crutches, I went back to the apartment and found Marie and all our things gone. I later borrowed Grandma's Pinto and went driving back up to see the village again by daylight. I checked the *morada,* but there was no one there. I went up to the well, slid the cover aside, and shone a high-powered flashlight within. I saw the bottom of the well, but Marie wasn't there.

I hobbled up to the dusty cross that now lay on the ground, stained darkly with my blood, and sat down on its severed stump, staring off toward the sun that lingered brightly over the Sangre de Cristos and wondering why Marie, my goddess, had forsaken me.

John Peyton Cooke *was born in 1967 and grew up nurtured by a steady diet of Stephen King and* Fangoria *magazine. His short stories have appeared in such markets as* Weird Tales *and* Christopher Street. *His novels include* The Lake, Out for Blood, Torsos, The Chimney Sweeper, *and the forthcoming* Haven. *He lives in New York City.*

Driven

BY

Kathryn Ptacek

My life is slowly being sucked out of me . . . bled away by my miserable existence, as if a vampire has attached itself to me. No, make that a spider. A spider's just as bad – she sits in her web, waiting for her prey, and when she captures it, she sucks the poor thing dry until there's only a husk left.

That's me . . . fast becoming the husk.

I study myself in the hall mirror and discover minute lines around my eyes that I know weren't there months ago. My skin looks dry . . . wasted. I could be ten years – fifteen years – older than I really am.

Dry . . . drying . . . dried . . . dust . . .

I take a ragged breath as I examine the handful of mail and my hands shake. I know what the official-looking envelopes contain even without tearing them open.

Past due.

Past due.

Past due.

You are X months late with payment.

We are turning your account over to collection.

We regret that you haven't contacted us . . .

We will be forced to . . .

And me with all of $38 in my checking account.

I crumple the envelopes suddenly, then carefully smooth the papers.

I don't know whether to cry or curse. I've done both in the months since Jack left.

It hasn't helped.

I've written letter after letter to my creditors explaining that I'm not trying to screw them out of payment and that I really intend to pay but that it will just have to be real slow, and the next week the dunning phone calls continue, the intimidating letters fill the mailbox. The calls are so bad now that mostly I leave the phone unplugged. *That* was disconnected twice in the past few months, and the electric company is threatening to shut me off.

Gritting my teeth, I toss the mail onto the hall table along with all the other unopened envelopes, including those from Jack.

I push back an errant strand and pick up the painting, my keys and purse, and slam out of the house. The glass panes in the door rattle.

I have plenty of time before I go to work, so first I'll drop the picture off to be framed. It's an oil that I was commissioned for months ago, and I finished it last week. It's not completely dry – the weather is too humid for that – but I can't wait any longer; I need the money. Time after time I'd started the painting, but it hadn't come together for the longest time. I'm not completely happy with it, but . . . I wish I had more time and energy for my art, but I don't; I'm lucky to get a bit done each weekend. And it's not easy being creative when you're depressed all the time.

My friends tell me to hang on, and I'm trying; I'm trying to have a positive attitude, trying to hope that things will change for the better . . . but it's hard . . . damned hard.

At the corner, I bear left. Ahead, a line of cars sits at a stop sign. There's no reason for this backup – there's not much traffic, and no pedestrians are crossing the street. I drum my fingernails on the steering wheel. I play with the electric windows, sliding first one, then the other up, then down. I adjust my seat, my rearview mirror and side mirrors, and just as I'm about to honk the horn, the convertible in front of me slides forward a few feet. I inch up, leaving my foot on the brake. A bead of sweat trickles down my back, and I lean forward to cool off. I'd turn on the air conditioning, but that overheats the engine. It's so hot these days; no rain in sight, with temperatures predicted to hover in the nineties for at least another week or so.

Suddenly something thumps me from behind, and I blink, for a moment not understanding.

Then I know: some idiot has smacked me. I leap out to inspect the damage.

The other driver, an older woman with wispy white hair, slowly emerges from her Jaguar. Her lower lip wobbles as she approaches me and she starts to cry.

'I'm so sorry. I didn't mean to hit you. I just thought you were going to move more. I'm really sorry. I'm so sorry. Really.' She wrings her hands, hands dotted with age spots, hands where the veins stick out in vivid relief.

I remember the last time I saw my mother – her fingers were all gnarled, and the veins stood out so prominently; when I had taken her hand, though, it had been cold, icy cold. I feel the anger build inside, and I lash out, almost screaming. 'You dumb bitch, why don't you watch what you're doing? Why don't you pay attention instead of fiddling with your radio or messing with your stupid hair? Lucky for you I don't have my baby in the car.'

I march off and, now that the cars in front of me are gone, drive off. Trembling, I glance back in the mirror and see the old woman sagging against the Jag. I bite my lip. I don't know why I blew up. There really isn't any damage to my bumper, and her car had the scrapes. I felt bad seeing her cry, but somehow that had made me angrier, made me really want to lash out.

And why did I say that thing about the baby? I don't have one.

I shudder. Maybe it's the heat. The heat and humidity.

I can't park by the frame shop, so I settle for a space in front of a building down the way. The walk back is hot, the asphalt underfoot sticky; rotting fruit from a nearby tree stains the sidewalk.

The guy behind the counter barely glances at me when I enter. He's on the phone and from the way his voice is lowered, it isn't with a customer. I wait for a minute, then two, then three. Finally, when I've been there over five minutes, I clear my throat.

'I gotta go. Call me back in a minute.'

I think our transaction will take longer than that, but I say nothing.

'Yeah?' the clerk asks as he approaches. His tone is surly, and it's obvious he thinks a customer is interrupting his life.

'I called earlier in the week – I had a hell of a time getting through, too; the phone's always busy.' I glare at him, knowing now why I kept getting a busy signal. 'I have this painting to frame, and the man I talked to said it would take only a few days.'

'Yeah, well, Dave isn't here.'

'Who's Dave?' I ask, baffled.

'He's the guy who frames. I don't know when he'll be back.'

'Can you give me an estimate?'

'I don't do frames.'

You don't do much, I want to point out. 'Well, don't you have a chart or something?'

'Yeah.'

It's such an imposition, I know, for me to expect the guy to do *something*.

The clerk takes the painting from me, and I slap his hand. 'Don't touch the canvas. You'll wreck it.'

'My hands are clean.'

'It doesn't matter. You can leave marks even if you just washed your hands.'

He starts to pick it up again, his fingers against the canvas, and I snatch the painting back. He grabs it, and one of his nails scrapes against pigment, leaving an inch-long scar.

All my hard work . . . 'You idiot. Look what you've done.' Tears brim my eyes as I cradle the painting. 'Forget it. Just tell Dave or whoever that I'll be back in a few days. And it won't be to have my picture framed, but rather to complain about you.'

'Fuck off, lady.' As he starts to turn away, he's already reaching for the phone.

I slam out of the shop and return to my car. Something official-looking flaps under the windshield wiper and I stare at it in disbelief. A ticket.

But why?

I glance around and for the first time see the hydrant. I groan. I hadn't even noticed it when I parked. I grab the ticket, nearly ripping it in half in the process, and thrust it inside my purse, then sit in the car and stare at the painting.

I can repair the damage; it isn't that bad, but . . . but it angers me. Why was he such a moron? Why wouldn't he listen to me? Why hadn't *Jack* listened to me? I take out my Swiss army knife and run the flat of a blade across the raised pigment to see if I can smooth it a bit. It looks worse than before. Suddenly I hate the clerk, hate what he did, hate the painting. I thrust the knife into the canvas, and smile as the canvas rips. I slash over and over, until it's practically in shreds; then I toss it into the backseat.

My hair straggles into my face, and I slap it back with both hands, unmindful of the open knife. When the point of the blade grazes my temple, I drop it, and it falls onto the floor. I lick my dry lips.

Everything these days frustrates me; little things just pile up and up and up, and bother me. Someone can say 'boo' and I'll either cry or get angry. I have to get control, have to get back on even keel, except that I don't know how to do that anymore, don't know what I can do to calm things down. Once my life was so orderly; now it seems utter chaos; I'm on a constant roller coaster that mostly heads down and down and down.

It's okay . . . I can do the painting again. Do it better this time. I can still get paid; that's the important part.

I start the car and wince as it threatens to die – and ease out onto the clear roadway, just in time to have someone in a red import race up close to my bumper and lay on the horn. As she swings around me, a teenage girl flips me the bird.

Give me a fucking break, I think. The girl hadn't been in sight when I pulled out.

My hands are trembling, I realize, as I park in the lot at work. I retrieve the knife and close it, slip it back into my purse. As I walk into the building, a blast of air conditioning hits me. Maybe this will cool me down, I think – in more ways than one. I greet the usual people in the outer offices. Most merely nod or keep their heads down, and my skin prickles. What's wrong?

I'm barely settled at my desk when the phone rings. It's my boss wanting to see me. I glance at my watch; I'm only a minute late. That isn't so bad; we've talked about it before, and he says he doesn't mind if I'm a few minutes late here and there because he knows I will make it up at the end of the day.

I smooth down my hair, powder my nose, and then slowly walk down the hall to his office and wait outside the closed door. I try chatting with Vickie, his white-haired secretary, but the woman abruptly excuses herself for the ladies' room.

'Come on, Carol,' Dick says, sticking his head out the door. His tone isn't jovial – it's polite, nothing more. I enter. The personnel manager is there as well, and several department heads.

There is no chair for me to sit in. None of others look at me.

I remain standing while Dick closes the door.

He walks around to his desk and sits down behind it. He picks up a letter opener in the shape of a small jeweled dagger. His expression is grim. 'I'm sorry, Carol, but we aren't happy with the work you've been doing for us.'

I blink at him. 'Aren't happy? But you gave me a raise last month at my yearly review.'

'I know, but there were problems then.'

'Why didn't you say something? I could have tried to improve or change or something. I can still do something.' I try to keep the eagerness out of my voice; I don't want to look like I'm groveling, even though I am.

He strokes the letter opener now, and I hope he cuts himself, hope he drips blood all over his precious month-end reports. 'I'm sorry, Carol, but we're just not satisfied with your performance. Over the past year you haven't shown the growth we expected; you're not as aggressive as we anticipated. And there's the little matter of the personal problems, too. That's taken away from your job, and impacted your performance here.'

Impacted? My problems – the 'little matter' of Jack has torn my life apart. Not 'impacted.' Why can't he even speak proper English? When it all began, Dick brought me into his office and told me how sorry he was, and how they all understood, and they would understand if I needed a day or two off here and there, etc. He had been so warm, so friendly . . . so two-faced.

'. . . and so we're going to have to let you go.'

'Let me go?' Somehow the words don't make sense to me. I realize I've missed other things he said, but it doesn't matter. Just the last words did.

I lick my lips, feel how dry they were, how dry my throat is.

Dry. . . drying . . .

Dick clears his throat. 'Al will take you back to your office, where you can clean out your desk, and he'll escort you from the building.'

'That's it? I don't get a warning? I don't get put on probation? You're firing me just like that? Without any warning whatsoever? You said before that you all understood about what was going on, you said that you'd cut me some slack, you said—'

'Carol, I said that for some time we haven't been—'

'I know what you *said,* Dick, but why didn't you let me know this before so I could have tried to work harder? Why did you just wait to spring this on me? Why?'

He starts to speak again, and I know what he'll say. We haven't been happy for some time, we haven't this, we haven't that – everything he spewed out just moments before he'll parrot over and over, as if he's nothing more than a tape loop.

'You'll have to surrender your key.'

I want to grab the little dagger letter opener and plunge it into his heart. If he has one. I would love that, seeing the surprise in his eyes as he tries to wiggle away from me . . . only I wouldn't let him. I'd twist the dagger in his chest and twist and twist and twist, and the blood would spurt all over me, and I wouldn't be so dry anymore.

He sits there watching me.

They are all waiting for my reaction, waiting for me to cry, to beg for my job back. The hell with that. I won't give them the satisfaction of me crying. Not that I feel like it; I don't think I have any tears left.

Numbly I yank my key chain out, and unhook my office key and fling it at him; it hits him squarely in the chest. My lips curl into a faint smile. My fingers shake so badly I can't get the other keys back on the chain, so I just thrust them into my purse.

I whirl and leave his office, brush past Vickie who has returned and half walk, half stumble to my office.

I know my face is red, can feel the heat of it, and I glance wildly around for a carton to put my things in. Vaguely I'm aware of Al lurking in the doorway. Probably wants to make sure I don't steal my desk or chair. Absurd! I've been a trusted employee, and now this . . . humiliation . . . this indignity.

Moments later Nora from accounting comes in, all apologetic and more than a little embarrassed, with a computer paper carton. She murmurs that she's sorry, slaps the container on my desk, then ducks out.

I jerk open my desk drawers, sweep the contents into the box. Silently I dare Al to challenge me on any of the contents. I pick up my coffee mug and toss it with the other stuff, then set my purse on top of everything. I pick up the carton and brush past him.

'I'm sorry—' Al begins.

'Yeah, I just bet you are.'

I walk through the building, aware that everyone is watching me now, aware that Al is trailing after me. What are they afraid I'll do? Destroy something along the way? Duck into someone's office and hide?

This is ridiculous.

But it is a ridiculous place, always has been.

He opens the door for me and I go out without thanking him, and walk stiffly to the car. I open the trunk and drop the box back there. Slam the trunk lid down. Open it again to retrieve my purse, then slam it. I get in my car and sit there, and stare at the building.

I can see some faces at windows here and there, and I wonder if Dick is watching. Good ol' Dick. Dick the Prick, we all used to call him behind his back. How much of that, I wonder now, got back to him? If I don't leave after a while, will he call the police and accuse me of trespassing? The thought is almost funny. One part of me wants to stay there and find out just what he'll do.

Another part of me wants to start up the car, press the gas pedal down *hard,* and just gun that sucker into the front of the building. I smile, envisioning the building's glass front shattering into millions of shards as the car smashes through it, imagine the satisfying crunch I'd make as I hit the receptionist's desk, imagine all the whirling papers and alarmed voices and fragments of glass and wood everywhere.

Fragments. Like my life. Everything is in pieces.

I can feel the tears now, feel their warmth creeping down my cheeks, and I pound the steering wheel with a clenched fist over and over until I know my hand is bruised.

I brush at the tears, and through their haze I see someone coming out into the parking lot. Sending the Gestapo, I tell myself, and back jerkily out of the parking space. I won't give them the satisfaction of seeing me cry. I blot at my tears with a tissue, wipe the sweat off my face and grimace.

Whoever it was goes back inside. No one watches now.

They're spiders, all of them. They've sucked me dry and thrown me out, just as they will with everyone else inside that building.

I slam on the brakes, take out the army knife, and run back to Dick's parking spot. I unfold the biggest blade and stab one of the tires. Nothing happens. I try again and glance nervously at the door. I don't have much time before someone comes out. The tire will take forever. I stand up and glance inside the Continental, then smile. I open the door and run my hand across the fine leather seat.

Then I bring the knife down and slit the seat open in one long, very satisfying tear.

I walk back to my car.

I pause at the driveway, wondering where to go. Home? To do what? Just sit and stare out the window and think about how miserable my live is and how I hate everything and everyone at the moment?

No.

Or I can just drive around. And maybe that will calm me a bit.

I switch on the radio, and frown at the music under the crackling. Yeah, that needs fixing, too.

I wheel onto the roadway, nearly sideswiping an A&P semi. I don't care. Let 'em wipe me out. It'll be less expensive that way, I think bitterly.

No husband.

No job.

No money.

And just how the hell am I supposed to pay my mortgage? How am I supposed to pay for groceries? At least the old sedan is paid for; that's something they can't repossess for nonpayment. At least I don't think so.

I drive blindly, not knowing where I'm going, not caring. I head out to the A&P shopping center and circle the parking lot, wondering if I should go into one of the stores just to be *doing* something, but all those things to be bought there will just remind me of how little money I have.

I head downtown then and creep past the video store and the pizzeria and the new Chinese restaurant. I haven't been out to eat in months – too expensive. And I'd always loved eating at the Chinese place.

Then I am past the frame place once more. I pull into a parking lot and stare across at the liquor store. I could buy something. Some wine. A wine cooler. A six-pack of beer. Something. I don't care to drink, though, and that angers me. I would like to get lost in an alcoholic haze right about now.

Maybe getting fired isn't such a bad thing, though. Maybe that will give me a chance to concentrate on my art. I'll have more time for painting; I can put up some of my business cards on bulletin boards around town. I'll call some of my old contacts, see if they need some artwork done for ads or whatever. There are ways . . . things to do. It isn't hopeless yet. I can't give up. Not yet. The husk still has some life in it.

I decide to leave, and wait while the vehicle in front of me sits at the stop sign. Another one, I think, and bite down on my lip.

The woman has a fancy new silver van filled with high school-aged kids. The woman, who keeps twisting around to make some point in her conversation, seems to have forgotten that she's blocking a driveway. Or perhaps she just doesn't care. I wait, and just as I'm about to honk my horn, the woman hops out of the van and, looking around to make sure no one sees, slips a flattened aluminum can under one of the landscaped shrubs. Then she climbs back into her van and turns right.

What the hell is that? I wonder. She can't keep a squished can in her precious van? Her brand-new van that cost nearly thirty grand, and which probably has a working radio and doesn't overheat when the air conditioning is on.

I bite harder on my lip, and the wound bleeds more.

I swing into the road, following the van, which swings left onto Ryerson. I turn left.

The van stops at the traffic light. I stop.

The van drives down Ryerson for a mile or so, and I trail behind, sometimes discreetly, sometimes not. I don't care if the woman sees me, if the woman knows I'm following her. I don't care. That fucking woman has tons of money and has nothing better to do with her life than to ferry kids back and forth, and I'm very sure *she* doesn't have to worry about phones being disconnected, and not having a job or money to pay her mortgage or buy groceries or do anything decent in her life, and I am fucking well sure that this woman never felt a creative urge in her body in all her vapid suburban life and that she can't tell an oil from a watercolor, and what the hell is she doing with such a nice, fine life when she doesn't deserve it?

The van is out on Main Street, now, and I follow. The woman stops at Maple, and one of the kids jumps out and waves. The other driver honks. I honk. The van starts up again and then stops half a block down. Another kid leaps out.

What? The kid can't even walk a few houses down? I ask myself incredulously, oblivious to the blood that runs down my chin from my lip.

The woman stops next at the Quik Check and runs inside, leaving the van idling. I park a row behind and watch. Moments later the driver returns, a small bag in her hands. She glances at my car, then away.

The bitch knows, I think, and I smile.

The van starts out again, and I follow. The other woman drives out to the streets by the country club, and I cruise behind her. She's been driving all over town, I realize, up one street and down another. Like an insect trying to find its way off a web.

I smile.

I'm not the husk, not the hapless prey in the web, I realize. *I* am the spider. I'm not waiting to get zapped by some human arachnid – I'm the eight-legged terror that glides along the silken strands of the web to rid it of these flies, these worthless things that clutter the world. Yeah, that's it.

What a predator I am. I am hunting prey . . . weak suburban prey. I grin into the rearview mirror at myself and am surprised to see the trickle of blood. I lick it away and concentrate on driving. I am very meticulous about putting my turn signal on far enough in advance and not tailgating. I don't want to be stopped by a cop. But I wonder what it would be like to nudge the van a little, just a little, just knock it a few inches forward, or maybe a foot, or maybe just slam full speed into the back and—

I want to see the terror in my prey's eyes.

The woman stops at another house, this one a really fancy one, and I wonder if it's hers. No. She pulls away again. The 'fly' seems to be going a little faster than earlier. Is she a little anxious? Good. Let her wonder what's going on. Let her worry like I always have to worry.

I glance at my watch and see I've been following the woman for over an hour now. My grin broadens.

I am hunting this woman, hunting down this moronic creature who has all the time in the world and doesn't know what it is like to paint an exquisite landscape, who doesn't know what it is to have her beloved husband leave her for some two-bit woman in his office, who isn't drying up before her time, who doesn't know anything about living.

Living. Yeah, this is real living.

I am smiling so widely now that it feels like my face is about to crack open. I lick my dry lips, wipe the sweat off my forehead.

I wish I had a gun. A nice handgun that I could take out of the glove box. I can smell the oil on it, feel its cold, metallic hardness. I would stroke the barrel, check the chamber, and then I'd raise it up to the windshield, and I'd imagine what would happen when I pull the trigger—

. . . the shattering of the glass . . . the sound of the bullet as it rips through the metal . . . the impact of the slug as it tears into the woman . . . the woman's scream . . . the blood and . . .

. . . the blood . . .

. . . all that blood from hapless victims to be sucked out of them . . .

. . . blood . . .

I taste something coppery on my lips – blood, I realize – and I blink. I glance at the van, then at the clock on the dashboard. Another hour has elapsed, and I have no idea where I've been or even how I've been driving. I don't remember a single thing. Nothing since I thought about the gun.

I wipe the sweat on my chin and my hand comes away red.

We are back on Maple, I see. I frown. Is it even the same van? Isn't that woman's van silver? This is blue-gray. Not the same. Or is it? Maybe it's a trick of the light. Maybe the van really is more blue than I thought earlier?

Maybe.

Or maybe this is a different van altogether.

And how long have I been following this one? How long have I thought it was the same van?

Hours.

Hours gone, hours out of my life.

I have wasted hours of my day.

Tears burn in my eyes, and I swallow heavily.

What's wrong with me? I thought I was coping well enough, and here I've gone and done this . . . stupid thing. I brush the tears away and back the car away from the van. I have to go home. I am falling apart, and I am scared.

At the stop sign I wait for the street to clear. I glance briefly in my rearview mirror as a red import pulls up behind me. Finally, it is clear, and I turn into the lane.

I don't want to think anymore about spiders and webs and prey.

I'll go home and take a bath – no, a shower; that's more invigorating – and I'll even wash my hair, and I'll dress in fresh clothes, and then I'll sit down at the dining room table with a pencil and pad of paper and list my options. I can apply for unemployment, get food stamps, ask my mom for money, sign up for one of those classes they always have for women left in the lurch – well, there are a lot of things I can do rather than wallow in self-pity.

I turn off Maple onto Main, the red car still behind me. It drives neither too fast nor too slow, and the driver seems to be watching me intently.

I swing onto Ryerson; the import follows. I go out to the A&P parking lot. The red car remains behind.

I force myself not to look in the mirror, not to think about the other car, and head back home.

But as I roll into my driveway, I glance back in the mirror. The red car still shadows me and is now slowing down.

I get out of my car, and just as I step into the house, I hear the *click* of a car door.

Jack had a gun, but he took it with him. It doesn't matter. There are other things around the house . . . my lair . . . a knife, a hammer, what's the difference – I know how to use them all.

The doorbell rings.

I stand in the hallway, not moving.

It rings again, and someone knocks.

Patience.

The door is unlocked. Sooner or later she'll try it.

Come into my parlor . . .

Kathryn Ptacek *has sold eighteen novels, and edited three anthologies (among them the critically acclaimed* Women of Darkness*); her stories have appeared in numerous magazines and anthologies. She also writes review columns for* Cemetery Dance *and* Dead of Night*, and is a member of Horror Writers Association, Sisters in Crime, and Mystery Writers of America. A full-time compositor at the* New Jersey Herald *(the local newspaper in Newton, NJ), she is also the editor/publisher of* The Gila Queen's Guide to Markets*, a market newsletter for writers and artists, and prepares market reports for HWA and* Horror Magazine. *She collects teapots and cat whiskers.*

Barbara

BY

JOHN SHIRLEY

'YOU don't do some guy, even some old guy, them motherfuckers are all NRA nuts, homie; you might think you get some old white dude can't do shit and he dust you up.' VJ is telling Reebok this while they stand in the bus shelter, watch people coming and going in the mall parking lot, late afternoon. California spring breeze is blowing trash by, couple of wax cups from Taco Bell.

'He got an AK in his walker?' Reebok jokes. He's out of high school now, still the class joker VJ thinks.

'You laughin', some of those old dudes are strapped big. Some senile motherfucker shot Harold's dog, all the dog do is run up on his porch. They got those M16's, that shit pops off, you cancelled.'

'So you think . . . it should be girls?' Reebok ponders, scratching his tag into the clear plastic wall of the kiosk with a house key. Key to his grandma's house. His mama left town with that white dude.

'Girls maybe armed, too. Most of 'em at least got that pepper spray, but you smart, you don't give'm a chance to use it, you take it away, put it in their eyes.' VJ nods to himself.

'Can't make her use the fuckin' ATM, she got pepper in her eyes.'

'I hear that. I hear that. We just jack the bitch from behind, is all, take her pepper away. Maybe later on, we clock her, too.'

'When we do it?' Reebok asks.

'Fuck it. What about that one?'

She knows that Avery loves her. There's no doubt about it. If he says, Barbara, don't call back . . . that means: Barbara, call back again; Barbara, don't give up. It was there in the catch in his voice. It was heartbreaking, really, how Avery suffered. He *can't* say what he means, not with his witch wife, that witch bitch, not with Velma looking over his shoulder. Busting his balls, excuse my French. Not letting his manhood emerge. His manhood trapped inside him. Avery should never have let Velma come into the office at all.

When Barbara had been in the office, it was beautiful, they'd share treats, and he'd smile at her in the way that meant, *I want you, even though I can't say so, and you know I do and I know I do; I want you.* It was so precious how all of that was in one smile! That was Avery. But Velma kept him on a leash like he's one of those little dogs with the hair puffed up over their eyes, little brown eyes like Avery's.

Coming out of the mall, Barbara's got the gift for Avery in her straw bag, the Italian peasant's bag she'd bought at the Cost Plus import place, and she's thinking maybe she should have charged the watch, because this was risky, she'd never stolen anything before, almost never, anyway nothing this expensive, and they could be following her out of the mall, waiting till she crossed some legal boundary, and it's not like they'd understand. *Love paid for it,* she could say to them, but they wouldn't understand anymore than Velma did. Velma was the one who had pushed Avery into firing her.

Barbara unlocks her car, her hands fumbling. Then she goes all cold in the legs when a man speaks to her, in that sharp tone, and she's sure it's a store cop. She turns, sees it's a black guy, very young, not bad-looking. Wants some money probably. He's going to tell her his car ran out of gas and he just needs gas money or one of those stories.

'I don't have any change with me,' she says. 'I don't really believe in giving money to people, it just keeps them on the streets.'

'The ho isn't listening,' says the taller of the two. How old are they? Maybe twenty, maybe.

'Lookit here,' the other one says, the one with the blue ski jacket, and he opens the jacket and shows his hand on the butt of a gun stuck in the waistband of his jeans. 'I said: Get in the car and don't scream, or I shoot you in the spine right here.'

In the spine, he says. I shoot you in the spine.

It turns out their names are VJ and Reebok. Reebok keeps talking about making her give him a blowjob. VJ says some pretty mean things about her looks and her age, though she's only thirty-eight and she's only about thirty pounds overweight or so.

VJ says, 'One thing at a time. She suck your dick. But just one thing at a time.'

Barbara's at the wheel of the Accord, VJ beside her, Reebok in back. He has a gun, too, a kind of oversized pistol with a long black metal box for the bullets. He calls the gun a Mac.

What would it be like to suck his penis? Would it be clean? He seemed clean. She could smell aftershave on them both. It's okay if it's clean.

She wonders why she isn't more scared. Maybe because they seem so ridiculous and amateurish. They don't really know what they're doing. That amateur stuff could make them even more dangerous; an officer had said that on *Cops.*

They almost drive by her bank, so she has to point it out, though she *told* them which one it was. 'There's my bank, if you want me to turn in.'

'You better be turnin' in.'

She changes lanes, cuts into the lot, kind of abruptly so that somebody honks angrily at her as she cuts them off. Then she glides the Honda Accord up to the ATM.

'You both getting out with me?' she asks as she puts the car in park.

'You just shut up, ho, and let us work on what we do,' VJ says. He looks at Reebok.

'I don't know. We both get out? That might look kinda . . .'

'Might look . . .'

'Neither one has to get out,' Barbara says, amazed at her own chutzpah. 'What you do is, you keep a gun on your lap under a coat, you watch me, and if I try to run or yell or anything, you shoot me. No wait – this is stupid! I can just give you the PIN number!'

They look at her with their mouths a little open as she digs through her purse, comes up with her Versateller card and an eye-liner pencil. Writes the number on the back of a receipt, hands it to VJ with the card. 'I'll wait here with Reebok. He can keep an eye on me.'

'How you know my name?' Reebok says with a whipping in his voice that makes her jump in her seat.

'You don't have to yell. I know your names because you said them to each other.'

'Oh.' He looks at his partner. 'Go own.' That's the way the word sounded. *Own.* She guessed it was *Go on.*

VJ starts to get out of the car. Then he turns back, takes the keys out of the car. 'Don't try any weird shit my man got a gun, too.'

'I know. I saw it. It's a big one.'

He blinks at her in momentary confusion. Then he gets out, goes up to the ATM. He puts the card in – it comes back out. He puts the card in – it comes back out. She rolls down the window.

'Whoa, ho, what you doin'!' Reebok barks at her from the back-seat.

'I'm just going to tell him something about the ATM.' She sticks her head out the window. 'VJ? You've got the card turned the wrong way.'

He turns it the right way around. It goes in and stays. He stares at the screen, punches the numbers. Waits.

Barbara's thinking. Aloud she says, 'Were you ever in love with anybody, Reebok?'

'What?'

'I'm in love with Avery; he's in love with me. But we can't see each other much. I see him outside his house sometimes.'

'What the fuck you talking about? Shut the fuck up.'

VJ comes back scowling, gets into the car.

'There ain't shit in there but forty dollar.' He holds up the two twenties.

'You check the account?' Reebok asks him.

'Forty dollars.' He looks hard at Barbara. 'You got another account?'

'No. That was all I have left. I got fired from my job a few months ago. You know how that is.'

'The fuck.' He's busy rooting through her purse.

'Just dump it out,' she says. 'It's hard to find anything unless you dump it out.'

He looks at her hard. He mutters something. Then he dumps it out on his lap. He finds the checkbook, checks it against the receipt from the ATM. Same account number. He doesn't find any credit cards. Any other bank cards.

'You can look through my apartment,' she suggests. 'It's not too far away.' She looks at Reebok. 'We might be more comfortable there. I have some cold pizza.'

'Girl,' VJ says with a different, patient tone, as if talking to an idiot, 'you been carjacked. *Carjacked.* We're not eating your motherfucking pizza. We carjacking.'

'We could sell my car for parts,' she suggests. 'You could strip it.'

'You got any jewelry at your house?'

'You can look, but I haven't got any, no, except junk. All I've got's a cat. Some cold pizza. I could get some beer.'

'The ho's retarded,' Reebok says.

'I think I'm the one doing the best thinking here,' Barbara points out. She spreads her hands and adds, 'If you want to rape me, you should do it at my house, where it's safe. If you want to strip the car we should go do that. But we shouldn't stay here because it might call attention to us, just sitting in the parking lot.'

VJ looks at Reebok. She can't read the look.

She decides it's time to make the suggestion. 'I do know where there's money. Lots of it. It's in a safe, but we can get it.'

Avery knows it's going to be a good one because his palms are clammy. He's sensitive to things like that. He looks at the clock on his desk. Velma is going to be in here in five minutes, with the outfit he got for her in that shop in Los Angeles, and his willy is already stirring against his thigh, with that sort of core sensation running through it, like a hot wire running back into his testicles, and his palms are clammy and the hair on the back of his neck is standing up, all from trying not to think about her coming through the door of his office with that outfit under her coat. She could be a bitch, and you could take that to the bank, but by *God* there was no one like her when it came to playing those little games that got his blood up. They had it down to, what, maybe twice a month now, and that was just about right. He was almost fifty, and he had to sort of apportion out his energy with this kind of thing. He needed that extra something to prime the pump, and for a woman of forty-five she sure could—

The phone rings. 'Beecham Real Estate,' Avery says into it.

There's a lady on the other end wants to know about his rental properties. Wonder what kind of underwear *you* got on, he says to her in his mind. Out loud he says, 'I can ask Velma to show the place tomorrow morning. It's a great little find . . . no, this afternoon might be kinda hard . . .'

The woman goes on and on about her 'needs.' Her rental needs. While he pretends to listen, Avery fantasizes about getting a line on some little cookie like this, a *young* one, giving her a house to live in at minimal rent in exchange for nookie once in a while. Trouble is, Velma goes over all the rental accounts. She'd notice the discrepancy. There's always a snag and it's always your hag.

But Velma was okay. She liked games, liked to do it in the office, in broad daylight. Long as the shades are down.

He remembers that girl in the Philippines when he was in the Navy. He shipped out two days after she said she was pregnant. Like that was an accident, her getting pregnant. But what a tail. That petite golden tail. And he remembers those paper lanterns she got from some Japanese sailor. The shifting colored light on the wall from those paper lanterns, swinging in the breeze coming through the mango tree while he worked that golden tail. Man.

Beeping tone tells him he's got another call coming in; he wriggles off the first call (love to answer your *needs*) and takes the second call, which is from his lawyer, the bloodsucking cocksucker. 'What you going to charge me for this call, Heidekker?' Avery asks, looking out the window to see if Velma's car's in the parking lot. Don't see it. That yellow Accord, who's car is that? He knows that car, doesn't he?

'No, I'm not charging you for this call,' Heidekker says. 'Now listen—'

'I've about had it with you sending me a bill every time you fart in an elevator with me, pal, I got to tell you.'

'Look, I just need you to sign the request for an injunction because I'm gonna run it over to Judge Chang in about an hour here—'

'Just scribble my fucking signature on it. Just get it done.' Goddamn it, now Heidekker's got him thinking about Barbara, and of course his dick starts shriveling up. He tries not to think about Barbara, it shoots his nerves to hell, seeing her hang around his house, watching him in the parking lot—

'I'm not empowered, you're going to have to sign. If you want to give me power of attorney some time, that might be a good idea and we could talk about that—'

'No, forget it, forget it, just—' There, that was Velma's Fiat pulling in. 'Just don't come over for half an hour or so. I won't be in. So, this paper going to do it all?'

'This injunction's all-inclusive – she may not follow you, watch you, call you, the whole shebang. Can't come within five hundred yards. There are laws about stalking now, and we can prosecute her on them if she tries anything cute. She'll end up doing time. Which might do her good because they'd send her to a shrink. You change the locks at the office yet?'

'No, that's tomorrow morning. She might have a key, if she copied it. Frank says I should be flattered. Hey, not by the attention I get from this girl, pal.'

'Anyway, we'll take care of it. I gotta go, Avery—'

'Hold on now, hold on—' Keep him talking a minute, it went with the fantasy for Velma to interrupt a business call. 'I gotta talk to you about this bill you sent me for last month, this is right on the edge of outrageous, here, Heidekker—'

'Look, we can go over it item by item, but I'm going to have to charge you for the time it takes to do that—'

The door opens; Velma's taking up most of the doorframe, unbuttoning her coat, her long red hair down over the white, freckled shoulders as she slips the coat away: freckles on the white, doughy titties cupped by the black lace corset, those thighs under the crotchless panties maybe a little heavy but when she's wearing crotchless red lace panties, who the fuck cares. Lot of makeup around her deep-set green eyes. Maybe she's got some crow's feet; maybe her butt's beginning to sag. But with the corset holding it all together in black and red lace, with her pink labia winking out from the golden-red bush, who the fuck, who the fuck, who the fuck cares . . .

'Get back to you later, Heidekker,' Avery says into the phone, hanging up.

'I had to have it. I want that woodie in your pants, Av. I was touching myself and thinking about you and I had to have it, I couldn't wait. I want it here and now,' she says in that husky voice she does. 'Give me that big woodie.' She traces her cherry red Revlon lips with the tip of her tongue.

'It's easy to misunderstand Avery,' Barbara's saying. They're in her car, in a corner of the parking lot of Avery's building. 'I mean, Avery's so gruff. It's really cute how gruff he is. I gave him a stuffed bear once, with a note, it said: "You're just a big old bear!" The way he talks is very short sometimes, and pretty blue, if you know what I mean, but he's really very, very sweet and sometimes he—'

'There any money in that place?' VJ interrupts, looking through the windshield at the little, sienna-colored office building. Kind of place built in the early seventies, with those chunks of rocks on the roof, some insulation fad. 'I think you frontin', girl, I don't think there's shit in there.'

At least, she thinks, I've graduated from *ho* to *girl*. 'He keeps a lot of cash in his safe. I think he's hiding it from the IRS. It was part of some payoff kind of thing for—'

'How much?' Reebok interrupted.

'Maybe fifty, maybe a hundred thousand dollars. It *is* quite a lot of money, isn't it? I never really thought about it much before . . .'

'That place kind of rundown, don't look like anybody in there doing that good.'

'The recession killed two of the businesses that were there, and it's a little place and Avery's the only one left and he owns the building and he's gonna renovate – he's really just incredibly smart about those things, he always has these great plans for—'

'*Damn* shut the *fuck* up about the man!' Reebok snarled. 'Mother*fucker!*'

'Fine, but just remember we can't go in there shooting because I don't want Avery to get hurt—'

'Ho, what the *fuck* you talkin' about – we step where we want, we got the motherfuckin' *guns*—'

'You need me. I know the combination to the safe.'

Reebok goes tense in the backseat and shoves his gun at her. 'And I know how to use this piece right here, you fuckin' white-tail bitch!'

'Then shoot me,' she says, shrugging, surprising herself again. But meaning it. She doesn't care that much, really. Velma has Avery and nothing matters except Avery. That's what people didn't understand. Avery belongs to her, and he is the cornerstone, and he is Man and she is Woman, and that's that, and people should understand it. 'I really don't care that much,' she goes on, shrugging. 'Torture me. Kill me. I'm not going to do it unless we do it my way.'

The muscles in VJ's jaw bunch up. He points the gun at her face.

She looks into VJ's eyes. 'Do it. Throw away the money.'

VJ looks at her for a full ten seconds. Then he lowers his gun and reaches into the back, and pushes Reebok's gun down.

Right on the desk. He was doing it to her right on the desk, and he was telling her he loved her. He had her legs spread, her bony knees in his big, rough hands, and he had his pants down around his ankles, and there were zits on her thighs, she was wearing some kind of hooker costume, and . . .

He was telling her he loved her.

Then Avery's head snapped around to look at them, his mouth open and gasping with effort, his face mottled, forehead drippy, and he blinked at them. 'She locked the office door . . .' Kind of blurting it. Then he focused on Barbara and realized she must have copied the keys.

Then – she can see it in his face – he realizes he's standing there with his pants down and his penis in Velma, who's propped on a desk with her legs spread, and two strange black guys are standing behind Barbara staring at him over her shoulder.

'Jesus Christ Mary Mother of God' is what comes out of him next as he pulls out his penis and grabs his pants, and Velma opens her eyes and sees Barbara and Reebok and VJ and screams.

Velma scrambles off the desk, hunching down behind it. Avery hits the silent alarm button, but it won't work; Barbara switched it off.

When Barbara was a little girl in Florida, she witnessed a hurricane. She was staying at her granddad's orange farm. Her grandma kept chickens, and Barbara looked through a knothole in the wall of the storm shelter and saw a chicken spreading its wings and being caught by the wind and the chicken was lifted into the sky and it disappeared up there, in the boiling air. Barbara feels now like there's a big wind behind her, pushing her into the room, only the wind is inside her, and she does what it wants to do, and it's carrying her around the room, like a tornado's whirling, carrying her around and around the desk, and it's howling out of her: *'Thats how she traps you, Avery! That's how she did it and she's dressed like a hooker and that's completely right because she is a whore, she's a WHORE who's trapped you with her cunt and she is an evil, evil WHORE!'*

Avery had his pants up and he was seeing Reebok and VJ come into the room and he was reaching into the desk drawer. Barbara is swept up to the desk by the wind feeling, and she *slams* the desk drawer on his hand. *'No.'*

Avery yelps with hurt, and when she hears that, something just *lets go* in Barbara; a spillway opens up in her and she thinks, *I forgot what feeling good feels like.* She hasn't felt this good since she was little, before some things started happening to her.

Now she finds herself drawn to the sound that Velma is making: Velma cursing under her breath as she hustles toward the side door to her office, thinking she's going to get to a phone, call 911.

Barbara looks VJ in the eye and says, 'Don't let her get away, she's got the money. *Shoot her in the legs.*'

VJ jerks out the gun – and hesitates. Velma's got her hand on the doorknob.

'Barbara, jeezus Christ!' Avery yells, clutching his swelling hand to his stomach.

'VJ,' Reebok says. 'Shit. Just grab her.'

'No, shoot her in the goddamn legs or we lose the money!' Barbara says, saying it *big,* the voice coming out of her with that stormfront behind it.

Then the thunder: the gun in VJ's hand.

Velma screams and Barbara feels another release of good feeling roll through her as pieces of Velma's knees spatter the door and embed in the wall and blood gushes over the carpet. Avery bolts for the door and, feeling like a Greek goddess, Barbara points at him and commands Reebok, 'Hurt that traitor with your gun! Hurt him! He's stealing everything that's ours! *Stop him.*'

Reebok seems surprised when the gun in his hand goes off –

maybe it was more a squeeze of fear in his fingers than a real decision to shoot – and a hole with little red petals on it like a small red daisy appears on Avery's back, then another—

Avery spins around, howling, mouth agape, eyes like a toddler terrified of a barking dog; Avery trying to fend off bullets with his pudgy fingers – she never saw before how pudgy they were – as Barbara reaches over and grabs Reebok's hand and points the gun downward at Avery's penis as his unfastened pants slip down. She pulls the trigger and the tip of his penis disappears – which she saw only that one other time, uncircumcized, with that funny little hose tip on it – and she shouts, *'Now you'rc circumcized Avery you traitor fucking that whore you pig!'*

Reebok and Avery scream at the same time almost the same way.

Then she notices Velma sobbing. Barbara crosses the room to Velma, picking up something off the desk as she goes, not really consciously noticing what it is till she's kneeling beside Velma, who's trying to crawl away, and Barbara's driving the paper spike into her neck, one of those spikes your kid makes for you in shop with a little wooden disk, still has some receipts on it getting all bloody as the nail goes *ka-chunk* into her neck three times, four times, and Avery is screaming louder and louder, so VJ turns to him and yells *'Shut the fuck up!'* and makes the top of Avery's head disappear at the same moment that Barbara drives the spike again into Velma *kachunk-boom!,* the nail going in right behind her ear, and Velma suddenly pees herself and stops flopping, right in mid-flop, she stops . . .

'Oh, *fuck,*' Reebok is saying, sobbing as Barbara gets up, moving through a sort of sweet, warm haze as she goes to the corner of the room and points at the cabinet that has the safe hidden in it and says, 'Forty-one, thirty-five and . . . seven.'

It's not until she's in the car, on the road, pulling onto the freeway entrance, that Barbara notices that she peed herself, too, just like Velma. That's funny. She's surprised that she doesn't really care much. She's just surprised at herself all day. It feels good; it's like on *Oprah* those women talking about doing things they never thought they could do, that people said they couldn't do, and how good they felt.

She has to change her skirt, though. She won't chance stopping by her apartment, but she'll send VJ into a Ross or someplace at that new mall out east of town, on the way – she's made up her mind they're going to Nevada, Mexico would be too obvious – and he can get her some clothes for them with some of the money from the safe, almost a hundred thousand dollars . . . They didn't have to do discount now, they could go to Nordstrom's.

But there was the problem of Reebok. His blubbering. 'You'd better quiet him down,' she tells VJ softly. 'The police are there by now, from all the noise, and they're going to put out an APB and they might have a description of the car from somebody, but I don't think so because no one was around, but even if they don't . . .' She was aware that she was talking in a rambling, on-and-on way, like she was on diet pills, but it didn't matter, you just had to get it out. You had to get it out eventually. '. . . even if they don't have a description, they're going to be looking for anything suspicious, and him sobbing and waving a gun around.'

'VJ,' Reebok says raspily, between gasping sobs, 'look what this crazy bitch got us into . . . Look what she done . . .'

'I got you into a hundred thousand dollars.' She shrugs and passes a Ford Taurus. 'But I don't think he should get any of the money, VJ,' she says. 'I had to do half the job for him, and he's going to panic and squeal on us.' She likes using that verb from old movies, *squeal.* 'I think you should drop him off somewhere, then we can go to Nevada and buy a new car for you, VJ, and some new clothes, maybe get you a real gold chain instead of that fake one, and you can have the watch I got in my bag, the watch I got for Avery, and some girls if you want, I don't care. Or you can have me. As much as you want. Then we have to think about some more money. I've been thinking about banks. I read an article about all the mistakes bank robbers make. How they don't move around enough, and all kinds of other mistakes, and I think we could be smarter.'

VJ nods numbly.

Reebok looks at him, blinking, gaping. 'VJ?'

VJ points at an exit. 'That one.' The exit's a good choice: Caltrans was doing a lot of construction there, though the workers had all gone home, so there's lots of cover, what with the earthmovers and all the raw wood, to hide what they are doing from people passing on the freeway, and there are places where the earth is dug out, to hide the body. VJ made a smart choice – he's the smart one of the two guys, smarter than she is, she decides, but that doesn't matter, because she is stronger than VJ in a certain way. That's what counts.

She's thinking all this as she pulls off onto South Road exit and onto a utility road, in the country, with the construction between the road and the freeway, and no one around.

She pulls the car up in a good spot. Reebok looks at them and then bursts out of the car and starts running, and she says, 'VJ, you know he's going to tell, he's too scared.' VJ swallows and nods, and gets out and the gun barks in his hand, and Reebok goes spinning. VJ has to shoot another time before Reebok stops yelling. Barbara, all the while, is watching the wind pinwheeling some trash by, some napkins from a Burger King . . . just trash blowing by . . .

Some more yelling. VJ has to shoot Reebok one last time . . .

She squints into the sky, watches a hawk teetering on an updraft.

VJ is throwing up now. He'll feel better after throwing up. Throwing up always leaves a bad taste in the mouth, though.

She wonders what VJ's penis will taste like. It will probably taste okay. He seems clean.

And VJ's smart, and handsomer than Avery, and much younger, and she knows they belong together, she can feel it. It's cute how VJ tries to hide it, but she can see it in his eyes when he thinks she's not watching: he loves her. He does.

***John Shirley** is the author of the horror novel,* Wetbones *(Zeising, 1992), to name his personal favorite. He is also a screenwriter, having adapted* The Crow *for the movies, and is currently working on the adaptation of Blake* Nelson's *Girl. One of the founding fathers of cyberpunk, Shirley has worked in every genre from men's adventure to erotica to suspense thrillers. His label-defying short fiction can be found in the collections* Heatseeker *(1989, Scream Press),* New Noir *(1993, Black Ice), and the upcoming* Exploded Heart *(Eyeball Books).*

Hymenoptera

BY

MICHAEL BLUMLEIN

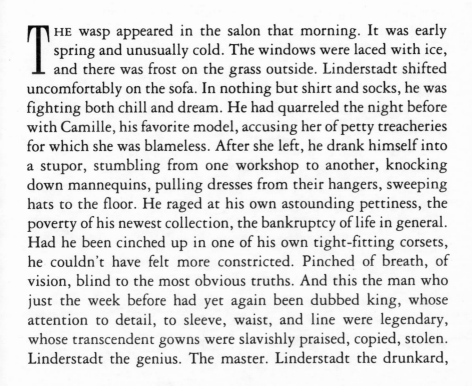

THE wasp appeared in the salon that morning. It was early spring and unusually cold. The windows were laced with ice, and there was frost on the grass outside. Linderstadt shifted uncomfortably on the sofa. In nothing but shirt and socks, he was fighting both chill and dream. He had quarreled the night before with Camille, his favorite model, accusing her of petty treacheries for which she was blameless. After she left, he drank himself into a stupor, stumbling from one workshop to another, knocking down mannequins, pulling dresses from their hangers, sweeping hats to the floor. He raged at his own astounding pettiness, the poverty of his newest collection, the bankruptcy of life in general. Had he been cinched up in one of his own tight-fitting corsets, he couldn't have felt more constricted. Pinched of breath, of vision, blind to the most obvious truths. And this the man who just the week before had yet again been dubbed king, whose attention to detail, to sleeve, waist, and line were legendary, whose transcendent gowns were slavishly praised, copied, stolen. Linderstadt the genius. The master. Linderstadt the drunkard, wrestling with his empire of taffeta, guipure, and satin, flailing at success like a fly trapped behind glass.

Dawn came, and sunlight appeared along the edges of the heavily curtained windows, penetrating the salon with a wan, peach-colored light. Linderstadt was on a couch at one end of the room, half draped with the train of a bridal gown he had appropriated from one of the ateliers. The wasp was at the other, broadside and motionless. Its wings were folded back against its body, and its long belly was curled under itself like a comma. Its two antennae were curved delicately forward but otherwise as rigid as bamboo.

An hour passed and then another. When sleep became impossible, Linderstadt staggered off the couch to relieve himself. He returned to the salon with a glass of water, at which point he first noticed the wasp. From his father, who had been an amateur entomologist before dying of yellow fever, Linderstadt knew something of insects. This one he located somewhere in the family Sphecidae, which included wasps of primarily solitary habit. Most nested in burrows or natural cavities of hollow wood, and he was a little surprised to find the animal in his salon. Then again, he was surprised to have remembered anything at all. He had scarcely thought of insects since his entry forty years before into the world of fashion. He had scarcely thought of his father, either, preferring the memory of his mother, Anna, his mother the caregiver, the seamstress, for whom he had named his first shop and his most famous dress. But his mother was not here, and the wasp most unmistakably was. Linderstadt finished his glass of water and pulled the bridal train like a shawl over his shoulders. Then he walked over to have a look.

The wasp stood chest high and about eight feet long. Linderstadt recognized the short hairs on its legs that used to remind him of the stubble on his father's chin, and he remembered, too, the forward palps by which the insect centered its jaws to tear off food. Its waist was pencil-thin, its wings translucent. Its exoskeleton, what Linderstadt thought of as its coat, was blacker than his blackest faille, blacker than coal. It seemed to absorb light, creating a small pocket of cold night right where it stood. Nigricans. He remembered the wasp's name. Ammophila nigricans. He was tempted to touch it, to feel the quality of its life. Instinctively, his eyes drifted down its belly to the pointed sting that extruded like a sword from its rear. He recalled that the sting was actually a hollow tube through which the female deposited eggs into its prey, where they would hatch into larvae and eat their way out. Males possessed the same tube but did not sting. As a boy he had always had trouble telling the sexes apart, and examining the creature now in the pale light, he wondered which it was. He felt a little feverish, which he attributed to the aftereffects of the alcohol. His mouth remained parched, but he was reluctant to leave the salon for more water for fear the wasp would be gone when he returned. So he stayed, shivering and thirsty. The hours passed, and the room did not heat up. The wasp did not move. It was stiller than Martine, his stillest and most patient model. Stiller in the windless salon than the jeweled chandelier and the damask curtains that led to the dressing rooms. Linderstadt himself was the only moving object. He paced to stay warm. He swallowed his own saliva to slake his thirst, but ultimately the need for water drove him out. He returned as quickly as possible, wearing shoes and sweater, carrying pencils, a pad of paper, and a large pitcher of water. The wasp was as he had left it. Had Linderstadt not known something of insect physiology, he might have thought the animal was carved in stone.

By the fading light he began to draw, quickly, deftly, using broad, determined strokes. He worked from different angles, sketching the wasp's neck, its shoulders and waist. He imagined the creature in flight, its wings stiff and finely veined. He drew it feeding, resting, poised to sting. He experimented with different designs, some stately and elegant, others pure whimsy. He found that he had already assumed the wasp was female. His subjects had never been otherwise. He remembered Anouk, his first model, the scoliotic girl his mother had brought home to test her adolescent son's fledgling talent. He felt as supple as he had then, his mind as inventive and free-spirited as ever.

He worked into the small hours of the morning, then rested briefly before being woken by church bells. In his youth he had been devout, and religious allusions were common in his early collections. But sanctimony had given way to secularity, and it had been thirty years since he had set foot in a church. What remained were the Sunday bells, which Linderstadt savored for the sake of nostalgia and a lingering guilt. It was a habit of his, and he was a man who held to habit.

The morning brought no visitors, and he had the store to himself. It was even colder than the day before. The wasp remained inert, and when the temperature hadn't climbed by noon, Linderstadt felt secure in leaving. His drawings were done, and his next task was to locate a suitable form on which to realize them. He owned hundreds of torsos of every conceivable shape, some bearing the name of a specific patron, others simply marked with a number. He had other shapes as well, baskets, cylinders, mushrooms, triangles, all of which had found their way at one point or another into a collection. As long as an object had dimension, Linderstadt could imagine it on a woman. Or rather, he could imagine the woman in the object, in residence, giving it her own distinctive form and substance, imbuing each tangent and intersect with female spirit. He was a pantheist at heart and expected to have no trouble finding something suitable to the wasp. Yet nothing caught his eye; not a single object in his vast collection seemed remotely to approach the creature in composition or character. It was enigmatic. He would have to work directly on the animal itself.

He returned to the salon and approached his subject. To a man so accustomed to the divine plasticity of flesh, the armor-like hardness and inflexibility of the wasp's exoskeleton presented challenges. Each cut would have to be perfect, each seam precise. There was no bosom to softly fill a swale of fabric, no hip to give shape to a gentle waist. It would be like working with bone itself, like clothing a skeleton. Linderstadt was intrigued. He stepped up and touched the wasp's body. It was cold and hard as metal. He ran a finger along one of its wings, half expecting that his own nervous energy would bring it to life. Touch for him had always evoked the strongest emotions, which is why he used a pointing stick with his models. He might have done well to use the same stick with the wasp, for his skin tingled from the contact, momentarily clouding his senses. His hand fell to one of the wasp's legs. It was not so different from a human leg. The hairs were soft like human hairs, hairs that his models assiduously bleached, or waxed or shaved. The knee and ankle were similarly jointed, the claw as pointed and bony as a foot. His attention shifted to the animal's waist, in a human the pivot point between leg and torso. In the wasp it was lower and far narrower than anything human. It was as thin as a pipestem, a marvel of invention he was easily able to encircle between thumb and forefinger.

From a pocket he took out a tape and began to make his measurements, elbow to shoulder, shoulder to wing tip, hip to claw, jotting each down in a notebook. From time to time he would pause, stepping back to imagine a detail, a particular look, a melon sleeve, a fringed collar, a flounce. Sometimes he would make a notation; other times, a quick sketch. When it came time to measure the chest, he had to lie on his back underneath the wasp. From that vantage he had a good view of its hairless and plated torso, as well as its sting, which was poised like a pike and pointed directly between his legs. After a moment's hesitation, he rolled over and took its measure, too, wondering casually if this was one of those wasps that died after stinging, and if so, was there some way he could memorialize such a sacrifice in a dress. Then he crawled out and looked at his numbers.

The wasp was symmetrical, almost perfectly so. Throughout his long career Linderstadt had always sought to thwart such symmetry, focusing instead on the subtle variations in the human body, the natural differences between left and right. There was always something to emphasize, a hip that was higher, a shoulder, a breast. Even an eye, whose iris might be flecked a slightly different shade of blue than its neighbor, could trigger a report somewhere in the color of the dress below. Linderstadt's success to a large degree rested on his uncanny ability to uncover such asymmetries, but the wasp presented difficulties. There was nothing that distinguished one side from the other, almost as if the animal were mocking the idea of asymmetry, of individuality, and, by inference, the whole of Linderstadt's career. It occurred to him that he had been wrong, that perhaps the true search was not for singularity but for constancy of form, for repetition and preservation. Perhaps what abided was commonality; what endured, the very proportions he held in his hand.

Linderstadt took his notebook to the main atelier to begin work on the first dress. He had decided to start with something simple, a velvet sheath with narrow apertures for wing and leg and a white flounce of tulle at the bottom to hide the sting. With no time for a muslin fitting, he worked directly with the fabric itself. It was a job normally handled by assistants, but the master had not lost his skill with scissors and thread. The work went fast, and partway through the sewing, he remembered the name of the order to which his wasp belonged. Hymenoptera, after *ptera,* for wing, and *hymeno,* for the Greek god of marriage, referring to the union of the wasp's front and hind wings. He himself had never married, had never touched a woman outside his profession, certainly not intimately. Some suggested that he feared intimacy, but more likely what he feared was a test of the purity of his vision. His women were jewels, precious stones to be admired like anything beautiful and splendid. He clothed them to adore them. He clothed them to keep them in the palace of his dreams. Yet now, having touched the wasp's body, having been inspired by a creature as unlike himself as woman to man, he wondered if perhaps he had not missed something along the way. Flesh begged flesh. Could such a lifelong loss be rectified?

He finished the dress and hurried to the salon. The wasp offered no resistance as he lifted its claws and pulled the dark sheath into place. The image of his father came to mind, deftly unfolding a butterfly's wing and pinning it to his velvet display board. The Linderstadt men, it seemed, had a way with animals. He straightened the bodice and zipped up the back of the gown, then stepped back for a look. The waist, as he expected, needed taking in, and one of the shoulders needed to be realigned. The choice of color and fabric, however, was excellent. Black on black, night against night. It was a good beginning.

Linderstadt did the alterations, then hung the gown in one of the dressing rooms and returned to the workshop. His next outfit was a broad cape of lemon guipure with a gold chain fastener, striking in its contrast to the wasp's jet black exterior. He made a matching toque to which he attached lacquered sticks to echo the wasp's antennae. The atelier was as cold as the salon, and he worked in overcoat, scarf, and kid gloves whose fingertips he had snipped off with a scissors. His face was bare, and the bracing chill against his cheek recalled the freezing winters of his childhood when he had been forced to stand stock still for what seemed hours on end while his mother used him as a form for the clothes she was making. They had had no money for heat, and Linderstadt had developed a stoical attitude toward the elements. The cold reminded him of the value of discipline and self-control. But more than that, it reminded him how he had come to love the feel of the outfits being fitted and fastened against his skin. He had loved it when his mother tightened a waist or took in a sleeve. The feeling of confinement evoked a certain wild power of imagination, as though he were being simultaneously nurtured and freed. What he remembered of the cold was not the numbness in his fingers, the misting of his breath, the goose bumps on his arms. It was the power, pure and simple, so that now, even though he had money aplenty to fire his boilers and make his rooms hot as jungles, Linderstadt kept the heat off. The cold was his pleasure. It was fire enough.

He worked through the night to finish the cape. When Monday morning arrived, he locked the doors of the salon, turning away the seamstresses, stockroom clerks, salesgirls, and models who had come to work. He held the door against Camille and even Broussard, his lifelong friend and adviser. Hidden by the curtain that was strung across the door's glass panes, he announced that the collection was complete, the final alterations to be done in private by himself. He went to his strongbox and brought back bundles of cash, which he passed through the mail slot for Broussard to distribute to the employees. He assured everyone that the house of Linderstadt was intact and invited them all to return in a week for the opening of the collection. Then he left.

Back in the workshop he started on his next creation, an

off-the-shoulder blue moiré gown with a voluminous skirt festooned with bows. He sewed what he could by machine, but the bows had to be done by hand. He sewed like his mother, one knee crossed over the other, head bent, pinkie finger crooked out as though he were sipping a cup of tea. The skirt took a full day, during which he broke only once, to relieve himself. Food did not enter his mind, and in that he seemed in tune with the wasp. The animal signaled neither hunger nor thirst. On occasion one of its antennae would twitch, but Linderstadt attributed this to subtle changes in the turgor of the insect's blood. He assumed the wasp remained gripped by the cold, though he couldn't help but wonder if its preternatural stillness sprang from some deeper design. He thought of his father, so ordinary on the surface, so unfathomable beneath. Given the chance, the man would spend days with his insects, meticulously arranging his boards, printing the tiny specimen labels, taking inventory. Linderstadt could never quite grasp his father's patience and devotion. His mother claimed her husband was in hiding, but what did a child know of that? By the time it occurred to him to ask for himself, his father had been dead for years.

The weather held, and on Wednesday Linderstadt wheeled one of the sewing machines from the atelier to the salon so that he could work without leaving the wasp's side. Voices drifted in from the street, curiosity seekers making gossip, trying in vain to get a glimpse inside. The phone rang incessantly, message after message from concerned friends, clients, the press. M. Jesais, his personal psychic, called daily with increasingly dire prognostications. Linderstadt was unmoved. He heard but a single voice, and it kept him from distraction. He wondered why it had taken so long to hear.

He stitched a sleeve and then another. Forty years of success had brought him to this, needle, thread, tubes of fabric fashioned together like artifacts for a future archeology. Barely a week before, he had felt on the verge of extinction. Ghosts had begun to visit, ghosts of past models, of deceased friends, of his parents. The more he had tried to capture his vision, the more it had eluded him. Juliet in satin, Eve in furs, the Nameless Queen, arrogant and imperious in stiff brocade. Sirens of impossible beauty, triumphs of yet another man's muddled desire. Success, it seemed, rested on vanity. Such was the sad lesson of his career. And after forty years he had tired of the pretense. He had seen too many Camilles, too many Martines and Anouks. Seen and not seen. He was better off with no one at all.

But now there was the wasp. The wasp was different. The wasp added a twist. Chitin was not flesh, six not the same as two, six legs and claws, six declinations of angle, line, and force. And wings, wings that were stronger and finer than the angel Gabriel himself, a painting of whom Linderstadt had used to model his '84 collection. Eyes too, compound eyes, able to see God knows what. And antennae, to sample the world's invisible delight. Linderstadt tried to imagine Camille as an insect, crawling down the runway, striking a pose. Camille on four legs, on six, Camille on her belly, inching along like a caterpillar. From that vantage his gowns were no more than cocoons, pallid reflections of a more vivid reality. His life's vision had suffered from being too petty. It was flawed by arrogance. His adoration of women was an insult, his lofty ideals of grace and beauty, sophistry. The way of his heart was simpler and more direct. It was rooted inside, just as the wasp was rooted there in his room.

Linderstadt thought again of his father. He was dressing for work, buttoning up his navy blue postman's jacket with the yellow piping around the cuff. He was talking about a moth he had found whose body looked exactly like a woman. Was he talking to Linderstadt's mother? Linderstadt couldn't remember. There was tension in the air, he remembered that. And something else. Rapture?

He finished the last seam and held up the dress. The shimmering moiré reminded him of a sea; the six-legged gown, of a creature delectably adrift. To a lesser talent the sleeves would have been a nightmare, but in Linderstadt's hands they flowed effortlessly into the bodice. Each one sported a ruffled cap and was zippered to aid in getting it on. Once the gown was in place, Linderstadt stepped back to have a look. The fit was uncanny, as though some hidden hand were guiding his own. It had been that way from the start. There were five gowns now. Five in five days. One more, he thought, one more to complete the collection. The bridal gown, his signature piece. For forty years he had ended every show with such a gown. Brides signified life. They signified love and the power of creation. What better way to signal his own rebirth?

The dress took two days, which Linderstadt knew only because he had paused at one point to listen to the Sunday bells. He was working on the veil at the time, a gorgeous bit of organza that looked like mist, sewing and thinking what a pity it would be to cover the wasp's extraordinary face. And so he had devised an ingenious interlocking paneled design that simultaneously hid the face and revealed it. After the veil he had started on the train, using ten feet of egg white chiffon that he gathered in gentle waves to resemble foam. Where it attached to the skirt, he cut a hole for the sting and ringed it with flowers. The main body of the dress was made of brilliant satin with an Imperial collar and long sleeves of lace. Queen, Mother, Bride. The dress was a triumph of imagination, technique, and will.

He finished Sunday night, hung the gown in the dressing room with the others, then wrapped himself in overcoat and scarf and fell asleep on the couch. Early Monday he would get up and make the final preparations to receive his public.

That night the cold spell broke. A warm front swept in from the south, brushing away the chill like a cobweb. In his sleep Linderstadt unbuttoned his coat and pulled off his scarf. He dreamed of summer, flying a kite with his father at the beach. When he woke, it was almost noon. The room was thick with heat. A crowd had gathered outside the store for the opening. The wasp was gone.

He searched the workshops, the stockroom, the offices. He climbed to the roof and looked in the basement. Finally, he returned to the salon, bemused and somewhat dazed. Near where the wasp had stood he noticed a paper sphere the size of a small chair. One side of it was open, and inside were many tiers of hexagonal cells, all composed of the same papery material as the envelope. Linderstadt had a glimmer of understanding, and when he discovered that his gowns had vanished, he realized his mistake. The wasp was not a Sphecida at all but a Vespida, a paper wasp. Its diet consisted of wood, leaves, and other natural fibers. It had eaten its own gowns.

Linderstadt surveyed the remains of his work. The nest had a delicate beauty of its own, and briefly he considered showing it in lieu of the collection. Then he caught sight of a bit of undigested material peeking out from behind the papery sphere. It was the bridal veil, and he followed it around the nest, where it stood on the floor like a fountain of steam frozen in air, unattached to its gown but otherwise intact. Outside, the crowd clamored to be let in. Linderstadt drew back the curtains and lifted the gossamer veil. The sun seemed to set it aflame. Like the smallest fragment of a memory, it recalled every memory. He placed it on his head. A smile played across his face, the first in months. His eyes shone. With everything gone there was nothing left to hide. A single thread would have sufficed. Drawing himself up, proud and erect, Linderstadt went to open the doors.

Michael Blumlein *is America's answer to J.G. Ballard. He is the author of* The Movement of Mountains *and* X.,Y., *and his short stories have appeared in such markets as* The Mississippi Review, Omni, Full Spectrum, *and* The Norton Anthology of Science Fiction. *His short story collection,* The Brains of Rats, *is scheduled for paperback release by Dell in 1996. He is currently at work on a new novel.*

The End of It All

BY

ED GORMAN

Sometimes the only thing worse than losing the woman is winning the woman.
—French saying
Embrace your fate.
—French saying

I GUESS the first thing I should tell you about is the plastic surgery. I mean, I didn't always look this good. In fact, if you saw me in my college yearbook, you wouldn't even recognize me. I was thirty pounds heavier and my hair had enough grease on it to irrigate a few acres of droughted farmland. And the glasses I wore could easily have substituted for the viewing instruments they use at Mt Palomar. I wanted to lose my virginity back in second grade, on the very first day I saw Amy Towers. But I didn't lose my virginity until I was twenty-three years old and even then it was no easy task. She was a prostitute and just as I was guiding my sex into her she said, 'I'm sorry, I must be coming down with the flu or something. I've got to puke.' And puke she did.

This was how I lived my life until I was forty-two years old – as the kind of guy cruel people smirk at and decent people feel sorry for. I was the uncle nobody ever wanted to claim. I was the blind date women discussed for years after. I was the guy in the record shop the cute girl at the cash register always rolls her eyes at. But despite all that I somehow managed to marry an attractive woman whose husband had been killed in Vietnam, and I inherited a stepson who always whispered about me behind my back to his friends. They snickered mysteriously whenever they were around me. The marriage lasted eleven years, ending on a rainy Tuesday night several weeks after we'd moved into our elegant new Tudor in the city's most attractive yuppie enclave. After dinner, David up in his room smoking dope and listening to his Prince CDs, Annette said, 'Would you take it personally if I told you I'd fallen in love with somebody?' Shortly thereafter we were divorced, and shortly after that I moved to Southern California, where I supposed there was plenty of room for one more misfit. At least, more room than there had been in an Ohio city of 150,000.

By profession I was a stockbroker, and at this particular time there were plenty of opportunities in California for somebody who'd managed his own shop as I had. Problem was, I was tired of trying to motivate eight other brokers into making their monthly goals. I found an old and prestigious firm in Beverly Hills and went to work there as a simple and unhassled broker. It took me several months, but I finally got over being dazzled by having movie stars as clients. It helped that most of them were jerks.

I tried to improve my sex life by touring all the singles bars that my better-looking friends recommended, and by circumspectly scanning many of the Personals columns in the numerous newspapers that infest L.A. But I found nothing to my taste. None of the women who described themselves as straight and in good shape ever mentioned the word that interested me most – romance. They spoke of hiking and biking and surfing; they spoke of symphonies and movies and art galleries; they spoke of equality and empowerment and liberation. But never romance and it was romance I most devoutly desired. There were other options, of course. But while I felt sorry for homosexuals and bisexuals and hated people who persecuted them, I didn't want to be one of them; and try as I might to be understanding of sado-masochism and cross-dressing and transsexualism, there was about it something – for all its sadness – comic and incomprehensible. Fear of disease kept me from whores. The women I met in ordinary circumstances – at the office, supermarket, laundry facilities in my expensive apartment house – treated me as women usually did, with tireless sisterly kindness.

Then some crazy bastards had a gunfight on the San Diego freeway, and my life changed utterly.

This was on a smoggy Friday afternoon. I was returning home from work, tired, facing a long, lonely weekend when I suddenly saw two cars pull up on either side of me. They were, it seemed, exchanging gunfire. This was no doubt because of their deprived childhoods. They continued to fire at each other, not seeming to notice that I was caught in their crossfire. My windshield shattered. My two back tires blew out. I careened off the freeway and went halfway up a hill, where I smashed into the base of a stout scrub pine. That was the last thing I remember about the episode.

My recuperation took five months. It would have been much shorter, but one sunny day a plastic surgeon came into my room and explained what he'd need to do to put my face back to normal and I said, 'I don't want it back to normal.'

'Pardon me?'

'I don't want it back to normal. I want to be handsome. Movie-star handsome.'

'Ah.' He said this as if I'd just told him that I wanted to fly. 'Perhaps we need to talk to Dr Schlatter.'

Dr Schlatter too said 'Ah' when I told him what I wanted, but it was not quite the 'Ah' of the original doctor. In Dr Schlatter's 'Ah' there was at least a little vague hope.

He told me everything in advance, Dr Schlatter did, even making it interesting, how plastic surgery actually dated back to the ancient Egyptians, and Italians as early as the 1400s were performing quite impressive transformations. He showed me sketches of how he hoped I'd look, he acquainted me with some of the tools so I wouldn't be intimidated when I saw them – scalpel and retractor and chisel – and he told me how to prepare myself for my new face.

Sixteen days later, I looked at myself in the mirror and was happy to see that I no longer existed. Not the former me anyway. Surgery, diet, liposuction and hair dye had produced somebody who should appeal to a wide variety of women – not that I cared, of course. Only one woman mattered to me, only one woman had ever mattered to me, and during my time in the hospital she was all I thought about, all I planned for. I was not going to waste my physical beauty on dalliances. I was going to use it to win the hand and heart of Amy Towers Carson, the woman I'd loved since second grade.

It was five weeks before I saw her. I'd spent that time getting established in a brokerage firm, setting up some contacts and learning how to use a new live phone hookup that gave me continuous stock analysis. Impressive, for a small Ohio city such as this one, the one where I'd grown up and first fallen in love with Amy.

I had some fun meeting former acquaintances. Most of them didn't believe me when I said I was Roger Daye. A few of them even laughed, implying that Roger Daye, no matter what had happened to him, could never look this good.

My parents living in Florida retirement, I had the old homestead – a nice white Colonial in an Ozzie and Harriet section of the city – to myself, where I invited a few ladies to hone my skills. Amazing how much self-confidence the new me gave the old me. I just took it for granted that we'd end up in bed, and so we did, virtually every single time. One woman whispered that she'd even fallen in love with me. I wanted to ask her to repeat that on tape.

Not even my wife had ever told me she loved me, not exactly anyway.

Amy came into my life again at a country club dance two nights before Thanksgiving.

I sat at a table watching couples of all ages box-step around the dance floor. Lots of evening gowns. Lots of tuxedos. And lots of saxophone music from the eight-piece band, the bandstand being the only light, everybody on the floor in intimate boozy shadow. She was still beautiful, Amy was, not as young-looking, true, but with that regal, obstinate beauty nonetheless and that small, trim body that had inspired ten or twenty thousand of my youthful melancholy erections. I felt that old giddy high school thrill that was in equal parts shyness, lust, and a romantic love that only F. Scott Fitzgerald – my favorite writer – would ever have understood. In her arms I would find the purpose of my entire existence. I had felt this since I'd first walked home with her through the smoky autumn afternoons of third and fourth and fifth grade. I felt it still.

Randy was with her. There had long been rumors that they had a troubled marriage that would inevitably disintegrate. Randy, former Big Ten wide receiver and Rose Bowl star, had been one of the star entrepreneurs of the local eighties – building condos had been his specialty – but his success waned with the end of the decade and word was he'd taken up the harsh solace of whiskey and whores.

They still looked like everybody's dream of the perfect romantic couple, and more than one person on the dance floor nodded to them as the band swung into a Bobby Vinton medley, at which point Randy began dancing Amy around with Technicolor theatrics. Lots of onlooker grins and even a bit of applause. Amy and Randy would be the king and queen of every prom they ever attended. Their dentures might clack when they spoke, Randy's prostate might make him wince every thirty seconds, but by God the spotlight would always find its ineluctable way to them. And they'd be rich – Randy came from a long line of steel money and was one of the wealthiest men in the state.

When Randy went to the john – walking right meant the bar; walking left meant the john – I went over to her.

She sat alone at a table, pert and gorgeous and preoccupied. She didn't notice me at first, but when her eyes met mine, she smiled.

'Hi.'

'Hi,' I said.

'Are you a friend of Randy's?'

I shook my head. 'No, I'm a friend of yours. From high school.'

She looked baffled a moment and then said, 'Oh, my God. Betty Anne said she saw you and – oh, my God.'

'Roger Daye.'

She fled her seat and came to me and stood on her tiptoes and took my warm face in her cold hands and kissed me and said, 'You're so handsome.'

I smiled. 'Quite a change, huh?'

'Well, you weren't that—'

'Of course I was – a dip, a dweeb—'

'But not a nerd.'

'Of course a nerd.'

'Well, not a complete nerd.'

'At least ninety-five percent,' I said.

'Eighty percent maybe but—' She exulted over me again, bare shoulders in her wine red evening gown shiny and sexy in the shadow. 'The boy who used to walk me home—'

'All the way up to tenth grade when you met—'

'Randy.'

'Right. Randy.'

'He really is sorry about beating you up that time. Did your arm heal all right? I guess we sort of lost track of each other, didn't we?'

'My arm healed just fine. Would you care to dance?'

'Would I care to? God, I'd love to.'

We danced. I tried not to think of all the times I'd dreamed about this moment, Amy in my arms so beautiful and—

'You're in great shape, too,' she said.

'Thank you.'

'Weights?'

'Weights and running and swimming.'

'God, that's so great. You'll break every heart at our next class reunion.'

I held her closer. Her breasts touched my chest. A stout and stern erection filled my pants. I was dizzy. I wanted to take her over into a corner and do it on the spot. She was the sweet smell of clean, wonderful woman flesh, and the even sweeter sight of dazzling white smile against tanned, taut cheeks.

'That bitch.'

I'd been so far gone into my fantasies that I wasn't sure I'd heard her properly.

'Pardon?'

'Her. Over there. That bitch.'

I saw Randy before I saw the woman. Hard to forget a guy who'd once broken your arm – he'd had considerable expertise with hammer locks – right in front of the girl you loved.

Then I saw the woman and I forgot all about Randy.

I didn't think anybody could ever make Amy seem drab, but the woman presently dancing with Randy did just that. There was a radiance about her that was more important than her good looks, a mixture of pluck and intelligence that made me vulnerable to her even from here. In her white strapless gown, she was so fetching that men simply stood and stared at her, the way they would at a low-flying UFO or some other extraordinary phenomenon.

Randy started to twirl her as he had Amy, but this young woman – she couldn't have been much more than twenty – was a far better dancer. She was so smooth, in fact, I wondered if she'd had ballet training.

Randy kept her captive in his muscular embrace for the next three dances.

Because the girl so obviously upset Amy, I tried not to look at her – not even a stolen glance – but it wasn't easy.

'Bitch,' Amy said.

And for the first time in my life, I felt sorry for her. She'd always been my goddess, and here she was feeling something as ungoddess-like as jealousy.

'I need a drink.'

'So do I.'

'Would you be a darling and get us one, then?'

'Of course,' I said.

'Black and White, please. Straight up.'

She was at her table smoking a cigarette when I brought the drinks back. She exhaled in long, ragged plumes.

Randy and his princess were still on the dance floor.

'She thinks she's so goddamned beautiful,' Amy said.

'Who is she?'

But before Amy could tell me, Randy and the young woman deserted the floor and came over to the table.

Randy didn't look especially happy to see me. He glanced first at Amy and then at me and said, 'I suppose there's a perfectly good reason for you to be sitting at our table.'

Here he was flaunting his latest girlfriend in front of his wife, and he was angry that she had a friend sitting with her.

Amy smirked. 'I didn't recognize him, either.'

'Recognize who?' Randy snapped.

'Him. The handsome one.'

By now I wasn't looking at either of them. I was staring at the young woman. She was even more lovely up close. She seemed amused by us older folks.

'Remember a boy named Roger Daye?' Amy said.

'That candy-ass who used to walk you home?'

'Randy. Meet Roger Daye.'

'No way,' Randy said, 'this is Roger Daye.'

'Well, I'm sorry, but he is.'

I knew better than to put my hand out. He wouldn't have shaken it.

'Where's a goddamned waiter?' Randy said. Only now did I realize he was drunk.

He bellowed even above the din of the crowd.

He and the young woman sat down just as a waiter appeared. 'It's about goddamned time,' Randy said to the older man with the tray.

'Sorry, we're just very busy tonight, sir.'

'Is that supposed to be my problem or something?'

'Please, Randy,' Amy said.

'Yes, please, Dad,' the gorgeous young woman said.

At first I thought she might be joking, making a reference to Randy's age. But she didn't smile, nor did Roger, nor did Amy.

I guess I just kind of sat there and thought about why Randy would sire his own daughter around as if she were his new beau, and why Amy would be so jealous.

Six drinks and many tales of Southern California later – Midwesterners dote on Southern California tales the way people will someday dote on tales of Jupiter and Pluto – Randy said, 'Didn't I break your arm one time?' He was the only guy I'd ever met who could swagger while sitting down.

'I'm afraid you did.'

'You had it coming. Sniffing around Amy that way.'

'Randy,' Amy said.

'Daddy,' Kendra said.

'Well, it's true, right, Roger? You had the hots for Amy and you probably still goddamned do.'

'Randy,' Amy said.

'Daddy,' Kendra said.

But I didn't want him to stop. He was jealous of me and it made me feel great. Randy Carson, Rose Bowl star, was jealous of me.

'Would you like to dance, Mr Daye?'

I'd tried hard not to pay any attention to her because I knew if I paid her a little I'd pay her a lot. Wouldn't be able to wrench my eyes or my heart away. She was pure meltdown, the young lady was.

'I'd love to,' I said.

I was just standing up when Amy looked at Kendra and said, 'He already promised me this one, dear.'

And before I knew what to do, Amy took my hand and guided me to the floor.

Neither of us said anything for a long time. Just danced. The good old box step. Same as in seventh grade.

'I know you wanted to dance with her,' Amy said.

'She's very attractive.'

'Oh, Jesus. That's all I need.'

'Did I say something wrong?'

'No – it's just that nobody notices me anymore. I know that's a shitty thing to say about my own daughter, but it's true.'

'You're a very beautiful woman.'

'For my age.'

'Oh, come on now.'

'But not vibrant, not fresh the way Kendra is.'

'That's a great name, Kendra.'

'I chose it.'

'You chose well.'

'I wish I'd called her Judy or Jake.'

'Jake?'

She laughed. 'Aren't I awful? Talking about my own daughter this way? That little bitch.'

She slurred the last two words. She'd gunned her drinks – Black and White straight up – and now they were taking their toll.

We danced some more. She stepped on my foot a couple of times. Every once in a while I'd find myself looking over at the table for a glimpse of Kendra. All my life I'd waited to dance like this with Amy Towers. And now it didn't seem to matter much.

'I've been a naughty girl, Roger.'

'Oh?'

'I really have been. About Kendra, I mean.'

'I suppose a little rivalry between mother and daughter isn't unheard of.'

'It's more than that. I slept with her boyfriend last year.'

'I see.'

'You should see your face. Your very handsome face. You're embarrassed.'

'Does she know?'

'About her boyfriend?'

'Uh-huh.'

'Of course. I planned it so she'd walk in on us. I just wanted to show her – well, that even some of her own friends might find me attractive.'

'You felt real bad about it, I suppose?'

'Oh, no. I felt real good. She naturally told Randy and he made a big thing over it – smashed up furniture and hit me in the face a few times – and it was really great. I felt young again, and desirable. Does that make sense?'

'Not really.'

'But they got back at me.'

'Oh?'

'Sure. Didn't you see them tonight on the dance floor?'

'Pretty harmless. I mean, she's his daughter.'

'Well, then you haven't had a talk with good old Randy lately.'

'Oh?'

'He read this article in *Penthouse* about how incest was actually a very natural drive and how it was actually perfectly all right to bop your family members if it was mutual consent and if you practiced safe sex.'

'God.'

'So now she walks around the house practically naked, and he rubs her and pats her and gives her big, long squeezes.'

'And she doesn't mind?'

'That's the whole point. They're in on this together. To pay me back for sleeping with Bobby.'

'Bobby being—'

'Her boyfriend. Well, ex-boyfriend I guess.'

Kendra and Randy came back on the floor next dance. If any attention had been paid to Amy and me, it was now transferred to Kendra and Randy. But this time, instead of the theatrical, they embraced the intimate. I was waiting for Randy to start grinding his hips into Kendra dry-hump style, the way high school boys always do when the lights are turned down.

'God, they're sickening,' Amy said.

And I pretty much agreed with her.

'She's going to try to seduce you, you know,' Amy said.

'Oh, come on now.'

'God, are you kidding? She'll want to make you a trophy as soon as she can.'

'She's what? Twenty? Twenty-one?'

'Twenty-two. But that doesn't matter, anyway. You just wait and see.'

At our table again, I had two more drinks. None of this was as planned. Handsome Roger would return to his hometown and beguile the former homecoming queen into his arms. Technicolor dreams. But this was different, dark and comic and sweaty, and not a little bit sinister. I could see Roger touching his nearly nude daughter all over her wonderful body, and I could see Amy – not a little bit pathetic – hurtling herself at some strapping college student majoring in gonads.

Jesus, all I'd wanted to do was a little old-fashioned home wrecking . . . and look what I'd gotten myself into.

Kendra and Randy came back. Randy abused a couple more waiters and then said to me, 'You having all that plastic surgery – surprised you didn't have them change you into a broad. You always were a little flitty. Nothing personal, you understand.'

'Randy,' Amy said.

'Daddy,' Kendra said.

But for me this was the supreme compliment. Randy Big Ten Carson was jealous of me again.

I wasn't sure where Kendra was going when she stood up, but then she was next to me and said, 'Why don't we dance?'

'I'm sure Roger's tired, dear,' Amy said.

Kendra smiled. 'Oh, I think he's probably got a little bit of energy left, don't you, Mr Daye?'

On the floor, in my arms, sexy, soft, sweet, gentle, cunning, and altogether self-possessed, Kendra said, 'She's going to try to seduce you, you know.'

'Who is?'

'Amy. My mother.'

'You may not have noticed, but she's married.'

'Like that would really make a difference.'

'We're old friends. That's all.'

'I've read some of your love letters.'

'God, she kept them?'

'All of them. From all the boys who were in love with her. She's got them all up in the attic. In storage boxes. Alphabetized. Whenever she starts to feel old, she drags them out and reads them. When I was a little girl, she'd read them out loud to me.'

'I imagine mine were very corny.'

'Very sweet. That's how yours were.'

Our gazes met, as they like to say in novels. But that wasn't all that met. The back of her hand somehow passed across the front of my trousers, and an erection the goatiest of fifteen-year-olds would envy sprang to life. Then her hand returned to proper dancing position.

'You're really a great-looking man.'

'Thank you. But did you ever see my Before picture?'

She smiled. 'If you mean your high school yearbook photo, yes, I did. I guess I like the After photo a little better.'

'You're very skilled at diplomacy.'

'That's not all I'm skilled at, Mr Daye.'

'How about calling me Roger?'

'I'd like that.'

I wish I had a big capper for the rest of the evening at the country club, but I don't. By the time Kendra and I got back to the table, Amy and Randy were both resolutely drunk and even a bit incoherent. I excused myself to the john for a time, and as I came back I saw Amy out on the veranda talking to a guy who looked not unlike a very successful gigolo, macho variety. Later, I'd learn that his name was Vic. Back at the table good old Randy insulted a few more waiters and threatened to punch me out if 'I didn't keep my goddamned paws' off his wife and his daughter, but he was slurring his words so badly that the effect was sort of lost, especially when he started sloshing his drink around and the glass fell from his hand and smashed all over the table.

'Maybe this is a good time to leave,' Kendra said, and began the difficult process of packing her parents up and getting them out to their new Mercedes, which, fortunately, she happened to be driving.

Just as they were leaving, Kendra said, 'I may see you later,' leaving me to contemplate what, exactly, 'later' meant.

After one shower, one night-cap, most of a David Letterman show, and a slow fall into sleep, I found out what 'later' meant.

She was at the door, behind a sharp knock in the windy night, adorned in a London Fog trench coat that was, I soon learned, all she wore.

She said nothing, just stood on tiptoes, wonderful lips puckered, waiting to be kissed. I obliged her, sliding an arm around her and leading her inside, feeling a little self-conscious in my pajamas and robe.

We didn't make it to the bedroom. She gently pushed me into a huge leather armchair before the guttering fireplace and eased herself gently atop me. That was when I found out she was naked beneath her London Fog. Her wise and lovely fingers quickly got me properly hard, and then I was inside her and my gasp was exultant pleasure but it was also fear.

I imagine heroin addicts feel this way the first time they use – pleasure from the exquisite kick of it all but fear of becoming a total slave to something they can never again control.

I was going to fall disastrously in love with Kendra, and I knew it that very first moment in the armchair when I tasted the soft, sweet rush of her breath and felt the warm, silken splendor of her sex.

When we were done for the first time, I built the fire again, and got us wine and cheese, and we lay beneath her trench coat staring into the flames crackling behind the glass.

'God, I can't believe it,' she said.

'Believe what?'

'How good I feel with you. I really do.'

I didn't say anything for a long time. 'Kendra.'

'I know what you want to ask.'

'About your mother.'

'I was right.'

'If you slept with me only because—'

'—because she slept with Bobby Lane?'

'Right. Because she slept with Bobby Lane.'

'Do you want me to be honest?'

I didn't really, but what was I going to say? No, I want you to be dishonest. 'Of course.'

'That's what first put the thought in my mind, I guess. I mean coming over here and sleeping with you.' She laughed. 'My mom is seriously smitten with you. I watched her face tonight. Wow. Anyway, I thought that would be a good way to pay her back. By sleeping with you, I mean. But by the end of the evening – God, this is really crazy, Roger, but I've got like this really incredible crush on you.'

I wanted to say that I did, too. But I couldn't. I might be a new Roger on the outside but inside I was strictly the old model – shy, nervous, and terrified that I was going to get my heart decimated.

By dawn, we'd made love three times, the last time in my large bed with a jay and a cardinal perched on the window watching us, and soft morning wind soughing the windbreak pines.

After we finished that last time, we lay in each other's arms for maybe twenty minutes until she said, 'I have to be unromantic.'

'Be my guest.'

'Goose bumps.'

'Goose bumps?'

'And bladder.'

'And bladder?'

'And morning breath.'

'You've lost me.'

'A, I'm freezing. B, I really have to pee. And C, may I use your toothbrush?'

In the following three weeks, she spent at least a dozen nights at my place, and on those nights when one or both of us had business to attend to, we had those lengthy phone conversations that new lovers always have. Makes no difference what you say as long as you get to hear her voice and she gets to hear yours.

Only occasionally did I pause and let dread come over me like a drowning wave. I would lose her and be forever bereft afterward. I was suffused with her tastes and smells and sounds and textures – and yet someday all these things would be taken from me and I would be forever alone, and unutterably sad. But what the hell could I do? Walk away? Impossible. She was succor, and life source, and all I could do was cling till my fingers fell away and I was left floating on the vast, dark ocean.

The eighth of December that year was one of those ridiculously sunny days that try to trick you into believing that spring is near. I spent two hours that afternoon cutting firewood in the back and then hauling it inside. Fuel for more trysts. On one of my trips inside, the doorbell rang. When I peeked out, I saw Amy. She looked very good – indeed, much better than she had that night at the country club – except for her black eye.

I let her in and asked her if she wanted a cup of coffee, which she declined. She took the leather couch, the leather armchair that Kendra and I still used on occasion.

'I need to talk to you, Roger.' She wore a white turtleneck beneath a camel hair car coat and designer jeans. There was a blue ribbon in her blonde hair, and she looked very sexy in a suburban sort of way.

'All right.'

'And I need you to be honest with me.'

'If you'll be honest with me.'

'The black eye?'

'The black eye.'

'Who else? Randy. He came home drunk the other night and I wouldn't sleep with him so he hit me. He sleeps around so much I'm afraid he's going to pick up something.' She shook her head with a solemnity I would never have thought her capable of.

'Does he do this often?'

'Sleep around?'

'And hit you.'

She shrugged. 'Pretty often. Both, I mean.'

'Why don't you leave him?'

'Because he'd kill me.'

'God, Amy, that's ridiculous. You can get an injunction.'

'You think an injunction would stop Randy? Especially when he's been drinking?' She sighed. 'I don't know what to do anymore.'

This was the woman I'd come back to steal, but now I didn't

want to steal her. I didn't even want to borrow her. I just felt sorry for her, and the notion was disorienting.

'Now, I want you to tell me about Kendra.'

'I love her.'

'Oh, just fucking great, Roger. Just fucking great.'

'I'm know I'm a lot older than she is but—'

'Oh, for God's sake, Roger, it's not that.'

'It isn't?'

'Of course it isn't. Come over here and sit down.'

'Next to you?'

'That's the idea.'

I went over and sat down. Next to her. She smelled great. Same cologne Kendra wore.

She took my hand. 'Roger, I want to sleep with you.'

'I don't think that would be a good idea.'

'All those years you were in love with me. It's not fair.'

'What's not fair?'

'You should have gone on loving me. That's how it's supposed to work.'

'What's supposed to work?'

'You know, lifelong romance. We're both romantics, Roger, you and I. Kendra is more like her father. Everything's sex.'

'You slept with her boyfriend.'

'Only because I was afraid and lonely. Randy had just beaten me up pretty badly. I felt so vulnerable. I just needed some kind of reassurance. You know, that I was a woman. That somebody would want me.' She took both my hands and brought them to her lips and kissed them tenderly. I couldn't help it. She was starting to have the effect on me she wanted. 'I want you to be in love with me again. I can help you forget Kendra. I really can.'

'I don't want to forget Kendra.'

'Deep down she's like Randy. A whore. She'll break your heart. She really will.'

She put two of her fingers in her mouth and began sucking.

She was quite good in bed, maybe even better technically than Kendra. But she wasn't Kendra. There was the rub.

We lay in the last of the gray afternoon and the wind came up, a harsh and wintry wind suddenly, and she tried to get me up for a second time, but it was no good. I wanted Kendra and she knew I wanted Kendra.

There was something very sad about it all. She was right. Romance – the kind of Technicolor romance I'd dreamed of – should last forever, despite any and all odds, the way it did in F. Scott Fitzgerald stories. And yet it hadn't. She was just another woman to me now, with more wrinkles than I had suspected, and a little tummy that was both sweet and comic, and veins like faded blue snakes against the pale flesh of her legs.

And then she started crying and all I could do was hold her and she tried in vain to get me up again and saw the failure not mine but her own.

'I don't know how I ever got here,' she said finally to the dusk that was rolling across the drab, cold Midwestern land.

'My house, you mean?'

'No. Here. Forty-two goddamned-years old. With a daughter who steals the one man who truly loved me.' A gaze icy as the winter moon then as she said, 'But maybe things won't be quite as hunky-fucking-dory as she thinks they'll be.'

Later on, I was to remember what she said vividly, the hunky-fucking-dory thing, I mean.

Kendra appeared at nine that same night. I spent the first half hour making love to her and the second half trying to decide if I should tell her about her mother's visit.

Later, in front of the fireplace, a wonderful old film noir called *Odds Against Tomorrow* on cable, we made love a second time and then, lying in the sweet, cool hollow of her arms, our juices and odors as one now, I said, 'Amy was here today.'

She stiffened. Her entire body. 'Why?'

'It's not easy to explain.'

'That bitch. I knew she'd do it.'

'Come here, you mean?'

'Come here and put the shot on you. Which she did, right?'

'Right. '

'But you didn't—'

I'd never had to lie to her before and it was far more difficult than I'd imagined it might be.

'Things get so crazy sometimes—'

'Oh, shit.'

'I mean you don't intend for things to happen but—'

'Oh, shit,' she said again. 'You fucked her, didn't you?'

'—with all the best intentions, you—'

'Quit fucking babbling. Just say it. Say you fucked her.'

'I fucked her.'

'How could you do it?'

'I didn't want to.'

'Right.'

'And I could only do it once. No second time.'

'How noble.'

'And I regretted it immediately.'

'Amy told me that when you were real geeky-looking you were one of the sweetest people she ever knew.'

She stood up, all beautiful, brash nakedness, and stalked back toward the bedroom. 'You should have kept your face ugly, Roger. Then your soul would still be beautiful.'

I lay there thinking about what she said a moment, and then I stalked back to the bedroom.

She was dressing in a frenzy. She didn't as yet have her bra on completely. Just one breast was cupped. The other looked lone and dear as anything I'd ever seen. I wanted to kiss it and coo baby talk to it.

Then I remembered why I'd come in here. 'That's bullshit, you know.'

'What's bullshit?' she said, pulling up the second cup of her bra. She wore panty hose but hadn't as yet put on her skirt.

'All that crap about keeping my face ugly so my soul would remain beautiful. If I hadn't had plastic surgery, neither you nor your mother would have given me a second glance.'

'That's not true.'

I smiled. 'God, face it, Kendra, you're a beautiful woman. You're not going to go out with some geek.'

'You make me sound as if I've really got a lot of depth.'

'Oh, Kendra, this is stupid. I shouldn't have slept with Amy and I'm sorry.'

'I'm just surprised she hasn't managed to tell me about it yet. She's probably waiting for the right dramatic moment. And in her version, I'm sure you threw her on the bed and raped her. That's what my father told her the night she caught us together. That I was the one who'd wanted to do it—'

'My God, you mean you—'

'Oh, not all the way. They had one of their country club parties, and both Randy and I were pretty loaded and somehow we ended up on the bed wrestling around and she walked in and— Well, I guess I tried very hard to give her the impression that we'd just been about to make it when she walked in and—'

'That's some great relationship you've got there.'

'It's pretty sick and believe me, I know it.'

I felt tired standing in the shadowy bedroom, the only light the December quarter moon above the shaggy pines.

'Kendra—'

'Could we just lie down together?' She sounded tired, too.

'Of course.'

'And not do anything, I mean?'

'I know what you mean. And I think that's a wonderful idea.' We must have lain there six, seven minutes before we started making love, and then it was the most violent love we'd ever made, her hurling herself at me, inflicting pleasure and pain in equal parts. It was a purgation I badly needed.

'She's always been like this.'

'Your mother?'

'Uh-huh.'

'Competitive, you mean?'

'Uh-huh. Even when I was little. If somebody gave me a compliment, she'd get mad and say, "Well, it's not hard for little girls to look good. The trick is to stay beautiful as you get older."'

'Didn't your dad ever notice?'

She laughed bitterly. 'My father? Are you kidding? He'd usually come home late and then finished getting bombed and then climb in bed next to me and feel me up.'

'God.'

Bitter sigh. 'But I don't give a shit. Not anymore. Fuck them. I come into my own inheritance in six months – from my paternal grandfather – and then I'm moving out of the manse and leaving them to all their silly fucking games.'

'Is now a good time to tell you I love you?'

'You know the crazy goddamned thing, Roger?'

'What's that?'

'I really love you, too. For the first time in my life, I actually love somebody.'

On the night of 20 Jan, six weeks later, I went to bed early with a new Sue Grafton novel. Kendra had begged off our date because of a head cold. I'm enough of a hypochondriac that I wasn't unhappy about not seeing her.

The call came just before two a.m., long after I was sleeping and just at the point where waking is difficult.

But get up I did and listen at length to Amy's wailing. It took me a long time to understand the exact message her sobs meant to convey.

The funeral took place on a grim snowy day when the harsh, numbing winds rocked the pallbearers as they carried the gleaming silver coffin from hearse to graveside. The land lay bleak as a tundra.

Later, in the country club where a luncheon was being served, an old high school friend came up and said, 'I bet when they catch him he's a nigger.'

'I guess it wouldn't surprise me.'

'Oh, hell, yes. Poor goddamned guy is sleeping in his own bed when some jig comes in and blasts the hell out of him and then goes down the hall and shoots poor Kendra, too. They say she'll never be able to walk or talk again. Just sit in a frigging wheelchair all the time. I used to be a liberal back in the sixties or seventies, but I've had enough of their bullshit by now. I'll tell you that I've had their bullshit right up to here, in fact.'

Amy came late. In the old days one might have accused her of doing so so she could make an entrance. But now she had a perfectly good reason. She walked with a cane, and walked slowly. The intruder who'd shot up the place that night, and stolen more than $75,000 in jewelry, had shot her in the shoulder and the leg, apparently leaving her for dead. Just as he'd left Kendra for dead.

Amy looked pretty damned good in her black dress and veil. The black gave her a mourning kind of sexiness.

A line formed. She spent the next hour receiving the members of that line just as she had done at the mortuary the night before. There were tears and laughter with tears and curses with tears. The very old looked perplexed by it all – the world made no sense anymore; here you were a rich person and people still broke into your house and killed you right in your bed – and middle-aged people looked angry (i.e., damned niggers) and the young looked bored (Randy being the drunk who's always wobbled around pinching all the little girls on their bottoms – who cared he was dead, the pervert?).

I was the last person to go through the line, and when she saw me, Amy shook her head and began sobbing. 'Poor, poor Kendra,' she said. 'I know how much she means to you, Roger.'

'I'd like to visit her tonight if I could. At the hospital.'

Beneath her veil, she sniffled some more. 'I'm not sure that's a good idea. The doctor says she really needs her rest. And Vic said she looked very tired this morning.'

The bullet had entered her head just below her left temple. By rights she should have died instantly. But the gods were playful and let her live – paralyzed.

'Vic? Who's Vic?'

'Our nurse. Oh, I forgot. I guess you've never met him, have you? He just started Sunday. He's really a dear. One of the surgeons recommended him. You'll meet him some time.'

I met him four nights later at Kendra's bedside.

He was strapping arrogant was our blond Vic, born to a body

and face that no amount of surgery or training could ever duplicate, a natural Tarzan to my own tricked-up one. He looked as if he wanted to tear off his dark and expensive suit and head directly back to the jungle to beat up a lion or two. He was also the proud owner of a sneer that was every bit as imposing as his body.

'Roger, this is Vic.'

He made a point of crushing my hand. I made a point of not grimacing.

The three of us then stared down at Kendra in her bed, Amy leaning over and kissing Kendra tenderly on the forehead. 'My poor baby. If only I could have saved her—'

That was the first time I ever saw Vic touch her, and I knew instantly, in the proprietary way he did, that something was wrong. He probably was a nurse, but to Amy he was also something far more special and intimate.

They must have sensed my curiosity because Vic dropped his hand from her shoulder and stood proper as an altar boy staring down at Kendra.

Amy shot me a quick smile, obviously trying to read my thoughts.

But I lost interest quickly. It was Kendra I wanted to see. I bent over the bed and took her hand and touched it to my lips. I was self-conscious at first, Amy and Vic watching me, but then I didn't give a damn. I loved her and I didn't give a damn at all. She was pale and her eyes were closed and there was a fine sheen of sweat on her forehead. Her head was swathed in white bandages of the kind they always used in Bogart movies, the same ones that Karloff also used in *The Mummy.* I kissed her lips and I froze there because the enormity of it struck me. Here was the woman I loved, nearly dead, indeed should have been dead given the nature of her wound, and behind me, paying only a kind of lip service to her grief, was Kendra's mother.

A doctor came in and told Amy about some tests that had been run today. Despite her coma, she seemed to be responding to certain stimuli that had had no effect on her even last week.

Amy started crying, presumably in a kind of gratitude, and

then the doctor asked to be alone with Kendra, and so we went out into the hall to wait.

'Vic is moving in with us,' Amy said. 'He'll be there when Kendra gets home. She'll have help twenty-four hours a day. Won't that be wonderful?'

Vic watched me carefully. The sneer never left his face. He looked the way he might if he'd just noticed a piece of dog mess on the heel of his shoe. It was not easy being a big blond god. There were certain difficulties with staying humble.

'So you know Kendra's surgeon,' I said to Vic.

'What?'

'Amy said that the surgeon had recommended you to her.'

They glanced at each other and then Vic said, 'Oh, right, the surgeon, yes.' He gibbered like a Miss America contestant answering a question about patriotism.

'And you're moving in?'

He nodded with what he imagined was solemnity. If only he could do something about the sneer. 'I want to help in any way I can.'

'How sweet.'

If he detected my sarcasm, he didn't let on.

The doctor came out and spoke in soft, whispered sentences filled with jargon. Amy cried some more tears of gratitude.

'Well,' I said. 'I guess I'd better be going. Give you some quality time with Kendra.'

I kissed Amy on the cheek and shook Vic's proffered hand. He notched his grip down to mid-level. Even hulks have sentimental moments. He even tried a little acting, our Vic. 'The trick will be to get her to leave before midnight.'

'She stays late, eh?' I said.

Amy kept her eyes downcast, as befitted a saint who was being discussed.

'Late? She'd stay all night if they'd let her. You can't tear her away.'

'Well, she and Kendra have a very special relationship.'

Amy caught the sarcasm. Anger flashed in her eyes but then

subsided. 'I want to get back to her,' she said. And Mother Teresa couldn't have said it any more believably.

I took the elevator down to the ground floor, then took the emergency stairs back up to the fourth floor. I waited in an alcove down the hall. I could see Kendra's door, but if I was careful neither Amy nor Vic would be able to see me.

They left ten minutes after I did. Couldn't drag Amy away from her daughter's bedside, eh?

In the next six weeks, Kendra regained consciousness, learned how to manipulate a pencil haltingly with her right hand, and got tears in her eyes every time I came through the door. She still couldn't speak or move her lower body or left side, but I didn't care. I loved her more than ever and in so doing proved to myself that I wasn't half as superficial as I'd always suspected. That's a good thing to know about yourself – that at age forty-four you have at least the potential for becoming an adult.

She came home in May, after three intense months of physical rehab and deep depression over her fate, a May of butterflies and cherry blossoms and the smells of steak on the grill on the sprawling grounds behind the vast English Tudor. The grounds ran four acres of prime land, and the house, divided into three levels, included eight bedrooms, five full baths, three half baths, a library, and a solarium. There was also a long, straight staircase directly off the main entrance. Amy had it outfitted with tracks so Kendra could get up and down in her wheelchair.

We became quite a cheery little foursome, Kendra and I, Amy and Vic. Four or five nights a week we cooked out and then went inside to watch a movie on the big-screen television set in the party room. Three nurses alternated eight-hour shifts so that whenever Kendra – sitting silently in her wheelchair in one of her half-dozen pastel-colored quilted robes – needed anything, she had it. Amy made a cursory fuss over Kendra at least twice an evening, and Vic went to fetch something unimportant, apparently in an attempt to convince me he really was a working male nurse.

More and more I slipped out early from the brokerage, spending the last of the day with Kendra in her room. She did various kinds of physical therapy with the afternoon nurse, but she never forgot to draw me something and then offer it up to me with the pride of a little girl pleasing her daddy. It always touched me, this gesture, and despite some early doubts that I'd be able to be her husband – I'd run away and find somebody strong and sound of limb; I hadn't had all that plastic surgery for nothing, had I? – I learned that I loved her more than ever. She brought out a tenderness in me that I rather liked. Once again I felt there was at least some vague hope that I'd someday become an adult. We watched TV or I read her interesting items from the newspaper (she liked the nostalgia pieces the papers sometimes ran) or I just told her how much I loved her. 'Not good for you,' she wrote on her tablet one day and then pointed at her paralyzed legs. And then broke into tears. I knelt at her feet for a full hour, till the shadows were long and purple, and thought how crazy it all was. I used to be afraid that she'd leave me – too young, too good-looking, too strong-willed, only using me to get back at her mother – and now she had to worry about some of the same things. In every way I could, I tried to assure her that I'd never leave her, that I loved her in ways that gave me meaning and dignity for the first time in my life.

Hot summer came, the grass scorching brown, night fires like the aftermath of bombing sorties in the dark hills behind the mansion. It was on one of these nights, extremely hot, Vic gone some place, the easily tired Kendra just put to bed, that I found Amy waiting for me in my car.

She wore startling white short-shorts and a skimpy halter that barely contained her chewy-looking breasts. She sat on the passenger side. She had a martini in one hand and a cigarette in the other.

'Remember me, sailor?'

'Where's lover boy?'

'You don't like him, do you?'

'Not much.'

'He thinks you're afraid of him.'

'I'm afraid of rattlesnakes, too.'

'How poetic.' She inhaled her cigarette, exhaled a plume of blue against the moonlit sky. I'd parked at the far end of the pavement down by the three-stall garage. It was a cul-de-sac of sorts, protected from view by pines. 'You don't like me anymore, do you?'

'No.'

'Why?'

'I really don't want to go into it, Amy.'

'You know what I did this afternoon?'

'What?'

'Masturbated.'

'I'm happy for you.'

'And you know who I thought of?'

I said nothing.

'I thought about you. About that night we were together over at your house.'

'I'm in love with your daughter, Amy.'

'I know you don't think I'm worth a shit as a mother.'

'Gee, whatever gave you that idea?'

'I love her in my way. I mean, maybe I'm not the perfect mother, but I do love her.'

'Is that why you won't put any makeup on her? She's in a fucking wheelchair, and you're still afraid she'll steal the limelight.'

She surprised me. Rather than deny it, she laughed. 'You're a perceptive bastard.'

'Sometimes I wish I weren't.'

She put her head back. Stared out the open window. 'I wish they hadn't gone to the moon.'

I didn't say anything.

'They spoiled the whole fucking thing. The moon used to be so romantic. There were so many myths about it, and it was so much fun thinking about. Now it's just another fucking rock.' She drained her drink. 'I'm lonely, Roger. I'm lonely for you.'

'I'm sure Vic wouldn't want to hear that.'

'Vic's got other women.'

I looked at her. I'd never seen her express real anguish before.

I took a terrible delight in it. 'After what you and Vic did, you two deserve each other.'

She was quick about it, throwing her drink in my face, then getting out of the car and slamming the door shut. 'You bastard! You think I don't know what you meant by that? You think I killed Randy, don't you?'

'Randy – and tried to kill Kendra. But she didn't die the way she was supposed to when Vic shot her.'

'You bastard!'

'You're going to pay for it someday, Amy. I promise you that.'

She still had the glass in her hand. She smashed it against my windshield. The safety glass spiderwebbed. She stalked off, up past the pines, into invisibility.

I didn't bring it up. Kendra did. I'd hoped she'd never figure out who was really the intruder that night. She had a difficult enough time living. That kind of knowledge would only make it harder.

But figure it out she did. One cool day in August, the first hint of autumn on the air, she handed me what I assumed would be her daily love note.

VIC
CHECK
FIGHT
$

I looked at the note and then at her.

'I guess I don't understand. You want me to check something about Vic?'

Her darting blue eyes said no.

I thought a moment: Vic, check. All I could think of was checking Vic out. Then, 'Oh, a check? Vic gets some kind of check?'

The darting blue eyes said yes.

'Vic was having an argument about a check?'

Yes.

'With your mother?'

Yes.

'About the amount of the check?'

Yes.

'About it not being enough?'

Yes.

And then she started crying. And I knew then that she knew. Who'd killed her father. And who'd tried to kill her.

I sat with her a long time that afternoon. At one point a fawn came to the edge of the pines. Kendra made a cooing sound when she saw it, tender and excited. Starry night came and through the open window we could hear a barn owl and later a dog that sounded almost like a coyote. She slept sometimes, and sometimes I just told her the stories she liked to hear, 'Goldilocks and the Three Bears' and 'Rapunzel,' stories, she'd once confided, that neither her mother or father had ever told her. But this night I was distracted and I think she sensed it. I wanted her to understand how much I loved her. I wanted her to understand that even if there were no justice in the universe at large, at least there was justice in our little corner of it.

On a rainy Friday night in September, in an apartment Vic kept so he could rendezvous with a number of the young women Amy had mentioned, a tall and chunky man, described as black by two neighbors who got a glimpse of him, broke into Vic Bailey's place and shot him to death. Three bullets. Two directly to the brain. The thief then took more than $5,000 in cash and traveler's checks (Vic having planned to leave for a European vacation in four days).

The police inquired of Amy, of course, as to how Vic had been acting lately. They weren't as yet quite convinced that his death had been the result of a simple burglary. The police are suspicious people but not, alas, suspicious enough. Just as they ultimately put Randy's death down to a robbery and murder, so they ultimately ruled that Vic had died at the hand of a burglar, too.

On the day Amy returned from the funeral, I had a little

surprise for her, just to show her that things were going to be different from now on.

That morning I'd brought in a hair stylist and a makeup woman. They spent three hours with Kendra and when they were finished, she was as beautiful as she'd ever been.

We greeted Amy at the vaulted front door – dressing in black was becoming a habit with her – and when she saw Kendra, she looked at me and said, 'She looks pathetic. I hope you know that.' She went directly to the den, where she spent most of the day drinking scotch and screaming at the servants.

Kendra spent an hour in her room, crying. She wrote the word *pathetic* several times on her paper. I held her hand and tried to assure her that she indeed looked beautiful, which she did.

That night as I was leaving – we'd taken dinner in Kendra's room, neither of us wanting to see Amy any more than we needed to – she was waiting in my car again, even drunker than she'd been the first time. She had her inevitable drink in her hand. She wore a dark turtleneck and white jeans with a wide, sash-like leather belt. She looked a lot better than I wanted her to.

'You prick, you think I don't know what you did?'

'Welcome to the club.'

'I happened to have fucking loved him.'

'I'm tired, Amy. I want to go home.'

In the pine-smelling night, a silver October moon looked ancient and fierce as an Aztec icon.

'You killed Vic,' she said.

'Sure, I did. And I also assassinated JFK.'

'You killed Vic, you bastard.'

'Vic shot Kendra.'

'You can't prove that.'

'Well, you can't prove that I shot Vic, either. So please remove your ass from my car.'

'I really never thought you'd have the balls. I always figured you for the faggot type.'

'Just get out, Amy.'

'You think you've won this, Roger. But you haven't. You're fucking with the wrong person, believe me.'

'Good night, Amy.'

She got out of the car and then put her head back in the open window. 'Well, at least there's one woman you can satisfy, anyway. I'm sure Kendra thinks you're a great lover. Now that she's paralyzed, anyway.'

I couldn't help it. I got out of the car and walked over to her across the dewy grass. I ripped the drink from her hand and then said, 'You leave Kendra and me alone, do you understand?'

'Big, brave man,' she said. 'Big, brave man.'

I hurled her drink into the bushes and then walked back to the car.

In the morning, the idea was there waiting for me.

I called work and told them I wouldn't be in and then spent the next three hours making phone calls to various doctors and medical supply houses as to exactly what I'd need and what I'd need to do. I even set up a temporary plan for private-duty nurses. I'd have to dig into my inheritance, but this was certainly worth it. Then I drove downtown to a jeweler's, stopping by a travel agency on my way back.

I didn't phone. I wanted to surprise her.

The Australian groundsman was covering some tulips when I got there. Frost was predicted. 'G'day,' he said, smiling. If he wasn't over sixty with a potbelly and white hair, I would have suspected Amy of using him for her personal pleasure.

The maid let me in. I went out to the back terrace, where she said I'd find Kendra.

I tiptoed up behind her, flicked open the ring case, and held it in front of her eyes. She made that exultant cooing sound in her throat, and then I walked around in front of her and leaned over and gave her a gentle, tender kiss. 'I love you,' I said. 'And I want to marry you right away and have you move in with me.'

She was crying but then so was I. I knelt down beside her and put my head on her lap, on the cool surface of her pink quilted housecoat. I let it lie there for a long time as I watched a dark, graceful bird ride the wind currents above, gliding down the long, sunny autumn day. I even dozed off for a time.

At dinnertime, I rolled Kendra to the front of the house, where Amy was entertaining one of the Ken-doll men she'd taken up with these days. She was already slurring her words. 'We came up here to tell you that we're going to get married.'

The doll-man, not understanding the human politics here, said in a Hollywood kind of way, 'Well, congratulations to both of you. That's wonderful.' He even toasted us with his martini glass.

Amy said, 'He's actually in love with me.'

Doll-man looked at me and then back at Amy and then down at Kendra.

I turned her chair sharply from the room and began pushing it quickly over the parquet floor toward the hallway.

'He's been in love with me since second grade, and he's only marrying her because he knows he can't have me!'

And then she hurled her glass against the wall, smashing it, and I heard, in the ensuing silence, doll-man cough anxiously and say, 'Maybe I'd better be going, Amy. Maybe another night would be better.'

'You sit right where you fucking are,' Amy said, 'and don't fucking move.'

I locked Kendra's door behind us on the unlikely chance that Amy would come down to apologize.

Around ten, she began to snore quietly. The nurse knocked softly on the door. 'I need to get in there, sir. The missus is upstairs sleeping.'

I leaned over and kissed Kendra tenderly on the mouth.

We set the date two weeks hence. I didn't ask Amy for any help at all. In fact, I avoided her as much as possible. She seemed similarly inclined. I was always let in and out by one of the servants.

Kendra grew more excited each day. We were going to be married in my living room by a minister I knew vaguely from the country club. I sent Amy a handwritten note inviting her, but she didn't respond in any way.

I suppose I didn't qualify as closest kin. I suppose that's why I had to hear it on the radio that overcast morning as I drove to work.

It seemed that one of the city's most prominent families had been visited yet again by tragedy – first the father dying in a robbery attempt a year earlier, and now the wheelchair-confined daughter falling down the long staircase in the family mansion. Apparently she'd come too close to the top of the stairs and simply lost control. She'd broken her neck. The mother was said to be under heavy sedation.

I must have called Amy twenty times that day, but she never took my calls. The Aussie gardener usually picked up. 'Very sad here today, mate. She was certainly a lovely lass, she was. You have my condolences.'

I cried till I could cry no more and then I took down a bottle of Black and White scotch and proceeded to do it considerable damage as I sat in the gray gloom of my den.

The liquor dragged me through a Wagnerian opera of moods – forlorn, melancholy, sentimental, enraged – and finally left me wrapped around my cold, hard toilet bowl, vomiting. I was not exactly a world-class drinker.

She called just before midnight, as I stared dully at CNN. Nothing they said registered on my conscious mind.

'Now you know how I felt when you killed Vic.'

'She was your own daughter.'

'What kind of life would she have had in that wheelchair?'

'You put her there!' And then I was up, frantic, crazed animal, walking in small, tight circles, screaming names at her.

'Tomorrow I'm going to the police,' I said.

'You do that. Then I'll go there after you do and tell them about Vic.'

'You can't prove a damned thing.'

'Maybe not. But I can make them awfully suspicious. I'd remember that if I were you.'

She hung up.

It was November then, and the radio was filled with tinny, cynical messages of Christmas. I went to the cemetery once a day and talked to her, and then I came home and put myself to sleep with Black and White and Valium. I knew it was Russian roulette, that particular combination, but I thought I might get lucky and lose.

The day after Thanksgiving, she called again. I hadn't heard from her since the funeral.

'I'm going away.'

'So?'

'So. I just thought I'd tell you that in case you wanted to get hold of me.'

'And why would I want to do that?'

'Because we're joined at the hip, darling, so to speak. You can put me in the electric chair, and I can do the same for you.'

'Maybe I don't give a damn.'

'Now you're being dramatic. If you truly didn't give a damn, you would've gone to the police two months ago.'

'You bitch.'

'I'm going to bring you a little surprise when I come back from my trip. A Christmas gift, I guess you'd call it.'

I tried working but I couldn't concentrate. I took an extended leave. The booze was becoming a problem. There was alcoholism on both sides of my family, so my ever increasing reliance on blackouts wasn't totally unexpected, I suppose. I stopped going out. I learned that virtually anything you needed would happily be brought you if you had the money, everything from groceries to liquor. A cleaning woman came in one day a week and bull-dozed her way through the mess. I watched old movies on cable, trying to lose myself especially in the frivolity of the musicals. Kendra would have loved them. I found myself waking, many mornings, in the middle of the den, splayed on the floor, after apparently trying to make it to the door but failing. One morning I found that I'd wet myself. I didn't much care, actually. I tried not to think of Kendra, and yet she was all I did want to think about. I must have wept six or seven times a day. I dropped twelve pounds in two weeks.

I got sentimental about Christmas Eve, decided to try and stay reasonably sober and clean myself up a little bit. I told myself I was doing this in honor of Kendra. It would have been our first Christmas Eve together.

The cleaning lady was also a good cook and had left a fine roast beef with vegetable and potato fixings in the refrigerator. All I had to do was heat it up in the microwave.

I had just set my place at the dining room table – with an identical place setting to my right for Kendra – when the doorbell rang.

I answered it, opening the door and looking out into the snow-whipped darkness.

I know I made a loud and harsh sound, though if it was a scream exactly, I'm not sure.

I stepped back from the doorway and let her come in. She'd even changed her walk a little, to make it more like her daughter's. The clothes, too, the long double-breasted camel hair coat and the wine-colored beret, were more Kendra's style than her own. Beneath was a four-button empire dress that matched the color of the beret – the exact dress Kendra had often worn.

But the clothes were only props.

It was the face that possessed me.

The surgeon had done a damned good job, whoever he or she was, a damned good job. The nose was smaller and the chin was now heart-shaped and the cheekbones were more pronounced and perhaps a half inch higher. And with her blue blue contacts—

Kendra. She was Kendra.

'You're properly impressed, Roger, and I'm grateful for that,' she said, walking past me to the dry bar. 'I mean, this was not without pain, believe me. But then you know that firsthand, don't you, being an old hand at plastic surgery yourself.'

She dropped her coat in an armchair and fixed herself a drink.

'You bitch,' I said, slapping the drink from her hand, hearing it shatter against the stone of the fireplace. 'You're a goddamned ghoul.'

'Maybe I'm Kendra reincarnated,' she smiled. 'Have you ever thought of that?'

'I want you out of here.'

She stood on tiptoes, just as Kendra had once done, and touched my lips to hers. 'I knew you'd be gruff the first time you saw me. But you'll come around. You'll get curious about me. If I taste any different, or feel any different. If I'm – Kendra.'

I went over to the door, grabbing her coat as I did so. Then I yanked her by the wrist and spun her out into the snowy cold night, throwing her coat after her. I slammed the door.

Twenty minutes later, the knock came again. I opened the door, knowing just who it would be. There were drinks, hours of drinks, and then, quite before I knew what was happening and much against all I held sacred and dear, we were somehow in bed, and as she slid her arms around me there in the darkness, she said, 'You always knew I'd fall in love with you someday, didn't you, Roger?'

***Ed Gorman** is the author of more than a dozen novels and three collections of short stories. He has been called 'The modern master of the lean and mean thriller'* (Rocky Mountain News), *'One of the world's great storytellers' (Britain's* Million*) and 'The poet of dark suspense'* (The Bloomsbury Review)*. His story here, 'The End of It All,' has been optioned as a feature film.*

Heat

BY

Lucy Taylor

WHEN the fire engines first begin screaming up Niwot Street, the man whose name I have forgotten is inside me.

He pumps away with workmanlike intensity as the sirens jangle the quiet. The hair on the back of my neck goes prickly and damp. Inside, it feels like a ball of cold the size of a fist is jabbing the wall of my uterus.

Tommy? Billie? One of those names that ends in a Y and sounds boyish, even if the owner is a portly carpet salesman with a capped smile and a wedding band.

Johnny? Jimmy?

No matter.

He grunts and bucks. I arch beneath him, so aroused that the rutting is painful, like trying to swallow water through swollen lips. So close to coming, to stilling the awful cold, that I can feel the twitch and pulse of an impending orgasm all the way up into my belly, but I can't make it, can't quite let go and thaw myself in this stranger's arms, and the sirens scream closer and closer, and I think, 'This time they're coming for me.'

They know.

But they don't, of course.

Not yet.

Not this time.

The man whose name I have forgotten heaves himself between my legs one final time, like one trying to break through a rawhide-tough hymen. I feel the shuddering squirt of his semen.

Then I'm off the bed and up so fast that his cock pumps out those last few drops onto the blue motel sheets and cum runs down the inside of my thighs.

'Jimmy,' I say. I can tell by the look on his face that I've guessed the wrong name. 'I have to go. This was a mistake. I don't even know you. I'm sorry.'

A few minutes later, I'm dressed and running to my car. Another fire engine passes, its siren like a strike of lightning along my spine, and I jump into the Volvo, peel away from the curb, and race in pursuit.

The fire engine leads me to a used bookstore in a rundown block of East Colfax. I can see the smoke, a furry plume shaped like a dust-bowl tornado, long before we arrive.

And then the flames. They lick and peel and crackle out windows and from fallen sections of wall. The fire is chewing and swallowing the building from the inside out, and every place it licks and laps collapses black and charred. I leave the car and approach as close as the firemen allow me, close enough that I can feel the heat rippling in the air like the bars of a molten cage. Enthralled, I watch this gorgeous gutting, the building getting fucked by the flames, and I long to be consumed entirely, reduced to ash and rubble.

By the fire.

By a man.

By desire that will gut and burn, devour me.

'Heat,' I whisper, and it's both prayer and plea.

Heat.

The other day I was doing my friend Shawna's hair, dyeing it that deep copper color that her husband, Robbie, likes, and I started talking about heat. What it feels like, what it can make you do, the men who've made me feel it. There've only been three such men in my whole life, among hundreds of lovers, and I've known it every single time, within the first ten seconds that I set eyes on them, when our auras intersected, our pheromones collided and entwined, when all was hot stars and sizzle.

Shawna laughed at my overblown description. She said, 'It sounds painful. How do you put it out?'

I told her you never really put it out, you just commit a hara-kiri of the heart, tamp down your burning insides, and go cold and empty for a time until you meet another man who makes your skin flame when he touches you and you start to burn again.

Shawna shook her head at that and spattered dark red droplets of henna dye. She said, 'This kind of heat – I've never felt it.'

I'm still amazed by that. It was as if Shawna had confided to me she was blind to color and saw rich crimson and plush purple and indigo and amber and jade all as dull shades of gray.

Heat – how could one live never having felt it? And not to feel it – how could one continue to live?

What it feels like – it feels like you've touched something live and electrical or accidentally injected a drug that's part hallucinogen, part poison. Your mind unravels. Your body feels limp, but you don't fall down because lust juices up your muscles, causes synapses to fire wildly, like a multiplicity of orgasms, while heat smolders in your belly and spreads down into the groin and up to twine around the heart like a kind of flaming kudzu.

It's been a long time now since I've felt that heat. My heart's going into hypothermia. I'm parched and achy and chill. I drive from Denver up to Boulder, watch the men stroll and prowl and saunter on the Pearl Street Mall, dozens, hundreds of them, all types and shapes and sizes, and some are all pumped lats and abs and some marathon-runner lean and others solid, amply padded, but I feel nothing – their cocks would be like rain-soaked straws, their touches tepid, they would give me nothing but impatience and frustration and grief.

I long for what I had before, the heat that surges and destroys, that consumes the soul and melts the heart so that it runs down, liquid, scarlet, to settle hotly in my pussy.

In my dreams lately, I see the fire turn into a man. Blazing and roaring, he bears down on me, seizes me in a searing kiss. Then I awaken in my bed alone.

From his tiny room up the hall, I can hear Colin tapping, tapping on his keyboard. The Famous Writer who simply hasn't been discovered yet. The austere and celibate *artiste.*

My God, how did we come to this?

How did we who used to smolder come to be so cold?

Three times in my life I've felt heat. The first time was a professional boxer named Zeke, all sinew and steel draped in sleek skin the color of smoky quartz. He was married to a woman down in Colorado Springs and had four children, but we fucked as if we were the last two people on earth and set up housekeeping in an apartment Zeke rented for me on Zuni Street.

The day the plastic surgeon told me it would take two operations to repair the damage Zeke had done to my cheekbones and nose, I packed a bag and moved in for a while with Shawna.

The second was Neal, an Italian model whom I seduced briefly into heterosexuality by proving I could fuck as wildly, with as savage an inventiveness, as any pierced and tight-rimmed hustler.

I left Neal because he came to love drugs more than me and because he snored and because he left the towels on the bathroom floor in steamy piles like pale blue turds and because I didn't like his aftershave and because I came home one night and found a teenage boy in my bed, a naked boy with an erection that reached all the way to his navel, and the only kind of cock I had to offer Neal was the one that had already pierced my heart.

The third is Colin.

Colin is different from Zeke and Neal. Colin is the only one who abandoned me before I could walk out on him.

Oh, he still lives in our apartment on Pascal Street. He's still there at breakfast and he always straggles home, even after getting drunk in one of those establishments where the clientele has literary pretensions, but he no longer shares my bed. He sleeps instead in the room he calls his office, a tiny coffin-shaped space which he's got filled with old magazines and newspapers and letters. Colin fancies himself a writer. He's always researching, taking notes, hoarding them away like a chipmunk storing up winter berries. So many books and newspapers and reams of paper, there's barely room for the cot he's pushed over into one corner of his cramped, cluttered nest.

Late into the night, which we used to fill by making love, I hear the peck-peck of the keyboard, like a psychotic hen. He writes of love but doesn't make it, describes passion but has lost the capacity to feel it. The writing has stolen his soul.

We used to be great lovers, Colin and I. Such great lovers that at first we seldom even resorted to the games that Zeke loved and upon which Neal insisted – the threesomes, the trolling for fresh flesh willing to be fucked by both of us, and then the toys – the polished leather whips, the cuffs, the gold chains affixed to nipple rings. It was almost a year before I even asked Colin to start hitting me, before I begged him to put his hands around my throat and choke in rhythm to his thrusts, but when we did those things – when we finally began to spice passion with pain, it was like someone throwing kerosene upon a fire. We were incinerated by it, we let go of work and friends, we withdrew from the outer world, lived only in the one of our own creating.

And that was when Colin drew away from me.

When he decided that writing was incompatible with passion, that art and sex were natural enemies. That was when I began to follow fire trucks and yearn to feel the flame.

'The funniest thing happened today,' I tell Colin, peering into his cluttered little nook where he sits scrunched before his Apple. 'I met a man in a bar on Colfax. We went to a motel and fucked and then I forgot his name. I didn't even make him use a condom. I wanted to have his cum still inside me when I came home to you.'

Colin's eyebrow rises, but nothing else. He stares at what he's written, leans forward to make some correction, strokes his chin.

'You bring me your promiscuities like a cat coming home with a mangled bird in its jaws. You may think it shows affection, but it only turns my stomach.'

I lean up against the door jamb, rub my hip against it so my silky dress slithers up.

'It didn't turn your stomach when you watched me fuck that man I found over in the Crosstown Bar? Or how about the woman we brought home that night from Larimer Square? Or your dear friend Luke from college? Or your ex-girlfriend? How sensitive we've gotten in our celibacy, my dear.'

'Please leave,' he says with chilly calm. 'You've said what you came to say. Now go.'

'I'll go,' I say, 'but you won't be able to write for wanting me. You'll imagine me in that stranger's arms, and you'll want me so much you'll want to carve out my heart with a dessert spoon. You'll want to *kill* me.'

Curse said, spell cast, I sulk my way into the living room to light a fire.

I sit before the fireplace in the living room and watch the flames curl up like orange pinion feathers of some exotic macaw. I strike a match and watch it burn down until it sears my fingers.

I was this flame, one time. I burned with just as fierce a heat, and Colin along with me. How could one relinquish that for any other mistress, muse? How could one come to fear the flame?

Colin fears it.

I remember waking up on the sheepskin rug before the fireplace and seeing Colin sobbing. 'Thank God, thank God, I thought I'd killed you. Oh, Jesus, I just lost track . . . it was like blacking out . . . and I was so close, I was coming and I just kept choking you and then I finally realized you'd stopped moving and . . . oh, God, I thought you were dead.'

I tried to comfort him, but he drew away.

And that was the last time he touched me.

A few weeks later, he admitted what I'd already guessed – that his terror came not so much from forgetting what he was doing, but from the fact that he *didn't* forget, that he was choking me and he wanted to choke me more, that for an awful moment as he felt my pulse grow weak beneath his hands, he longed as much to kill me as to come, that death and orgasm commingled in an overpowering lust.

He had fought it off, though, and I had lived.

Nor was he ever able to understand why I wasn't grateful.

What keeps me sane, if sanity is what this is: long masturbatory sessions and prowling for men to pick up, take to a motel or into a park, and fuck.

And I go to fires. There's a fire station only a half mile away on Wilson Street. Sometimes if I'm quick enough I can follow the last departing engines to the blaze. There is a strange seductiveness to the writhing, licking of the flames. I wonder if the firemen feel it, if, unknown to any but themselves, they bring erections to the blaze.

Over time, I watch the burning of a department store, a warehouse, a private home, imagining that it was I who lit the flame, that it isn't lust that crazes me, but simple madness, fire love.

And then I wonder if it isn't the same thing.

Sleep is yet another kind of scalding.

The man whose face is made of fire turns my dreams to tinder.

He's Zeke and Neal and Colin, he touches that part of me that's never touched, that even when I'm fucked past the screaming point, never ignites the cold core of my being. His cock is a torch reaching my heart. I long for him to burn away my insides.

The whips, the blows, the sweet and painful kisses of fist and lash, these were always an attempt to thaw that cold part, to reach the frozen, icy center.

But not just any man will do. Only those three, my personal erotic Trinity. Only those men whose fire somehow ignites my own, who burn at the same level of heat that I do. With these few men I fuck with heart and mind and soul and pussy. With the others it was just a brief insertion of cock into cunt, tab A into slot B, shake well and stir, and close the door on your way out, thank you, sir.

The fire in the grate goes cold.

And Colin keeps on tapping, tapping. Late into the night I can still hear his fingers on the keyboard.

A week later, I go at night to an abandoned building I've passed many times on my way to and from Colfax. I park around the corner, slip inside. In the daytime this place is hideous, a rubble-strewn eyesore in a neighborhood to match. In the dark, however, there's a weird, unnatural beauty to this monstrosity. The moonlight weaves an eerie luminescence through broken windowpanes, off cracked and peeling walls. It reminds me of an underwater temple, ruined and abandoned, yet full of mystery and leftover grandeur.

It will burn like a piece of cardboard soaked in kerosene, which is what I use to start the blaze.

I stay as close as I dare, retreating only when I hear the sirens.

The building dies in minutes, its fragile walls collapsing, tumbling in.

What have I done?

While the firemen put out the remaining hot spots, I am left as before, shivering in the shadows, the dark place in my belly sheeted over with ice, the cold a hard lump in my belly like a dead child.

I go home.

Thinking somehow I must change Colin's mind. I must make him want me. Make him burn.

Colin greets me at the door with a drink in his hand and these unpardonable words:

'I've thought it out. I'm leaving.'

'You can't! What have I done?'

'Nothing. Everything.' He looks exhausted. 'Ever since you told me about the man in the motel, the man whose name you couldn't recall, it's like you hexed me. I can't write about anything but you. With him. With other men. It's an obsession that blocks out everything else. I have to get away from you.'

'No!' I pull him to me, and for one melting instant he clings to me and I can feel his hardness, but when I reach for him, he pushes me away.

'You're drunk,' I say.

'Not drunk enough.'

'And angry at me.'

'Yes.'

'Then let me feel your anger. Hit me. Anything you want. Just make me feel something.'

'Tomorrow,' he says, and for just an instant I have hope. But I've misunderstood. 'I'm leaving,' he says, 'tomorrow. Just as soon as I get some sleep.'

And he staggers to the cot and falls across it.

Glacial cold, intolerable.

While Colin snores, I dribble gasoline across the piles of newspapers, the manuscripts, the newspapers that I scatter at the door. Then I step back and light the match.

And throw it.

There is a roar, which I wasn't expecting, and an almost instantaneous leaping erect of the flames. Colin's shirt ignites at once. He roars and flails to his feet, slapping frantically at his burning clothes.

He looks up and sees me just as I slam the door in his face.

It's only for a few seconds that I'm able to hold the door shut against Colin's panicked assault, but that is all it takes. The newspapers must have blazed at once, the cot, the manuscripts. He's trapped in a book-lined oven.

I can feel the heat behind the door and Colin's blows, less powerful now. He's screaming something – my name? – and I step back from the door, fling it wide.

Inside the flaming furnace, the man made of fire whirls. He gyrates and high-steps, he thrashes and writhes – he's an off-kilter, blazing gyroscope, a flaming top with carrot hair. His clothes, his hair, whole hunks of his anatomy, are gorgeously ablaze.

I watch this hideous spectacle, this dance of agony, and I realize suddenly that I'm still ice inside. Worse now than ever. That nothing in this world can ever warm me again.

Except the flame.

My cold heart feels like shattered glass. With every beat, shards slice into my throat, my lungs. The hair on my arms starts to singe, but I'm freezing next to the fire.

I cannot bear the cold. Not for another moment.

I hurl myself through the doorway, into the embrace of the man made of fire.

I want him inside me. *Now.*

***Lucy Taylor** is a full-time writer whose short fiction has appeared in such markets as* Little Deaths, Hotter Blood, Hot Blood: Deadly After Dark, Cemetery Dance, Pulphouse, *and* The Mammoth Book of Erotic Horror. *Her collections include* Close to the Bone, The Flesh Artist, *and* Unnatural Acts and Other Stories. *Her novel,* The Safety of Unknown Cities, *was recently published by Darkside Press. A former resident of Florida, she lives in the hills outside of Boulder, Colorado, with her five cats.*

Thin Walls

BY

NANCY A. COLLINS

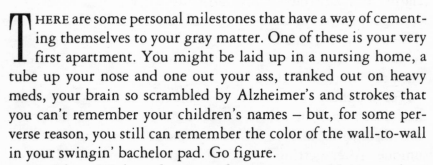

THERE are some personal milestones that have a way of cementing themselves to your gray matter. One of these is your very first apartment. You might be laid up in a nursing home, a tube up your nose and one out your ass, tranked out on heavy meds, your brain so scrambled by Alzheimer's and strokes that you can't remember your children's names – but, for some perverse reason, you still can remember the color of the wall-to-wall in your swingin' bachelor pad. Go figure.

Me, I *know* I'll never forget my first apartment. No matter how hard I try.

The name of the complex was Del-Ray Gardens. Don't ask me why. I never saw anything that even vaguely resembled a growing thing – much less a garden – the entire eighteen months I lived there, unless you count the dismal courtyard dominated by a cracked swimming pool that bred mosquitoes and scum.

The Del-Ray was old. It had been built at least a decade or two before my own conception, back when the school had been a simple state college. No doubt the Del-Ray, with its double-decker motor-hotel layout and muckleturd stucco exterior, was initially designed for the tide of GI Bill-funded married students who began to pour into the campus just before the Korean War. By the time I moved in, during the fall of '79, the only thing the Del-Ray had going for it was its proximity to the campus. It was literally a three-minute walk to and from school. And for someone like myself – who found attending classes the bitter pill one must swallow if you want to enjoy college life – the situation was ideal.

I moved in during my junior year. I'd spent my freshman and sophmore in one of the dorms and was sick to death of having to share the bathroom with three other people and not being (technically) allowed visitors of the opposite sex after nine in the evening. The Del-Ray was nearby and, at a hundred a month plus utilities, definitely within my budget.

I moved in all by myself – since all I owned in the world was a couple of plastic milk crates full of paperbacks, a double mattress (no box springs), a manual typewriter, a blow dryer, a digital alarm clock, a portable black-and-white television set, and a popcorn popper, it was hardly a Herculean task. So what if I didn't have a chair to sit in? I was on my own! I had my very own place to party in! Although what I found waiting for me quickly dampened my youthful high spirits.

For one thing, I discovered that the previous tenant had left a half-dozen eggs in the refrigerator before pulling the plug a month or so back. Needless to say, the clean-up experience was unique. After getting the kitchen straightened out, I walked down to the Hit-N-Git on the corner and bought some macaroni and cheese and a couple cans of tuna for my first meal in my new home. My mother had been thoughtful enough to endow me with some of the old pot vessels and dishes she'd been meaning to replace, so there was a strange feeling of domestic déjà vu as I spooned my evening's repast onto my old Daffy Duck plate.

As I sat, cross-legged, on the floor of the living room, my back resting against the cheap plywood paneling, I smiled contentedly and imagined the empty walls covered with blacklight posters and lined with bookcases full of paperback sf, the bedroom doorway draped by a glass-bead curtain, while a stereo system cranked out Alice Cooper and Kiss at volumes loud enough to put even more cracks in the Del-Ray's crumbling stucco facade. I imagined all my friends nodding their heads and checking out the decor, toking weed and swigging beer and saying, 'This place is really cool' or—

'Who told you you could turn the fuckin' channel, you motherfuckin' cocksucker?'

The voice was so loud, so *close,* I actually jumped, thinking someone was in the room with me.

'You weren't fuckin' watchin' it! You were fuckin' asleep!'

'Bullshit! I was fuckin' watchin' the fuckin' TV!'

'Like fuck you were! How could you be watchin' the fuckin' TV when your fuckin' eyes were closed?'

'I was just restin' my fuckin' eyes, you dirty cocksucker!'

By this point I realized I was, indeed, very much alone in my apartment. What I was hearing was coming from next door. Both voices were male, more than a little intoxicated, and seemed to belong to older people – guys my dad's age, if not older. Although the television in question was indeed turned up fairly high – something I'd grown used to in the dorm and had learned to ignore – I was unused to people yelling at the top of their lungs.

'Don't call me that again, Dez! I told you before about callin' me that!'

'I'll call you whatever the hell I want to call you, damn it!'

'God damn you, Dez, shut the fuck up!'

'You shut the fuck up, you dirty cocksuckin' piece of shit!'

I crept to my front door and opened it, peering out into the courtyard. To my surprise, none of the other tenants were visible. Was it possible no one else could hear what was going on in the apartment next to mine?

'Shut up, old man! Go to bed!'

'You fuckin' piece of shit!'

'It's time for you to go to bed, Dez!'

'You think you're so fuckin' smart!'

'Shut your fuckin' mouth and fuckin' go to bed!'

'Don't you touch me, you queer piece of shit! I'll fuckin' kill you if you fuckin' touch me, you queer motherfucker!'

Suddenly there was a loud thump, as if someone had just thrown a duffel-bag full of dirty laundry against the other side of the living room wall. Then another. And another.

I yanked the door back open and headed to the apartment across from mine, intending to borrow the phone to call the police. My heart was hammering away in my chest as I knocked on the door. After a few seconds I could hear the bolt being shot back, and a man I recognized as one of the English Department teaching assistants peered out at me.

'I'm sorry for interrupting your dinner, but I need to use your phone—'

The T.A.'s eyes flickered over my shoulder to where my apartment door was standing open. 'You in 1-E?'

'Yeah. I just moved in this afternoon. Look, I need to call the cops—'

'You can use the phone if you like, but I'll warn you right now – they're not going to come. At least, not right away, and only then if two or three other people call in to complain.'

'What do you mean?'

'It's just Dez and Alvin again.'

'Are you sure? About the cops not coming, I mean?'

The T.A. laughed the same way my dad laughs whenever he talks about the IRS. 'Believe me, I know.'

That was my first exposure to my next door neighbors, Dez and Alvin.

Over the next few months, I got to know quite a bit about them, although I never learned their last names. Most of the information was absorbed unintentionally, as there was no way I could avoid listening to their nightly harangues. During the day and afternoon they were usually quiet – although dormant might be a more accurate term. I quickly learned that their screaming matches, while loud, were usually brief and seemed to follow a schedule. They would start arguing about the time the five o'clock news came on, building to a crescendo around Johnny Carson's monologue.

I had signed a lease, like a fool, and I knew that I'd never be able to find anything as close to campus and as cheap as the Del-Ray, so I gritted my teeth and decided to ride it out as best I could. I spent a lot of time going to double-features, timing it so I wouldn't get home until Dez and Alvin had finished their alcoholic kabuki theater for the night.

Although I heard them on a daily basis, I didn't lay eyes on Alvin and Dez until my second week at the Del-Ray, and that was by complete accident.

It was about two on a weekday afternoon. I had gone to the Hit-N-Git, the twenty-four-hour convenience store down the block from the Del-Ray. There was a tall, thin man dressed in cranberry-colored synthetic pants – cheap Sans-a-Belt knock-offs – and a synthetic silk shirt with pictures of sailboats lithoed all over it, trying to microwave a burrito.

He reeked of cheap perfume, bologna, and gin so strongly I could smell him from two aisles away. Although he was probably forty-five, he looked a lot older than my dad. His hair, which had once been red but had faded to an unattractive carroty orange, was arranged in that style peculiar to older white trash homosexuals: one part bouffant and one part rooster comb. As he headed for the cashier to pay for his burrito, I glimpsed a bruise under his left eye, covered by liquid foundation makeup that was a shade darker than he was. It suddenly dawned on me that I was staring at one half of the notorious Dez and Alvin. Probably Alvin. Dez's voice was deeper, heavier, and seemed to belong to a much older man.

While at the counter, Alvin bought a pint of gin – the kind with the yellow label that just says GIN in big block letters – and a pint of equally generic vodka, then lurched out the door, leaving his microwave burrito sitting on the counter. The cashier, a Pakistani exchange student, simply shrugged and tossed the food in the trash.

I didn't spot Dez until that same weekend, when I made the mistake of inviting a couple of friends over to my groovy new pad. The last couple of weekends Dez and Alvin had gone out drinking at some bar, and I made the mistake of thinking this was something they did every weekend. Nope. Just those immediately after Dez's Social Security and Alvin's welfare checks arrived.

I managed to round up a kitchen table and enough chairs to attempt a dinner party, of sorts. So I invited George and Vinnie over. George and Vinnie were a gay couple I'd known since my freshman year. George was a theater major studying set design, while Vinnie was interested in architectural engineering. Really sweet, funny guys. Loads of laughs.

I made spaghetti and garlic bread (one of the few things I knew how to cook), and George and Vinnie brought a bottle of chianti. I'd just cleared the dishes and we were sitting around discussing the latest gossip when the living room wall shook so hard it dislodged the Jagermeister mirror I'd bought at the Spencer's in the mall the day before and sent it crashing to the floor.

'Don't touch my shit!'

'I didn't touch your shit! Nobody ever touched your fuckin' shit!'

'You're a lyin' sonofabitch, Alvin!'

'Shut up, old man!'

'Don't you touch me, you queer motherfucker! You touch me again, I'll kill you in a fuckin' minute! I don't give a fuck who you are! I'll fuckin' kill you, you fuckin' piece of shit!'

'Shut your fuckin' mouth!'

'Shut your mouth, you fuckin' queer! You're a fuckin' piece of shit, that's all you are! Hell, you ain't even a piece of shit! Queers ain't human!'

George pushed back his chair, his eyes never leaving the living room wall. 'We'd – umm – like to stay and chat awhile, but Vinnie and I really need to get home . . .'

'I'm really sorry about this, guys. Honestly I am . . .'

'I ain't got no use for fuckin' cocksuckers like you! All you queers ought to die! Leave us normal people alone!'

'Shut up, Dez! Nobody wants to listen to you!'

'I'm gonna kick your fuckin' ass!'

'Just try it, old man!'

'Honey, not as sorry as we feel for *you*,' Vinnie whispered, hurrying to follow George to the door. They both kept eyeing the wall as if they expected Dez and Alvin to come busting through it like trained tigers jumping hoops of fire.

Just as George opened the door, Alvin and Dez's slammed shut. All three of us stood on tiptoe and peeped around the corner of the jamb. A short, thick-set man in his sixties – with what was left of his gray hair in a military-style buzz cut – was weaving toward the parking lot and the general direction of the Hit-N-Git's late-night liquor supply. He wore a short-sleeve dress shirt and a pair of badly wrinkled slacks that, from the back, looked like he was smuggling well-fed bulldogs.

'Who – or should I say *what* – is that?' stage-whispered George.

'I guess it's Dez. He lives next door with Alvin, the guy he was fighting with.'

'I've heard of closet cases – but this one takes the cake!' Vinnie marveled.

'You don't think he's gay, do you?' I wondered aloud. 'I mean, I know Alvin is . . . But Dez looks like one of my dad's old army buddies. Maybe they're just roommates.'

George gave me a look he reserved for particularly dense straight people. 'Honey, are there any two-bedroom units in this dump?'

'Uh.'

'Besides, I've heard stories about this couple. No one's ever mentioned their names or where they live exactly, but I'm pretty sure these are the same guys. They're hardcore alcoholics and they've been living together since the early sixties.'

'You've gotta be kidding! How could two people who hate each other's guts so much stay together under one roof that long?' I shuddered. The very idea was impossible to visualize – kind of like my grandparents having sex.

Vinnie shrugged. 'Hey, my parents spent the last ten years of their marriage like they were fighting the Vietnam War, not raising a family in suburbia.'

'This whole scene's too much like my own folks,' George agreed. 'It's weirding me out. Why don't you come visit us next time? I don't think I could handle having to listen to those closet queens screech at each other again.'

As you may have guessed, that was my one and only attempt at having friends over to my new place. Thanks to Dez and Alvin, I never once got to throw a wild and crazy college student-type party while I lived there. The possibility that they might crash the party in hopes of scoring free booze was enough to deep-six any plans I might have entertained.

I was amazed at how quickly Dez and Alvin had become a part of my life, even though I had yet to say anything to them and didn't really want to. Frankly, Dez scared the hell out of me. As far as I could tell, neither of them worked, and the only time they left their apartment was either to go to Hit-N-Git to buy liquor and cigarettes, cash their welfare checks, or go to the hospital emergency room. I soon realized that the long-term residents of the Del-Ray viewed Dez and Alvin as elemental forces outside the ken of Mankind. You stood a better chance of controlling the weather than changing their behavior.

Still, I often wondered what kind of hold Dez and Alvin held on the landlord. Surely enough people had complained about them over the years? I finally got an answer to this question when Dez nearly burned down the apartment complex one afternoon.

I arrived home after classes to find a couple of fire trucks pulled up outside the building, the smell of smoke and chemical fire extinguisher heavy in the air. A group of my fellow tenants were gathered in the courtyard, around the scum-pool, watching from a safe distance as a couple of firemen outfitted in heavy water-proofed canvas coats filed out of 1-D.

Dez was sitting on the staircase that led to the second-floor apartments, looking like a pickled fetus poured out of its jar. He was blinking in the afternoon sun and staring at things like he didn't know where he was, his face grimed with soot, but not so much that I couldn't make out the gin blossoms covering his cheeks and nose.

'Found what started it,' one of the firemen said, holding up a smoking piece of debris that looked like a cross between a frozen pizza and a hockey puck. 'Apparently he put it in the oven without taking it out of the box.'

Just then an older man shouldered his way through the crowd.

He was dressed in slacks and a golf shirt as if he'd just hurried off the seventeenth hole. 'What's going on here?!? I'm the owner, somebody tell me what's happened—?'

As the fire chief explained the situation – pointing in Dez's direction – the man who claimed to be the Del-Ray's owner rubbed his face the same way my Uncle Bill used to whenever he was trying to hold his temper in front of company. The moment the firemen left, the owner stalked over to where Dez was sitting and began yelling at him, although at nowhere near the volume I knew Dez was capable of. It was only then – seeing them face to face – did I realize they were blood kin.

'For the love of God, Dez, what the hell did you think you were doing?!? You're gonna put the insurance on this dump through the roof. I promised Ma I'd make sure you always had a place to live, but I've had about all I'm going to outta you! You fuck up one more time, and you're out on your ass, you hear me? And that goes for Alvin, too!'

I expected Dez to start shouting back at him, but to my surprise he just sat there and took it. His head wobbled on his neck and he began blinking his eyes real fast. I couldn't tell if they were tearing from the smoke or the chewing-out. After the Del-Ray's owner left, Dez levered himself off the steps and shuffled back into the apartment. A couple of minutes later Alvin showed up. Apparently he'd been out cashing a welfare check.

'Omigod! What the fuck did you do, Dez?'

'I didn't fuckin' do anything, you piece of shit! You're always accusin' me of doin' shit and I don't do nothin'!'

'Don't you lie to me, old man! Look at this place! Look at it! What did you do, Dez? What did you do?'

'You weren't here to fix my dinner, so I fuckin' fixed it myself!'

'You fuckin' ruined dinner, didn't you? Ruined it for everybody! See what you've done?'

'Shut up, you fuckin' piece of shit queer cocksucker!'

That particular argument got so violent that Alvin ended up in the emergency room and Dez in the lockup. Alvin was out of the hospital in two days, but Dez was sentenced to thirty for resisting arrest when the cops finally showed up. The entire apartment complex heaved a collective sigh of relief, and the Del-Ray became – for a time – a relatively quiet place.

Then Deke showed up.

I don't know where Alvin found Deke. I wouldn't rule out the underside of a large rock. Deke was considerably younger than Alvin and a few years older than myself. I guess he was twenty-five, although he didn't look particularly youthful. He was medium height, skinny, with shoulder-length, greasy hair and a droopy mustache that did little to help his weak chin. He was ferrety-looking and had all the twitchy mannerisms of a crack addict. He had one pair of filthy, raggedy jeans and an infinite number of sleeveless T-shirts and gimme-caps that promoted either Jack Daniels, Lynyrd Skynyrd, Copenhagen, or Waylon Jennings.

Where Dez had been somewhat scary, Deke gave me the out-and-out creeps. At least I knew Dez left his apartment only in times of extreme duress, such as the kitchen catching fire and the vodka running out. Deke, however, seemed the type who could suddenly manifest in the middle of my bedroom some dark night, steak knife in hand.

One day I came home early to find Deke hanging out in front of the Del-Ray, apparently waiting for Alvin to get back from the liquor store. When he saw me he grinned in that way guys who they think they're a ladies' man do.

'Hey, you're that lit'l gal that lives next door to Alvin.'

I grunted something noncommittally affirmative and tried to move past him, but he attached himself to me like toilet paper to a boot heel. He loomed over me as I stood by my front door, keys in my hand, exposing yellow, crooked teeth in a disturbingly feral grin.

'I been noticin' you, y'know. You live here alone, right? I thought you might wanna go out or something—?'

I maneuvered my keys so that they jutted from between my knuckles. Since there didn't seem an easy way out of the situation, I decided to take the bull by the scrotum, so to speak. 'What about Alvin?' I asked. 'Won't your boyfriend mind?'

Deke's face colored and he sputtered for a minute. 'I like girls! I ain't no fuckin' queer!'

'That's not what I hear,' I replied, determined not to open my door until Deke had cleared the vicinity.

'It's a damn lie! All I let the old fag do is suck my dick!'

It was then I realized what Alvin saw in Deke. No doubt he reminded him of Dez as a young man.

'Deke!'

Deke jumped like he'd been bit. Alvin was headed toward us clutching a grocery sack, and he didn't look at all happy to see Deke standing so close to me.

'Get in this house right this fuckin' minute and leave that girl alone!' he hissed.

Deke complied instantly, going in ahead of Alvin, who lingered on the threshold long enough to fix me with a venomous stare.

That night I started sleeping with a butcher knife under my pillow.

When Dez came home after his thirty days, I expected Deke would disappear. No such luck. While Deke didn't exactly live with them (I'm not sure if Deke actually lived *anywhere*), he sure as hell was over there a lot. And, to his credit, Dez didn't like Deke any better than I did.

For one thing, Alvin obviously preferred the younger man to Dez, always deferring to what Deke wanted to watch on television or – more important – the kind of liquor Deke liked. This, apparently, was a big sore spot for Dez. Dez was a vodka man. Deke, on the other hand, favored rye. Once Dez came home from jail, every fight more or less began like this:

'There's nothing to drink in this fuckin' house!'

'Don't you start that again, Dez! You know perfectly well there is rye in the fuckin' kitchen!'

'Like fuck there is! I ain't drinkin' that stinkin' shit!'

'Then don't drink it! I don't care! I didn't fuckin' buy it for you, anyway! I bought it for Deke!'

'I ain't drinkin' no god-damn rye! Rye is for no-good fuckin' punk cocksuckers!'

'Shut up, Dez!'

'You shut your mouth, you fuckin' queer!'

'Don't call me names in front of Deke!'

'I want my vodka, god-damn it! Vodka's what real men who are normal and like women drink – not fuckin' rye! Rye is a queer cocksucker drink, you god-damn piece of shit!'

Et cetera, et cetera, et cetera.

It was the end of the semester and most of the Del-Ray's tenants had already bailed for the summer when the sad and sordid love triangle finally collapsed. I knew it was destined to come to a bad end, but I was rather surprised by it nonetheless.

I'd been out late, partying with some friends at one of the local dives. It was almost three in the morning by the time I got home, only to find a couple of squad cars and an ambulance outside the Del-Ray, their sirens silent but the bubble lights still spinning. I sighed and rolled my eyes. No doubt another quarrel about the rye and the vodka.

The door to 1-D was standing wide open, light spilling out into the courtyard. In order to reach my place I had to walk past theirs, but the way was blocked by a beefy patrol officer with a walkie-talkie squawking to itself.

'I'm sorry, miss, but I'm afraid you can't go in there.'

'I live next door. I'm just going home, Officer.'

'Oh.' The patrolman stepped aside.

I was fumbling my keys out of my handbag when I heard the officer clear his throat. 'Uh, excuse me, miss? I know it's late, but Detective Harris wants to know if you could step inside for just a moment?'

What the hell. I shrugged and followed him into Dez and Alvin's apartment. It was the first and only time I'd ever set foot in it. It was exactly the same as my own one-bedroom, except that the floor plan had been flipped over. The only furniture in the living room was a swayback red velveteen sofa, an overstuffed easy chair that sported tufts of horsehair from its split seams, and a huge wooden Magnavox 'entertainment center' that looked like a coffin with a picture tube.

Dez was sitting in the easy chair, wearing baggy khaki pants and a dirty undershirt. He was staring at the snow rolling across the television screen, muttering darkly to himself. If he noticed that the room was full of uniformed police officers, his eyes didn't acknowledge it.

A weary-looking man in a rumpled suit and an equally rumpled raincoat, a badge fixed to the lapel, came out of the kitchen. 'Excuse me, miss. I'm Detective Harris. I'm sorry if we're keeping you from going to bed, but I need your help.'

'I'll try. What's wrong? Where's Alvin?'

Detective Harris looked even wearier than before. 'I'm afraid he's dead, miss.'

'Oh.'

'I'm sorry. Was he a friend of yours?'

'No. I don't think Alvin had any.'

'Well, he had at least *one.* We were wondering if you could tell us his name—?' Detective Harris pointed to the bedroom. I pushed open the door and peered inside. There were a couple of paramedics packing up their gear and discussing the upcoming baseball season. There was only one bed in the room – and it was surprisingly narrow. Sprawled across it were two nude bodies. Deke's head looked like a dropped pumpkin, while Alvin had an electrical cord wrapped around his neck tighter than a Christmas ribbon.

'Do you happen to know the name of the younger man?' Detective Harris asked, pulling a much used notepad out of his coat pocket.

I nodded mutely. I'd never seen real-live dead bodies before.

'And?'

'Deke. His name is – was – Deke.'

'Deke what?'

I blinked and looked away from the murder scene, feeling oddly disjointed. 'I – I don't know. All I ever heard him called was Deke.'

Detective Harris nodded and scribbled the information down in his notepad. 'Thank you, ma'am. You can go now.'

'Did Dez do it?'

'Looks that way. He used a steam iron to bash in the younger man's head, then strangled his partner with the cord. Then he called the police.'

That part kind of surprised me. Not that Dez had done it; but who would have imagined Dez and Alvin owned an iron?

The beefy patrolman escorted me back out of the apartment. As we passed in front of the TV, Dez suddenly stopped mumbling and lifted his hands to his face. I could see now that his wrists were cuffed together.

'Darling.'

I was surprised at how his voice sounded at normal volume. It was a little bit like Walter Cronkite's. Dez's bloodshot eyes wandered the walls for a second before settling on me.

'He was calling him darling.' Dez's meaty ex-marine's face looked like it was in danger of collapsing in on itself. His eyes grew unfocused and began wandering again. 'Who's gonna fix my dinner now?'

That night I slept without the butcher knife for the first time in weeks.

I got to read all about the tragedy next door in the local paper. According to the confession Dez gave the police, he had passed out in front of the television after a couple pints of vodka, so Alvin and Deke decided to have sex in the bedroom. Dez woke up unexpectedly and staggered in, surprising them in the act. Apparently the sight of Alvin and Deke together threw Dez into a murderous rage. The rest I already knew. The newspaper didn't say if Dez claimed he 'despised all queers,' but I don't doubt it came up in the conversation. It did give Dez and Alvin's last names, which I've long forgotten, and mentioned that they'd been sharing the same apartment since 1958, the year before I was born. The mind boggles.

Alvin wasn't even in the ground (or cremated or whatever the hell the county does to people too poor and unpopular to be given a real funeral) before Dez's brother had workmen in to renovate the apartment. By the end of the month there was an elderly retired couple living in Dez and Alvin's old space. They were real sweet and clearly devoted to one another and were complete teetotalers. They had a wiener dog named Fritzi that barked now and again, but outside of that they were polite, quiet neighbors.

When my lease was up I decided to move out. It just wasn't the same anymore. End of an era, you could say. It definitely gave me a unique yardstick for measuring my future neighbors, that's for certain.

But sometimes I can't help but think of Dez and Alvin. I'm pretty sure there must have been something like love between them, a long time ago. Maybe it was because, all the swearing and screaming and threats aside, Dez and Alvin rarely came to actual blows. And I can't get the picture of that narrow bed out of my mind. Despite the hate, self-loathing, and mutual resentment, there was something between them, even if it was the companionship that exists between fellow alcoholic burnouts.

I can imagine what it was like: years before I was born, a handsome marine walked into a bar that self-respecting men, much less marines, weren't supposed to know about and saw a redheaded young boy who was destined to be the love of his life. They had everything ahead of them, and all that mattered was their love. All lovers are invulnerable, sealed away from the harsher realities of life by their shared passion. At first. But society and its rules and expectations somehow find a way of eating through the protective bubble. And if you're not careful, it's real easy for love to curdle into resentment and anger; happiness into misery.

I'd like to think they knew something like joy before they turned into two bitter, miserable excuses for human beings, snapping and snarling at one another like animals sharing a cage that's way too small. Or a bed that's way too narrow.

Love sucks. It makes fools and slaves of us all.

But being alone and unloved is worse.

Just ask Dez and Alvin.

Author's Note: *The above story was inspired by the Raymond & Peter underground tapes (the* Best Of . . . *collection now available on CD from Ectoplasm Records) and her own experiences with the late, great 'Mr Snoopy' of Memphis.*

Locked Away

BY

Karl Edward Wagner

It was a small gold locket, late Victorian, shaped as a heart, usual period embellishments, pendant from a heavy gold chain. The locket came as part of a lot of estate jewelery for which Pandora had just made a successful bid. She was quite pleased with her purchase, although she had had to bid very high. She generally did well on her buying trips.

Pandora Smythe – she had taken back her maiden surname – owned and managed an antique shop in Pine Hill, North Carolina, a sort of sleepy college town now overrun with development, yuppies employed by the numerous white-collar industries, and retirees from up North. Pandora was English by birth and couldn't complain about newcomers, especially since they enjoyed spending too much money for antique furnishings to grace their new town houses and condos, erected where a year before all had been woodland.

Her shop was, not unsurprisingly, named Pandora's Box, but it did a very good trade, and Pandora employed three sales assistants, one of whom she would take with her on buying trips.

Pandora Smythe had peaches-and-cream complexion, angular but pert features, was rather tall, jogged daily to preserve her trim figure, was blonde and green-eyed, and nearing thirty. Her two vices were an addiction to romance novels and sobbing through vintage black-and-white tear-jerkers on rented video cassettes.

She wished she were Bette Davis, but instead she was a sharp businesswoman, and she had made only two mistakes of note: She had married Matthew McKee and stayed with him for most of a loveless year despite his open philandering and drunken abuse of her. She bought a locket.

It had been a good day at the shop. Doreen and Mavis had managed very well; Derrick had seen to the packing and delivery of the larger auction items – some very good and very large Victorian furnishings and a few excellent farmhouse primitives, which would be stuck in the back of Volvo wagons before the week was out. Pandora carried back the case of jewelery herself, chiding herself for having paid too much, but that bastard Stuart Reading had been keen for the lot as well. Probably would have fetched far more as individual pieces, but the day was long, and most of it was costume, worth more as antique pieces rather than any intrinsic value.

'Ooh! I love those jade earrings!' Mavis was peering over her shoulder as Pandora sorted through her trove across her desk.

'Take them out of your salary, then.' Pandora gave them a quick look. 'I'll want fifty dollars for them. About turn of the century. And that's green jasper, not jade.'

'Then I'll only give you thirty dollars.'

'Forty. That's gold.'

'Staff discount. Thirty dollars. And I have cash.'

'Done.' Pandora passed the earrings to Mavis. She could have had the fifty easily from a shopper, but she liked her staff, liked Mavis, and there was more here to turn a handsome profit than she had thought. Eat your heart out, Stuart Reading.

'Here's the thirty.' Mavis had dashed for her handbag.

'A sale. Put it in the cash drawer.' Pandora was sorting the cheaper bits from items which might demand a professional jeweler's appraisal. Of the latter there were a few.

'Here. I quite fancy this.' Pandora lifted the golden locket. An inscription in Latin read *Face Quidlibet Voles.*

Mavis examined it. 'Late Victorian. Gold. Yours for a mere two hundred dollars.'

'I've *already* purchased it, Mavis.' Pandora fussed with the gold chain. 'Give us a hand with the clasp.'

Mavis worked the clasp behind her neck. 'You going to keep it for yourself?'

'Maybe just wear it for a few days. How does it look?'

'Like you need a poodle skirt to go with it.'

Pandora faced an antique mirror and arranged her hair. 'Feels good. Think I'll wear it for a bit. As you said, should fetch two hundred dollars. Solid gold. Look at the workmanship.'

Mavis peered into Pandora's cleavage. 'I can't make out what the lettering means. Face something voles? That's silly. Voles are cute. Got them in my garden. Industrious little rodents. Better than having squirrels chewing up the bird feeders.'

Pandora studied her reflection. 'Problem with gold. A well-worn locket. And I haven't had Latin since a school girl.'

'Let's open it up and see what's inside!' Mavis fumbled with the catch. 'Should be a lock of hair or some old portraits.' She tried again. 'Shit, it won't open.'

'Stop tugging!' complained Pandora. 'I'll manage once I'm at home.'

Pandora took a long shower, wrapped herself in towels and terry cloth robe, made a small pot of tea, added cream, two sugars, and a bit of lemon to her cup, flicked on the television, curled up on her favorite couch, snuggled under a goose down comforter, and waited for her hair to dry. Her hair was too straight for her liking, so she preferred not to use a blow dryer.

The television was boring. The tea was good. She fiddled with the catch on the gold locket – she hadn't been able to work the chain clasp before showering. The hot water had done the trick. The locket snapped open.

Inside, nothing. Pandora was somewhat disappointed.

Feeling the fatigue from her buying trip, she set aside her teacup and fell into sudden sleep.

She was wearing a schoolgirl's gym slip. Two of the sisters were holding her arms, as she was bent over a desk. A third sister flipped up Pandora's skirt and yanked down her chaste white cotton knickers. Sister brandished a wooden ruler. The other girls in the classroom stared in frightened anticipation.

'You were seen touching yourself,' said sister.

'I'm an adult businesswoman! Who the hell are you?'

'You've only made it all the worse.'

The ruler smacked her bottom. Pandora yelped in pain. Again and again the ruler came down. Pandora began to cry. Her classmates began to titter. The ruler continued to whack her reddening buttocks. Pandora screamed and tried to escape the tight grip of the other two sisters. The beating continued.

She felt a rush of orgasm.

Pandora gasped and sat up, almost overturning her teacup. Dizzily she finished it, noticed the locket had closed. Must have done it while asleep. No more strong tea at bedtime. She removed the towel from her head and brushed out her hair. Strange dream. She had never attended a Catholic school. Her parents were C of E, she was secular humanist, in currently politically correct jargon.

Her buttocks hurt. In the mirror she saw welts.

By morning there was nothing to remark upon. Pandora shrugged it off to lying on a rumpled bathrobe and an agitated imagination. She let her staff run the shop, while she sifted through the classifieds and notices of upcoming sales. Doreen got an easy seven hundred dollars for the heart-of-pine table, poorly restored and purchased at a tenth of that. Pandora began to feel better, but still made an early day of it. She thought of Doreen and Mavis as Bambi and Thumper from that James Bond film. Derrick was perhaps James Bond. They could mind the store.

She put on a pink baby-doll nightgown – she had a weakness for fifties nostalgia – curled up in her bed and began reading *Love's*

Blazing Desire by David Drake, her favorite romance author. She fidgeted with her locket.

It opened.

Pandora was wearing a white cone bra and a white panty girdle attached by garters to beige stockings. Her party dress was somewhere in the back seat of a '56 Chevy, and she was on her knees on the cemetery grass.

Biff and Jerry were in a hurry, as the cops patroled this strip, looking for teenagers getting their thrills. They'd just dropped their jeans and Y-fronts. Standing beside the car, they were letting Pandora give them double head.

She couldn't take them both all the way into her mouth at once. She gave each cock a quick deep throat, alternating by sucking in both heads, tonguing them rapidly, while she jerked them off separately, fingering her cunt from outside of the tight chastity belt of her panty girdle. She'd told the boys that she was on the rag, because neither had thought to buy rubbers.

Biff was yelling: 'Gawd! Gawd! Gawd!'

Jerry said: 'Shut up, douche bag! You'll get the cops on our ass!'

Pandora said nothing, making only slurping and sucking sounds. She couldn't completely close her lips over both cocks, and saliva was drooling down her chin and onto her bra.

Jerry grunted and Biff repeated: 'Gawd!' Their cum gushed into Pandora's mouth faster than she could swallow, spraying over her face. She gobbled down the sticky, salty tide, sucking in both cocks as they grew limp, all the while rubbing her fingers against her cunt outside the elastic barrier of her panty girdle. Her orgasm came just as she accepted both flaccid cocks all the way into her throat.

Pandora choked and sat up in bed, still cradling the romance novel. She had never even ridden in a '56 Chevy, had no real idea as to what one looked like. Saliva covered her cheeks and chin. She wiped it with a tissue. It smelled like semen. It tasted like semen. It was semen.

The locket had closed.

Pandora was useless at the shop the next day. She went home at lunch, complaining about a touch of flu. Her workers expressed sympathy: she hadn't looked well. Mavis reminded her of a country auction this coming Saturday, which Pandora and Derrick meant to attend, and said that Stuart Reading had phoned before she got in. Pandora said that Stuart Reading could get stuffed, and then she went seeking a warm shower. Perhaps she was coming down with flu.

The shower was just what she needed: hot, steaming, relaxing taut muscles. Toweling off, her fingers brushed her locket. It clicked open.

Pandora was in a steamy men's locker room, and she was wearing only a jock strap. White, elastic, no bulge over her crotch. Not so for the others in the locker room: male hunks, dripping sweat, jock straps bulging.

Pandora yipped as one of them flipped her on the ass with his rolled towel. 'So, if you want to play football with the big boys, then you have to bend over.'

They forced Pandora to kneel onto a weight bench. Seconds later a soapy cock was pressing into her ass. Pandora cried out as the head popped into her and its length was stuffed brutally to the balls. The man began to thrust into her ass violently, urged on by cheers from the others. Pandora gasped but endured the pain. After a few minutes she felt his cock strain and pulse, spurting cum into her rectum.

The second entry was not as painful, and the man came quickly after a few rapid thrusts. The third cock was thick and long; the man fucked her ass slowly while the others yelled for him to hurry up. The fourth man seemed to come forever. The fifth was in and out of her ass in a minute. The sixth took his time and paused to drink a beer. By the seventh her ass was sore and bleeding, but he reached into the pouch of her jock strap and massaged her pussy. The eighth followed suit, playing with her clit. By the ninth Pandora finally had her orgasm.

She was lying across her bed. The locket was closed. Her ass was in agony. She stumbled onto the toilet seat in extreme urgency. There was a little blood and a great spewing of mucus from her ass as she sat down on the seat. Later, she cleaned herself, then tugged off her jock strap. She did not own a jock strap. To the best of her knowledge.

Pandora made an emergency call to her therapist, scheduling an appointment for the next day. Dr Rosalind Walden had been very supportive during the dark months of her broken marriage. Pandora felt she could help her understand this series of nightmares – if nightmares they were.

Dr Walden was a trim brunette, with rather short hair (a salon cut), close to Pandora's height, and looked more a successful career woman than a psychiatrist. Today she was wearing a loose business suit ensemble of dark linen and black hose. Pandora felt comfortable with her and gratefully sank onto her couch.

Later, Dr Walden said: 'So you think these dreams are associated with this antique locket. Why not then just get rid of it?'

'I think I may enjoy these fantasies,' Pandora confessed.

'You are recovering from a dysfunctional marriage, during which your former husband physically and sexually abused you. I think there may be a part of you who enjoys being the victim. We need to explore these repressed needs. But now, let's have a look at this locket.'

Dr Walden bent over her, fumbling with the catch. Pandora liked the brush of her hands against her bosom. 'I can't work it.'

'Let me.' Pandora clicked open the locket.

Rosalind was already leaning over her. She bent her head closer and kissed Pandora softly on the lips. In a moment their tongues were wriggling together.

Breathless, Rosalind broke off their kiss and turned to pull off her panties. Pandora was surprised to see that she wore a black garter belt. She tossed the lacy black panties onto the floor by the couch, then quickly sat astride Pandora's face. She raised her skirt, looking into Pandora's eyes. 'You want my pussy. You know you want my pussy. Tell me that you want my pussy.'

Rosalind had shaved her crotch for a thong bikini line. It smelled of musk and faint perfume. Her pussy lips were already engorged and spreading.

'I want your pussy.'

'Say it louder! You won't be able to beg in another second!'

Pandora shouted. 'Yes! Please! I want to eat your pussy!'

Rosalind lowered herself onto Pandora's face, silencing her with a gag of flesh. Pulling her skirt to her breasts, she watched Pandora's face as she rocked back and forth against her tongue. She squeezed her breasts as she rode Pandora's face, shoving her clit against her nose.

Almost smothered, Pandora worked her tongue twirling around Rosalind's clit and into her vagina. Her pussy was salty but sweet with juices. It excited her. She could feel her own pussy growing wet. She felt Rosalind come onto her mouth, almost choking her. After a brief spasm of ecstasy, Rosalind began to ride her face all the harder. Pandora's cunt grew hotter and wetter. She tried to masturbate herself, but Rosalind's legs restricted her arms, and she could not reach inside her skirt.

The second time Rosalind came was violent enough to trigger Pandora's own orgasm.

Pandora sat up from the couch. The locket was closed.

Dr Walden was making a few notes. 'Repressed sexual fantasies are common to all of us, and it's not unusual for patients to experience them involving their therapist.

'Oh, would you like some coffee? You fell asleep for a moment there.'

'I'm all right.'

'Well, are you sure you can drive? I've written out a prescription here for something that will help you sleep at night. Most likely job worries and travel stress have created sleep deprivation, causing these repressed fantasies to emerge in REM sleep. Try these for a week. If they help, I'll renew the prescription. If not, we may need to consider an antidepressant. In any event, don't hesitate to call me at any time.'

'Thank you.' Pandora recovered her handbag from the floor beside the couch. There was a pair of lacy black panties lying beside her bag. She quickly slipped them into her bag as Dr Walden wrote out her prescription.

Derrick Sloane was at her door at six in the morning. Pandora pulled on her robe and let him in.

Derrick looked embarrassed. 'You'd said to come around at six, and I hadn't heard different. So. Here I am. Right on time. Are you feeling all right? Flu can be nasty. If you want to sit this one out, I can go wake up Mavis and let Doreen keep shop while we're at the auction.'

'No. It's just that my shrink gave me some sleeping pills. I'll just get dressed. Would you please make the coffee?'

'Didn't even know you saw a shrink.'

Derrick was familiar with her kitchen and had a cup waiting for her when Pandora finished dressing.

'Thanks. This will help. I can't miss this auction.'

Derrick made better coffee than Pandora could. He was taller than she was, in his twenties, well versed in antiques, and very well built. Ideal for lifting and loading heavy pieces at auctions and moving them about the shop. He was darkly handsome, and Pandora rather fancied him, but suspected he was gay. At least, he'd never made a move on her or the others at her shop, and Mavis was to die for.

It was a bright spring morning, and Pandora felt much better with the coffee. She had pulled on some faded blue jeans and scuffed Reeboks, a T-shirt advocating saving whales, and a denim jacket. Derrick had buttered toast for her, and she munched this as she carried her plastic mug to the van.

Derrick had on black Dockers, a Graceland T-shirt, and a light jacket of black leather. That would get hot once the sun was high. Pandora glanced at her watch. They were running a bit late, but should be there in fine time for the viewing.

Derrick moved the van along swiftly. Pandora admired his shoulders. Yes, they reached the pre-auction viewing with good time to spare. It was an 1880s farmhouse whose heirs wished to liquidate along with all properties, and Pandora knew for a fact that the house was a treasure trove.

Of course, Stuart Reading was there, mingling with the other dealers and the mundanes. He sidled up to Pandora. He was a balding sixty-something with a paunch and reek of pipe tobacco.

'Sorted out that lot of jewelery from the Beales' estate yet? I see you're wearing her locket.'

'Whose?'

'Tilda Beale. You outbid me for the lot, inasmuch as I was only interested in a few of the pieces. I can offer you a very good price on the few I'm interested in. The jasper earrings?'

'Jade. Already sold.'

'Chrysolite, actually. Do you still have the necklace of carnelian and bloodstone? The matching earrings? Come, give me a good price, and I won't bid against you on that pokeberry-dyed spindle bed you have your eye on. And I do have a buyer in mind for them, so you can get the bed without my overbidding, and we'll both profit.'

Reading peered at the locket, pulling it away from Pandora's bosom, much to her distate. '*Face Quidlibet Voles.* Do what thou wilt. Aleister Crowley. Where on earth did she acquire this? Wore it always. Probably family motto. Consider selling it?'

'The necklace and earrings are for sale, of course. Not the locket. What do you know of Tilda Beale?'

'You should do your homework, my dear, if you're to stay afloat in this business. She was a maidenly spinster who never had an impure thought. A matriarch of our church.' Reading was a Southern Baptist. 'Passed on at age one hundred three. Wonderful woman. Won't be any more like her.'

'No impure thoughts?'

'If she ever had any, which I doubt very much, she kept them locked away in her heart. Hey, they're about to start. Will we cut a deal?'

They did, and Derrick and Pandora carried off the heirloom spindle bed in triumph.

After unloading the bed and the rest of Pandora's purchases, Derrick suggested that they stop off at his place for some champagne, which he'd been saving since his team lost the Super Bowl. Pandora was in high spirits after a successful auction and from selling the necklace and earrings to Stuart Reading at an exorbitant price – his buyer must be daft.

'Super!' she said. Was Derrick making a move? Perhaps she had been wrong about him.

Derrick actually had several bottles of champagne in his fridge. They went through the first one rather quickly with some Brie cheese and Ritz crackers – Derrick apologizing all the while. He said he'd run out of peanut butter and Velveeta. They both exploded in laughter. Derrick opened a second bottle.

'This locket,' said Pandora, after a glass too many. 'What do you make of it?'

'Still wearing that? Woman's picture and a lock of hair. Saw it at the auction with the rest of the lot last week.'

'But it's empty.'

'Mistake somewhere. Doesn't matter. Let's have a look.' Derrick fumbled with the clasp.

'Let me,' said Pandora, and the locket opened.

By the end of their kiss, Derrick was pulling off her T-shirt. She pulled off his. She was wearing a bra, he wasn't. He removed that as well as her jeans, she followed suit, and after minimal fumbling, their clothing was all in a pile and so were they.

'Do you mind if I tie you?' Derrick asked.

'*What?*' Pandora was dazzled by the champagne.

'Just a little gentle bondage. A real turn-on. It helps me drive you to new heights of passion.'

Bad line from one of her romance novels, but Pandora was ready for anything now. Derrick's cock was starting to straighten, and she realized she had been wrong in considering him gay. There must be ten inches there, if she helped him along.

'Sure. If it pleases you.'

Derrick opened a drawer full of many ropes and things. Pandora obediently stood with her hands crossed behind her back as he tied them.

'Let's see how close these elbows can come together.'

'That hurts!' Pandora whimpered, as another rope pulled her arms together brutally. Another rope passed around her back and breasts, pinching them cruelly.

'You'll get used to it,' said Derrick. He had passed a length of rope in several turns about her waist, tightly cinching a few turns through her cunt and ass. 'Your pussy is already getting wet, so you know you enjoy this. Now, walk into the bedroom and lie down on the bed.'

Derrick tied her ankles together and then her knees. He rolled her onto her stomach and tied a short length of rope between her ankles and wrists, drawing them together in a tight hog-tie.

Pandora was clutching her ankles and in some pain. Her back was bowed, her breasts raised from the bed. This wasn't gentle bondage, but she had gone too far now.

'But how can you screw me like this?'

'Down the throat, babe. Open wide, bitch, if you ever want to be untied.' He stood beside the bed and grabbed her hair.

Derrick's huge erection was suddenly bouncing against the back of her throat as Pandora tried to engulf it. She thought of the movie she'd seen about Mr Goodbar or something. She was completely helpless. Maybe this was all in fun.

Derrick was excited and came very quickly, filling her throat with his long blasts of cum. He grabbed her head and slammed her face again and again against his crotch, yelling obscenities at her all the while.

When she had sucked out the last drops of cum, he withdrew from her mouth. Pandora was in real pain from the brutal hog-tie. 'I think this game has gone on long enough. Please untie me.'

'I think you talk too much.' Derrick was rummaging through their clothes. He folded her panties into a neat wad, soiled crotch leading as he pushed them into her mouth and tied them there tightly with her bra.

'Just to keep the cum inside while I plan the rest of our evening.'

Pandora rocked back and forth on the bed, helpless, only able to make muffled grunts.

Derrick rolled her onto her side. He wound another long length of rope around her back and encircling her breasts. He tied the ropes in a tight tourniquet around each breast. Pandora's breasts quickly swelled from the stricture. Derrick seemed pleased by the effect of her bulging, reddening breasts. Then he clamped clothes pins onto her nipples.

Pandora made muffled sounds through her gag.

Derrick watched her writhe about while he smoked a cigarette. Rising, he rubbed the cigarette out on her ass. Her screams were lost into the panty-bra gag. Derrick lit another cigarette.

'Like that, bitch? Here's another game we'll try.'

Derrick brought a candle from his dinner table, lighted it, and began to drip hot wax onto Pandora's tortured breasts. She made frantic sounds through her gag.

Her pain turned Derrick on, and his cock hardened quickly. He stroked it over her breasts and face as the wax dripped onto her red and swollen breasts. 'I think I'll come up your nose and see if you can breathe cum.'

Pandora's eyes pleaded. The gag was already choking her.

'Maybe later. Let's see how you like this.' Derrick ejaculated onto her agonized breasts, following the spurts of cum with hot candle wax, sealing it to her flesh. 'Which is hotter, bitch?

'Thought you'd enjoy that. Now try this.'

Derrick rolled her back onto her belly, then violently jabbed the burning candle stub into her ass, wedging it between the ropes that bound her crotch.

'If you lie still and don't make a fuss about the hot wax running over your ass and slit, maybe I'll blow it out before it burns all the way down.'

He pushed his cigarette against her other ass cheek, lit another, and sat back to watch. He took a large knife from the drawer and tried its edge.

Pandora was in agony, but she wriggled her body against the

rope that ran through her cunt, rubbing her clitoris as hot wax dripped into the crack of her ass. The flame scorched her wrists as the candle burned down. Soon it would be scorching her ass cheeks. She writhed harder, rubbing her clit against the rope. The flame had reached her ass.

It took forever to reach orgasm, but she did.

The locket was shut.

Pandora staggered up from Derrick's sofa.

Derrick was carrying a tray of tea things. 'Hope you like herbal teas. This one is one of my favorites. Do you take honey? This will help you wake up. You've been out for an hour. You really shouldn't mix auctions with flu.'

Derrick was wearing an apron. He set the tea tray down on the table beside the sofa and began to pour. 'Oh. And this is my friend, Denny. He came home while you were in slumberland.'

Denny was a handsome, muscular blond of just past twenty, perhaps. He waved and said the usual pleasantries as he accepted a cup of herbal tea. Then he said: 'Derrick told me you've been at it since six this morning. No wonder the nap.'

'Glass of chablis helped,' said Derrick, sipping his tea. 'And Pandora shouldn't have insisted upon helping with the lifting – women's lib or not.

'We'll see you safely home once you've finished. You really do need to take a few days off from the shop. We guys can run it. We worry about you. Flu can be much worse than just a bad cold.'

Derrick drove Pandora home. Pandora thanked him and Denny, locked her door, undressed, broke away the wax that still clung to her breasts, took a pill, then passed out on her bed.

It was a Sunday, so she slept through. By dusk she was stumbling about the house in her robe, stirring a mixture of black coffee, sugar, and brandy to wash down the aspirin. She followed that with a straight brandy, then collapsed onto her favorite couch.

Probably flu. Her joints ached. As if she'd been tied in severe restraint. Flu. Lifting. Overwork. Fresh as a daisy come Monday morning. Maybe take the day off, as Derrick had suggested.

Probably made a fool of herself passing out like that. More vitamins, more jogging, no champagne. Chablis?

There had been no champagne. Derrick had only stopped at his place to check his mail and feed the cat, and Pandora had wanted to make a phone call. Glass of chablis? Maybe.

Blackout. Whatever. Flu. Overwork. Losing it.

Pandora felt the urge and plopped very carefully onto the porcelain throne, for her ass was very painful. After some straining, she felt much better. Then she noticed the candle stub floating in the bowl. She flushed and fled her bathroom as she was still screaming.

'Bitch! Bitch! Bitch! Sanctimonious Baptist bitch!' Pandora tugged at the gold chain of the locket as she stumbled naked into her bedroom.

'Bitch! You locked all your sexual fantasies away in your heart! Bitch! Bitch! You just waited! You fucking bitch!'

Pandora was in no state to work the clasp. After several tries she managed to snap the chain, chafing her neck in the process. She threw chain and locket onto the floor. The locket snapped open. She started to smash it with her bare foot, but it was only a locket with a lock of hair and a portrait of a young woman of another century.

Pandora sat down on her bed. She covered her face in her cradled hands. 'Wasn't you. It's me. I'm losing it. Can't hold back my fantasies any longer. Don't even want to. I won't be like you.'

Pandora washed away the thin string of blood from her neck. Looking into her mirror, she admired the red tattoo of a heart upon her left breast. She had blocked it out of her mind, but now she remembered getting a little tight, walking past the tattoo parlor, feeling daring, feeling the needle drilling into her skin. She wondered what else was missing from her blackouts and where the fantasies began. The last beating her husband had given her put her in the hospital for three days. Dr Walden had told her it was a severe concussion.

It was growing late, but the singles bars were open and sure to be hot. Pandora carefully dressed herself in black hose and garter belt, black panties and platform bra, and a clinging black tube dress and black stiletto heels. The low cleavage and push-up bra showed her heart-shaped tattoo to good advantage. She hadn't felt at all embarrassed when she purchased all of this, she now remembered: She'd felt brazen and had smiled at the clerk in a way that had made the girl nervous.

This was the first time Pandora had worn the ensemble. At least, she thought it was.

She carefully put on her makeup, brushed her hair, as she wondered what to do next. There was a small stain like an old scab on the hem of her dress, but she cleaned that away without much trouble. Maybe she should wear the red outfit instead.

Dr Walden had said to call at any time. After the singles bar, perhaps. She could ask Dr Walden for her opinion. Tonight or another night.

She opened a drawer and dropped the switchblade into her black sequined handbag. Frowning, she removed it, pressed the release button: mechanism well oiled and functioning, blade sharp and clean. Satisfied, she returned the switchblade to her handbag. She remembered buying it as part of a carton of bric-a-brac at an estate auction. Like with the locket. She remembered cleaning off the blood last time she put it into the drawer. Or was that just another fantasy?

The knife was real.

Derrick might be fun. Later.

And Mavis. Delicious.

No more the victim.

Karl Edward Wagner *graduated from the University of North Carolina School of Medicine, practicing psychiatry briefly before becoming a full-time writer. He has written or edited over forty-five books, including fifteen of* The Year's Best Horror Stories, *six books in the Kane series, and two collections of contemporary horror fiction. Karl died of heart failure on October 13, 1994. 'Locked Away' was one of his last stories written.*

Loop

BY

DOUGLAS E. WINTER

You'd better hope and pray
That you'll wake one day
In your own world . . .
—Shakespear's Sister

YOU know this dream. It takes you by the hand and leads you out of the wilderness of your office, away from the paper-patterned desk and ever ringing telephone and into the first of the many hallways. Your secretary is smiling, not at you, but at the air somewhere to the left of you; her telephone receiver is balanced between shoulder and ear, and you hear her talk of dates and times and places. The weekend, always planning for the weekend: a dental appointment, a son's soccer practice, a tryst is a darkened motel room. You wish for a new lie to tell her, but your wrist pokes the Rolex President from beneath the embroidered initials of your starched white cuff and you give the timepiece that practiced impatient stare. The bank, actually a savings and loan, will close at four, and you tell your secretary what you usually tell her. She nods without losing her smile and talks on.

You know these hallways, too. A flurry of birds swoops from the canvas at the first corner. The open doors, although there are few of them, offer glimpses of the other offices, identical furniture and file cabinets, the same gilt-framed trophies on display: subdued photographs of wives or husbands, diplomas from the finer law schools, certificates of admission to the proper courts. This hallway leads to another, and then another, and at last you are wandering the lobby, nodding back to the receptionist before ducking into the men's room.

You relieve yourself of the afternoon's cups of coffee, knowing that more will be needed if you are to finish writing the brief that even now, with luck, the word processing department is retyping. But you are thinking far ahead – never a good sign.

You must not forget the Kleenex. You pull five, six sheets from the dispenser, fold them neatly into a square, and tuck them into the inner pocket of your Paul Stuart suit coat.

Now you are ready. You take a last look into the mirror, squaring the knot of your tie and drawing in a stomach-tightening breath. The man who looks back at you seems tired but knowing, in control of his own destiny and that of his clients.

You wonder why it is that mirrors always lie.

The clock is running, and Delacorte, if anything, is punctual. He has thirty minutes for his errand and enough paper waiting on his desk to keep him busy half the night. He drags a comb through his hair, carefully buttons his double-breasted jacket. He decides to wash his hands again, and tosses the wad of paper towel the length of the washroom, a swish, before he exits. The receptionist waves a farewell to his call of 'Back in twenty,' and then he is riding the elevator to the pavement.

The streets of the capital have no names. In this quadrant, letters run in alphabetical order, absent the J, from south to north, while numbers count ever higher east to west. Some mad Frenchman is responsible.

Delacorte needs no grid systems, no tourist maps, no directions. He has made this pilgrimage nearly every week for the past year, and his eyes may as well blink closed. It is no longer a walk but a migration. He prefers the east side of 13th Street, crossing at I Street to enter Franklin Park, where he endures the usual gauntlet of broken men: gristled faces, shriveled bodies, brown-bagged bottles. An elderly black woman wearing a mottled DuRag maneuvers her shopping cart in an endless circle, stopping on occasion to rearrange the newspapers inside. At a bench near the fountain sits a man Delacorte knows only as Ernie, for this is the name sewn above the pocket of the gray-purple Texaco jumpsuit that is apparently his only clothing. Ernie smiles at the sight of him and asks for bus fare – the same question, the same words, he offers each time Delacorte has passed. Delacorte slips a dollar from his wallet and presses it into Ernie's trembling hand: 'Go home,' he tells Ernie, the same advice he has always offered. Ernie nods and sits back down on his bench.

On the far side of the park is 14th Street, across which waits a brownstone enigma, the liquor store and its angled alley, the last remnants of the invasion of mirrored glass and marble facade known as urban renewal. To the south was once a block of bars and burlesque clubs, bookstores and model studios, a shadowland tended mostly by women, frequented mostly by men. Now it is a furrow of bright concrete dwarfed by multistory monoliths. Inside these buildings are law firms and lobbyists, bankers and businessmen, the endlessly expanding hive of frantic worker bees. Delacorte looks both ways before crossing.

The windows of the liquor store offer the wet dreams of beer and bikini teams, but Delacorte isn't buying. There is time for three dollars, no more, no less. He thinks himself invisible and veers into the alleyway, takes the ten or so footsteps that lead to the decrepit portico lurking at its north side. Into the doorway, into the dark.

The smell, as always, astounds him, a stew of stale breath and sweaty armpits, Lysol cleanser and spent semen. He calms his surging stomach and looks down the waiting avenue of booths; one day, he is certain, he will meet someone here whom he knows. Though he does know the bull-necked Jamaican who minds the cash register; he knows him rather well, in the same way that he knows the man whose jumpsuit name tag reads Ernie. Most every weekday he hands each of them dollars.

Today Delacorte deals three portraits of George Washington onto the countertop and takes three stacks of quarters in return. He drops eleven of the quarters into his jacket pocket; the twelfth he holds between thumb and forefinger as he nods a wordless thank-you to the man at the cash register. A woman known as Taylor Wayne hovers at the man's shoulder, twisted in some impossibly alluring contortion across a glossy poster, nearly life-size, fully nude. Last week it was a woman known as PJ Sparxx, and the week before that, a woman known as Aja: the ever blonde, ever naked, ever willing. They mean nothing to him.

His favorite booth is 7: truly a lucky number, for it was there that he met her. It happened years ago, before the video monitors were installed, when the backs of the doors of each booth were laminated with tiny white-speckled screens onto which robot projectors tickered their five- and ten-minute film loops. There was no sound, not yet. It must have been 1978, 1979 – that long ago. He had come to this place only once or twice before, for reasons that he could not even begin to explain: an impulse, a vague need, idle curiosity. He thought of the visits as a kind of vulgar release, the kind of sex, like that with the occasional secretary, that could be appreciated and despised – quick and easy and forgettable.

But he could not forget her. One look, and he belonged to her, just as she, in time, would belong to him. There was no title on the tattered remnant of a film box that had been taped to the door of booth 7. She was nowhere to be seen in the lurid photographs on its splayed front and back. She was not even a featured player; those roles were reserved for the long forgotten and now, perhaps, long dead. The centerpiece of this loop was a threesome, a man and two women so blonde and tanned and athletic as to be almost indistinguishable as they coiled in urgent pantomime on a spotlit, silk-skinned dais. Around them in huddled, humping shadows lurked the minor players in this filmic orgy, quaffing imaginary wine from empty bottles and biting at plastic grapes. She was but one of them, a shadow within shadows – set dressing, nothing more than fleshy backdrop, until the closing seconds of that short reel, when the featured trio, momentarily spent, untangled their knot, the women kissing each other gently as the Adonis stood, reaching up into the darkness for a bottle. A portly gray-haired celebrant rises from his decorous deed, flaccid pencil of a penis flapping beneath a furred belly, and through a trick of the light she is exposed, alone, no longer something but someone: a person. She is young, no doubt underage – fifteen, sixteen years old, corn-bred in some Midwest nowhere, Nebraska or Iowa, run away from the usual things: alcoholic mother, abusive stepfather, boring high school. She is too thin, her hips sharp and pointed, her breasts flat and tiny. Her hair is blue black and Dachau short. But her pose, the vague and vulnerable gesture: the pose has it own purity, its own perfection. She reclines into the shadows, helpless, waiting, wanting, wishing . . . for you. You must stand in the tiny booth, the sudden erection cramped and painful.

The film spools from end back to beginning, and you push more quarters into the mouth of the meter and wait patiently through the minutes, the images blurring into a kind of meaningless newsreel until she appears again, and again, and again, and here, in this dark confessional, you visit her each day, feed quarter after quarter into the coin box bolted to the plywood wall, the clank of the metal a kind of overture, an expectant signal that brings your mind and body awake with total intensity, watching but not watching this ten-minute loop of grainy film until you know its every nuance, and hers: those timeless twenty seconds from shadow to light to shadow again. The sagging carcass of her partner, tilting forward, bottle in hand, and in his gray wake the sliver of alabaster skin that widens into the pair of adolescent breasts and then into the upper torso of a woman, head turned aside, looking not at the camera but to some vision that just escapes your sight off-frame, and then the first breath, almost a sigh, that raises her nipples and her shoulders, her left arm moving back, her hand, invisible, seeking some purchase on the pillows beneath her, lips parting, a look both pliant and puzzled and then, with a second breath, her leg angling up and then the pose, the sublime pose, and darkness.

You watch her and you watch her and you watch her and then, one day, she is gone. Taped to the door of booth 7 is a shiny new cardboard box, and inside, when you sit, disbelieving, hoping, praying, and offer a shiny quarter to the coin box, the projector whirs out a new film, a different film, something called *Hardcore Hookers.* You watch with dutiful resignation, but of course she is not there. You ask the man at the cash register – at the time, a scowling Filipino troll whose throaty laugh collapsed into a cough. 'Gone,' he said. You even offered him money, but he knew nothing about the film, nothing but 'Gone, gone.' His hand waved to the door, as if the reel itself had arisen from the wet darkness of the booth and slouched out into the alley.

Years later, scrounging the racks of dusty boxes in a place called Top-Flite Video, just off Times Square in the ragtag reach of the Port Authority Terminal, you found and bought that first Super 8 film, even though you owned no projector. Just touching the plastic reel was enough to bring back the vision, and with it that feeling, the one like no other, the one that took you out of this world and into hers. The loop, you learned, was called *Roman Hands,* and though the foxed yellow carton listed the names of its stars, none of them was hers. But by then you didn't need to know her name. She was famous.

The years had passed with increasing intensity. These were the 1980s – your thirties – and you measured them with money. You lived the law, slept the law, worked the partnership track until there was no doubt that you would be among the tenured few. The visits to Peepland slowed, and as the weeks multiplied into months, and the months into years, you finally brought an end to what you saw as a boyish fling, the last gasp of adolescence. It was like visiting your mother's grave, a desire that in time became an obligation and at last lost all vestiges of sentiment. Once you dated a woman who reminded you vaguely of her, but in bed, her body folded beneath you, she did not transform. Her kisses were dry, her breath stale. As you slid into her, there were gasps, not silence. Sooner or later you had to call her by name: Jane it was, or Jean. Janine. In the morning, when you woke up next to her, you wanted to cry. You bought her breakfast instead, and never called her again.

In a few months you met Melinda, our lady of investment banking; Melinda of the business suits and wire-rimmed glasses, forever clinking glasses of chardonnay and daring you to unfurl that braid of ash blonde at the nape of her neck. Her voice filled your silence and, for a time, even touched that silence inside, the place in your mind and heart and gut where only the picture people walked and talked and made love in silent shadows.

Melinda, who stole into your life on a rainy afternoon, late in April or early in May, and who left, not at all quietly, almost four years later. Melinda of the Georgetown condominium; Melinda of the Nordic Trac; Melinda of the unwanted pregnancy; Melinda of the career that mattered most.

Melinda, whose photograph you need to bring back memories of her face.

Your first wife, Melinda.

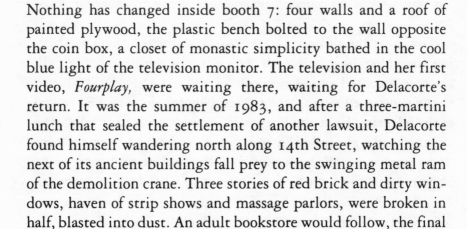

Nothing has changed inside booth 7: four walls and a roof of painted plywood, the plastic bench bolted to the wall opposite the coin box, a closet of monastic simplicity bathed in the cool blue light of the television monitor. The television and her first video, *Fourplay,* were waiting there, waiting for Delacorte's return. It was the summer of 1983, and after a three-martini lunch that sealed the settlement of another lawsuit, Delacorte found himself wandering north along 14th Street, watching the next of its ancient buildings fall prey to the swinging metal ram of the demolition crane. Three stories of red brick and dirty windows, haven of strip shows and massage parlors, were broken in half, blasted into dust. An adult bookstore would follow, the final domino, and the block would be cleansed, made ready for secretarial pools and stock options.

Whether his footsteps were impulsive or merely inevitable, he found the alleyway and escaped the August sun in the dank solace of Peepland. The old ways came back to him too easily. The crumpled dollars from his pants pocket were transmuted into quarters, and he made his way to booth 7 with nervous certainty: that she would be waiting, that she would be gone, and disappointment settled into his gut as the video played out its plotless episodes, the random collision of anonymous bodies in anonymous rooms. The male star, a mustachioed Ron Jeremy, plied his smirking sex play on a series of listless bodies until one dollar, two dollar, three dollar, four brought on the final scene, the gigolo and his latest conquest, a slutty Amber Lynn, tangling the sheets of a soundstage bed. Through an angle of light, a French maid enters, black fishnets and white ruffles, and feigns surprise with a silent surge of her lips. A latticed door is the shield through which she peers at the writhing couple, whose contortions urge her own fingers to touch her breasts, her stomach, and at last between her legs. There is no doubt that it is her. The hair is brunette, a shag cut, like Fonda in *Klute,* and she is no longer thin but lean, her stance effortless and athletic and all so knowing as she works open the buttons of the insipid uniform, unveils a budding body, still so young, so pale, so fragile and yet so willing: her mouth and at last her taut darkness taking in her fingers with such singleminded joy.

This time she did not escape him. Delacorte insisted on buying the video, haggling with the clerk until, after a phone call, the man accepted a hundred dollars, cash. As Delacorte returned to the sun-baked street, tape tucked beneath his arm, he blinked at the relentless light and knew with a sudden certainty where the visions would go, coiled in black cases, unleashed from the rundown storefronts, the back alley theaters, the bygone houses of the holy and sent into the living rooms, the bedrooms, the dens of suburbia, where video decks in the thousands, the millions, would loop out her secret life and, in time, make it public.

Her name is Charli Prince. It is a new name, taken for her headline role in the Vivid Video production known as *Air Force Brat.* Or perhaps the name was always hers, but only now, in her newfound fame, is it worthy of revelation. For her very first film credit, a seven-minute Swedish Erotica loop in which she gave a dreamy blowjob to a dusky construction worker, she was known simply as Cherie. The loop ran in booth 12 of Peepland for five weeks in the winter of 1980: Hostages held in Iran, Reagan's election, the space shuttle taking flight. Then came a series of loops for Pleasure Principle Productions in which she took third or fourth billing as Cheri Redd. Her hair was long and wicked, thickets of crimson fire that she flung furiously from side to side as men in ones and twos were taken into her mouth and then her vagina before spilling necklaces of pearly white across her throat and chest.

When he first heard her voice – that throttled cry of 'Yeah, yeah . . . *yes*' cut short by gasps so pained that she may as well have been knifed – she was known as Lotte Love. He was huddled in what he hoped was a clean seat at the Olympic Theatre at 15th Street, just below H Street; a bank building now towers over its grave. He was watching her first feature film, directed by Radley Metzger and called *Carnal Souls.* Though Metzger's films have found a skewed legitimacy, this one seems to have disappeared, with rare and usually oblique references in the filmographies. For years Delacorte had to settle for two weatherbeaten publicity stills, found in a pricy collector's catalog; in 1989, after his biotech clients consumed their leading competitor, he bought a 16mm print. His memories of the movie, except for those of her scene, were muddled by the years, but the story was one he could not forget. A church organist, played with coy perfection by Kelly Nichols, fellates the hunky parish priest and then leaves a small midwestern farm town in shame, reckless with remorse, only to die when her car plunges from a bridge. Awakening in purgatory, she expiates her sins through a series of triple-X encounters with other lost souls. One of the dear departed – none other than Lotte Love – laments having never made love to a woman, and Kelly has no choice but to comply.

It is one of his favorite scenes. She takes Kelly to the floor like a famished lion, not so much kissing as tasting her, from mouth to breasts to cunt and then back again. Her lips are fuller now, pouty and stung by bees. Her complexion is clear, burnished carefully by sun or sunlamp, and those blue eyes shine with a singleminded desire. The red of her hair is brighter, slashed with black. She owns the scene; she controls each gesture, each movement, even when she lies supine, Kelly's fingers inside her.

He remembered one other thing about *Carnal Souls.* It was that night, early in the eighties, that he entered the bookstore next to the Olympic and began to buy the magazines. Not many of them, not at first, just one or two each month: *Adam Film Quarterly, Triple X World* and the rest, devoted to the burgeoning adult movie trade. Searching, ever searching, for photos of her, and rewarded again and again as she flashed and fondled and fucked her way out of obscurity and into his eager heart. In *Gent* she straddled a jockstrapped football player, teasing his erection with her cheerleader's pompons; in *Knave* she sucked the spike heel of a Nazi-uniformed prison matron. Her wrists were circled with rope in *Bondage Life;* she knelt, her buttocks striped with welts, in *Submission*; she glistened, in red and in black, in *Latex Lovers Guide.*

In the January 1986 issue of *Gallery,* she shed the skin of Lotte Love to pose as the 'Girl Next Door' from Missouri, Sherry Ellen Locke: birthdate 6/11/64, passions for cowboy films, white chocolate, the Indy 500. He might not have noticed but for the pose on page 103: the tilt of her shoulders as she leaned over the hood of a vintage Ford Mustang, the careless but knowing thrust of her chin and breasts and hips. It took only a second look, and by then it was obviously her.

Her hair was straight and silky, insufferably blonde, the kind of blonde that mingles silver and white; her breasts had inflated to ripe and impossibly firm grapefruits. A deep tan, cooked under California sun, was slit with the blue stripe of a T-back bikini bottom. On the following pages she is beyond glorious, bending and twisting in white garter belt and stockings, draping a poolside lounge chair in nothing but high heels and suntan oil, spreading her legs wide for all to see.

With each new magazine, each new video, each new vista, she opens herself to you, shows you some wisdom in a world of skin and muscle, nylon and silk, latex and rubber, leather and chain, where the unknowable is expressed by the down of blonde peach fuzz, a taut stomach, tensed thigh. She is immaculate and she is invincible, a wingless angel, unreachable perfection – and she is insatiable. She is now called Sherilyn, as you learn when paging through an issue of *Video Xcitement,* your fingertips bruised with cheap newsprint. You order her solo video from Southern Shore and watch her undress and dance to the distant sound of rock 'n' roll while the picture fades into sunsets and at last a silver dildo.

She is Cher Lucke when going wall-to-wall with Jamie Gillis in Hollywood Video's *Ultrafoxes.* She is Cheri in *Naughty Night* and *Creampuffs 2.* In a video from B&D Pleasures, she is title material: *Sherri Bound.* Her costars are Kiri Kelly, a docile, bleach-maned submissive, and a whipmaster by the name of Jay Dee, a potbellied graybeard with a taste for riding boots and those bygone clichés of the S/M underworld. When he calls her 'slave' you nearly laugh, for there is no doubt just who is master here; she owns the camera, and everything that it sees.

It is your local video store that announces her to you as Charli Prince. There, in rental offerings hidden between the covers of a three-ring binder, awaits the erotic elite, and in *Air Force Brat* she took her rightful place among them. The next night you selected her tryst with Tracy Adams and Tyffany Minx in *Flirtysomething,* a video by Insatiable Gold. You watched her mouth, her eyes, for a clue, some knowing smile, a nod and a wink that would tell you she is acting, that she knows you are watching, wishing, wanting as her voice called to you in her trademark 'Yeah, yeah . . . *yes*' and she pulled herself, and you, to orgasm.

With each new tape, some of them purchased, others rented and copied, but all of them made part of your collection, there is a revelation: the seductive debut on Active Video with the bombshell blonde known, like so many of her sisters, by a single name, in this case, Savannah; the intensity of her interracial licking at the lips of Heather Hunter; and the desperation of her cries in the closing moments of *Deep into Charli,* in what *Adult Video News* describes as 'her first anal encounter.'

You find yourself thinking about her at the least likely moments, and this, of course, means that you are in love. You are taking the deposition of a grim-faced young mother, her child the slobbering, brain-dead victim of a pharmaceutical cartel's multi-million-dollar mistake, and just as you ask again about this woman's history of venereal disease, you flash on the notorious set piece from *Ultimate,* the video that gave your secret love her first fifteen minutes of fame, that took her from the furtive shadows and into the public eye, and the look of absolute abandon that shone from her face as the five thick-muscled, over-endowed men closed in on her, forming the points of a star. Two of them penetrate her, front and back. A third dips his cock into her wide and waiting mouth. Her hands grasp the risen gristle of the fourth and fifth, pulling at them in a frantic rhythm that seems, like her body, to pulse, to move slowly from pattern to passion to pageantry as she brings them simultaneously to climax.

It is this scene, impossible to imagine, that replays again on the night that you bedded Alice, the sister of your tennis buddy's assistant at the Ex-Im Bank, and during the following nine months of life together you found no moment as fulfilling. Later you wondered why it took that long to find Alice's flaw, to understand that subtle imperfection. Perhaps you were distracted. There was so much work to be done as the mergers and acquisitions tumbled into bankruptcies and dissolutions – and there was so much yet to be seen.

For here in booth 7, she is yours, and you are hers. She looks out at you from the pulsing screen, licks her willing lips, and smiles her never ending smile. 'Yeah, yeah . . . *yes.*' Smiling on the bed, the sofa, the divan, the lounge chair, the carpet, the hardwood tile, the pool table, the kitchen table, the lawn, the leaves, the desert, even the blacktop of an outdoor basketball court. In the car, front seat and back. In the flatbed of a pickup truck; in the cab of an eighteen-wheeler; in the trough of a concrete mixer. In the swimming pool, in the Jacuzzi, the tub, the current, the tide. Under a shower of water and, yes, once, of urine. 'Yeah, yeah . . . *yes.*' Smiling as the deeds are done by her and to her, smiling as the nipples and the pussies and the cocks are pushed into her mouth, taken by her hand; smiling as the handcuffs are secured, the cloth gag thrust between her lips, the lashes laid across her buttocks and her back; smiling as the kisses descend, ascend, linger, the wet red tongues lick and lap; as the come shots are replayed in slow motion, the favorite target her face, though of course her breasts and so many times her stomach are bathed in the essence of her worshipers.

Smiling. Always smiling.

'Yeah, yeah . . . *yes.*'

Delacorte slips another quarter from his pocket. The television monitor, inches from his face, hums with white noise that dampens the sound from the booth next door, a riot of muted moans and then a tinny voice that declares, 'I'm coming . . . I'm coming' as the screen blinks its message, red on blue, summoning Delacorte to insert another coin. Once, wondering just what his quarters might buy, he timed the tape loop, the gift of twenty-five cents. It was a meaningless gesture. Inside the booths there is no inflationary spiral; his coins buy ecstasy just as cheaply now as then. It is the ecstasy itself that has spiraled, crossing over from the darkness, out of the grainy loops of film, out of the thing called pornography into something new and different, something called adult entertainment. From this journey came a new ecstasy, a strangely cleansed and sanitized ecstasy, bright and shining moments of orgasmic glory in videotapes of startling clarity made by cameras that peered and probed from every angle. A world where lovers, should he say fuckers, practiced safe sex and portrayed no violence. A world where friends, lovers, even husband and wife, might watch. A world where a vision might rise from the shadows and walk into the light.

In the year before the accident, the name, the face, and, of course, the perfect body of Charli Prince sped across the pages of the magazines, the covers of videos, the screens of televisions.

Suddenly she was everywhere: not a week went by without another sight of Charli Prince. Aerosmith's new music video. The cover of *Penthouse.* Lingerie modeling for *Elle,* swimsuits for *Inside Sports.* A brief feature in *Entertainment Weekly.* A cameo on Letterman. Brian De Palma was quoted in *Daily Variety*: He would cast Charli Prince in his next movie.

She was no longer seen but shown. She was being covered with clothes. Her lips and tongue were open, but forming words – words and sentences.

Whether she fled or was forced from the light of this nude dawn, Charli Prince stole quickly back into the darkness, making of all things some tawdry horror film, an erotic thriller for the mad Italian Gualtiere. Why she should have settled for this role is as mysterious as her fate. In the footnote focus of *Hard Copy* and *Inside Edition,* there was only the somber suggestion that making an R-rated film could somehow give her a new life, something that was lacking in an X-rated world. The smirking irony, the undertone of vicious glee, burned at your heart. De Palma never had his chance to work with Charli Prince, to stalk her with his Steadicam, to make her his victim. Giacomo Gualtiere, for whatever reason – an agent's instinct, the Tallis script, a favor owed – was there first and last and forever.

In an instant, she was a goddess.

In another instant, she was dead.

But love never dies. Love fills the little closet, the one with the lock, in the guest bedroom of your riverfront Victorian in McLean; and this is no ordinary love, not the love of gestures, of flowers and sentimental greeting cards. This is a love that is hard fact, love that can be sorted and counted: fifty-four videos, seventy reels of film, magazines in the hundreds. Two calendars, a sheath of promotional stills, the cover of that Pearl Jam CD. A poster of her, the famous wet bikini in the boardroom that inflamed feminists and, no doubt, the passions of ten thousand college boys, looks down upon this testament of your love.

Everything is here, from that first loop of film to the final performance. Delacorte found that video at his local Blockbuster, not hidden behind a ring binder, but displayed openly on the shelf for all to rent and see: *Death American Style.* The laconic narrator, who once sang beach boy ballads and starred in an NBC made-for-TV movie, offers homilies about gun control and capital punishment to a cavalcade of atrocities, many of them real, some of them staged. There, following George Holliday's amateur video of the beating of Rodney King – fifty-six times in eighty-one seconds – is the in-store camera recording of a Korean convenience store owner as she shoots a fifteen-year-old girl in the back of the head. Hotel balconies collapse amidst New Year revelry; religious communes are set afire by the FBI. United Airlines Flight 232 cartwheels into flames in a crash landing at Sioux City, Iowa. Pennsylvania State Treasurer R. Budd Dwyer, facing a prison sentence for bribery, calls a press conference, thrusts a .357 Magnum into his mouth, and blows out the back of his head. On the set of *Twilight Zone: The Movie,* Vic Morrow is decapitated by a crashing helicopter, the two refugee children torn from him, and from us, forever. Suffering and pain, fire and blood, images without context, killings without cause or effect, killings without meaning but for their moment, the moment that they are recorded, the moment that they are seen.

Then, saving the best for last, is the outtake from *Bloody Roses,* as a clapboard introduces scene and take, and in an instant Charli Prince is there, she is alive and she is moving in high-heeled wonder toward the camera, toward you, on a soundstage somewhere in Salt Lake City, and it is the final week of shooting, you know that from your file of news clippings and obituaries, and Giuseppe Tinelli is at the camera and he frames her in medium close-up, struggling from the arms of a tall brutish Italian whose stage name is George Eastman, and from somewhere off camera the culprit comes, igniting from the cartridge of the rigged stage pistol, as her left hand circles Eastman's forearm, then pushes away, spinning her back toward the camera, toward the super-heated discharge that erupts in the darkness, even as she takes a single step, moving into the overloaded blank that rockets from the barrel of the gun and spits its dull fragments of metal into her suddenly heaving chest, that tunnels through her too quickly for even the unblinking eye of the lens to record, that sprays the air with blood and flesh, that spins her around and sends her falling down even as the cameraman moves miraculously to close-up and that is when her lips move, and although there is only silence, there is no sound, you can hear her voice, you can hear her calling 'Yeah, yeah . . . *yes*' before her mouth fills with blood, before all is red, hemorrhaging from her nostrils in a flood as she sprawls, kicking, onto the floor, and the camera holds the shot, never letting it go as her lungs seek air and her chest heaves once, then again, and then and then and then is still.

Delacorte could not help himself; he stood, pants tenting as his hard-on rose in triumph. Then he took the remote control, stabbed at its buttons, rewound the scene to its beginning.

He unzipped his pants and pressed the slow-motion.

You knew then that your love could never die. You kept the rental tape until the copy you ordered arrived, and you paid the late fee with a gold card and a smile. You asked after a laserdisc of *Death American Style* and the clerk expressed doubt, though he had heard about the possibility of a CD-ROM. He would check and let you know.

For weeks you watched the tape, fast-forwarding through the mayhem until you reached the ninety-minute mark, and you studied this fifty-five-second smear of colors, you ran it back and forth, you ran it in slow motion, frame by frame, at double speed, in reverse, until you knew its every brilliance and blemish, the odd streak of light that flares into the upper left-hand corner of the frame at the seventeen-second mark; the black spot of the entry wound that appears at twenty-four seconds, preceding her first jerking response by almost two heartbeats; each frame has its own story to tell, and you sit and you watch until there is nothing left to know.

Then you put the tape into your closet and you wait and you wait but you know too well what has happened, and you need no sullen peepshow counterman to tell you: 'Gone.' It is the end, it is over, and at night, as you fight for sleep, you imagine how the next night will end, and the night after that, how a parade of taut-bodied, long-legged goddesses will serve your every need and be gone when you awaken, ready for another day of work. But the next night is spent with Sally, and in the morning, eyeshadow smeared and body smelling of sweat, she talks with Delacorte about commitment, and the night after that he spends alone.

After Sally there is Kate, who likes to play Harry Connick CDs and wants you to wear a condom; and after Kate there is the new paralegal, Alyson, and after Alyson is a brief meeting with your managing partner, who reviews the firm's policy on sexual harassment. You are thinking about Alyson, about the clipped fingernails, the mole on her left shoulder, why she never wore lipstick, when you hear about the videotape. It is idle conversation, overheard in a bar, a half whisper at your shoulder, a laugh, somewhere in the shallow background of pennies for thoughts and pickup lines, but you sat in a circle of suits, talking about tax codes, unable to turn and ask, unable to say even a word. Later you doubted what you had heard. You tried not to think about it, but the thoughts were unrelenting, the thoughts would not stop promising that it was real. It was not long afterward that you saw the words, or something very much like them, in print. The city's underground newspaper spoke them, loud and clear, in a derisive rant on the missing links of Americana: aliens in Hangar 18, Dillinger's penis, JFK's brain, mimed moonlandings, dead drug-addled crooners and, yes, of course, a certain video.

True lies, all of them, the stuff of tabloids and talk shows and too many cocktails. Still: you had money, and you had time. You rented the post office box and you placed the classified ads here and there and you waited and you waited, but you didn't have to wait long.

The letter was postmarked ROCHESTER NY, but the telephone number was from a suburb of Pittsburgh. You did not believe, you knew it was a hoax, a con, but you made the call, and the call made you wonder, and the wonder brought on the hunger, and the hunger was for love. It wasn't long before you said yes.

It was the most expensive video you have ever seen: $200 for the viewing and then the plane fare to Chicago, nearly two thousand quarters. What it bought you was a darkened motel room near O'Hare, a half circle of seats facing into a television screen, and a squat Hitachi videodeck whose clock blinked out 12:00; it was the first time you had watched her when you were not alone. You paid your money to a shadow and you sat down in the closest of the chairs. An older man, someone's grandfather, arrived five minutes late and nervous; he coughed, too loudly, and shrugged inside his frayed corduroy jacket. The other two men were friends, acquaintances, huddling like conspirators in the corner to your right; they looked pretty much like you, and would not meet your eyes.

'Gentlemen,' said the voice of the shadow. 'Please be seated.' And seated you were, with an uneasy atmosphere of embarrassed expectancy that divided you from the others more convincingly than the wooden walls of booth 7 could have done. You leaned toward the television and its veil of gray haze as the shadow reached the cassette into the videodeck. Then there was nothing left for you to do but what you do best: watch.

On the videotape there is no sound, though from somewhere in the room comes a sharp intake of breath, whether of shock or sudden desire you do not know, as the picture rolls, steadies, blurs, then steadies again and finds focus. It is grainy, fourth- or perhaps even fifth-generation, like the signal of some distant television station, transmissions from the end of the world, and it is a view in black and white, from a fixed position, high above, no doubt mounted on the ceiling, peering down from an angle slightly to her left.

For she is there. She lies before you, eyes closed, palms upward, legs spread ever so invitingly – and nude. You squint but cannot quite make out her expression, though you are certain that it is a smile. The video jumps, its only edit, and you now look upon a close-up of a single sheet of paper, an official-looking document, a form marked in ink with circles and checks, the outline of a human form, and handwriting and a signature. You ignore its codes and comments, searching for the box with her name:

Charlotte Pressman. A cold and anonymous name, as cold and anonymous as her corpse.

You let the words find your lips as the picture jumps again and the fixed camera angle returns, and now you know her, every inch of her, you know her gray and mottled skin, her deflated breasts, her matted tangle of hair, as the deputy medical examiner closes in, scalpel in hand, to dance this last dance.

The striptease of flesh begins. From the left shoulder cutting downward, then the right, and then a single stroke of the blade along her stomach, a ragged letter Y. The folds of skin are taken in his hands, and the layers of her outer flesh are peeled back, revealing the glories within: strips of muscle, yellow pouches of fat, wet bone. In a frozen forever, man and metal probe the shattered breastbone, forceps dip and pull at her broken heart. A silvery rotary saw descends and, when its work is done, the glistening organs are pulled out one by one, examined and weighed and catalogued as you hear the voice, the voice that has been speaking for minutes but only now is heard: pancreas, unremarkable; adrenals, unremarkable; spleen, unremarkable. The flat voice, the drone of a dial tone – unremarkable, unremarkable – as he reaches deep inside her, to the places that tongues and pricks could not venture, and with each touch takes more and more until at last she is a gutted husk. But there is, of course, more: The swift pass of the scalpel from ear to jaw to ear, and her face is peeled back, flimsy and forgotten, before the saw spins again and shears the top of her head. The gray mass is lifted, weighed – unremarkable, unremarkable – and the drama is done. At last you have seen all of her.

You stand and you walk away, out of the room, out of the hotel, out of Chicago, and you hear the voice of one of the men behind you, wondering aloud about the price of a second showing. But there is no price, not one that you can afford; you have only your quarters, and you will always have her:

She is faceless; she is nameless; she is meat.

Each week you returned to Peepland; each week for the first month, once or twice or three times a week and now it is every day, every afternoon, that you leave your desk and you walk the few short blocks to this tiny outpost, the last of its kind in this city, and you trade your dollar bills for quarters and you find your way to a booth, more often than not this booth, lucky 7, and you sit in the darkness and you look through the window of the video screen and you see the naked, the women and the men, you see them rage and rut, and you see nothing there for you, nothing at all, nothing but the lean face of Delacorte reflected in the glass, looking back at you.

In time, the loop will run out, and Delacorte will raise himself up off the bench, and he will return to the office, squaring the knot of his tie, ready to sit behind his desk and take his telephone calls and revise his brief well into the night. But you: You are alone, and although you are waiting and you are watching, there is nothing left to be seen.

When what your last quarter bought you winds down to blue, then nothing, you lean your forehead against the monitor, feel its light and warmth fade into black. Your eyes, trapped in the vanished picture, look into the darkness and offer their plea. But there is no escape.

You sit in booth 7 and you watch the black screen, waiting for the shadow to move, the shadow to shift from darkness into light and then never find the darkness again. You realize then how very much you want to cry, to find the way that tears are made, but of course, as always, your cock has wept for you.

You take the fold of Kleenex from your pocket, wipe the red and swollen tip of your penis and then your hands. In the moment before you stand, ready to open the door and step back into the world, you let the Kleenex fall to the floor, where the life that was inside you trickles down a crack in the cold concrete.

for David J. Schow

***Douglas Winter** was born in 1950 in St Louis, Missouri, and has since gone on to become a partner in the internationally based law firm of Bryan Cave and the author or editor of nine* *books, including* Stephen King: The Art of Darkness, Faces of Fear, *and* Prime Evil. *He has published more than 200 articles and short stories in such diverse markets as* The Washington Post, The Cleveland Plain Dealer, The Book of the Dead, Harper's Bazaar, Cemetery Dance, Saturday Review, Gallery, Twilight Zone, *and* Video Watchdog. *He is a winner of the World Fantasy Award and has been nominated for the Hugo and Stoker. A member of the National Book Critics Circle, his forthcoming projects include a critical biography of Clive Barker and an epic anthology of apocalyptic fiction entitled* Millennium. *Doug makes his home in the suburban splendor surrounding our nation's capital with his lovely wife, Lynne, and their differently-abled Pekineses, Happy & Lucky.*

ABOUT THE EDITORS

Nancy A. Collins is the author of *Paint It Black, Walking Wolf, Wild Blood, In The Blood, Tempter* and *Sunglasses After Dark.* Her collected Sonja Blue Cycle, *Midnight Blue,* was published in omnibus format by White Wolf in early 1995. She won the Horror Writers of America's Bram Stoker Award for First Novel and the British Fantasy Society's Icarus Award. She is also the founder of the International Horror Critics Guild. Nancy is currently working on the comics and screenplay adaptations of *Sunglasses After Dark* and the fourth installment in the Sonja Blue Cycle, *A Dozen Black Roses,* and a romantic dark fantasy called *Angels On Fire.* She currently resides in New York City with her husband, anti-artiste Joe Christ, and their dog, Scrapple.

Edward E. Kramer is a writer and co-editor of *Grails* (nominated for the World Fantasy Award for Best Anthology of 1992), *Confederacy of the Dead, Phobias, Dark Destiny, Elric: Tales of the White Wolf, Excalibur, Tombs, Forbidden Acts,* and many additional works in progress. His original fiction appears in a number of anthologies as well. His interest is not confined to the printed word, either. Ed has written and photographed for the music industry for over a decade, and has hundreds of articles and photos published. A graduate of the Emory University School of Medicine, Ed is a clinical and educational consultant in Atlanta. He is fond of human skulls, exotic snakes, and underground caves.

Martin H. Greenberg is widely known as the leading anthologist in several popular fiction markets with more than 600 books to his credit. He is Professor of Regional Analysis, Political Science, and Literature and Language at UWGB. Marty is an elected member of the International Institute for Strategic Studies in London and an elected Fellow of the Consortium on Armed Forces and Society of the University of Chicago. He has served as a Scholar-Diplomat at the United States Department of State and has traveled widely in the Middle East. Marty has also served as Vice-President of the Science Fiction Research Association and is the series editor of publishing programs at Southern Illinois University and Greenwood Press.